vow of hell

CLARA ELROY

Vow of Hell

Editing: Editing4Indies
Proofreading: Amy Briggs
Cover Design: The Pretty Little Design Co.

They say the vows you take on your wedding day are sacred.

Mine are drenched in greed and hatred.

A beautiful lie hiding the ugly truth lying beyond.

Saint Astor is the big bad wolf I'm trying to run from.
He is the only one that can see beyond my veil of deception.
The only one who has the power to break me into a million pieces.

My forbidden crush, coming to life in the form of a nightmare.

I had a plan to escape from the crutches of a loveless marriage.

Fall in love with someone else.

But when that turns sour, the media's golden boy comes to collect.

And I can't do anything except lay my soul at his feet and hope he doesn't burn it.

NOTE

Vow of Hell is a full-length, interconnected standalone that features strong language, sexual scenes and mature situations which may be considered triggers for some.
Reader Discretion is advised.

PLAYLIST

"Goosebumps"— Travis Scott, HVME
"Gimme What I Want"— Miley Cyrus
"Okay"— Chase Atlantic
"Into It"— Chase Atlantic
"Devil Inside"— CRMNL
"Stargazing"— Kygo, Justin Jesso
"GREECE" — DJ Khaled, Drake
"All Mine"— Plaza
"Do I Wanna Know"— Arctic Monkeys
"Bad Idea"— Ariana Grande
"Safety Net"— Ariana Grande
"Let Me Love You"— Ariana Grande
"Kiss And Make Up"— Dua Lipa, BLACKPINK
"Hotter Than Hell"— Dua Lipa

For every flawed soul.
Your imperfections make you beautiful.

The path to paradise begins in hell.

— DANTE ALIGHIERI

PROLOGUE
ARIADNE

"**H**ey, are you okay?"
The words barely registered in my brain as I downed my fifth shot of the night. The burning liquid traveled down my throat, lighting up my insides and making the betrayal that lingered in my heart pale in comparison.

"Aria, I'm talking to you." A hand wrapped around my upper arm, tugging me back.

I hissed as half of the amber liquor ended up missing my mouth, finding the low neckline of my black dress more appealing. Cursing under my breath, I set the glass on the bartop and turned to face my cousin.

"I'm fine, Daphne. Gosh, this was supposed to be a fun night out, but you're acting like a mother hen," I said, grabbing the handful of napkins she shoved my way.

"Well, excuse me for being concerned. You've been downing shots like they're water ever since we got to Bella's. Is something wrong?" She pursed her red lips as she perched her ass on a clear barstool.

Her white leather skirt made it difficult for her to sit comfortably, but Daphne prioritized her appearance over anything else. I didn't understand why. She already looked like perfection personified with her tall and slim build, long brown locks, and warm hazel eyes. A put-together version of me. She could wear a trash bag and still catch the eye of every guy in the room.

"Nothing's wrong." I held back a shuddered exhale as I finished wiping my chest. Daphne wasn't the kind of person who took no for an answer, though, so I threw her a bone. "Grandma Chloe came in for a visit this morning, and you know how she is. I didn't even have any time to drink my coffee in peace."

I still remembered how my nostrils stung when my first sip ended up going out my nose and not down my throat. They'd ambushed me. My parents and her, my family had hand-delivered news I never thought I'd ever hear as a woman living in the twenty-first century.

"Ohh." Daphne winced, giving me a *you poor girl* look through furrowed brows and signaling for another round of shots. The bartender eyed me wearily every time he passed alcohol my way. My stubby height made me appear younger than I was.

"Yeah," I muttered back.

"That woman thinks she's better than everyone. Her air of superiority could probably suffocate the royal family, I swear. I despise how she looks down on your mother just because she doesn't have the same stuffy upbringing as her husband. Not that I have anything against Uncle Dorian, but..."

I tuned out as Daphne continued to ramble.

A flurry of squeals hit my right ear when an Ariana

Grande song pounded through the speakers, and girls scrambled to dance like someone was chasing them. Over the dance floor, lit chandeliers hung from the ceiling, and heavy Swarovski crystals decorated the metal branches. Their reflection gleamed off the shiny onyx floor, making it seem as if transparent jellyfish were floating underneath all the dancing bodies.

I honed in on a couple at the far right, mesmerized by the graceful moves of the blonde. Passion spilled from her limbs. Every twirl and twist was fluid, in tune with the music. She knew what she was doing. A smirk lit up her face as she ground against the curly-haired guy on her back who had his eyes closed as if he was in pain while holding her.

They looked like two stars burning bright only for each other, so in love, they captivated looks dripped in jealousy left and right.

That was what I wanted—minus the jealousy. Evil eye was a real bitch.

That something special.

A love so deep it lit up my world. I wanted a kaleidoscope of pinks and reds, not dull grays and blues. I wanted what my parents had, what this couple had, not what I was supposedly destined to get, according to my grandma, a cynical romantic and ruthless businesswoman.

"Don't you agree?" Daphne's voice pierced through the fog in my brain, and when I turned back, I found her waiting for my answer.

"Yes." I nodded, the movement sending my head spinning. "Totally."

"Really? So, I should balance a stack of books on my head and belly dance naked for a team of football players while they're competing in the Super Bowl?"

"Well, I bet they would appreciate *that* distraction."

"Aria! You're not listening to me." She smacked my forearm, and I hopped off the stool, laughing.

"Sorry, love." I grabbed my clutch from the bar, hauling the silver strap over my shoulder. "I really have to use the bathroom."

"Fine." Daphne huffed out a breath, crossing her arms. "But don't be too long. I don't want to stay here alone."

As if her being alone was even possible. I could already see potential suitors hovering nearby, like vultures eyeing their next meal. Nevertheless, I dipped my chin in agreement before turning around.

I kept my eyes glued forward as I made my way past the crowds of people to the dingy hallway bathed in red light because I didn't want to glance at the couple again. I didn't want to be reminded of everything I'd lost.

It wasn't like I had any claim to anyone in the first place, just girly fantasies pieced together by years of watching my parents' love for one another. Never in my wildest dreams had I thought the same people who built the delicate vessel of my ideals would be the ones who'd shatter it as well.

My chest burned as emotions swelled again.

Emotions. Emotions. Emotions.

I hated emotions. I was so fucking tired of them. Everything felt heightened through your lows, plunging you deeper into a murky abyss, fully equipped with a whole separate aura that dimmed your light. It bent and snapped, in tune with the events of my life, and occasionally morphed, bleeding other people's hurt into my character.

An empath with a flair for the dramatics. That was me and all the baggage that came with me.

I rubbed my hand over my chest as I closed in on the

bathroom door. I needed to pee, down five more shots, and I'd be so wiped out I wouldn't even remember my name by the end of the night.

With that plan in mind, I slipped inside, taking in the white-tiled walls bathed in the same neon red light that showered the hallway and the graffitied stall doors. Loopy designs covered the entire surface, beautiful in their chaotic nature.

I was splashing my neck with some cool water when the film of silence broke, and weird sounds invaded my eardrums.

Pants, moans, flesh hitting flesh.

Sucking in the droplets of water donning my upper lip, I snapped my head to the mirror, focusing on the noise. A groan sliced through the thickened air. A very loud, very satisfied, and very male groan. The kind that was breathed into your ear as a hand fisted your hair, straining your neck, and making your body tingle in the most delicious way possible.

My nails dug into the edges of the porcelain when I noticed two sets of feet peeking through the cubicle on the far left. Shiny black Louboutins bracketed a pair of oxfords, spread on either side as the door creaked with movement.

Well, at least two people were having a better night than I was.

Snapping back into action, I finished lathering my hands and ignored the ever-increasing tightness between my legs. What was wrong with me? I was acting like a creep, listening in on strangers getting it on.

"Oh my God, Saint." A high-pitched voice bounced off the walls.

My feet froze on the floor, my body turning into ice at the name that escaped the girl's mouth.

"You're stretching me so much it hurts, but it feels so good, baby."

"I am not your baby, Caroline. Thought I made that clear from the start. I'm using you just as much as you're using me," a gruff reply came, and the door started rattling harder.

A sudden wave of bile traveled up my throat when I recognized his voice. As if there were many guys named fucking Saint to begin with, but no, I needed that second seal of confirmation. The seal that tied the bow on the fucked-up present named Saint Astor.

He was a walking, talking contradiction with an extended list of sins.

The self-proclaimed Hugh Hefner of our city.

Talk of his antics still painted the streets of Astropolis red even though he was closing in on turning thirty-one.

"Did you know that Saint Astor used to throw monthly orgy parties? It was the scandal of the century, but I heard he still hosts one every now and again, and apparently, girls line up to attend."

"I heard that he trashed his parents' home after his six-figure football deal with the Raptors got dropped. The police had to get involved, and according to their neighbors, he got arrested. His father was even considering suing him."

"Ever since his spinal cord injury, he's been on a downward spiral. He bought a mansion up north, and they say he spends all of his days drowning in a bottle of bourbon."

Obviously, that last rumor wasn't true. He was too busy drowning in girls. The very same day, I found out my family wanted to marry me off to him. At the very same club I attended. I didn't believe in coincidences, and I didn't believe in letting people make a fool out of me, especially immature boys.

My exhales turned sharp as the girl's pants turned heavier, husky with pleasure. A fog clouded my brain, and I didn't have any control over my feet as they rushed to the cubicle, and my palm smacked the abused stall door.

"What do you think you're doing? This is a public restroom, and I would very much appreciate using the bathrooms without contracting chlamydia." The sentence left my mouth before I had time to think it over.

The noises ceased as if I'd pulled the plug, and an equally loud stunned silence stood in the wake.

"Something you probably haven't done in a while. There are four more stalls. Go use one of them, bitch," Caroline replied, and blood rushed to my head.

I didn't know why he and another girl got my soul churning.

It wasn't jealousy.

It was anger at his audacity. That instead of reaching out and talking to me, he went out of his way to show me how this would work.

Pain ricocheted down my wrist as I slammed my hand on the door again. "I'm gonna call security if you don't get out of there, and do you really need one more scandal, Saint?"

It would be so easy to turn around and walk away, but frustration clawed at my chest. It wasn't solely aimed at him. He was simply the last spark I needed to blow up. My power was stripped away, tied to a snotty rich boy who couldn't get his life together.

Anxiety and satisfaction twisted my belly in knots when I heard Caroline whine and the sound of a zipper being tugged up. My words made an impact because he didn't want to land in further shit.

That was what got us there in the first place.

That and my desperate family, I guess.

My feet hadn't properly touched the ground when they stunned me with the announcement. After my twelve-hour flight from Europe, I found them all sitting around the dining table as if they were discussing their battle plans. Mom, Dad, and dearest Grandma Chloe.

Unsuspecting, I'd stepped into a minefield.

A whoosh of brute air hit my face, and I stumbled back as the door swung open. My heartbeat faltered when his frame filled the doorway, taking up every inch of space with his bulky body. A white T-shirt stuck over his pecs like a second skin, and black cigar pants clung to his long legs, straining over his... member.

I quickly pulled my gaze up only to find amber eyes glaring at me like they wanted to take me up in flames with the intensity of their whiskey stare. Pure, unadulterated disgust veiled the green specks breaking through the liquid gold. Anger coated his curled upper lip, and annoyance bled from his pores as he ran a hand through his mussed, fair hair.

"Who the fuck sent you?"

I vaguely heard his words as I felt my body buzz in an unfamiliar way. Shivers broke down my spine when I caught the line of his jaw clenching, remnants of a red lipstick clinging to his neck like a brand. A wave of anger hit when he spoke again.

"So now you lose your voice? Isn't that convenient?" His lips tugged up in a cruel smirk that had me blurting out the first retort that came to mind.

"Everyone loves a good train wreck, Saint. Pulling your

gaze away can prove to be difficult." I cleared my throat, masking the catch in my voice.

"Is that why your pupils are dilated? You know, if you wanted to join us, you could've just asked. Caroline loves to share, isn't that right?" Saint threw a hand over the blonde's bony shoulders, crushing her body to his. His voice was flat, but his eyes were looking to ruin me. As if I was the one in the wrong.

"You're disgusting," I spat, letting the influx of hatred that swelled in my chest out.

Indifference swam in Saint's gaze. "And you're dismissed. Tell my father he can shove his curfew up his ass, and if he sends any more people like you my way, I will sue him for harassment."

What?

I stared at him blankly as the words took a minute to sink into my brain.

He thought his father sent me?

To keep an eye on him and report back?

"You don't remember me?"

Saint's eyes squinted as he looked me over, from the top of my head to the tips of my strappy heels. His gaze tingled in the most delicious way possible. It was like ice spread in my veins, evaporating when he shook his head.

"I haven't seen you before, peeping Tom, but you clearly know me."

My lungs expanded, and I took in a breath. "As I said, everyone loves to watch a disaster unfold. You must be on to your eighth headline of the week."

My retort didn't impress a bored Caroline who'd taken to scrolling on her phone as Saint and I had our verbal spar.

She rolled her eyes before talking over us. "Oh my God, Saint, let's go already. We can head to my place."

Saint didn't pay her any mind, though; he was too engrossed in this back and forth. In pulling as much as I was pushing. He dropped his hand from Caroline's body, and she huffed, stepping back.

"What's your name?"

I pursed my lips, not knowing whether I wanted to laugh or cry.

I had a habit of acting before thinking things through.

I thought he knew me or at least knew *of* me. We weren't strangers. Hell, we saw each other in every other fashion week. Fleur and Falco were two of the biggest fashion houses in the world. There was no escaping each other, especially now that our parents had agreed to a merger.

But why would someone like Saint care about little old me? Why look at the short brunette with curves in all the wrong places when he had Candice Swanepoel look-alikes at his beck and call?

"Brigette." I gave him my middle name, feeling like he had to earn calling me by my actual name.

It didn't make sense. My brain was a jumbled mess of hormones and emotions, but our playing field wasn't level, and the game hadn't even started yet. I'd take whatever leeway I could get because guys like him didn't change in a day. The more space between us, the better.

Hopefully, I could find a way to get out of this before my clock ran out.

"*Brigette.*" He rolled my name on his tongue, his voice a touch husky and a lot seductive. Caroline blended into the background as my world focused on him when he stepped into my space. "You can't stand by a landslide and get out unscathed. You will eventually fall, and when you do, hope there's someone there to catch you and not judge you."

Two red splotches bloomed in my cheeks. I felt the heat traveling from my face and unfurling down my neck when he raised a hand in the air, curling a finger around one of my brown curls.

I stopped breathing altogether. Saint's face was so close, I saw the golden flecks in his eyes glittering with inexplicable mirth. His annoyance bled into dry humor. Watching me squirm was too enjoyable.

Somewhere along the way, the tables turned, and I didn't like it.

Not one bit.

"Think before you speak, Spitfire. It'll take you a long way." He tugged on the strand, making a hiss fall past my parted lips, and he let go with a chuckle.

I hated his laughter. I hated it because it made him even more attractive than he already was. Saint had dimples on both of his cheeks, giving him a boyish aura despite having crossed that threshold several years ago.

"Fuck you." My body trembled as I pulled back.

"Thanks, but no thanks, jailbait. I'm all set up for the night," he said, and then much to my horror, he pulled his wallet from his back pocket and threw me a wad of fifties. "There, that should be enough to buy your silence. You didn't see me here tonight, did you, sweetheart?"

I bit my lip to keep from crying out as I cradled the cash against my chest.

He was rude, mean, and vulgar.

And he was supposed to be my future husband.

Resentment and irritation mixed in the pit of my stomach until a cocktail of unpredictability stood in its wake.

He brought out the worst in me in under ten minutes.

"This." I held up the money between my pointer and middle finger before dropping it at his feet. "Would be enough to buy anyone's silence. Respect, though? That's earned. I have plenty of people to catch me if I fall, but you? Who do you have?"

Nothing was more satisfying than watching his faux smile drop, his expression shattering like his fragile reality. "What the fuck do you want?"

It was my turn to smirk as I made a U-turn, giving them my back.

To be free.

"Nothing from you."

CHAPTER ONE
ARIADNE

Five months later

"You need to call it off, Ariadne," Mom said as she poured some piping hot coffee in two cups. "The longer you wait, the harder you're going to make this on each other."

I toyed with my phone, avoiding her gaze like the plague.

I didn't want to have this conversation. I heard the ticks of an invisible clock hanging over my head, its daunting shadow crowding my every move.

"Why would I break up with my boyfriend? We're doing great." I shrugged, wrapping my hands around the mug she placed before me.

Lydia Fleur saw past the bullshit, though.

She arched one brown brow in response, shutting me down with a single look. Mom knew me like the back of her hand, which could be because I was always attached to her hip as a kid.

That was the way it was in our family. My sister Irena

was a daddy's girl, and I stuck to Mama. In looks too, we were like two drops of water; bushy brows, chestnut locks, heavy lashes shielding dark eyes, and a slight crook on our noses betraying our Greek descent.

"Because you are betrothed to another man. What you're doing isn't right. You're stringing the poor guy along."

"I am not marrying Saint," I sing-songed, the sentence flowing past my mouth like water. "Also please stop saying *betrothed*. This is not medieval England."

I'd repeated the same tune about a thousand times the past three months, but they still hadn't drilled that fact into their heads. My grandma could've signed whatever papers she wanted. This was my life, and I wouldn't be forced into doing anything I didn't want.

"Trust me, there is nothing else I want more than for you to choose your own future, but there is nothing we can do, honey." Mom took her seat on the opposite side of the kitchen aisle. The afternoon sun sliced through the bow windows, giving us a perfect view of my parents' garden... well, more like my dad's garden.

It was the biggest in Astropolis.

He took huge pride in it, planting all kinds of seasonal vegetables and fruits amidst all the sugar maple trees. The grounds were losing their vibrancy by the day as summer made room for fall.

"Now, you know I don't like bad-mouthing your grandma even though she has her quirks, but she's doing this for the best."

I tried to stop my eyes from rolling. I really did.

Mom loved talking shit about Grandma, and I didn't fault her to a certain extent, so I let her comment slide. Ignorance was bliss sometimes.

"For whose best? The company? Because she certainly wasn't thinking of me when she went ahead and signed a seven-figure contract, basically selling *me* to become richer."

"Fleur has been going downhill for a while now. She had no choice, and the Astors presented her with a good deal. A merger and a marriage, guaranteeing equal division of all assets."

"It has been going downhill because they refused to adapt to modern times. Online stores are not just for retail shops. The sooner they realize that, the better. Diversity is also key. We're missing out on huge markets."

Mom bobbed her head, her chestnut locks falling over her shoulders as she agreed with my statement. "Look at the bright side of things, *glukia mou*. You can implement all those things you're talking about. Marry Saint, and you'll have a bigger say in the company than Grandma Chloe." She went back to singing her original tune, calling me sweetheart in Greek as if that would butter me up.

At first, I didn't understand why my mother wasn't appalled by the news of this sham of a marriage. She was my biggest cheerleader, always encouraging me to follow my dreams and use my voice.

You're a lion, not a mouse, Ariadne. You are what you exude; bleed power and people will treat you with respect.

I caught on pretty quickly, though. Everyone craved what they couldn't have, and while I looked at my mom like she hung the moon, she was still mortal, and we were all flawed.

Lydia was forced to be a stay-at-home mom, taking care of my sister and me when all she wanted was to be involved in the business as well. Grandma Chloe never allowed it. It had been more than thirty years since my parents married, but in her eyes, Mom would always be the unwanted, pregnant Greek girl Dad tugged along with him after a wild summer in Mykonos.

Yes, that was how I was conceived.

And I was blessed with listening to that particular story every time the bickering between those two started.

"What do you know, you Greek whore?"

"Well, more than you, you uptight Karen."

The names they called each other after a full-blown fight one night when I was seven rang in my ears. I wasn't supposed to have heard them, but who can stop an eavesdropping child?

"Can't you see that she's doing the same thing to me that she tried to do with Dad? He was supposed to marry Saint's mom, but because that didn't work out, I'm supposed to pay the price?"

Mom's palms tightened around her ceramic cup at the reminder of the turbulent past. It killed me knowing that she prioritized her power game over my happiness and her dignity.

"I choose to look at the positive. This isn't an ideal situation, but it is for the best. You'll even get to put your fashion degree to use right after you graduate college. Not many young adults have a job lined up for them, especially in your field. Acknowledge your privilege, Ariadne, and stop whining."

I was way more fortunate than probably ninety-nine percent of the population on this planet, I would admit that. I was grateful for the life I led, but at the same time, I couldn't help but wonder what it would feel like not to be in the public eye so much.

The media loved young, rich heirs, especially ones who

came from families that led the fashion world. They picked apart every little interaction, every uttered word, pulling at the threads until they spun a story so good, they could sell it for millions.

I held back a wince when I thought about what I'd said to Saint four months ago, kicking him down when he was already nine feet underground. I blamed the alcohol running through my system that night for my appalling behavior.

Who was I to dictate his actions?

I avoided him like the plague after secondhand embarrassment settled in the next day while I was hugging the toilet bowl and retching like my guts were on fire. It was an all-around lovely atmosphere as Irena held back my hair.

"Where did your mind wander off to?" Mom snapped me back to the present. "And why are you turning red? Is it an allergic reaction?"

Of course, now that she'd pointed it out, I felt myself turning even redder.

"No." I shook my head, chugging what was left of the coffee in my cup. "It's a bit warm here. You know Dad likes to set the thermostat up too high."

"I didn't know you were that sensitive to warmth." She eyed my flaming cheeks with suspicion.

My phone pinged before I could reply, and I thanked the Lord for the distraction. I pulled it up, eyeing the text from Harry, saying he was on his way.

My boyfriend and I met at my college graduation in May. He was there for a family member of his, and we stumbled across each other, had a good laugh, one thing led to another, and we exchanged numbers. We were friends for two months before we started dating in August.

He was *nice*. Never tried for more until I gave him the

green light, but the more time passed, I could tell he was getting impatient. Rough touches, clipped answers, a short fuse, and a low tolerance for repeated questions. There was no spark between us, just friendship that grew into fondness, and in a way, a sort of defiance for me.

Harry was my way out.

He was my scapegoat, the one who was supposed to keep me safe from a future I had no say in.

"Bodies change as we grow older, Mama." I tossed out a half-assed excuse, dropping my phone in my clutch as I pulled my seat back. "Anyway, it was lovely catching up, but I really have to go. I have a date."

That judgmental frown pulled over her features again, and I averted my gaze, busying myself with pulling my beige peacoat on.

"Is it *him?*"

"No, it's Saint," I drawled, hating how her eyes lightened. "Yes, it's Harry, my boyfriend, whose name you should know by now, seeing as we've been dating for three months."

"Three months is peanuts. Besides, it won't go on for much longer."

"Goodbye, *Mom.*"

Lydia sighed heavily as if I was the reason for all her wrinkles, and bid me farewell too, dropping in the usual complaint that I was sure every Greek mother had from their child. "One of these days, you need to come over for some cooking lessons, Ariadne. You're way too thin."

I was a healthy one hundred and forty-seven pounds, a little overweight for my height, but I humored her, knowing that this was a war I would never win. Besides, cooking lessons meant she'd probably make Moussaka, and saying no to that was blasphemous in my book.

"Will do," I said, dropping a kiss on her cheek on my way out. "See you in a few days."

"Excuse me, I asked for medium, and this might as well be raw."

I sank lower in my seat as Harry complained to the server. It wasn't so much about what he'd said that made me uncomfortable. It was about the underlying rudeness in his tone.

"I'm sorry, sir, we'll fix that right away," the flushed guy replied, and from the way his hands shook as he took Harry's plate, I could tell he was relatively new.

"And make sure it doesn't happen again. This is a three Michelin star restaurant, for God's sake, and every other weekend there's a different problem with your dishes."

My eyes widened as he went on, hammering the poor worker for a measly mistake. Yes, every other weekend, he had something to complain about. I thought he was picky with his food, but now I was starting to believe he liked being a dick to the staff.

"I-I'm really sorry. I'll talk to the chef immediately," the server stuttered, the flush spreading to the tips of his ears and disappearing under a mop of auburn hair.

"Actually, I would like to speak to the manager."

"That's enough," I spoke up, and both men turned to me. I hit Harry with a frown before turning to smile apologetically at... *Ben*, according to his nametag. "That won't be necessary, Ben. We would appreciate it if you could just tell the chef to cook the steak for a little while longer."

I clamped down on my jaw when Ben turned to Harry,

waiting for confirmation and simultaneously recognizing him as the figure of authority. Much to my relief, Harry nodded, and the server left, stringing a line of apologies.

My boyfriend's usually charming smile was downturned today, and his sparkly blues were extra frosty as lines creased his forehead, donned by black curls on either side of his temples. He was a sight to behold, especially in a restaurant where the median age of every customer was above fifty. Long straight nose, full dark eyebrows, and a taut body wrapped in a Bellini suit.

Not to forget, one hell of a temper too.

"What was that about?" I asked, noticing we had captured the attention of several other guests.

"What was what, Aria? Don't I have the right to complain when they get my order wrong?" Long fingers wrapped around the stem of his wineglass as he sloshed the red liquid around before taking a sip.

I held back an annoyed sigh as I glanced around the restaurant once again. Harry insisted on dining here because a buddy of his owned the place. And while the interior didn't look bad with its checkered floors and arched wooden ceiling, it was a bit outdated. It attracted precisely the same kind of crowd too. Filled to the brim with gossiping married couples who thankfully returned back to their overpriced meals.

"Of course you do." I continued, some of the intensity seeping out of my voice. "But you don't have to be rude about it. You all but chewed that boy out. The manager card, really?"

Harry bit down on his lower lip, and I felt his leg shake under the table before he gave a resigned nod. "I'm sorry for being such a dick. Today has been challenging to say the least."

It seemed like every day was challenging for him.

As soon as the thought entered my head, I felt guilty. People had shitty periods that stretched for quite a long time. It was just that except for our initial meetings, I'd only seen flashes of charming, sweet Harry. The mean, broody one was a constant companion, though.

Sighing through my nose, I kept my thoughts to myself, deciding to hear him out.

"I figured that much." I reached out, threading my fingers with his on the table. "We can talk about it if you want."

"I'd rather not bore you with the details. A deal at work I've been trying to strike for a while didn't work out, that's it."

"I'm really sorry." I squeezed his hand. "It sucks when all your hard work goes down the drain. I remember when I had to redo my final project for design class a few months ago because my partner bailed on me last minute, but guess what?"

His eyes flicked up at my question. "What?"

"The result was better than the original idea. Don't worry, babe. This deal might've not gone through, but there will be plenty of others that will."

A small smile took hold of his lips, and he brought my hand up, kissing the back of it. "You're right. After all, the people who can resist the charm of Harry Shaw are few and far between."

A strained laugh bubbled out of my throat in response to his. Harry's eyes lit up with mirth, and I instantly recognized the direction his mind had taken. Down the valley of my breasts and then farther south.

A curl of anxiety festered when I detached as the server came back with Harry's food. I wasn't asexual. I had needs like most people in the world, but I also didn't feel completely comfortable performing any of the things he was dreaming of, and probably watched on the regular with a PornHub Premium subscription.

Could be because I was of legal drinking age, and my vagina was still uncharted territory. Could also be that I was overweight, hence my reluctance to show any part of it. No matter what Mama said, I knew my body was not up to par with today's beauty standards.

We did other stuff, of course. You could only hold off a hungry shark for so long, but my V-card was still very much intact.

"My new bathtub was finally installed yesterday," Harry said, cutting into his steak with precision. "I got us some lavender Epsom salts to inaugurate it properly."

"Is that so?" I raised a brow, taking a big gulp out of my wineglass to wash down a bite of salmon.

"Yes, installed a TV on the opposite wall too, so you have something to look at while I eat your sweet pu—"

The white wine ended up going down the wrong pipe.

Did I ever mention that in addition to being ridiculously good-looking, Harry also had one of the filthiest mouths ever?

So why was it that it did nothing for me?

A headache split my forehead as I forced the liquid down my throat, holding back my violent coughs so I didn't sound like a dying whale.

"Are you okay?" Harry watched me with a wicked grin on his face.

"Just peachy." Sarcasm dripped off my tone as I calmed down. "How many TVs does your house even have now? I swear there must be one in every room."

"Movie buff, I can't really help myself."

I'd guessed as much already. Every other conversation we had contained at least one mention of Quentin Tarantino and Steven Spielberg.

I cleared my throat one more time, playing with the edges of my dark red dress. It was the perfect shade and cut, fit for seduction as it wrapped tightly around my chest and flared out over my stomach, disguising any imperfections.

I wasn't planning on making him wait much longer. At this point in our relationship, sex was expected of me, and I'd run out of excuses, but this time, I truly couldn't go. I had work in the morning.

"Well..." I started, and Harry's eyes flashed when he caught the dejected sound of my voice. "While that definitely sounds tempting, I'm afraid I can't come by tonight."

His jaw locked.

My heart started drumming faster.

Please don't break up with me. I need a buffer.

My mind betrayed me again, and I chided myself by digging my nails in my palms. Harry was more than just a shield I could use against my marriage from Astor.

He was sexy, bright, and had an amazing career in front of him.

At the age of twenty-eight, he was working his way up the ladder of The Alsford Group, one of the top real estate companies on the East Coast. Their CEO had invested the money he'd made from a break-out app, and they'd grown exponentially.

My boyfriend. He is my boyfriend, and I need to start showing up more.

"My father," I blurted out before he could get a word in. "I'm catching a flight to Milan with my father early tomorrow morning to scout a new supplier overseas. I'm only an intern at the moment, but he insists on showing me the ropes as early as possible."

Someone call the plumber because the tap won't shut off.

Gosh, I was acting like a child, having to excuse herself to her elders.

"Is there something you would like to tell me, Aria?"

The smile on my face was turning painful. "No, why would you say that?"

"We've been dating for months," he nudged again, but he wouldn't catch me slipping up.

"I'm well aware."

"Three months, more specifically, and you've only come over a handful of times. Is it me? Is it something I did, or maybe you're not attracted to me?"

There was a hint of vulnerability in his tone, and my throat closed up as I looked him over.

Gorgeous, bright, sexy.

Don't ruin this, Ariadne. Insecurities be damned.

"Oh my gosh, no. I'm so sorry I ever gave you that perception. You're amazing, Harry, seriously. The timing has been a little off these past few months, that's all. A lot has been going on down in the Fleur headquarters, and it's been keeping me busy."

Technically, it wasn't a lie.

Dad insisted on having me around ever since I graduated. Instead of having me work in the design department like I wanted, though, he kept shoving me into all these corporate roles that did nothing to nurture my creativity.

Harry considered my words. I could see the wheels behind his eyes turning, determining whether he believed me or not, but the doe-eyed look on my face left no room for dispute. I might've been a virgin, but I wasn't naïve. I knew how to play men. After all, eight years of reading smutty romance books had to leave me with something.

"And when do you get back from Milan?" he grumped, reluctantly accepting my excuse.

"On Saturday. I'll be gone for a week."

"All right, but once you get back, you're mine for the whole weekend. Deal?" He held out his hand, and despite the knots that twisted my stomach, I placed mine on his.

"Deal."

CHAPTER TWO

SAINT

There was no way I'd get to work on time today.

And my father was none too happy about it, judging by the silence on the other end of the speaker when I called to tell him I'd be late for the early morning meeting he had scheduled.

"I knew I couldn't count on you."

My jaw locked at his condescending tone, but I couldn't say anything because I kept proving him right again and again. It wasn't like I craved his approval. I was branded as the disappointment of the Astor family years ago. Disputing the label wasn't in my immediate plans.

They could talk all they wanted, but we all knew the truth.

It was unspoken and sat on our monthly family dinners like an elephant we all tried to forget existed. I wore the disappointment tag and flaunted it proudly. After all, when you gave the absolute minimum in life, you could only go up from there.

"What was it this time? Another party, or a trip to the

Bahamas with money you didn't work for?" He blew out an angry breath, and I could hear pacing on his side of the receiver.

"No, actually, it was a wake-up call from a brunette with an incredibly generous rack and tight, wet—"

"Enough, you-you crude *child*." I could almost picture how purple his face was turning, and a grin took over my face as a result. I might've been stuck in traffic, but at least I was entertained. "Chloe Fleur will be here in five minutes. I don't have time for your bullshit right now, but you best believe we're going to talk about your work ethic at length."

"I couldn't give less of a shi—"

"You don't give a shit about inheriting Falco, huh? Well, what else are you good at, Saint?" He cut me off again, and my knuckles turned white, my grip turning slick around the steering wheel. "You have no other fucking talents. The least you can do is put your business degree to work."

The vein in my forehead pulsed as the long line of cars moved a single inch.

The bad mood Brenna (or it could've been Jenna) sucked out of me this morning was coming back with a vengeance. A good for nothing dependable shit. That was what you turned out to be when life dealt you with a spinal cord injury three years in your NFL career.

Guess you really shouldn't put all your eggs in one basket.

Even if that basket ended up making you seventy million dollars richer.

Two inches.

The cars inched forward at a sloth's pace, and I was one more ignorant comment away from flooring the gas and causing irreversible damage to the silver Aston Martin. Rain poured from the skies today too, painting the whole town gray, battling down on the depression that hung all around the nine-to-five job holders like an infection.

We held the title of the City of Stars when you could actually see the stars only a handful of days per year. It was almost as if whoever named this town was aware of the darkness hiding underneath all the glittering gold.

"I won't be able to make it in five minutes," I choked out, any remnants of humor wiped out. "I'm stuck in Astropolis traffic hell."

"Then come straight to my office when you arrive. Consider yourself on probation, Saint. You fuck up one more time, and you're out. Killian will inherit everything."

My brother was more interested in watching paint dry than in Falco.

"That's not really your decision to make, Noah *Kane*."

We all knew who held all the power, and that certainly wasn't my father. He liked to bark a lot as rabid chihuahuas did, but his bite was equivalent to the overgrown rats too.

My mom, Celia, was the majority shareholder at Falco. Dad had just lucked out by marrying rich, changing his family name to Astor, and pretending his past didn't exist. He was a small fish in a big pond, not some great white policing the goddamn ocean like he thought.

"Don't call me that."

"Don't threaten me."

"Be here fast. I'll be waiting for you," he barked one last time, abruptly hanging up on me.

I ripped the earbud out, dumping it on the passenger seat, and turned the car off as it didn't seem like I'd be going anywhere any time soon. And what was I, if not an environmental activist? Fashion sucked up more energy than aviation and shipping but somehow was always overlooked.

Plastic straws were more important.

Drumming my fingers in tune with the music on the windowsill, I stared out the windshield. The sky looked like heaven's gates had opened, and God was showering us with his wrath. It was raining cats and dogs, and I was starting to hear the pitter-patter of hail the more time went on.

My father had been singing the promises of retirement for the past four years, ever since I started working at the company. The longer I stayed, though, the more I understood he was just blowing smoke up my ass. He had no plans of leaving, at least not until he'd made sure I was as much of a miserable fuck as him.

Competition was clearly in our blood, and we had fun outperforming each other. In a way, it made the fact that I would be selling out fashion shows and not football arenas more bearable.

I couldn't physically tackle anyone, but mentally?

I thrived on that shit.

Starting the car back up when the row started moving again, I winced when I felt a slight twinge of pain as I stepped on the gas. Bad weather always made my injury more sensitive for some reason. According to my physiotherapist, it had to do with barometric pressure or something like that. I had to put up twice the effort to make my limp stand out less during the winter.

It was annoying and at times painful, but I wasn't complaining. At least I could still walk after my accident. Not many people could say that after a spinal cord contusion. It didn't affect my performance in the bedroom, not in a way that mattered anyway, so there was that. I once had a girl tell me she and her friends were afraid I'd been crippled after not showing my face for a year after the fact.

I fucked her until *she* was damn near crippled and sent her on her merry way the next day, ready to spread the news that I was indeed still in my prime.

Not a lie, and not the full truth either.

Dots.

I couldn't see anything but dots as I lay on my back, a massive weight crushing my body to the ground.

Bright, flaming orbs ravaged the clear night sky blowing everything else out of the water with their sheer magnitude. It was almost as if I could feel them inside me, blazing a path of destruction up my spine and spreading like toxic vines of a broken reality to the rest of my limbs.

That split-second detachment after the blow settled in. I couldn't feel anything, but at the same time, I couldn't stop feeling.

The air was crisp, heavy with the promise of upcoming despair. The soil was moist and crumbling underneath my dirt-covered fingers. And the stench of sweat tickled my nose as the defenseman still hadn't realized that I wasn't moving... that I was paralyzed.

"Hey, get off him," a teammate yelled, *and my bones groaned as freedom settled in.*

One blink and all the sensations rushed back in like water bursting through the floodgates. There was no more night sky view, only a singeing pain and ringing sound in my ears as all hell broke loose.

Paramedics swarmed all around me, trying to get me to respond. I couldn't, though. I was frozen behind a sheet of ice that only allowed waves of pain to register in my brain.

Red-hot paralyzing agony.

"Is he going to be okay?" I heard my coach ask as he hovered over the paramedics.

The lulling of sleep wanting to alleviate the ache didn't allow me to listen to their response, but the grim faces of the men surrounding me carried through all the way to the hospital and would play a permanent role in my nightmares years later.

Employees smiled and waved at me as if they didn't think I was the byproduct of nepotism as I made my way to the glass tower housing the Falco headquarters. I didn't bother returning the sentiment, except for dropping a kiss on Nina's cheek before heading to my father's office. She had been his assistant for years now and probably the only person in this whole building who didn't hate my guts.

I knocked before entering but didn't bother waiting for a response. I was feeling like a grade-A asshole today.

Two equally shell-shocked faces swung in my direction when the door closed with a thud behind me. I moved farther in with a swagger in my step and a fake smile on my face.

"Is this him, Noah?" Chloe Fleur smoothed the fabric of her suit jacket, addressing my father.

"Saint Astor, in the flesh, ma'am," I said, and her eyes glossed over as I tugged her hand up to my lips.

"Oh my, you've really grown up, haven't you?" She patted my cheek with her other palm, examining me almost as if she was looking at a product line through her calculating blue eyes.

I straightened up, throwing her a crooked smile as I did

so. "I would hope so, seeing as I am turning thirty-one next year."

"Quite the jokester too; must have gotten that from your mother."

"All my best traits come from her."

I heard Dad sputter in his coffee beside us.

"What about tardiness? Does that come from her too?" She smoothed her gray hair, and her brow wrinkled further. "It's an unspoken rule to never keep a lady waiting, Saint. Especially one who is looking to do business with you."

I was ready to ask her to point out the lady in the room, but judging by my father's twitchy pinky, that wouldn't end well.

"You'll have to excuse me. I'm feeling a bit under the weather. Changing seasons and all will do that to you."

I was lying, and she smiled at me in a way that told me she could smell my bullshit from miles away. Chloe Fleur was a cunning woman. It came as a surprise to me when my father told me they were in the talks of a collaboration. Fleur was one of our biggest competitors, and if we managed to play our hand well, we'd end up with a huge win on our hands.

A rush of anticipation hit me.

I wasn't sold on running Falco. It wasn't what I dreamed of doing growing up, but I did enjoy winning. I enjoyed it so much so, I managed to climb up the corporate ladder at work in two years, from intern to CFO, and six months later COO. It was through hard work and determination, not favoritism like ninety percent of the building here thought.

"You're excused. I do hope you show up on time for our next meeting. I know someone who's dying to meet you."

"I'll make sure to bring a Sharpie then." I crossed my

legs, resting my hip on the chair opposite hers. I'd signed everything from tits to pets during my rise to fame.

"A what?"

"He'll be here, Chloe. I promise." Dad cut in before I could ruin this more from him.

"I'll hold you to that." Chloe nodded, and he visibly relaxed in his seat. "It was nice seeing you again, Noah. You too, Saint, but I'm afraid that's all the time I have for today."

Bet all she had planned was to go home and listen to Michael Bublé while a poor immigrant had the displeasure of rubbing her back.

Everyone in the industry knew Chloe Fleur had retired a long time ago, only meddling occasionally in her son's affairs. It struck me as odd they sent her to negotiate.

My father and I both shared Chloe's sentiment, bidding her farewell as he rounded his glass desk, escorting her to the door.

When he turned back to me, any semblance of warmth had vanished from his eyes as I made myself comfortable on the leather armchair Chloe had vacated.

"Is it my imagination, or was this more of a *social* meeting rather than a business meeting?" I asked, toying with Newton's cradle that was resting a few inches away from his splayed agenda.

"How would you know? You weren't here to listen to it."

"Well, for one, I doubt Chloe Fleur aka the fashion industry's matriarch"—as dubbed by the media—"would be doing any kind of business talk without an army of lawyers present. And two, she addressed us as if we were best fucking buddies reconnecting over a cup of coffee." I looked pointedly at the clear empty cups on his desk.

Realizing I had a point, he pressed the intercom. A few

seconds later, his second assistant, a leggy blonde, swooped into the room, clearing the cups and cookies from the table.

Some business meeting.

It seemed more like an elders' convention.

My father wasn't nearly as old as Fleur, but the dusting of white all over his scalp and the wrinkles—he injected with Botox every four months—along his eyes betrayed that he was well over his fifties.

"We met at the conference room, and of course, seeing as you were an hour late, you didn't manage to catch any of our talk. Besides, we've always been close with the Fleur family. Don't you remember we spent some summers together when you and your brother were younger?"

"You mean when I was eleven?" I deadpanned. "The only thing I remember from then was watching Killian trying to fit his fist in his mouth as a toddler."

Killian Astor was a delinquent in the making ever since he was born.

A part of the reason I never took my father's threats seriously when he threatened to cut me out of the will was because if anyone was worse than me, it was that little fucker.

My brother was eleven years younger than me—a surprise baby—but he already inspired fear where I brought disgust.

"I'm supposed to be interrogating you, not the other way around." My father finally snapped, ripping Newton's balls away from me. Frustration gleamed in his gaze, so like mine, it sometimes hurt to look at him. It felt like I was looking at a mirror. Disappointment hugging me at every turn like an unwanted mistress.

My palms turned to fists as I held back. Many of the

people who worked here wondered how Falco ran like a smoothly operated machine when the people who managed it were like two loose cannons that blew up in each other's presence. I remembered exactly when and why my relationship with my father turned disastrous—more than it was anyway.

It happened when I was drafted by the Raptors, and I told him I had no intention of passing on the dream of my life to take over Falco. He'd screamed at me for hours on end until he lost his voice. I couldn't help but put the blame on him for what happened.

It was illogical.

He wasn't the one that tackled me within an inch of my life. He wasn't even at the game.

But I couldn't forget how much he despised that I'd defied him.

That I'd tainted our name by becoming a jock, *a brute, a beast.*

"Men like us don't get our hands dirty. We don't settle for millions when we could have the fucking world. Who's going to continue the legacy now? Are you going to let some rando walk in and steal what the Astor family worked so hard for?"

His real presence eclipsed the one in my thoughts as he continued talking, oblivious to the dark turn of my thoughts. "What you did today was unacceptable. Being the boss's son doesn't make you immune to the rules, Saint. You have to come to work at the same time everyone else does and, most importantly, leave last!"

"I know it doesn't." I clenched my jaw so hard my teeth hurt. "I informed you that I wanted to take today off, though. *You* insisted I come."

"You're not really sick. You look fine to me. So, tell me, what reason do you have to request the day off?"

"You know what today is." The objects on the desk rattled as I slammed my palm on it.

The very day he rejoiced in my pain. Sat by my hospital bed with a smile while I lay paralyzed next to him, my head pounding as if an army of elephants had stomped all over it. He may have not been the cause of my accident, but he'd adored every second of it. Noah Astor loved being proven right more than he loved his own sons.

I fucking loathed the curl of his lips as he sat once again, proud of his handiwork. Proud he could push my buttons and make me snap, something no one else could do.

"The only thing I know about today is that we had an important meeting concerning billions of dollars' worth of profit, and you missed it." He flipped through some stack of papers in front of him. "Now, don't you have to work?"

Don't feed into his hand, don't let him win.

Up and go, and don't look back unless it's to laugh while something he loves gets destroyed.

"Always a pleasure talking with you, Father," I said, making my way to the door without glancing back.

"I'll send Yelena over in a bit to brief you on the latest updates on the Fleur case."

"Don't bother. I'll be taking the rest of the day off."

"Saint," I heard him hiss, and the blood under my skin warmed. "I told you, you are not tak—"

I let the door slam shut behind me with a satisfying thud.

CHAPTER THREE
ARIADNE

W as I in heaven? I couldn't take my eyes off the striking fabrics surrounding me. Red, lilac, gold, blue, any color you could imagine, I was surrounded by it. Some were shiny, reflecting the artificial light of the room and filling the space with luster. Others were delicate like spun silk.

I was running my fingers through soft velvet when a voice spoke up from behind. "Are we going to be here long? I'm bored to death."

With my heart in my throat, I turned around, relaxing when my sister's face filled my view. "You insisted on coming, Irena. No one forced you."

"Duh, you were going to Italy aka pasta, pizza, gelato, gondola rides... need I go on?" She spun a finger through a strawberry-blond lock.

At sixteen, Irena was already a head taller than me with long lashes framing aqua blue eyes. It should be illegal to look this good at her age, but she was one of the lucky ones that skipped through the awkward teenage phase. Her bone structure was enviable, all sharp cheekbones and plump lips. At least we had that last thing in common.

Ina had gotten the best of both worlds.

A French princess with a south European flair.

"We came for business." I rubbed my face, repeating the same sentence for the thousandth time.

"The only business I've seen you do so far is feel up fabric pieces to the point where I'm starting to get uncomfortable."

She might've not gone through an awkward teenage phase, but she sure as hell didn't skip the bitchy one.

"We're at Antonietta Tasutti's, one of the biggest fabric distributors in the world. They have everything from wool to sea silk. Do you know how rare that is to find?"

The place didn't look luxurious from the outside or the inside, with its warehouse-like architecture, but it certainly was iconic. A designer's dream, nestled in the countryside of Milan, Italy.

She rolled her eyes at me, adjusting the Rayban's on her head and crossing her arms over the red sundress she stole from my suitcase. "No, but I'm sure you're about to tell me."

"I sure am." I smiled as I spun around in my Aquazzura pumps.

Excitement bubbled inside me as I walked over to the small display of sea silk, checking if Irena was following me. She was, albeit the pep in her step wasn't as pronounced as mine.

"It comes from some type of endangered Mediterranean clam, hence the name. Very few people left in the world know how to harvest it. Weaving sea silk is an art form that's slowly dying in a way. Most won't ever get to see or touch it in person."

"Well, why don't they pass the knowledge along? I bet a lot would be interested. Everyone loves rare stuff. It's like a status symbol. People in Astropolis would pay gold for this stuff."

I nodded. There was nothing money couldn't buy, and when you had more than you could spend, impulsive purchases were the least of your worries.

"You see, that's exactly the reason. They keep it a secret for fear of environmental damage because if there's anything we humans excel at, it's destroying the planet."

We both stopped when we reached the table that held the small patch of copper cloth. It was mesmerizing really. Half of it was dark, and the other half that was exposed to the light flowing in from some overhead windows glowed gold.

"Wow, that is really pretty." Irena exhaled next to me, reaching to touch the threads.

"It is, isn't it? When I first saw it, I thought it would definitely be something mermaids would wear. 'Cause it's *sea* silk, get it?"

That got a snort out of her. "My God, you're such a nerd."

"Hey!" I slapped her arm, slightly offended.

"Have you been reading another one of your faerie porn books? Is that where you keep getting all these ideas from?"

My cheeks heated up, remembering how I'd once forgotten my Kindle at my parents' house, and Irena called me up the next morning ready to learn all about fae male wingspans.

"It's called being creative. Maybe you should try it sometime."

Irena laughed good-naturedly, prompting me to do the

same until she tilted her head, seriousness glazing over the humor in her eyes.

"I don't think I tell you this often enough, Aria, but I really admire your passion for your work. I might make fun of you, but I sometimes wish I was more like you."

"What do you mean?" My laugh got stuck in my throat.

If anything, there had been plenty of times when I wished I was more like my little sister. Fiercer, more confident, unbothered by anyone's opinion of her.

I was brave behind a phone screen. Social media was like a playground I'd mastered. That was what happened when you went viral at sixteen. But real life was different. You couldn't hide your flaws behind filters, and you couldn't edit out weak or unflattering moments.

"I wish I had something I was passionate about too. Wish I was as capable as you. You didn't get a single dime from Mom and Dad after you turned eighteen; paid for college out of your own pocket."

"You like ice-skating, plus you're still sixteen, honey. You've got so much time ahead of you. I went to college with kids that changed their majors like three times. Trust me, no one has their shit together until they're at least well into their thirties."

Her eyes widened, and I cursed under my breath.

I was making it worse.

"Their *thirties*?" She cocked her head, looking at me as if I'd grown two heads.

"What I meant to say is that what you're feeling is normal and something even adults experience. And a little advice from your big sister; enjoy this period of your life, be carefree while you still can."

"Easy for you to say. You're Ariadne Fleur, fashion

expert extraordinaire." She snorted, rolling her eyes at my online title.

I was a busy girl with a booming social media presence and an internship at Fleur. My niche was sharing fashion tips and advice, and so far, it was going great. Four years in the industry had gotten me enough brand sponsorships to secure an apartment in the East Village with a nice view of the ocean and an exclusive interview with Marcello Bolzano. I'd almost fainted when I got the email saying he'd love to be interviewed by me.

"Hey, don't be so glum. If push comes to shove, you can always be the Venus to my Serena Williams." I bumped Ina's shoulder with mine, wiggling my brows. "The Solange to my Beyonce."

"Why thank you for being so generous as to share the spotlight."

"What's having a famous sister good for?" I winked.

Silent footsteps from behind alerted us of a third presence, and we spun around just as soon as Dad spoke up. "What are my two favorite girls talking about?"

Darian Fleur had an imposing presence. He could make a room stop with a single word. He didn't demand respect; he owned it. When he spoke, everyone listened, but when he was around his girls, he melted. There was something was so endearing about watching a powerful man turn into a puddle around his wife and kids.

"Aria's faerie porn," my sister blurted out of nowhere, and I felt my cheeks warm under Dad's blue gaze.

I elbowed her just as Dad asked me, "What are you teaching your sister?"

"Nothing, I swear! If anything, she's the one corrupting me."

"Yes, blame the little guy."

I glared at her, and she threw a devilish smile my way as Dad came to stand between us, throwing an arm over both our shoulders and guiding us farther inside the warehouse.

"Come on, you two can fight later. I have something I would like to show you."

"What is it?" Irena quipped as we came to stand in front of a wall filled with racks of white lace.

Bile rushed up my throat at the sight of all the white. I had to use some similar Venetian lace when we were tasked with making a wedding dress in class. It was probably one of the worst projects I'd ever presented.

They say you attract what you fear.

No wonder church bells played on loop in my mind like haunting lullabies.

Dad felt me stiffening against him and rubbed his palm down my arm in a comforting manner. I glanced up, gluing my eyes to his blond hair. I didn't want to know what I'd find if I gazed into his eyes.

Expectations. So many of them wrapped around me, sinking my heart to the bottom of my stomach like an anchor.

I didn't want Saint. I didn't want to marry someone who didn't love me and never would. We could be real. A guy like Saint would never settle for a girl like me.

We came from the same class, but we couldn't be more different.

I made clothes, and he stripped them off supermodels.

"It's not what you think," Dad whispered, kissing the crown of my head. Irena didn't know. No one did, but Mom, Dad, Grandma, and Saint's family, since they were the ones setting the pace of our story.

"So." He straightened up. "While we are here for business per se, I also wanted to get your mother a little something. If she asks, though, we only came to check on a fabric supplier because they were lagging behind on production, all right?"

"You want us to lie to Mom?" Ina asked.

"I want you to help me surprise her. Our anniversary is coming up next month." He rubbed his hands. "And I was thinking of renewing our vows, a little intimate ceremony just the two of us. We never really got to enjoy our wedding day when we were young."

A saccharine-sweet taste bloomed in the back of my throat as Irena gushed over Dad's words. I fucking adored my dad. Growing up, he'd go the extra mile every day by bringing my mom roses or chocolates and taking her on spontaneous trips every few months. Dad was a good person and a devoted husband in a way most men weren't.

Was it too much to ask for a relationship like that?

"You're working hard to win the husband of the year award, I see," I murmured.

"I like being consistent." He laughed, dropping his arms from around us, and strutted forward to palm the lace. "Lydia is going to need a dress."

"Don't you think it would be best if she picked one herself?" I knew where he was going with this.

He slid his gaze my way, hitting the nail straight in the head and confirming my thoughts. "I think she'd love it if her daughter designed one for her."

"I'm down," Irena inserted herself in the conversation.

"You'd probably wrap her up with the lace like a burrito and secure the fabric with two pins," I snarked, taking my blood back for exposing my questionable reading preferences to Dad.

She flashed her tongue at me.

Dad was accustomed to our bickering, so he didn't pay it any mind, just scanned me carefully before continuing. "Honey, Grandma Chloe and I have been talking, and we think it would be great if you took on a more permanent role in the company. Alessandro would love to have you on his team. He was very impressed by some of the sketches you submitted for the last spring collection."

"He was?" I quirked a brow. "He didn't use any of them."

"Maybe he was intimidated that you'd sweep the creative director position off his feet," my sister mused.

"That's not true. Alessandro has years of experience on me."

"Is it not? There's a reason you have such a huge following on social media, and no, it's not only because you have a perky butt."

"Irena!" My God, she was set on embarrassing me in front of Dad today. My fingers ventured to the hem of my white mini dress and pulled down on the edges.

"What? It's true." She shrugged. "But anyway, your DIY looks are amazing. My friends always bug the shit out of me about how they'd love to buy one of your dresses, especially that Cinderella-inspired ball gown you made with the lights, which I'm gonna be wearing to prom this year." She batted her lashes as if to say, *pretty please.*

An influx of pride made me puff out my chest. Putting your art out there for people to judge was a vulnerable process, and while you couldn't please everyone, it felt fucking amazing when all your hard work was validated. Hours in front of a phone screen to build an audience, sleepless nights to sketch and sew, thousands of dollars spent on getting the right material and equipment.

Talent was only one-half of the equation.

"You can have it under one condition," I offered, and she raised a silky brow in question. "Be a good errand girl and fetch me some water. I forgot my bottle in the car."

She eyed me with defiance in her eyes, but after a hair toss, she spun around. "All right, but I'm getting your matching heels too!"

I shook my head, watching her skip to the door. Irena was talented, and she didn't even know it. She could pull the tension from a room with a single word.

I almost forgot about the weight of Dad's words until we were left alone.

As much as I craved to believe that they wanted me around because they believed in my artistic vision, I knew that wasn't the case. I wasn't born yesterday. I was my mother's daughter, and Lydia Karanikolaou-Fleur wasn't easily fooled.

Once the coast was clear, I turned to Dad who was looking at me expectantly. My throat felt as if someone had force-fed me a packet of dry rice cakes, and the words refused to flow out. I'd dreamed of working at Fleur ever since I was a kid. God had a funny way of granting wishes, though. He gave you what you wanted, but there was always a cost.

One I wasn't willing to pay this time around.

"Daddy, I'm honored that you want me to make Mom's wedding dress, I would love to, but I'm afraid I'm going to have to pass on the permanent position at Fleur."

He blinked at me differently and took a step back as if

rewinding my words in his mind. "What are you talking about, Ariadne? Why?"

"Grandma Chloe doesn't want me there because she thinks I'm talented; she wants to control me. It would be so much easier to marry me off if my life also depended on the success of Fleur."

I could tell he got my point but had a hard time digesting my thought process. We both knew what Chloe was capable of, though I wouldn't put this past her.

"You're really set on this, huh? You won't even meet the boy, get to know him? I will support whatever decision you make, but giving this a try wouldn't be so bad."

If only he knew I had met him, and it had ended disastrously.

"Why do you even care so much? You'll be perfectly fine. Fleur is not your only source of income anyway."

"It's not just us that will be affected, Aria. We have thousands of employees around the world."

A pang of guilt made a mess of my insides. "Great, add that to my conscience too." I retreated when Dad reached out to hold my shoulders. They had no right to put the blame for their past mistakes on me. "No. How about instead of talking to me, you talk to your own mother? She's the one responsible for this. Chloe is the one that used the company's funds to buy herself private islands and villas in the Caribbean. And now, all of a sudden, she's the savior, and I'm the bad guy because I don't want to be *sold*?"

Dad scrubbed a hand down his face in exasperation. Duty and loyalty crackled in him like a fiery whip, setting his thoughts ablaze. He couldn't put himself in my shoes, though. After all, what harm could come from giving it a go once?

Most girls would kill to marry someone like Saint Astor, but he wasn't for me. His attitude and his past made us an impossible match.

Or more accurately, a match made in hell.

"I know. I know. You're completely right, Aria, but I can't change the past, only the future. Like I said, I will support whatever decision you make." I stayed put when Dad reached out once more and let him take me in his hug. "You're my kid, darling. Your happiness comes first."

I embraced the peace that washed over me like a soothing balm and held it close, knowing it would be brief. Dad was a minuscule step on my way to freedom. It was the stubborn women in my life I had to be worried about.

"Thank you, Daddy. Besides, I already have a good thing going online, and I'm going to be setting up an online shop soon. Who knows, someday we might even get to have Fleur two point O."

I'd been working on having my own side-hustle a year before graduating, sponging up as much information as I could about the whole process, and I was finally ready to take the plunge.

I hung on to the optimism, using hope as a stepping stone.

CHAPTER FOUR

ARIADNE

"Are your friends expecting me too?" I asked, fixing my green skirt over my legs as I got out of Harry's Lexus.

I regretted wearing my ivory booties, seeing as the roads were all muddy and filled with puddles. September was not a good month for Astropolis, a far cry from the warm weather still harboring Italy.

I shut the car door behind me, meeting Harry outside.

"They're not exactly *my* friends. They're my boss's friends. He invited me to go out with them since I managed to sell a commercial property above the asking price."

"That's awesome. Look at you, climbing up the corporate ladder." I tried to muster up some enthusiasm for my response, alas I didn't quite make the cut when the black in his eyes overpowered the blue.

When I texted him earlier today saying I had gotten back from Italy, I didn't realize he'd make good on his deal a few hours after my plane landed. I barely had time to water my plants before Harry rushed to my apartment, insisting he'd missed me and I should go out with him tonight.

"Come on, babe, we'll stay for a bit, and then we can head back to my place, huh?" He didn't give me a chance to reply.

Harry's fingers clamped around my wrist, and I forced my legs to work, following him to Siren's Grill. The restaurant was tucked right next to an MC club, judging by the alarming number of Harleys parked upfront. I couldn't help feeling like a child, dragged around by her boyfriend, so I put some more pep in my step. I didn't want Harry's boss thinking I didn't like them.

"You don't have to yank my arm like that. I can walk fine on my own," I hissed once we made our way inside.

Siren's Grill was buzzing with energy.

Waitresses with tubes for tops glided over the wooden floors as they served over-fried chicken wings and plates teeming with nachos and melted cheese. Crowds were gathered around the red pool tables on the back, eager to see who'd win in the most boring sport ever, in my opinion. And the bar was full as men and women alike downed beer like it was a healing agent.

I guessed in a way it was. I definitely needed some alcohol in me if I was to get any socializing done in my state. Whenever I was tired, I tended to clamp down on the world with clipped answers.

Harry's grip tightened, and I winced as his fingernails dug crescents into my skin when he pressed a kiss into my cheek.

"Be good," he cautioned through a smile, leaving a slither of annoyance to foster in my mind. My teeth clashed when he wrapped his arm around my waist, creasing my lilac blouse.

Deep breaths.

Don't snap.

Deep breaths.

Today is his day. His pushy behavior can be chalked up to nerves. Being invited out by your boss is a big deal no matter who you are.

I repeated that mantra in my head as we rounded up to a group of five people who were on the far left of the dark wood bar, right next to one of the pool tables.

First thing I noticed? How freaking tall everyone was. I was like a midget amongst giants. Even the girls, a blond bombshell and a brunette with hooded eyes, had to be at least over five feet eight. Two towering stoic figures stood next to them. There was another man. His back was turned as he racked a pool table, but I barely glanced at him once we gained the attention of Harry's boss.

"Harry, you made it!" A man with mussed brown hair broke off from the lot, abandoning a nacho chip in a guacamole bowl and meeting us halfway, clapping Harry on the shoulder. "I thought you couldn't come tonight!"

"My appointment at the dentist got postponed last minute," Harry said, nodding at me. "My girlfriend also wanted to go out tonight, so I thought I'd bring her along too."

I swung my head to his boss to avoid strangling him for forcing me to participate in his lie. A bright hazel gaze was waiting for me when I did so, taking me in with unabashed interest that had my cheeks flaming.

"Hi, Ariadne Fleur," I greeted with a tired smile.

"Ares Alsford." He gripped my palm but didn't shake it.

Instead, he leaned down and pressed a kiss on the back of it, prompting me to giggle at the chivalrous move. Ares's blinding teeth were on full display as he glanced up at me, ignoring the way my boyfriend stiffened. "Lovely name, Ariadne, does it mean anything?"

He was dripping with charm and slowly gaining the attention of the rest of the gang as they came closer to greet us.

"I'm not sure, but I know there was a Greek princess named Ariadne."

"Well, you certainly look like one."

"Simmer down, Casanova," a deep voice drawled, and I had to take a step back to look all the way up at the newcomer. "Her boyfriend *is* right there."

My arteries pumped blood faster as I took him in.

He came back to me like pieces of stained glass. Every feature left its own impact and stole my breath away altogether. His golden eyes were the first to pop out behind the haze, wicked and hungry like a lion's. His sharp cheekbones and plush lips tainted berry red as if he'd drunk too many glasses of wine were next, before his nose broke off some of the perfect symmetry of his face. Straight with a slight bump on the middle, that only made him appear a bit roguish. Tainted the appearance of the perfect-looking saint.

Except when you looked beneath the surface, there was something sinister about him. From the mocking curl of his lips to the way his suit hugged his body tight as if he liked downsizing because everyone's gaze was immediately drawn to his taut muscles. Saint was huge. One of the biggest men I'd ever seen and just as intimidating. I hadn't come across him ever since the start of summer at my graduation outing, and I wanted to keep it that way.

He couldn't remember. He was wiped out drunk.

"Ariadne." My name on his lips set my heart beating faster.

Okay, so he must've overheard it. Or maybe he remembered my face because we used to see each other a lot when we were younger.

"Or was it *Brigette*? Which name do you like to go by these days?"

My slick palm fell from Ares's grip and slammed against my side like dead weight. The background blended into muted colors as I focused on playing it cool.

"You remember."

Way to go. Very cool.

"I do." His voice was bone-dry, and I could see the dislike running deep in his eyes. He studied me like I was another species he got to ridicule for the night.

"Remember *what*?"

My peripheral vision sharpened once more, and the world came rushing back one word, laugh, note of music at a time. The familiarity between Saint and I had enraptured everyone's attention, especially my boyfriend's as if we were a bad reality TV show. Harry had dropped his hold on me, now standing a whole foot away, and I hadn't even noticed.

"Don't get your panties in a twist, *Larry*." Saint laughed, the sound deep and husky before answering his question. "I've known little Aria here since she was young. We had the pleasure of bumping into each other at every fashion event there was."

So, he remembered that too.

"My name is *Harry*," my boyfriend reminded, sizing Saint up, not quite biting into his story.

"My apologies," Saint said, swirling the wine in his glass, not sorry at all.

"Alrighty then," a female voice called out from behind Ares, and I noticed it was the blond girl I'd seen before, smiling warmly at me, one hand curled around her swollen belly. "I'm Eliana, this is my husband, Leo, and that's Sonia, Ares's girlfriend."

She pointed at everyone individually, and I could've kissed her for breaking up a disagreement that could've led down a slippery slope. Together with her husband, they made for a breathtaking couple, and a memory rattled in the corner of my mind as I caught Leo's unruly light brown curls, and green eyes. They were the couple that was dancing/on the verge of fucking on the dance floor at Bella's.

I kept that knowledge to myself as I introduced myself back.

They welcomed us to their place on the bar, and Ares convinced me to order one of the beers he insisted they brewed themselves. Harry and Ares both slipped into a natural conversation as the girls gushed over my outfit, helping dilute my nerves whose source of existence was standing just a few feet away, casting a daunting shadow over my head.

"Green and purple, I'm impressed. Never thought those two colors would mesh well together, but you're rocking it girl," Eliana said, knocking back her orange juice as if it was a shot.

I didn't have the heart to tell her there was a difference between lilac and purple. You didn't correct a pregnant lady; I'd learned that the hard way when Irena was still in Mom's belly.

"Right?" Sonia shared her sentiment, "You gotta tell me

where you got them! I'm totally ripping your outfit off. Hope you don't mind."

"I actually make my own clothes," I said with an apologetic smile. "But I could totally suggest some dupes if you'd like. Quite a few of my friends from college have their own shops—"

"Yo, dude are we gonna play, or are you going to keep sucking on your wife's neck?"

I blinked.

Saint Astor cut me off.

My nostrils flared, and I drew circles on the base of my thumb to avoid using my hands in ways that were *not* friendly by any means. Like, say flipping him off real good.

"You feeling extra bitter today, Astor?" Leo knocked back, keeping his ass still firmly planted on his stool and Eliana between his legs, his arms reaching around her stomach.

I shifted in my seat to glare up at him, but Saint ignored me as if I wasn't even there.

He shrugged, taking a sip of his wine before answering. "Extra disgusted is more like it. You'd think you two would've calmed down after popping out Bella and now expecting your second kid." Saint's eyes sparkled when Eliana turned beetroot red, but she gave back as good as she got.

"As if you don't do worse on a daily basis, manwhore."

A wave of laughter floated from a few bikers some tables over, contradicting the dread that took over in my stomach. What about this man duped my body into thinking it was free-falling? Why did I care what he did or who he did it with?

I tightened my palm around my cold beer, appreciating

the coolness. It must've been a sense of responsibility, a bull-shit link that formed the day my grandma broke the news about her impending plans for us.

Nothing more.

"I'm starting to think we should have a room on call for you," Saint joked, choosing to go down the selective hearing route.

"Stop teasing my wife, fucker." Leo tugged Eliana back to him by her belt loop and dropped a kiss behind her ear when she drifted a few steps away self-consciously. "Only I'm allowed to do that."

Eliana threw him a half-hearted glare, but she settled deeper into his arms, half-sitting on his lap as she turned back around to face us. "To answer your question, Sainty. No, he won't play. I like him where he is."

"Bummer, I was looking forward to whopping his ass. Your husband is all talk and no action, Narcissus."

Narcissus and Sainty.

They had nicknames for each other.

My path used to cross with Saint every other month when we were younger. He always eclipsed everyone else with his light. He had a sarcastic sense of humor that was perceived as a charming and attractive personality trait when he grew older. I saw the shift in the room once he'd turned eighteen. Suddenly every woman eyed him like hungry sharks in an aquarium, and the men left green trails in their wake.

I'd never managed to gain his attention, and maybe that was what led me to utter my next words. Remnants of some weird infatuation ever since I was young with the most sought-after man in all of Astropolis.

"I'll play."

The smile on Saint's face froze when I spoke, and it took a dip as he turned his body my way, his long legs almost clashing with mine. "You know how to play pool, *Brigette*?"

I held back a wince at the name, and Sonia popped in on my behalf. "Why do you call her that?"

"Inside joke," I murmured so he didn't have a chance to spill the truth. Ignoring Saint's raised brows, I plowed forward with my newfound braveness. "And yes, I do know how to play."

I had no idea how to play.

Drumming his fingers along the surface of his wineglass, he nodded once, running his gaze from the tips of my toes to the crown of my head. The nape of my neck heated in response as if someone stroke a match up my spine in line with the speed of Saint's nod.

There was something seriously wrong with me.

I was craving his attention when I should be running away.

"Let's go then, Spitfire. Outshining a Fleur comes easy to Astors. Let's see how long you last." He used our decades-old rivalry to fuel the fight between us. Our families were the crème de la crème of our community and were pitted against each other at least once a week.

"Challenging me while at the same time calling me a Spitfire? Now you're just begging to lose."

"A fierce temper can also lead to a quick burn-out," he commented flatly, taking the lead and the last word as he headed for one of the pool tables. "Come on."

I bit my bottom lip in frustration, glancing at the place where Ares and Harry had been a few minutes ago and found nothing but vacant space. I kept losing track of my boyfriend.

"They slipped to the owner's office," Sonia clarified, noticing my mystified expression. "Something about a sale."

I ignored the guilt that slithered into my conscience like a snake and thanked her, hopping off my stool and following Saint. Harry was the one that made me tug along, only to abandon me and go talk shop with his boss.

"So," Saint started as he bound up to the cue sticks on the wall, and took two out. He turned around and held one in my direction, giving instructions at the same time. "This is a cue stick, and what you want to do is hit the balls with it."

"And the goal is that they slip inside…" I countered, leaving my sentence hanging for a bit until his eyes narrowed. "The pockets?"

He brushed closer, and I strained my neck to look up at him. Saffron and vanilla tickled my nose, his scent wrapping around me like a python. I sucked my bottom lip in my mouth, an insane corner of my mind wanting to know what it tasted like. What *he* tasted like.

Saint's eyes dropped, and he got closer, his stick—*cue stick*—touching the tips of my pointed booties. "Or slip outside, whatever tickles your fancy."

"Now you're just trying to misinform me."

"I thought you knew how to play, Spitfire." He arched a brow.

Annoyance slammed home at the nickname. It wasn't inherently mean, but the way he said it made it sound so. All condescending and scornful. "Stop calling me that."

"But you're so quick to come alive, like an angry fire. In a condensed form." His hand came down to ruffle my hair, and embarrassment wrapped around me like a vise. He was treating me like a child, reminding me of the nine-year age gap between us.

I knocked his hand off with a glare, ignoring the way my skin tingled, and he chuckled, giving me space. "Go ahead. Ladies first."

Right.

I faced the red pool table, eyeing the faint scratches on the brown edges that showed the wear of time on it. All I had to do was bend down and kick the white ball, so all the others spread.

Seemed easy enough.

"Need some help?" Saint called out behind me, sensing my inner struggle.

"No." I leaned forward until I had a fish-eye view of the table.

I did know how to do it. I'd watched plenty of movies with pool scenes. You set your thumb underneath the stick, you pushed it back and forth a couple of times, and when you were confident enough, you *shot*.

I squeaked and stumbled back when the white ball not only shot all the other colored balls but also shot *off* the table. As in, I literally made an inanimate object fly. A few laughs floated in the air from the people next to us, and I side-eyed them until they looked away.

"Well, that was plain sad." My live commenter couldn't help but pop in as he retrieved the ball I'd blasted off.

"Shut up," I bit back.

Saint set the ball back on the table and came to stand behind me. I snapped my head in his direction, but he forced me to look straight by placing his hands on my shoulders. "Come on, at least give yourself a fighting chance, sweetheart."

"What are you doing?"

"Feet apart." He knocked some space between my legs

with his foot, and I complied numbly, hyper-aware of his hard body pressed against mine. "You need to distribute your weight evenly between both legs. And then when you bend over, keep your back straight, don't arch it."

He fucking bent me over and leaned down on top of me.

My lungs let out air as we both went down. Saint Astor, blanketing me, his arms stretching over mine as he took control of my movements.

I could feel him.

I could feel him every-fucking-where.

His body heat seeped into my back, like a living thing, urging me to comply and lay motionless while he took what he pleased.

"Saint," I warned, but he hushed me.

"Now, when you hit the ball, there's no need for excessive force. Sometimes slow and steady does it." His hot breath rained fire on my cheek, his lips a hair's breadth away. "Go on, shoot your shot, Spitfire."

A blind person would've shot a better shot than me in my state. I couldn't concentrate for shit, so I took a deep breath and the leap to tell him what had been on my mind since the last time I saw him.

"Saint, I'm sorry about that da—"

"No need to apologize for saying what was on your mind." He cut me off *again*, his voice losing its previous warmth. I was shivering beneath him, and I didn't know whether it was because I was cold, or way too turned on when I shouldn't be.

It was wrong.

So, fucking wrong.

"I was drunk and mean without reason—" I started only to get shut down a third time.

"I was having sex in a public bathroom, sweetheart. You technically did have a reason." He paused for a brief second, and his nose nudged the side of my face. "I want to know something though."

I knew I shouldn't ask, but I did. "What?"

The pulse on my temple throbbed when he feathered his lips over my skin, lowering his head so he could speak directly into my ear. "Was it just the fact that I was breaking the law that riled you up, or was it something more?"

"Why would you say that?" My brain apparently hadn't gotten the memo that I was at a disadvantage and should shut up.

"You're not the most straight-laced person I've met."

"You barely know me," I said matter-of-factly.

"I know enough." Saint trapped me down harder, still swinging the stick back and forth, a veil of deceit for the public's eyes. "I know most girls that are in a committed, loving relationship wouldn't let me do what I'm doing to you right now, Spitfire."

Jesus Christ, they wouldn't.

My boyfriend was a few rooms away.

A coppery tang filled my mouth as my teeth ravaged my bottom lip, my nerves getting the best of me. Was I really this starved for attention? I should've done the right thing and pushed him away, but I didn't want to. My whole body was buzzing with excitement, rendering my brain useless.

"Do you want an oral depiction of our current position in case your mind is too hazy to comprehend it?" he continued, pressing me down harder. The tips of my breasts were flush against the top of the table, my shame burning as red as the scarlet surface.

"You're bent over the pool table. Barely visible because

my body is covering almost all of you, and your ass is rubbing all over my crotch while you're straining your neck, probably —" Saint's tongue teased the tip of my ear, and I shuddered in response. "No. *Definitely* aching for me to grab your hair while you let me take the reins like a good girl. A sight to behold for your little boyfriend, ain't that right, Spitfire?"

I was a fucking fool for allowing this. The way saliva pooled in my mouth was borderline unfaithful. Five more minutes of his rough palms on my skin, his mouth on my ear, and the imminent heat between my legs, and I'd be drooling all over the counter. I'd be an exhibition for everyone to behold, titled: *The effect Saint Astor has on people. Deadly with his words, lethal with his body.*

"Saint!" Leo's warning call slipped through us like a hot-wire.

I thought I heard a groan, either his or mine, as Saint reluctantly detached his front from my back. Goose bumps were left in his wake, my skin raised as if it wanted to keep him there. His heat was deceiving, creating a false sense of protection that all but fled out the window when I twisted and saw Harry emerging from a corridor with Ares.

Saint's golden gaze was there too, ready to marvel over his work of art. My flaming cheeks, bloody lip, and wild hair. He'd made a mess out of me, and I hadn't talked back. I laid there and took it.

I gasped when some of the lust-infused smog cleared from my head.

What did I do? What did I *let* him do?

In damage control mode, I moved a step to the left, using his body as a shield while I smoothed down my hair and shirt that had pooled dangerously low in the front. Saint watched me with an inquisitive gaze and a smirk I craved to wipe out.

"You have more to say?" I hissed.

He shrugged, and I was surprised that he stayed put as I fixed myself up, shielding me. "Your name means most holy, by the way. But guess you're as much of a sinner as the rest of us."

I paused as his words sunk in, hooking deep into my soul.

I'd wanted to apologize, make things right because no matter what our families demanded, Saint didn't owe me anything. What he wanted was to humiliate me and put my character into question. And he succeeded, I'd fallen into his trap like a willing prey, blindfolded and hands tied behind my back.

Dull entertainment filled his face when he caught the doubts swimming in my eyes. The predator was in full display as he gave me his back, prowling back to his friends who witnessed my derailment like I was a mere bump on his road.

Harry's laughter rang in the air like a wind chime, and they both joined the group at the same time as I wilted on the wooden flooring, gathering myself.

My family's wish and my defiance.

CHAPTER FIVE
SAINT

"Y ou're an asshole, you know that?" Leonardo's voice filled my left ear, and the sound of waves and seagulls attacked my right.

The liveliness my parents' limestone mansion lacked on the inside, you could find in abundance by taking a peek at their backyard. All rolling greens, tennis fields, golf courses, most amenities you found in a fucking amusement park, and a never-ending infinity pool that blended in with the view of the Atlantic ocean on the horizon. Birds chirped in trees, and the world didn't seem all that gray for one second. As much as I hated this cold piece of brick and mortar, I thrived on open spaces... and filling my father's balcony with ash.

I puffed on a cigarette, a tradition of sorts. I had one every time before a meeting with daddy dearest, just enough green rolled into the cancer stick to carry me through the mind-numbing conversations.

"Pot calling the kettle back much, Bianchi?" I blew out a plume of smoke, watching it get lost in the blue sky, and rested my ass on the cold railing.

"Do you like her?"

"Who?" I focused on the ashy taste that filled my mouth, urging the weed in my system to go into effect faster.

"As if you don't know who I'm talking about," he countered, and the memory of soft curves fought to creep its way into my mind. "The girl you almost fucked right in front of everyone last night."

"Leo!" I heard a high-pitched voice shout in the background and held back a grin.

Eliana Roux, straightlaced as ever, insisting her kid didn't pick up on any kind of bad language, which resulted in me walking out of their house half-broke every time I visited. Swear jars had to be the invention of *Baby Boss* wannabes with the impulse control of nuns.

Leo muttered his apologies, probably moving to a different room, judging by the shuffling on his end. "She has a boyfriend, in case you missed it. And he is one of Ares's best employees."

"Yes, I know. That Larry guy."

"Harry."

"Whatever."

He was as insignificant as his name.

The little spitfire had that breakthrough yesterday too. The pivotal scene in her Hollywood flick when she realized she would have let me fuck her in a second if there was no one around. It would've ended with her orgasm and tears when she realized she was nothing more than a glorified cheater.

We all had our vices, and a firm hand was hers. Dirty words whispered in her ear. All in all, the excitement, lacking from her life. I couldn't imagine Larry being that much of a roller-coaster ride. He was more interested in sucking Ares's dick all night than paying any attention to his girl. The way she melted beneath me was pathetic. All that fire inside her evaporating into a cloud of mist.

A little girl with a superiority complex.

I didn't know why I'd confused her for my father's lackey. She was way too young and way too quick with her words. He never hired people who talked back. It was a sign of either leadership or in her case, stupidity. We needed neither in our company. For nine-to-five jobs with a median salary, you only hired sheep that asked *"How high?"* when you told them to jump.

The blue blood in her veins was unmistakable. A quirky fashion sense, and a judgmental attitude. My social circle in a nutshell.

"Do what you must do, but don't fuck this up for Ares. It took him quite a while to get up on his feet after his parents died last year."

"Relax, Bianchi, your boyfriend is going to be okay." I put the joint out, dropping the remains on the white concrete tiles of the balconette. "I don't have any desire to touch the jailbait. She's fresh out of college."

It was true... in part.

Ariadne Fleur was constructed like a wet dream. All curvy lines, soft angles, and a proud face with lips that would look wonderful wrapped around my dick as her mascara pooled down her cheeks. Everything about her screamed femininity when I observed her around my friends last night. Her movements were graceful and satiny. She laughed at every joke and chewed like she had a fucking secret.

I would be impressed if I wasn't raised by the same people she was trying to be like. There were two versions of her. One that strived for perfection and acceptance, and one that craved power and freedom.

Except you couldn't have the best of both worlds. When your head grew too big for your body, everyone had the tendency to chase after you with growling chainsaws, forcing you to hide behind a mask of plastic smiles and mind-numbing weather talk, because uniqueness was offensive.

She was too young. It was too easy to trap her under societal norms.

"And you'll do well to remember that."

"Trust me, I'm reminded of it every time she opens her mouth." I heard the shuffle of footsteps beyond my father's office door, signaling the end of my current conversation and the start of mental torture for half an hour. "Gotta go, asshat. Kiss Bella for me."

I wasn't the biggest fan of kids, but Isabella Bianchi was a little shit after my own heart. She had the biggest grin, expressive blue eyes like her mother's, and curly brown hair like her father's. She looked more like Eliana appearance-wise, but in character, she was a mini Leo, with a sharp tongue since the age of three.

Killing the line, I plowed back to the room at the same time the door slammed open. The fear in my old man's eyes when he noticed my figure blocking the light from outside gave me a boost of serotonin as I waited for him to speak first.

"Fuck, you're here early."

I walked over to the glass alcohol cart as he passed by to sit in his cushy, leather chair. Being in his home office reminded me of one of those old black and white films where mafiosos gathered to discuss who they were going to kill next. He always kept the black curtains drawn like some sort of vampire, and the stench of cigar hung heavy in the air, clinging to the wooden library, stacking books that were a few decades old.

"Figured you'd be mad enough about Killian's latest addition to his body, so I cut you some slack." I poured myself a double shot of whiskey in a tumbler, not bothering to fix one for him.

"Don't remind me. If that boy gets any more tattoos, he's going to start looking more like an ex-con rather than someone who belongs in high society."

I hid my amusement behind a sip as I came to stand in front of him. My little brother already had five tattoos at nineteen, and he didn't seem to be stopping anytime soon. Unlike me, he took the smart route and enrolled in Berkeley, shitting all over this town and its residents.

Who knew? Maybe one day I'd join him. Sunny shores, *free the nipple* movements, and no overbearing family members sounded like my version of heaven.

"Sometimes, I feel like you still live in the eighties," I replied, already filling up my glass for a second time.

"I wish I was," he countered, thumbing through a stack of files in one of his drawers. "Things were much simpler back then. Only two genders, children obeyed their parents, and women were more inclined to stay at home."

"Is there a particular reason you called me here on a Sunday, or was it just to listen to you go on about your chauvinistic and homophobic view of the world?"

He paused in his search, his brows furrowing as he got a closer look at some papers before pulling them down and setting his gaze on me. Empty and dull like the twin barrels of a loaded gun.

"Sit down."

"I'd rather stand."

"All right then. Take a look at these while standing." He smoothed down his white polo shirt as he threw the file my way. It slammed on the edge of the desk, signifying the end of our bickering like two schoolgirls who showed up at prom wearing the same dress.

Plucking the butter-yellow folder, I set my glass down as I flipped it open, blowing through the useless first few pages quickly only to come to a stop on the fourth.

Definitive Merger Agreement. The title stood out in bulky, bold letters, beckoning me to read further, so I did. *Agreement and Plan of a merger dated as of October 21, 2021 (the "Agreement"), among Falco Holdings Limited, an Astropolis Company, and Fleur S.r.l....*

What?

My gaze sliced to my father's. He was looking at me with a raised brow and a look that said, *how would you like to sit now?*

I did. Only because the file weighed a fucking ton, and I had a lot of pages to get through, and slightly because I couldn't believe what I was reading. A merger between Falco and Fleur? I was rarely caught off guard.

Sure, there were successful examples of mergers between companies in the same field, i.e., Exxon and Mobil, Disney and Fox, and a ton of others that had been flushed from my mind the second I graduated. But in a merger, there was always a considerable chance of things heading south. Incompatible business cultures, and in the case of Falco and Fleur, different target audiences. Their designs were... sweeter, more fun, whereas we were classified as business casual.

Who the fuck thought this was a good idea?

I tapped my Oxford on the floor the further I read the

pre-merger steps. It would be easier for me to believe a unicorn that farted golden coins existed, rather than Chloe Fleur and Noah Astor relinquishing any kind of control. One more page flip, though, and I had the answer to that question and wish I'd gone for a vodka Red Bull instead to give me wings so I could escape this horror show.

"What the fuck is this?" I asked, forcing myself to inhale and exhale and hold my shit together. I did not just read what I thought I read.

"What do you think it is?"

I glanced down one more time at one of the terms written in bold black, a line slashed underneath, highlighting the importance of every word. I read it painstakingly slow, making sure the little Spitfire yesterday hadn't injected me with some type of venom that made me dream shit up.

But no. There it was, her name *Ariadne Brigette Fleur*, written right after mine, *Saint Astor*, in a marriage clause. I couldn't be seeing this right. How high was I? Surely, mixing weed with Glennfidich before eating breakfast would have an effect.

I blinked once.

Twice.

Nope, still there.

"I think it's you officially losing your fucking mind." My gaze darkened, and my father's tanned skin turned pink the more I stared at him. "News flash, this is not the eighties, old man, no matter how hard you get at the idea of the past. Why the fuck am I looking at a merger between Falco and Fleur, and why is there a marriage clause?"

F.F.—Fucking Freaks, Fake Fucks, Fucking Fools, Father Fuckers, Fist Fucks, Foot Fetish... I could go on for days, but the moral of the story, even the acronyms that resulted from the mashup of our brand names, confirmed that this was a dumb as shit idea.

Picking lint off his shirt, he regarded me as if I was a temperamental child, which only made me want to strangle him more. "So we can increase profits, expand our market share, streamline the inheritance of our wealth, diversify our products. Take your pick of a letter."

"Win the competition between you and Darian Fleur too?" I chose a letter that wasn't in his alphabet.

"I don't know what you're talking about."

He sure as hell did. Mom was once in a relationship with Darian Fleur, way before either Killian or I was born. That didn't stop the media from bringing up the topic whenever they were spotted on the same catwalk front lines, though. It also didn't help that my parents' marriage lacked the splendors of love. There was a silent but palpable competition—at least on my father's side.

"Sure, you don't." I chose to leave it at that and not get sidetracked, peppering my words with a cold smile. "You can't promise any of that will happen. You might be confident enough in your own skills, but their business has been failing. A merger guarantees equal say."

"Unfortunately, the old hag wouldn't hear any mentions of an acquisition, but we can revive whatever they've lost, rebuild and rebrand them. Don't worry about that," he crowed, delighted that I wasn't flat-out denying him. "Equal say was the main driving force behind Chloe's decision to pursue a marriage clause. She said something about some shady business practices she'd heard about me, all lies of course, and this being my promise to them. The Fleur girl is young and naïve, though. She'll walk into our hands like a lamb to the slaughter."

70

"What does the fact that she's young have to do with anything? You'd still be giving up full control of our company." I cocked my head, questioning how many brain cells he had left. It couldn't be more than five.

Not that seeing his dream fail seemed like a bad thing. If that ever ensued, I would be the first to laugh at his misery, but it wouldn't give me the same satisfaction as making it happen myself. That would drive the wedge deeper into the blood-soaked wound.

"You've had plenty of experience with women—sometimes much older." He brought up the fresh past with a pointed look, drumming his fingers on the armchairs. "I trust keeping her in her line won't be too hard for you. And you don't have to stay married to her forever. There is a clause that the marriage has to last only five years."

Obviously, he'd never met Spitfire. She was malleable, but there was searing heat inside her that made her impulsive and thus unpredictable. It would take a lot of effort to get her to behave. An effort which I wasn't willing to invest in a petulant child.

"So, I lose five years of my life, so your ass can get to have his cake and eat it too." His nostrils flared at my language, but I cut him off before he could speak. "Should I start looking for mental asylums?"

"If you'd read on, you would see that I won't remain head of Falco. Following you and the Fleur girl's wedding, you two will be the ones calling the shots."

My gaze sliced back to the papers, and indeed he was telling the truth.

"You—you..." I stuttered. I never stuttered. Taking a deep breath, I cleared my throat and tried again. "You agreed to this?"

"I did. As much as you don't like to admit it, Saint, you are a lot like me. You run a tight ship when it comes to business. Some of our most successful campaigns happened right after you took control of the marketing department. And even though you'll improve with time..." He gulped, and his forehead shone with a sheen of sweat underneath the warm yellow lighting of the room. "I believe in you."

It took him some time to utter those four words. Never thought I'd see the day where he'd be kissing my ass. At least not before I locked him up in a retirement home. I reveled in his discomfort, leaning back in my seat and downing the remaining alcohol in my glass. "Well, don't just stop there. I'd love to hear more about how amazing I am."

His lips thinned, and he kept on going as if I hadn't spoken. "And that girl—"

I cut him off. "Her name is Ariadne, something you should know if you intend for me to marry her."

"Yes, yes, Ariadne. She has quite an eye for design, graduated from Dane University too, and has a following on social media we could use to our advantage. She's not completely inadequate."

I didn't know that.

Then again, until five months ago, I remembered nothing about this girl other than her bushy brows when she was younger. She got teased relentlessly for her unibrow. Now, bushy brows were the trend.

"Hm... that does make signing my life away to her for five years better. She could feature me on her Instagram, and I could become famous too." Sarcasm dripped off my tongue like absinthe.

My father threw his head back, heaving a dramatic sigh. "What more do you want, Saint? You'll have Falco and Fleur at the palm of your hands, a relatively pretty wife, and a title that comes with respect. You're not being held at gunpoint. You're gaining the world. And after a few years, you can get rid of the dead weight."

He tried to sell me his idea, cocksure I would bite into it because he always thought he was the smartest person in the room, leaving little to no space for growth. He was used to getting what he wanted when he wanted.

I admitted it wasn't a bad idea per se. I had everything to gain and nothing to lose. My most prized possession out of this would be my father's pride. Noah Astor thought he was gaining a win at Darian's expense. Losing from his own son never crossed his mind.

I could turn my back on him now like he did years ago to me when I wanted to go through more physical therapy classes and get back on the field. But he crushed any hope I had of that happening. Physical health was the biggest deal for any NFL team. Reputation was a close second. I obviously lacked the first one, and daddy dearest made sure my name was dragged through the mud at my lowest point. Leaking my location to the press, talking about my worsening health condition, and fueling the flames of my supposed alcoholism during his interviews.

Taking something that belonged to him filled me with an unsated bloodlust. Destroying the sole thing he lived and breathed for, now that made my black heart soar.

Tit for fucking tat.

It seemed like the little spitfire was about to be caught in some actual fire.

"Beg for it." I tested my luck, wanting to see how far he would go to see this through. To see how bad it would hurt in the end.

I watched like a hawk as his eyes widened, reveling in every little moment from the tick of his jaw that matched the rhythm of his pulsing heart to his fists balling so tight, I knew he'd draw blood.

"Are you crazy?"

"On the contrary, you're asking me to do something crazy. I want to hear you say please, and then maybe I'll consider it."

His mouth dropped open and closed several times. I kept an amused frown pasted on my face as he battled an internal war. To beg, or not to beg, that was the question. Slowly, the man in front of me clasped his hands together on the table, his mouth set in a firm line, and gritted his teeth before he spoke.

"Please, Saint, I am begging you to marry Ariadne Fleur so we can close this deal. A billion-dollar deal that will be the beginning of a new area for Falco. Heights you've never imagined before are waiting for us."

Every word was stressed as if his life depended on this. I rolled some crushed ice I stole from the glass in my mouth, letting him sweat it out. My tongue turned numb, enough for me not to feel any pain as I bit down on it, a last attempt to hold off on this madness.

But who was I kidding?

Burning down the reputation of all firstborns was my calling.

"I want to talk to Ariadne first," I said, getting on my feet. "I'll make no promises unless I know she agrees to this too. I won't ruin a girl's life because of your selfish reasons."

My father's jaw locked when I evaded the request, but even he had to know you couldn't force someone into marriage anymore. Reluctantly, he nodded, his eyes screaming bloody murder as I turned my back on him, heading for the heavy oak door.

"We're meeting with them on Wednesday, eight o'clock sharp." His voice rang with warning behind me.

"See you there, old man."

CHAPTER SIX
ARIADNE

H e dumped me."

"What?" My sister's stare was comical as I dropped the news on her while we were both out riding. Ina was frozen, a strong gust of wind, and she would fall over.

I couldn't have told her earlier, not when the whole family was together. Sundays were spent in Grandma Chloe's ranch, south of Astropolis, and I didn't want to give Mom the satisfaction of being right and making Grandma's hopes resurface. I'd skipped the last few trips here, but when Dad called me that morning, I couldn't refuse.

Spending a day watching horses gallop on a field sounded so peaceful after the night I'd had. I already felt ten times lighter as I rode Storm; a beautiful thoroughbred mare with a black coat. Irena rode Fury, Storm's younger brother, and we both made our way down the smoky moun-tain armed with matching puff jackets over our riding outfits.

"Harry broke up with me," I repeated, not quite

believing it myself still. Fury's strides became uneven as Irena's posture relaxed, and I warned her to sit up straight.

She snapped up, taking hold of the reins more firmly, keeping her steely blue gaze clipped on mine. "What do you mean he broke up with you? I thought everything was going fine. You two looked so cute together."

"I refused to sleep with him."

It was as simple as that, really.

After the shit show with Saint yesterday, my mood was shot, and everyone could tell. I ruined Harry's night and made Saint's brighter. I couldn't fucking act as if nothing happened. Leo, Eliana, and Sonia had all witnessed my embarrassing moment of weakness, where not only my body turned to mush, but my brain as well.

Harry deserved someone better. He deserved a girl's whole heart, not scraps of it. Despite my dislike for certain aspects of his character, he *was* a catch. Just not the right catch for me. When he gave me the ultimatum that I either stayed at his place last night or went home and never saw him again, I didn't have to think twice about my choice. I was cranky and annoyed. Harry had a point, but I also had the right to relax after a twelve-hour flight.

Nevertheless, I never kept my end of the deal. So when he bid me goodbye with a backhanded *"have a nice life"* comment, I didn't even blame him. I expected some tears, yet I was only slightly bummed as I ordered an Uber to drive me home.

"I mean good for you for keeping your boundaries..." Ina bit her lip before she hit me with the dreaded question. "But are you ever planning on losing your V-card? I mean, Harry is a very nice guy. It seems kinda dumb to break up over something so trivial."

"You met him one time, Ina," I grumbled. "And I'm just waiting for the right person. I don't understand why it's the societal norm to lose your virginity at seventeen, and if you don't, you've somehow failed in life."

"I don't think you've failed in life. I'm just wondering how you managed to get through college... *untouched*." She chose her words carefully. "I mean don't you have urges? I know I do. We have a new exchange student from England, and he is *scrump-dilly-icious*, like a young Robert Pattinson."

Did I not have urges?

Of course, I did. I brought out the big guns last night in the form of a purple vibrator with a suctioning option because I couldn't sleep. It made me see stars. Golden eyes lingered amongst the night sky as well, enjoying the show like a perverted unwanted guest.

My hormones were at an all-time high. And I would admit, one more reason I didn't want to have sex with Harry was because he wasn't the reason for the slip and slide between my legs. The thought of losing my virginity to one man while thinking of another would haunt me for the rest of my life.

"College was such a blur for me. I was so focused on perfecting my craft and building my career that I didn't have time to think about anyone in a romantic way." I confessed. I had flings, but none of them stood the test of time. "And you know, I once read in a tabloid that Robert Pattinson loved licking Kristen Stewart's armpits when they were intimate."

Irena blanched. "Did you have to ruin my dreams like that?"

"I'm sorry, kid, but no Robert Pattinson look-alikes for you until you're at least forty," I joked, and we both knew it. She could do whatever she liked as long as it was safe and consensual. Our parents had drilled *the talk* in our heads since we were old enough to walk.

She rolled her eyes at me, and I wondered if she ever got headaches because she seemed to do that a lot. "So, how are you feeling? Mad, sad, angry?"

My teeth chattered when the wind picked up, and Storm started galloping faster down the trail. I had no right to feel mad after *he who shall not be named* broke through my walls with such little effort.

"Not particularly, I'm... relieved. Harry and I were much better as friends, even though I don't think we're ever going back to that."

Not even a full five seconds after the word *relieved* was uttered, we heard additional horse hooves ahead of us. We both strained to see who was coming as Grandma Chloe broke through the mist before us on top of Savannah, an Arabian purebred.

She was liberty riding, no gear at all, experience bleeding through her flawless posture. Being in her presence made me stand straighter. Whether it was because I was bracing for something or craved some sort of validation from the world-renowned matriarch, I didn't know.

"Grandma, we were just heading back. What are you doing here?" Irena asked when she neared, pushing between the two of us until she was in the middle. Storm was slightly spooked by the abrupt guest, so I patted her mane, calming her down.

Grandma's face held a few wrinkles. Regular Botox treatments and refusing to smile or frown helped her out. Despite her insistence on looking younger, she kept her hair natural. A gray, almost whitish color that didn't look half bad in combination with her crystal blues and her dark brown outfit.

"I came to ride with you girls, but I'm afraid your mother is asking for you, Irena. Something about a call from Mr. Pierce."

"Isn't that your math teacher?" I asked, an amused frown on my face at the panicked look in her eyes. "What did you do this time?"

"It wasn't my fault, okay? He got an exercise wrong, and then when I corrected him, he got mad." She blew out an angry breath. "Ugh, total small dick energy, who knows what lies he's said this time!" Muttering a string of curses—my sister had a mouth on her—she took off ahead of us, her frame steady, as Fury sprinted the rest of the way.

I couldn't hold back my laughter when Grandma's horrified gaze clashed with mine. My ugly snorts only served in making her glare intensify as she shook her head.

"This isn't funny, Ariadne. She has to learn to rein in her words. You do not swear your way out of situations, but I guess that's the kind of upbringing you can expect from your mother."

My amusement dissipated in a sigh. *Here we go again.* "Don't start again, please. Irena is a kid. Let her be one."

"Well, all right. Don't come to me when her bad habits develop into something worse."

Trust me, no one is coming to you.

My grandma had a lot to say about everyone else, but she failed to look in the mirror. I needed to exercise more, my dad was too stubborn, my mom too crude, and Irena too immature, according to her. She had an opinion about everything and carried herself as if she was a deity.

"Where are you going?" she asked once I continued forward.

"Home, it's almost lunchtime," I clarified.

"You can wait a bit longer," she said, turning toward the mountains and nudging her head left. She wanted me to ascend the mountain *again*.

Yeah, no. I was hungry, and the temperature had dropped significantly, mist crawling all around us like slithering snakes. It was worse when you glanced up. Visibility was pure shit.

Grandma caught my denial in the air and *tsked* at me. "Come on, I have a car waiting for us at the top and two stable boys to take care of the horses. I need some time in the wilderness after spending the entire day in Lydia's presence. You're not going to leave an old lady alone, are you?"

Rolling my eyes, I pushed my hips forward in the saddle, and Storm got the message, striding alongside Savannah. "Sometimes, I think you two secretly love each other. There's no other explanation. You've been singing the same tune for twenty-one years now and still haven't gouged each other's eyes out."

Grandma scoffed, and I marveled at how effortlessly she went up the hill with no gear. From what Dad told me, she used to ride professionally when she was younger and took part in horse races. "I don't despise her, I got used to her over the years, but I can't say I enjoy being in your mother's presence either. Nor does she like being around me. I guess you could say one thing I appreciate about Lydia is how straightforward she is."

"See, you do agree on something after all."

"Not just one thing, as of late... but *two*."

"You're pulling out all the stops today, huh? Go on,

surprise me. What else do you two agree on?" I asked, digging my own grave.

"You, marrying Saint Astor."

The groan that escaped my mind was immediate. I was tired of hearing his name... and thinking about it. "I walked right into that one."

"I'm going to try to change your mind one last time, Ariadne. And if you still don't agree, then I will let it go, I promise. All I ask is that you pay attention to what I have to say."

"The answer is still going to be no, but go on."

If it finally got her to leave me alone, then, of course, I would listen. It would be as if I was in the mall, late November, and "All I Want For Christmas Is You" was playing through the speakers. I'd heard the same tune a thousand times once more wouldn't hurt.

"So, as you know, Fleur is facing major economic problems—"

"Yes, I do. Just like I know you have other sources of income, not as big, but just enough so you won't be able to tell the difference in the quality of your life." I tapped the side of my boot to my horse, making it go faster.

We were all starting to sound like broken records.

Her nostrils flared at being interrupted, but she didn't say anything. I held all the power. "That's the thing, Ariadne. *We* do now, but we won't for long."

"What do you mean?"

"I..." She started, staring far ahead. "A few years back, I went into business with some bad people. I was promised a very hefty reward if I followed through with my end of the deal."

"Which was?" The chill in the air seeped into my skin.

"That I signed away all of my properties and businesses if I couldn't pay up. And I did... I did pay my end of the deal, but the contracts I signed with them... there were loopholes."

I was dumbfounded for a second.

Completely fucking numb down to my bones.

Storm kept moving even though I sat still as an ice sculpture on top, staring at my grandma like she'd grown a second head. She hadn't told me this before, not when she first breached the topic.

"You did *what*? What was that hefty reward that had you do such a thing? Didn't you have a lawyer look over the contracts first?"

"The lawyer was paid off by them. I realized that way too late." Her cheeks pinkened, and I was guessing it wasn't just because of the cold. "The reward doesn't matter. Trust me, Ariadne, for your own good, you don't want to know. What you have to know is that we need the Astor's help."

Was she lying to me? She was capable of stooping quite low if it meant getting what she wanted. This shit didn't happen in real life. It didn't happen to me—*a twenty-one-year-old virgin*, whose life was as exciting as watching paint dry behind the scenes.

"Well, you're still going to owe them even if I do marry, Saint. Do you think they're going to allow you to finesse any more money from the company?"

"No, but the company will be the only source of revenue we will have left because I missed the deadline, Ariadne. I was supposed to pay my debts two weeks ago, and now? Now, they're coming to collect."

"And if you refuse? You can take them to court. If you were in the right, you could find a way out." I tried to reason with her. I didn't like where this was going.

"If I refuse, they're going to collect more than just properties. There is no way out with these people."

"Who the hell did you do business with the fucking Russian mob?"

Her silence spoke plenty.

I didn't know if it was indeed the mob or not, but I couldn't be far off. Whoever it was, they yielded immense power and had public figures like the likes of my grandma shivering at the mere thought of them. I was shocked when I shouldn't have been. Backdoor deals and shady people weren't a new thing for the elite. You didn't get to the top by being decent, and the matriarch of the fashion world was certainly anything but.

I'd witnessed plenty of times when Grandma Chloe made people cry with her harsh critique. Some of my own body image issues stemmed from her thoughtless words. She was like a real-life Miranda Priestly, with a side of Rosetta Cutolo, apparently.

"What do you want from me?" I asked dejectedly.

Storm got irritable beneath me. I was acting like dead weight, giving mixed signals with my movements. I straightened up, although falling off a horse didn't seem like such a bad thing at the moment.

I didn't *want* to marry Saint. I was so insignificant to him. He didn't remember who I was until I made a scene. And at Siren's Grill yesterday, he ignored me for the rest of the night, cozying up to a Brazilian girl with gravity-defying tits and an ass that reminded me of two volleyballs.

"Be there on Wednesday. I've already told you the details of the meeting. Talk to Saint. *Try*. Don't do it only for me, but also for your parents and Irena. Their future is hanging on your shoulders, Ariadne."

No pressure.

At least she had the decency to look guilty. I was going to be paying for her fuck up. We both knew it. There was no way in hell I'd let anything happen to my family.

I made her promise that she wasn't lying as we neared the parked Range Rover waiting for us. She acted appalled for two point five seconds, but I showed her I wasn't buying it, so she skipped the dramatics and swore on her late husband's grave.

I believed her.

The desperation in her voice was real and raw, and I was so screwed.

So fucking screwed.

Saint Astor was going to chew me up and spit me out.

CHAPTER SEVEN
SAINT

I singled her out by her outfit.

She was wearing a bright blue dress today, drowning under layers of tulle, strutting toward the Falco headquarters like she was living her catwalk dream.

Ariadne Fleur was many things, but at least boring wasn't one of them. From her eccentric fashion choices to her wild curls framing her heart-shaped face and curves that she did a stellar job at hiding under layers of fabric, she bled personality and allure with every step she took. She appeared demure on the surface, but if you lit the wrong fuse, she would scorch you in seconds, spilling impulsivity by the buckets.

I rolled the window of my G-Class down, half tempted to scream *"Get in, loser, we're going shopping"* at her, but I figured that wasn't the best way to approach someone you needed a favor from. I'd try taking the civil route first—no matter how ridiculous she looked wearing a haute couture dress on a normal workday.

My honk drew everyone's attention, including hers, as

she rotated in place, her eyes fleeting to mine like magnets. A healthy flush spread down Ari's cheeks when she found me already looking at her. She did that a lot—blushed like a schoolgirl. Unfortunately for her, young inexperienced girls weren't on my list of fetishes.

"Fleur," I drawled, beaconing her closer so we wouldn't have a conversation ten feet apart.

She looked like she wanted the ground to swallow her whole as people stared and bounded over, keeping her steps short until she was standing next to my car door.

"Astor," she hissed lowly, throwing her hair over her bare shoulder. Bold choice considering it was freezing. "Couldn't wait to welcome me until we were inside, or you missed me too much?"

"Surprised you showed, Spitfire. Apparently, I overestimated your boyfriend's hold in your life." I didn't much care about him, it wouldn't be the first time a couple broke up because of me, but there was a reason I never proposed to any of those girls.

"You know nothing." Her lashes lowered, shielding her eyes.

"But I'm about to learn everything. There are no secrets between a husband and a wife, right?"

I lost track of my mouth, something primal tightening in my gut, anticipating the verbal spar that was bound to follow. There was no reason to tiptoe around it. We both knew what we were here for.

"Keep your voice down," she muttered, glancing at the crowd that didn't pay us any mind.

I leaned back on my seat, fisting the steering wheel and revving the engine, impatience flying through me. "Get in," I ordered. "We aren't going to the meeting."

"What? My grandma said—"

"I don't care what Chloe or my father said. This is between you and me."

The old farts would have to stop playing God for a hot minute. They'd sit in a conference room, wait, and wait, and wait, until panic took hold, that not just one, but both of us refused to show. Their brilliant minds would be put to question for one whole day until they found out the verdict of our *private* meeting.

"I don't think—"

Still not following instructions. Her jaw locked when I spoke over her. "Unless you want your grandma to die a thousand deaths when I ask you if you prefer missionary or doggy style, swallowing or spitting, lights off or on, then you will get in the fucking car."

A stain of embarrassment marred her cheeks again, and I was disappointed to confirm I couldn't look away as she seethed, tapping her cream heel on the pavement. "You wouldn't dare."

"Try me, Spitfire." I met her stare head-on until she retracted her gaze first. "How can I marry you without knowing if our sexual preferences are compatible or not."

Fucking *with* Ariadne Fleur was higher on my priority list than actually fucking her. We all had our different ideas of foreplay, and watching her carefully controlled expressions melt in the vinegar of my words was mine.

A car whose parking space I was blocking honked in the background, getting more restless as seconds flew. I didn't budge, looking at Ariadne with raised brows. Her fight dissolved in seconds, public outcry winning the waging war inside her, and with a last glare and a string of curses that sounded comical coming out of her proper mouth, she started for the passenger seat.

The bottom of the SUV reached her waist, but I had a feeling she would slap my hand away if I tried to help her, so I watched as she struggled to get in the car, huffing like she ran a marathon when she settled into her seat.

"Where the hell are we going?"

I gunned it out of there as soon as she was buckled in, not lingering to test my luck and see how much longer it would take for the asshat behind me to crash into me. Ariadne squealed when Nyx and Erebus—my two black Dobermans —made their presence felt, panting all over her back seat and stealing occasional licks.

"Oh my God!" Her high-pitched scream, in combination with the dogs' excited barks, pierced my eardrums. "What are those?"

The sensory overload made it hard for me to focus on driving, and I narrowly missed a car, causing the driver to flip me off as I sped past him. I growled under my breath, throwing my left arm behind her seat to put an end to the chaos and grant Ariadne some space to gather herself. I barked a command for the dogs to sit, and they obeyed, their tails still wagging furiously when I glanced at them through the rearview mirror.

"They're called dogs," I deadpanned, grateful that my eyes didn't stray from the road to look at her fluctuating chest and feral eyes caressing the side of my jaw with primitive fear. "The one on the right with the red collar is Nyx, and on the left with the blue is Erebus."

The dogs' pants got harder at the sound of their names, and a small whimper escaped Aria's mouth as she leaned as far as her seat belt allowed her to, glancing over my forearm with slight curiosity.

"Could've fooled me. They look more like mini-sized bears." Her voice was tiny, but she grew bolder, resting her palm on my bicep, informing me she wasn't scared anymore. "A little warning that there are other living *creatures* in the car would've been nice."

"They're trained guard dogs. They don't bite unless I tell them to," I countered, grinning wolfishly.

I drew back, sticking my hand back on the gear stick, and watching out of my peripheral vision as she drew closer to Erebus, the calmer out of the two. He bobbed her outstretched hand with his snout, and she giggled when he started licking her fingers like a love-sick fool that couldn't help but take to her immediately.

"Very original," Ariadne quipped, over her initial panic, resting back on her seat once bonding time was over. "I see why you would need guard dogs, though. Breaking hearts on the daily is bound to have an impact on your life as well."

She wasn't wrong. I had my fair share of attempted break-ins. None of them made it, seeing as my house was more secure than Fort Knox. I learned my lesson the hard way when I found a naked stranger waiting for me in my bed after returning from practice one day. But since then, I made sure to up my security. The dogs were a bonus, plus they were damned cute when they were puppies and helped me stay active.

My phone rang as I opened my mouth to reply, and we both glanced down at the same time, watching my father's name flash on the screen. I clicked the mute button, but then Ariadne's phone started buzzing not long after.

"Ignore it," I said, and she huffed in annoyance at being

ordered around. "This is between you and me, Spitfire. Let them foam at the mouth for a little bit."

She surprised me by agreeing and dropped her phone back in her mini-bag. It seemed I wasn't the only one that was frustrated by the turn of events. The deal was too good to pass up, but a premeditated marriage never crossed my mind. *Marriage never crossed my mind.* Period.

The Promenade, Astropolis's riverside park, came into view when I took a turn down Beacon street. It was a five-minute drive from work, two depending on how many speeding laws you broke. During the warmer months, they sometimes hosted free movies and concerts, but on a cold Wednesday morning, there was barely anyone, save for a few joggers and boats bobbing in the water.

"Are we going to the park?" Ariadne asked when I slowed down, and Nyx and Erebus became more hyper. "I'm not properly dressed for this weather. I thought we were going to be inside."

After pushing the lever up, I glanced at the exposed expanse of olive skin. Her tits were on the smaller side, which was why she managed to pull off this dress without looking trashy. Still didn't excuse the fact that it was East Coast fall time, and she was risking freezing to death for the sake of her Instagram feed.

Yes... I caved and Googled her. Not one of my proudest moments, ogling a twenty-one-year-old's social media pages, but she posted religiously—two, maybe three times a day. Sponsored posts, thirst traps (like that red bodysuit picture in Crete before her grandparent's home that had me rubbing one out at three a.m.). I said a silent sorry to her Nan and Pop, so I'd stop feeling like a pervert.

It didn't work.

"You can have my jacket." I shrugged out of my Parka, throwing it her way.

It hit her straight on the chest, and I thanked the Lord for the first time in years. I didn't need to be lusting after my too young, soon-to-be fiancé.

"What will you wear?" Aria asked.

"I'm wearing a sweater. You have a strapless dress on. I'll be fine," I said, getting out before she could say another word and bounding over to open her door.

She looked at me through narrowed eyes as she shrugged the jacket on, not making a move to get out. "Aw, is Saint Astor being a gentleman today?"

"Can't have people saying I broke your legs before you even step foot in a church." The hive mentality was real. I was the media's golden boy, but at the first sign of fragility, they exploited anything they could get their hands on. If there was a medal for losing your credibility the quickest, I would've won a long time ago. The last thing I needed to be branded as was an abuser. That shit stayed with you. "What did your parents even feed you that stunted your growth this much?"

She pursed her lips but took my offered hand. "The way you're going at it, I don't think we're making it that far."

I wrapped an arm around her waist, trying not to laugh at the way she leaned back as far as she could, lowering her to the ground beside me. She was tiny, two heads shorter than me, but the way she didn't stutter when she spoke back gave her more presence than her chipmunk build ever would.

Spitfire stared up at me, her chin tilted up in defiance, and I didn't take my hands off her immediately. My body was drawn to her familiar heat and the slight shiver that betrayed what her mouth would never dare utter.

"You never answered my question, you know. Saturday night while you were making yourself comfortable on my—"

"What question?" she growled, her breath leaving her body with a shudder.

"What drove you to me at Bella's?"

"Too many coincidences on short notice." She avoided my gaze.

"You thought I was fucking that girl just to spite you," I translated for her.

I was over that scene. It ended with getting my dick wet and my lust somewhat sated anyway, but I kept going back to it. Ever since Noah told me about the deal with the Fleurs, the wheels in my brain started turning. It didn't take much to put two and two together and figure out why Spitfire was so prone to outbursts of jealousy.

She knew before me. Five whole months.

The notion that Chloe Fleur was the one who pushed for marriage was turning more absurd by the day. Through acquisition or even a merger, she could get what she wanted without throwing her granddaughter to the wolves. My father pushing to control my life, on the other hand, was more believable. It wouldn't be the first time, and certainly not the last.

After years of crazy, I wanted a quiet life, and I was willing to walk the extra mile to get it. Ariadne Fleur most certainly did not fit in my plans. Nothing that was planted in my life by him did. Things my father touched were stained beyond repair.

"Your trust issues wound me." I clutched my hand over my heart, my tone laced with enough sarcasm for her to push me off, pursuing her bow-shaped lips as if she was readying to spit her venom.

I didn't wait to hear it. Rolling my shoulders, I opened the back door when the dogs became restless, scratching against it. They burst outside with excitement, tongues hanging out of their mouths and tails slicing through the air. Nyx and Erebus didn't take long to locate Aria behind me, taking to her like moths to a flame.

She leaned down—not much, seeing as my Dobermans were half her height—and scratched behind their ears as they took turns licking her face when she said the magic word —*walkies*. The edge of her dress was getting dirty from the muddy ground, but it was a welcome change of pace. Most girls that met Nyx and Erebus freaked out.

Well, to be fair, they weren't welcomed as warmly. My dogs didn't like strangers—especially ones that tiptoed out of my house at three am.

"It was a lapse of judgment, and I was very drunk and emotional. I don't expect you to stay celibate, as you shouldn't expect that of me. This is a business transaction at the end of the day," Aria clarified once we got the dogs leashed. I handed her Erebus since he didn't tug on his.

I wasn't going to be her gatekeeper, and I sure as hell wasn't going to be pushing for exclusivity. If she wanted to fuck anything with a pulse, she could, but I didn't know how prone little miss priss was to running her mouth. I needed someone I could trust by my side, not someone who would sing like a canary because the dick was too good. I hoped fraternizing with Astropolis's upper class was enough to teach her to look beyond the Crest-white smiles and notice the rotten breath of depravity lying beyond.

"Glad we're on the same page, Spitfire. You're going to

have to drop your steady dick, though. We wouldn't want him leaking anything to the press unless he's okay with the idea of an open relationship and will agree to sign an NDA."

An emotion I couldn't quite put my finger on ran through her eyes, the brown irises turning hazel when the sun shone through the overcast clouds, but it was swiftly masked with disgust. "My God, you're as crass as you are an ass."

I paused, masking my smile by remaining impassive. "I'll let it fly since it was an entertaining insult."

She rolled her eyes, giving Erebus a pat as he walked calmly beside her. Nyx, on the other hand, was too busy getting distracted by squirrels and kept trying to bolt. "In case you didn't know, not everyone is as good at throwing people out of their lives like used tissue paper."

"Everything can be achieved through practice." I plastered a nonchalant grin on my face.

"Some of us have feelings and get attached," Ariadne spoke slowly as if I was a stubborn kid.

"Some of us also agreed to a merger that comes with a bonus of a legally binding marriage for five years and a non-disclosure agreement." I challenged her by replicating the same annoying tone, looking down my nose. "So, if *some of us* can't adhere to the rules, there's still time to run."

Unconsciously her steps *did* get quicker like she was trying to escape reality.

"I *still* haven't agreed, so let's not talk like this is a sealed deal." She scowled up at me. "I'm surprised *you're* even considering it. Saint Astor settling down, the miracle of the century. How will you survive without your bi-weekly orgy parties?"

"For someone I've only talked to a handful of times in my

life, you sure know a lot about me."

"You're kind of a celebrity among us mere mortals. I don't know if you've noticed."

"So are you. An even bigger one based on your number of followers."

"You don't have any social media accounts, so that's not a good measure of unit. And I'm a fashion influencer and critic, hardly the same thing. People don't obsess over my life like they do yours." She worried her bottom lip, alerting me that being put under a microscope as well wasn't her idea of fun. "You literally have a Wikipedia page. All I have is Famous Birthdays, and they even got my star sign wrong."

How the fuck did the conversation even get to star signs?

Losing ground so early on wasn't a good sign. I could blink, and the next thing I knew, she would be analyzing the compatibility chart between Leos and whatever sign she was. Reading people and steering them in the direction of my choosing came easy to me. Ariadne was like an open book, young and impressionable, but somehow she wound up holding the reins.

Could be because for the past twenty minutes, my mind couldn't stop conjuring all sorts of fantasies about how her impeccable skin would feel like under my fingertips. She had one of the best complexions I'd ever seen, tan and dewy as if she moisturized ten times a day.

"I don't have all day," I said tersely, willing some of the previous frost between us to build up again. "Tell me, Spitfire, what made you show up today? You just graduated, your career is taking off, and your boyfriend—while he seems like the bore of the century—is a solid guy according to Ares's praise."

We came to a stop on the off-leash section of the park,

and I stretched my arm out after setting Nyx and Erebus free to run around with the other dogs. When I turned back, I caught Spitfire staring at me, her bold brown brows pulled together, shielding her stormy eyes.

"I could ask you the same thing," she countered. "You could have any woman you want with a snap of your fingers. You're already successful, *and* you can't stand the sight of me from what I've gathered. What are you looking to gain, Astor?" She pointed an accusatory finger at me.

It was an avalanche of setbacks that led to my distaste for my future wife. It started with a snowball that grew into an ice storm overnight. Admittedly, running her mouth was *her* only mistake. Being my father's pawn—even an ignorant one —was the final nail in the coffin, sealing any type of fondness away in Pandora's box full of unspeakables.

"The company," I said truthfully, keeping my intentions to myself.

"Me too." Aria piggy-backed off my answer. "The success of my company and the future of my family."

Ah, that's where you and I don't mesh, Spitfire.

Ruin, destruction, and perish were wonderful synonyms that ranked higher up on the list for all the things I had planned for Falco and Fleur. Success didn't even make the list, actually. Challenging Bezos, Musk, and Gates for best CEO didn't turn me on as much as it did my father.

"Greed, then," I stated the driving force behind our arranged marriage.

She tucked a stray curl behind her ear, and I let my eyes roam over her soft curls. Her hair glimmered red wherever the rays touched, full and shiny like they'd never seen a flat iron in their lifespan. "Do you think God is going to punish us for making a mockery out of such a sacred matrimony?"

I was already shaking my head. "I think God tapped out a long time ago on us, sweetheart."

We spent the rest of the morning hashing out the details of our upcoming union on a bench next to running water. I probed to see how much of a problem she would be when it came to running the company autonomously. Not much, considering she had no love for the business that promoted the art. I temporarily dropped the topic of her boyfriend when she threatened me with a Christian Orthodox baptism to appease her Greek side of the family. And we agreed on her moving to my house for the first year when the attention of the public would be at its peak.

After that, each one would go on their own merry way, meeting only when the occasion arose. She had her life, and I had mine.

"So that's it then... we both agree to this? You'll be my husband, and I'll be your w-wife," she stuttered, seemingly having a hard time believing what she was saying.

My tongue ran across my teeth, a deep, unsettling ache unfurling in my ribs. I watched, fascinated as Ariadne's demeanor shifted so fast it almost gave me whiplash. From confidently negotiating with me to cowering at the realization that we weren't exchanging empty words. They were a promise sealed with the responsibility of a united empire hanging over our shoulders like a dreaded boogeyman.

I couldn't believe it either. The whole thing went over too smoothly as if the Big Bang blew up one second and the universe was created in a day. Where there was darkness, I could now see pulses of light. Hope at the end of the mother-fucking tunnel in the shape of a spitting fire that made agitation course through me like lactic acid after a hard workout.

"Till we both shall stand each other, Ariadne."

CHAPTER EIGHT
ARIADNE

The world threw up all over my marquise cut ruby engagement ring in zero point five seconds after Saint and I went public with our decision. I was flooded with calls from every single living relative and friend, and I bet even the dead ones were rolling in their graves.

Irena wouldn't speak to me for a week because I hadn't told her anything about it. The longest she'd ever held a grudge, and she still wasn't completely over it. I didn't blame her, but I didn't trust myself not to break down and spill the truth if she cornered me.

My confidence and rationality were mere caricatures of what they used to be. Fear conquered my ink-black sky, and with nowhere to flee, I kept to myself, drowning in doubts. Irena was my bouncing board, my sister and best friend, and I didn't want to ruin her naive view of our family. Mom also begged me not to tell her anything, and I agreed as long as Irena got to choose her own future.

Grandma was, of course, floating on cloud nine. Right

along with my mother, that was finally getting her blood back, living vicariously through me. And Dad almost burst a vein when I told them, looking at me like I'd grown a second head that took over the decision-making.

Thankfully, it wasn't too hard to explain my *"relationship"* with Saint to the rest of the family, seeing as we had known each other for years beforehand. We played our hand with the whole rekindling of our friendship story when we stumbled across each other at a bar and eventually fell in love, iterating the same thing over and over again whenever someone asked.

Our front was fragile, though not many bought it.

Unplanned pregnancy was the resounding winner of explaining our rash decision, and I was sure Irena thought I'd cheated on Harry. In six months' time, my cousins, news outlets, and eighty percent of my comment section under my posts expected to see me with a swollen belly.

I shivered at the mere thought of babies. They were cute, don't get me wrong, but having one at my age? Hell fucking no. My *giagia* would have to live sordidly disappointed for a while longer. Or maybe forever.

My marriage was a sham, and my fiancé didn't give a shit about how I got off as long as it didn't have anything to do with him. I never thought I'd see the day when a guy didn't expect sex from me when I was pressured about it for most of my adult life.

As if my sick mind needed any more ammunition to think there was something wrong with me. My constant need for validation was my biggest flaw, but I was working on it. So, who cared if Saint avoided me like the plague, threw the engagement ring at me as if I was diseased, and didn't help me with moving whatsoever?

His loss, not mine.

I took my sweet time transferring my belongings to his hulking mansion, soaking in the last few moments I'd have with my beautifully decorated two-bedroom apartment.

Saint's house stood on a ten-acre lot, surrounded by wrought iron fences with spiky ends that made you think twice about trespassing and ivy crawling between the long black stakes, providing the privacy that the main building lacked. Windows and exposed structural elements like metal plates and turnbuckles linking huge wooden beams added to the unique architecture of the home. Still, it blended in well with the landscape of the North Ridge neighborhood, mostly filled with the homes of local politicians, celebrities, and athletes.

Rolling my last suitcase behind me, I tried not to linger on the fact that the asshole wasn't even here to welcome me and joined the pudgy, gray-haired housekeeper, Mrs. Adkins, at the entrance below the sky bridge. It connected the main house to another section of the home he'd instructed his staff to show me to. In essence, we had whole separate wings. So the only way I'd ever catch a peek of him inside of the house would be if I developed a finely honed X-ray vision.

"Miss Fleur, how are you this evening?" She greeted me while the engine of my Prius cooled in front of the garage.

"A little bit tired, but this is the last of my luggage finally." I motioned to the bag, and she was already on her way, tugging it away from me. My arms and legs felt like jelly after hauling bags around for the whole day, so I didn't protest.

"You go ahead to the kitchen and have some lemon soup while it's still hot. There's some banana bread in the oven too. I'll take care of sorting your clothes and run you a bath," she instructed as we both stepped inside the wide staircase.

Thank God for miracles like her. My mom didn't like having help around the house. She was old-fashioned in that sense, so we were taught to do everything ourselves, but after driving around all day, I was grateful for the helping hand.

"Thank you so much, Ms. Adkins. You really didn't have to do anything," I expressed my gratitude once we reached the threshold.

It was split in three different directions. The left side leading to the kitchen, judging by the sweet aroma that made my stomach grumble, the right to the living room, and behind us, there was the suspended pathway that led to my wing. Warm lights decorated each edge of the aisle, spilling outside of the double-pane glass walls.

"You don't have to thank me, Ms. Fleur. I'm just doing my job. After all, Mr. Astor instructed the staff to accommodate you as best as we can."

"He did?" I smoothed the hem of my knitted dress, glancing at my feet.

"Yes!"

Of course, he did, assigning his responsibilities to other people like a proper brat. A six-foot-five inch, two hundred and ten-pound brat that was used to getting his way. I wouldn't make it easy for him, wouldn't let him know how much his aloofness bothered me. If Saint Astor didn't care to climb my walls, I wasn't tearing them down so he could stroll inside.

"Now, go." Mrs. Adkins pushed my aching body toward the kitchen. "Your plate is on the table."

With one last smile, I took to the adjoining hall, my ears buzzing with the aftermath of a busy day. I could probably fill up my daily quota of steps by going from my room to the kitchen in this monstrosity of a house, but for all of its impracticality, it was gorgeous.

A secluded haven tucked in the outskirts of the suburbs, with pine trees and rolling mist as a backdrop, massive stone gas fireplaces, and windows in every corner bringing in tons of natural light that showered the industrial-inspired interior with warmth.

When I imagined Saint's place, I always envisioned something cold and impersonal to match his personality, but I was pleasantly surprised. I liked small places. They made me feel safe, and while the house was big, the wooden beams on the ceiling gave it a homey feel.

"So, you're really in love with this girl? You haven't talked about her once, *not one time,* and all of a sudden, you expect me to be fine with the fact that you're getting married in two months?" an unimpressed voice spoke from the kitchen as I neared the threshold.

I caught two built shadows lining the walnut flooring, and one was pacing back and forth. I didn't recognize who it was, so I stopped, palming the wall as I leaned forward.

"You don't have to be fine with it. You're not the one marrying her." Saint's familiar dry tone made a comeback as he finished his sentence off with a loud yawn.

It was well after twelve a.m., I didn't know what they were doing still up. They certainly weren't waiting for me since they were talking *about* me.

"Stop being a cunt, you know what I mean. When did you two meet? How long have you been together?"

I couldn't count on both hands how many times we were asked that question the past week, and because I was tired of being discussed behind my back, I made my presence known, tackling the cliché inquiry as I stepped into the room.

"We met at Carrousel du Louvre in Paris, during a Céline show. I was twelve, Saint was twenty-one and too busy chasing after every model in a skirt, so it's safe to say it wasn't love at first sight. That would be *very* illegal." I scrunched my nose, and both men in the room snapped to attention.

They were separated by the granite kitchen aisle, Saint with his back to me sat on a metal stool, and the other guy had stopped pacing, his eyes, blue with specs of that signature Astor gold, honed in on me. He looked exactly like a young version of Saint, save for the tattoos peeking beneath his loose, black button-up. I couldn't see them in full, but I caught lines of intricate illustrations curving over his wrists.

"Also, very disgusting," he said huskily, his rasp sending shivers of unease down my spine.

I felt outnumbered as I stood in a room with the Astor brothers. They had definitely made a name for themselves in Astropolis. The manwhore and the delinquent. The latter being Killian, seeing as he had the innate talent of getting into fights every other day while we attended high school.

Fine company I was keeping these days.

Threads of panic resurfaced in my brain, a constant companion of mine, causing my stomach to knot painfully whenever the topic of my future breached the conversation. I wasn't a person who lived in the moment. I was a planner. I had goals, dreams, visions. And none of them included getting married to a guy nine years my senior.

"Ariadne," Killian caved first with a greeting.

"Killian." I smiled tightly as I walked over to Saint, who stiffened when I set my hand on his broad back.

A second later, a reflex reaction kicked in, and he wrapped one thick arm around my shoulders, crushing me against his side. We'd been through the motions what felt like a thousand times by now, but a jolt of heat traveled down my belly at his touches. Even sitting, he was taller than me and had to bend down to kiss the top of my head. His warmth was comforting, fostering a false sense of protection because we shared the same secret.

"You two know each other?" Saint asked his brother as I burrowed myself into his chest, playing the role of the loving wife.

"We attended Crestview around the same time," Killian clarified, raking a hand through his dirty blond hair. His eyes shifted between us as if we were a puzzle piece he was trying to solve, the idea of love at first sight, being exclusive to fairy tales in his mind. "I didn't know you were here, Ariadne. Your fiancé failed to mention that too."

Like he did your existence.

The unspoken words shifted in the air, bouncing off my mental shield as if they were solid, like the fabricated charm Killian was hiding behind.

"I just got here, actually. I set my own work hours, and tonight I was running a bit late." The lie flew off my mouth like butter.

"Aria was in *Vogue's* best-emerging designers' list; her work's amazing," Saint butted in, saying all the things a supportive significant other should.

Except... I'd never told him that.

My head snapped up to find a smile pasted on his face, a seemingly genuine one, no sarcasm hiding along the dimples in his cheeks. It was gorgeous—everything about Saint was gorgeous as if he was tailor-made for seduction and greatness. A golden boy, enamoring crowds of thousands, be it with his athletic abilities or for more simple-minded folks like me—his face.

I clutched on to that slight indication that he wasn't as indifferent toward me as I thought he was. Saint's breath bearing down on my face began to feel like a cooling stream, carrying my juvenile infatuation with him to the surface.

Our web of deception was rooted in the truth, and the story of our first meeting wasn't a lie. He didn't see me, but I couldn't take my eyes off him. Saint Astor was a forbidden crush that came to life in the form of a nightmare.

"Gee, that's amazing," Killian said extra loud. "It's not as if she's a Fleur and has connections."

The last half of his sentence was barely audible, and I wished my ears were playing tricks on me. I glanced down before looking at Killian's unapologetic face, swift and brutal in his judgment. My mouth dropped open, a reply I couldn't take back on the tip of my tongue, but Saint beat me to it.

"And you're an Astor, but that hasn't stopped you from failing almost all of your classes this semester," Saint argued on my behalf. "No one likes a champagne socialist, despite what LA might lead you to believe. Apologize to Aria."

My gaze bounced between the two of them as they stared each other down. Saint's arm tightened around me when I started to retreat, but Killian took his sweet time turning to me, his anarchical nature pleading him not to back down.

"Sorry, Aria. Seems like my brother's sense of humor is keeping company to the stick that's shoved up his ass," he bit out a hybrid mix of an apology and insult that had my lips tipping up.

Killian Astor was really something. You couldn't help

but admire his ballsy nature even when he was offending you.

"That's all right. The joke was lost in translation. It happens," I cut in before this could continue any further, a breath of relief leaving my lungs when the brothers averted their eyes from each other. I idly drew circles over Saint's shirt as I tried to salvage the situation. "Did you fly in from California today?"

I migrated to a safer topic, and it worked as Killian's shoulders loosened, and he nodded. "I got here like an hour before you. So, on that note." He grabbed his phone, placing it in his back pocket. "If you'll excuse me, I'm off for the night. I'm dead tired."

"Of course." My smile was tight. "You should go lie down."

The atmosphere was tense as we wished Killian good night, and he departed down the hallway. As soon as he was out of sight, Saint dropped his hold on me as abruptly as Killian had left, all part of the act. My heart fluttered in my chest, but I didn't pay it any mind, keeping my back straight as I faced him.

"Please, don't speak on my behalf again. I had that under control, and I'm pretty sure your brother hates me right now."

Talk about a first impression.

Feelings were like drugs, deceptive in their glory. While it *felt* nice that Saint took my side, I didn't need him fighting my battles. I had enough open fires in my life as it was.

"If someone disrespects you, they're disrespecting me, Ariadne. I defend what's mine, even against my brother." The nonchalant look was back, his face a painting of apathy as he twisted his phone in his hand.

"Yours?" There was that weird flutter again in my womb.

"Mine," he replied curtly, getting on his feet. "However unorthodox our situation is, you're a reflection of my character. You do know the saying 'show me your friends, and I'll tell you who you are,' no?"

One step forward, ten steps back. It seemed to be a theme with Saint and me. All the happy bird chirps in my head turned vicious, their off-key melody flooding every crevice of my brain.

He was concerned about what light *my* reputation would paint him in?

A burst of crazed laughter spilled from my mouth as I strained my neck to look at his face. "I do. What about all your other female friends? Are they a reflection of you too?"

"They're not my friends. They're tight holes for my dick to sink into." He shrugged. "And vice versa for them. I'm nothing but a walking, talking orgasm."

My lip curled.

This guy had some serious issues... and so did I, for lusting over him. It was his good looks, plain and simple, but they wouldn't last him forever.

"I think your vanity says a lot more about you than people's opinions of me."

"You'd think so, wouldn't you?" A glimmer of anger broke past his facade of boredom, and I took a step back when he advanced forward. "Have you talked to your boyfriend at all lately? Asked him about the scene he caused outside of Ares's home yesterday?"

"What?" I asked, dumbfounded.

I hadn't heard from Harry ever since he abandoned me in front of Siren's Grill, which was two weeks ago but seemed like a whole lifetime. I didn't tell Saint we'd broken up, but I also never reinforced that we were in a relationship. I didn't want him thinking I was home alone while he was out sleeping with everything that walked.

"He went there looking for me, Spitfire, drunk off his ass calling both of us, especially you, very *colorful* names." A shiver of shock pinched between my shoulder blades, and I cowered when he bent his legs so he could drop closer to my face. "*Larry* should be grateful I wasn't there because instead of nursing him back to sobriety like a very patient Ares did, I would have given him the fight he so desperately wanted and bashed his teeth in like he deserved."

I was at a loss, trying to find the right words and flailing like a fish out of water, so Saint took it as an indication to continue talking. "I'll give you one more chance to leash lover boy. If he harasses my friends again and takes both of our names in his mouth, it won't be pretty. Am I clear, Spitfire?"

We stared at each other, Saint's face backing his cold-blooded statements, mine a mask of stupefaction at the turn things had taken.

"Crystal," I whispered, my brain still playing catch up.

This felt like a karmic intervention, telling me to run before the engagement party tomorrow, officially binding my life to this frustrating male for five years. Ever since I met him, it had been one bump after the other and potholes filled with humiliation on my end.

My God, his friends must think I'm such a mess.

A chill spread down my arms, and I rubbed the length of them as Saint straightened his spine, blinking at me. I thought I saw surprise gleam in his expression, but it was gone when he nodded at me. "Good. Have a good night, Ariadne, and make sure you use all of the layers Emily laid out for you. We've had some issues with the heating on the east wing, but it's getting fixed tomorrow."

With a last glance, Saint ate up the distance to the exit in seconds with his long strides, and I didn't digest his words until after he left, cursing under my breath.

Despite everything, I tried to eat, but I couldn't hold more than two bites down, anxiety already filling up the empty space in my stomach. So, I retired to my new room, barely taking it in, in the darkness, and collapsed on the bed, feeling cold, hungry, worried, and utterly alone.

The first night in Saint Astor's home set the tone for the days yet to come.

CHAPTER NINE
ARIADNE

I spent the morning of my engagement party working on a wedding dress that wasn't mine. I put together a Pinterest mood board for inspiration and started on some sketches, ignoring the way my hand trembled around the pencil.

Drawing was the best therapy to get rid of any residing anger, and I held a lot of it lately. At my fiancé, my grandma, my mother, my fucking ex.

You're a slut. Who gets engaged a week after breaking up with their boyfriend?

It's because he's rich, isn't it? Nothing gets a girl spreading her legs faster than a rich dick.

I could pay you if it would convince you to suck my cock.

The second I got my phone out, cocooned by my comforters yesterday, Harry beat me to it with an onslaught of angry texts that had my blood boiling. By the way he was acting, you'd think *I* was the one that dumped him and not the other way around.

The joke was on Saint, though. I preferred the cold last night and early this morning because I was ready to burst. It was as if I was on a submarine trying to climb out of a trench by being agreeable and passive, but it was only sinking me down deeper, crushing me with its immense pressure.

I wasn't going to let assholes with egos bigger than their dicks ruin my life. Making a sacrifice for my family didn't mean I needed to lay down my soul for everyone to walk over.

So after I was done with work, I got in the shower, shaved, scrubbed, moisturized, and made sure I spent enough time in there so the hot water supply ran out. Saint was going to need a cold shower after tonight, anyway.

"My God," Mrs. Adkins breathed as we both looked at my reflection in the full-length mirror by the closet. "You look absolutely stunning, Ms. Fleur."

I smiled at her compliment, a boost of confidence making me sit up straighter. In all honesty, it was the dress I had on that was absolutely amazing. The A-line number had a plunging neckline that made my boobs stand out, a cinched waist, and a flaring skirt featuring individually stitched-on feathers. Actual flecks of gold sewed into the fabric glimmered as they caught the artificial lighting of the room.

"It's a vintage Fleur dress," I said. I couldn't stop petting the cloth that tightened around my waist and skimmed perfectly over my hips. "My mom wore it to her own engagement party."

"The dress *is* pretty, but on you, it looks sensational." The middle-aged woman laid it on thick. "Gold is your color. It complements your skin tone well. You look like a Greek goddess with your black curls," she said as she gathered my hair, throwing it over my shoulder so my back was exposed.

Warmth dug its way into my heart as I released a breathless laugh. I did look good. After all, I had a shit ton of makeup on, perfectly highlighted cheekbones, and a sharply contoured nose. It was hard to go wrong with this much reinforcement.

I could see her vision... behind a thick cloud of smoke, but still, I could, and I wouldn't beat myself up over it today. My body wasn't perfect, my chest not as full as I would've liked it to be, my hips too round, my belly not flat enough, but I didn't let myself linger on my flaws. Not tonight.

Instead, I focused on the things I *did* like for once.

My skin glowed with a healthy flush, my eyes looked huge, bracketed by heavy lashes and smoky eyeliner, and my lips were plush, painted a light baby pink. Also, the six-inch heels I had on made me feel powerful.

Not quite an Aphrodite, but I'd take Hera.

Her husband was far from monogamous too, so we had a lot more in common than just looks.

I had to suck in my stomach a little as Mrs. Adkins tried to zip me up, but she stopped halfway when a cool voice sounded from the closet's entrance, making my exposed skin prickle.

"I got it from here, Emily." Saint swaggered into the room, his eyes rapt on me. "You can leave."

I clutched the low front of my dress, catching where his gaze had dipped in the mirror, and tried not to blush at the way Mrs. Adkins left with a pep in her step, thinking this was a case of a taken broom.

"Did no one teach you to knock before entering a room?"

I questioned, raising a brow at the designer-clad devil. "I could've been naked."

It was unfair how well he filled out his navy suit. It should be illegal for football players to even wear suits and for husbands to be more attractive than their wives, but oh-fucking-well, here we were.

He didn't bother answering immediately, slipping closer until his pine-needle scent tickled my nose. His fingers found the zipper, and my spine straightened at the skin-to-skin contact.

Light amusement danced on his face at my fidgety nature, and he shook his blond head. "It's nothing I haven't seen before."

Of course.

"*Fucking Zeus,*" I mumbled under my breath, and his brows knotted in confusion.

"What?"

"I... it's an expression Greek people use. They usually replace God with Zeus. My mom does it, and it's something my sister and I picked up on as well," I rushed to explain.

If my extremely religious orthodox *giagia* was hearing the bullshit I was spewing, she'd smack me over the head, but I'd literally die of mortification if Saint knew I referred to him as Zeus. Even if it was for all the wrong reasons, I knew the cocky bastard would find the positive in it.

"I've been to Greece multiple times. I've never heard anyone say that." He shook his head, fingers still fumbling with the zipper.

"Are you zipping or unzipping the freaking dress?" I changed the subject before I made a fool out of myself—any more than I already had—almost breaking my back when his pinky caressed my spine.

His answering laugh was a touch amused and a ton mocking as he finished fastening the dress. A whoosh of air escaped my mouth as the confining fabric forced my insides to relocate in order not to burst at the seams. My mom was a lot slimmer at my age, and we didn't have time to tailor the dress to fit me.

I bit my lip when the mirror started resembling the enemy again, filling my head with dark thoughts, and shuddered when Saint's hands molded around my waist. He stood tall behind me, like a dark looming figure as we looked at each other's reflections.

Future husband and wife.

We were like yin and yang—polar opposite appearances, a virgin and a manwhore, a confident man, and a woman who could use some of the poise that dripped with his every movement. Perhaps the single thing that tied us together was our similar upbringing.

"What's eating away at you, Ariadne?" he asked in a rare moment of ceasefire.

Everything. I wanted to reply.

I fear that I'm making the worst mistake of my life. That you're going to ruin me from the inside out before our first year together is even up. That I'm attracted to you, even though I shouldn't be, because you'd never want anyone like me.

I had so much to say, but I felt muzzled. The merger was already signed, my fate already sealed by my own doing. I couldn't complain now, not when I had everything to lose.

One more tricky clause Noah Astor insisted on having in the contract?

If either one of us requested a divorce before our five years were up, we would not only be opting out of the marriage but also the company. And I knew Saint wouldn't miss an opportunity to get rid of me, so I shut my mouth, slipping away from his drugging hold.

This was a game of survival I intended to win at any cost. For my family.

"I didn't give you my engagement present," I exclaimed, and he arched his brows, placing his hands in his pockets.

"I think you're confused. It's other people who are supposed to be giving us presents."

I shrugged, reaching for the black-tie box on the wooden closet shelf next to me, and extended it to him. Curiosity sparked in the upturned tilt of his lips, and I realized even Saint got excited for gifts when he grabbed it from me.

"Since I have your family's ring," I ran my thumb over the ruby stone subconsciously. "I wanted you to have something of mine tonight. I sewed you this black and gold tie, so we can match."

I played with my skirts as he opened the box, taking a peek at the tie. The contrast between the colors made for quite a statement piece, as the bold gold flowers sat on a black subtly striped background.

Saint ran one long finger down the middle before pulling it out and curving an inquisitive brow. "*You* made this?"

I nodded, and my stomach clenched when he smiled, his dimples coming out. A rush of boldness worked its way through my body, and maybe it was because Mrs. Adkins had compared me to a Greek goddess, but I wanted to touch him, and I didn't hold back.

Running my hands up his chest, I felt a delicious ache spread inside my womb when Saint's breath quickened and pupils dilated, tracing my movements. Taking the tie from his hands, I worked it around his neck, forcing him to look up as I tightened it... maybe a smidge too much when his hands dropped on my waist again, until our bodies were flush, the tie caught between our torsos.

"I can't have my fiancé looking basic."

Saint pierced me with a satirical look, and I worried if he could feel my heart almost beating out of my chest. Sugar, spice, and all things wicked, his scent was intoxicating, and I wanted to taste the mint in his mouth when his teeth came out like a predator.

"Let's go then, Ms. Fleur. We have crowds to woo."

SAINT

"What is your fiancé wearing?" Mom magically appeared by my side at the edge of the dance floor, a blue silk number dripping over her body and clashing with her fair hair.

A rancid cloud of perfume hung heavy in the air; Mugler, Dior, Falco, and a bunch of other high-end brands tickled my nose. I'd sneezed about five times since we got to the glitzy hotel where we'd booked the reception and was developing a mean headache.

The latter wasn't only due to the mixed aromas.

I didn't do people, least of all the people who were in attendance today.

All the blue bloods of Astropolis were invited, and their veneered teeth shone as they cross-examined rumors the entire night. Weddings and funerals were *the* place to spill the tea in our society. Everyone showed up because the gossip would be too hot to miss, not because they gave a shit.

I glanced at Ariadne, dancing with her friends under the

sparkling chandeliers in the middle of the marble, checkered floor. They were a breath of fresh air amidst the stiff Barbies surrounding them, possessing more rhythm in their pinkies than everyone else here did in their entire body.

I couldn't stop looking, even though I really should. No one could. She had about a dozen gazes fixed on her, from lusty men to envious women. It was that dress that made her look as if she'd descended from the heavens, the finest damned jewel in the room.

I snatched a champagne glass from a passing server to cool off before replying. "Clothes."

Unfortunately.

Celia Astor gave me a blank stare, raising her manicured hand so she could steal my alcohol away. I heaved a heavy sigh, knowing there was nothing I could do. I was on probation whenever she was around. I had a murky past with my amber-colored bottles at home, and Mom freaked out whenever I drank in her presence.

"Cut the sarcasm, Saint. Her boobs are almost popping out. Aren't you embarrassed that she went out like that? At your engagement party, no less?"

My eyes flew to Aria again, but nope her boobs were still very much tucked in.

Unfortunately, times two.

You could still tell they were there, perky and perfect like two pears waiting for a bite. I bit my lip instinctively, imagining it was something plumper.

Fuck, I was suffering from a case of blue balls. It'd been more than a month since I last had sex, seeing as problems sprouted like mushrooms wherever I went, and I was feeling the drawbacks like a recovering addict.

A recovering sex addict. It was ironic since my need for it

had severely diminished the past few years, but Miss Ariadne showed up, and I was gearing up and ready to go.

Jesus, I understood why women often said we men were predictable. Give us a girl in a skimpy dress, her makeup pretty but natural, skin soft like butter and bouncy curves, and our entire assessment shifted in seconds.

Shaking my head, I flushed the thoughts from my brain. The last thing I needed was to get hard in front of my mother. "What do you want me to do? Police what she wears? I have no problem with what she has on, this is her day, and she looks the part."

Her mouth dropped open to fight my statement because a world where mothers didn't fight their kids even when they were thirty was impossible, but she was interrupted before she could.

Lydia Fleur, Aria's mom, popped up on my other side, smiling warmly at me as she caressed the length of her red gown. "She does, doesn't she? My Ariadne has great taste."

My head started pounding harder when I recognized the incoming battle of the exes that was about to commence.

Holding back a groan, I smiled back at my mother-in-law, who Ariadne had an uncanny resemblance to, and brought her hand to my lips for a kiss. Even though I was picturing railing her daughter four ways into heaven since I saw her in the closet, my manners were still stellar.

"Mrs. Fleur."

"Saint, darling." Lydia's smile was calculating as she acknowledged and bypassed me just as quickly, latching on to my mother and layering her words with an extra touch of frost. "Celia."

"Lydia." Mom replicated her tone next to me, shuffling closer.

"You had something to say about my daughter's dress?" Lydia continued when I dropped her hand, her features frozen.

Oh, for fuck's sake, I was in the middle of two scorned women, and I couldn't even get some alcohol to chase down their bitterness for one another.

"I just don't think recycling material is classy. Wasn't that the dress you wore in your own engagement?" The crease between my mother's blond brows got deeper when she looked at Ariadne again.

"You mean the one where my fiancé actually showed up?" Lydia chirped, and even I could feel the burn.

Sighing, I scrubbed a palm down my scruff when my mom gasped. Not only had they both been with the same guy, but Aria's dad also abandoned my mom cold turkey on their engagement day.

There was nothing incestuous about it, but it still grossed me out.

"He already got you pregnant out of wedlock. I'm guessing abandoning you too would've damaged his reputation beyond repair," Mom seethed, giving as good as she got.

I noticed a few women had stopped dancing and started staring, waiting for the impending showdown. Taking a step forward, I inserted myself between them before this escalated to scratching or hair pulling.

"Ladies—" I intervened but was cut off by the subject of their decades-old beef.

"What's going on here?" Darian Fleur swaggered in, looking at his wife for clarification.

Lydia glued herself to her husband and answered at her leisure, waiting to see if my mom would say anything. "Celia doesn't like Ariadne's dress," she eventually snitched.

Darian's eyes widened in surprise, oblivious as a mule. "What? Why? It's a vintage Fleur. There have been thousands of articles written about it."

"Well, it's a bit tacky. I see Celia's point." My dad popped up behind me too. Not one to miss out on all the action, and I was closed in from all directions.

"Did you just..." Lydia gasped in outrage, looking at all of us. "Did he just call my daughter tacky?"

"I said the *dress* was tacky. In my opinion, the gown Celia and I sent over for her to wear was more appropriate for a setting such as this." Dad kept it going, enjoying the thunderous atmosphere.

It was game time whenever Darian and he took opposite sides in a fight.

"Maybe you should keep your opinions to yourself," I suggested, my mouth set in a cruel sneer. "Insulting the host is not going to do you any honors unless you'd like to find yourself kicked out."

His neck flushed as I berated him in front of Aria's family. Mom had said some petty shit too, but at least her words came from a place of hurt (and fuck, okay, maybe I had a bit of a soft spot for the person who carried me for nine months), Noah Astor just loved to see the world burn.

Lydia Fleur gave an uppity huff behind me, and Mom had betrayal painted on her face, wondering why I didn't join them in bashing my fiancé. I didn't have a particular attachment to Spitfire, but bashing my future wife wasn't my idea of a good time, no matter how unwanted she was.

"Now, I trust you'll be able not to kill each other if I leave you alone for two seconds." I swung my head sharply on either side, satisfied once I received nods from both of them.

Leaving the Brady bunch behind, I made my way past the dancing bodies in the ballroom, treating everyone that tried to talk to me like air. Aria's hips had stopped swinging hypnotically when a slow pop song burst through the speakers, and everyone paired up.

She rubbed her arm, unbeknown that a guy was approaching from the left, but he made a U-turn when he found me glaring at him, ready to break his limbs if he touched her. It was fascinating how she could pull such possessiveness from me.

I'd never been in a serious relationship. I'd fucked around plenty and had some steady partners, but we were never exclusive. If they could blow my world out in under five minutes, they stuck around. That was my rule of thumb. Since it hadn't happened in a while, there had been no one.

Maybe it was the fact that she was going to be my wife in a month's time that had animosity crawling through me. Ariadne was forced on me, but I didn't refuse. A sense of responsibility hummed under my skin, some primal male fondness that craved to own and protect.

"Spitfire." I caught her arm when she tried to slip away, turning her around, her dark tresses settling in unruly waves around her. "Care to give me this dance?"

Her eyes narrowed in question. "You want to dance? I assumed standing rigid like a marble statue the whole night was more up your speed."

"You inspired me," I drawled, pulling her close.

Aria went stiff as a board in my arms, suspicions swimming behind her browns as if I'd dip her and drop her on the floor. I hedged on, ignoring her distrust, and placed her arms around my shoulders, raising her slightly off the ground so she could reach up.

Her minty breath hitched, blowing a surprised puff over my neck when our bodies went flush. I could feel the heat of her exposed valley through the crisp linen of my shirt, and the break-off of her raised peaks cresting against my pecs.

"Is this really necessary?" she hissed, tightening her hold on me so she wouldn't fall flat on her ass. "People are watching."

"Let them." I clamped my hands over her hips, reveling in the sweet curves I found there, and ducked my head to whisper over her lips. "Half of the married couples in here wouldn't touch each other with a ten-foot pole. You have wives that have most probably slept with more pool boys than you can count, and men blowing through prostitutes left and right. A show is all they want, lust after something they can't have."

Aria's lashes fluttered over her pretty eyes. I didn't know what it was, but the lid I was keeping over my attraction for her was cracking open the more we were in proximity. I couldn't stop thinking about licking that pink lipstick right off, discovering if it tasted as it looked. Like strawberry cream, waiting to be lapped up.

"We don't have it either. I don't know if you realize, but what you just described is about to be our future." She kept her voice low as we spun about the rest of the dancing bodies. "A slightly altered version, of course. I wouldn't sleep with any pool boys, and I'd don't think you need to pay for sex."

No, I didn't. Sometimes it sickened me how readily available it was.

"I might not have a ten-foot pole, but I think my eight-inch one would suffice, and I guess touching you with it wouldn't be the end of the world."

To fuck with her, my hips dove ever so slightly forward as I dipped her out. Aria trembled, catapulting toward me sooner than the beat required, and stared at me with her jaw almost hitting the floor.

"What are you saying?"

"That I don't find you repulsive. Take the compliment, Spitfire."

"Well, I'm honored to be part of that ninety-nine, point nine percent of the female population in Astropolis that you find attractive, Saint," she said, sickeningly sweet, a faux smile pasted on her face as she waited to gouge my reaction.

"You're welcome," I mocked.

She held her head high as I moved us around, our bodies closer than socially acceptable. We'd garnered a ton of attention, everybody waiting for a sliver of affection between us.

Ariadne's breaths came out in short pants once I spun her out, the air around her filling with golden halos, and slammed her back into me, my hands cupping her face.

The ember between us grew more vicious.

"We're going to make quite a few headlines tomorrow," she whispered but stayed put, letting me lead.

"Kiss me then." Her eyes flared up at my words, and I didn't know where the fuck I'd pulled them from. "Give them something to talk about because if we don't, they still will, for all the wrong reasons."

"Like what?"

Proximity drew sweat from her palms. She clutched my dress shirt tight, creasing it in her little fists, one side of her wanting to throw me off, the other begging to delve into the wild.

"Like we're a weird fucking couple that didn't exchange a single touch on their own engagement party. You flinch every time I get close to you, Spitfire. *The world* is watching, not only our family and friends. Everything you do and say is going to be picked apart for bored housewives to spread rumors about."

Her chest caved with the realization that her life wasn't hers anymore. That was what marrying everyone's favorite headline got you. Scrutiny by the buckets. The Fleur's were better at shielding their kids, so I was sure this seemed alien to Ariadne. Having to measure every word before it left your mouth and think about every movement and gesture was no easy feat to get used to.

"So we have to kiss to prove that we're in *love?*" She spat the last word out as if it was blasphemous. There was a deer caught in headlights look in her eyes that sprouted a burst of laughter from me and a scowl from her.

"Could you relax? It's just a kiss. You're acting like I'm gonna eat you out on the table for all the guests to see."

Her teeth pierced her lower lip. "Stop being so crass—"

My hand traveled to her hair, and I gripped it near the base of her head. Instead of going through multiple rounds of insults, I tilted her head up and slammed my lips onto hers, shutting her up with my *so crass* mouth.

Ariadne froze in my arms, and our bodies were suspended for a few moments as we got a feel of each other. Ample softness beaconed my teeth to sink in her lower lip, and when her breath met mine, it charged the air with electricity I could taste. Cinnamon and oranges bloomed on my tongue when she let me blow past her defenses and into the crevice of her mouth.

My ears rang, a vicious symphony that distorted all the noise around me until all I could hear was her. I wanted to make it good for her, so good she felt guilty at night when she imagined my face between her legs as she masturbated to the thought of what she craved. The hot-blooded male in me had a silent but palpable competition with her boyfriend and took pride in knowing *Larry* didn't make her as flustered as I did.

Ariadne's tongue tangled with mine, giving back tenfold once she was out of her stupor. Her body trembled as she held on to me, her fingers tangling on the nape of my neck, causing our teeth to clash as our mouths battled each other.

I felt her fight spreading from my head to the tips of my toes, paying special attention between my legs. Heat filled my dick, and I pressed her belly to the swell on my trousers, my other hand shackling her tulle-covered hip.

"Saint," I ate up her gasp with another thrust of my tongue, exploring the stormy sea that was Ariadne Fleur.

A spitfire with hackles of steel.

No match for the fire that built in my gut, though. A slow aching burn ravaged through tissue and bone as I kissed her like I was starved, not giving a shit that everyone had their eyes glued on us.

My fake fiancé was a closet freak. Despite her resistance at first, her body trembled with adrenaline as she palmed my jaw in her shaking hands. There was no way Spitfire had a ton of experience. She kissed like a schoolgirl after her first date, sloppy and just filthy enough to make removing my mouth from hers a struggle.

I dragged the kiss out, lessening the intensity, and when I was finally sated, I pecked the corner of her damp mouth before pulling away. Her eyes were slammed shut as I allowed for some distance, but I still reveled in her flush and the rawness of her lips. They were bright red, and I was wearing her lipstick on my mouth like a goddamn fool that needed to get his priorities straight.

"Spitfire, are you okay?" I asked when she still hadn't opened her eyes.

The song changed to a fast-paced beat again, but we stood unmoving, catching our breaths. Her lashes split after she released a loud sigh, rewarding me with the molten brown color of her irises.

"Perfect." She nodded, running her gaze down my face as she stripped my hands from her body. I let go reluctantly. "I'm... I'm going to go sit down for a while. I'm a bit tired from all the dancing."

I nodded, needing my space to memorize the sentence *look, but don't touch*. We went in opposite directions, and I downed two champagne glasses, now that I was free of supervision. On my third, I took a peek at where she was sitting, her eyes glued to her phone, and I knew immediately who she was texting.

She was biting her lip, shielding her screen so her nosy cousin wouldn't see, and acid burned down my throat. Nothing turned me off more in this world than desperate girls chasing after dangerous dicks for a thrill.

CHAPTER TEN

ARIADNE

"Bitch, what the hell was that?" Daphne cornered me the second she got the chance. My eyes flicked to Irena, who was sitting next to her, sipping her chai tea latte and looking at us through narrowed eyes. "First, you break the news of an engagement out of nowhere. Let me tell you, I was offended that you didn't tell me anything, especially when your fiancé is Saint *freaking* Astor. Then you dodge my calls for weeks. I mean, I get why you would be busy with such a hunk. The way he kissed you on that dance floor was so, *ugh*." I kept my laugh to myself when Daphne's eyes rolled to the back of her head. "My man was one step away from hoovering your soul up. That little boy you were with before him could never. What the hell even happened to that guy?" She looked at me expectantly, removing her blue scarf and picking up her coffee cup.

I squirmed in my seat, willing Nyx and Erebus to finish their puppuccinos faster, so we could leave. I wasn't planning on meeting them. We bumped into each other at Starbucks near my old apartment after getting the dogs a treat, and Daphne forced me to sit down so we could catch up. At least I got Mom's dress from my trunk and gave it to Irena so she could drop it off for me.

She had a lot of thoughts about that kiss, as did I. A whole lotta feelings too that I kept under wraps when Saint disappeared as soon as we got home. I had no right to ask where, but I had a pretty good idea.

"Oh, we broke up a while ago."

Irena choked on her sip, and another notification lit up my phone screen, making my stomach churn with nerves. I patted Nyx's back, holding on to their leashes tighter as they ate their treats.

"A while ago, as in three weeks ago?" My own sister threw me under the bus.

"Three weeks?" Daphne's eyes widened, grasping on to new gossip. "Damn, girl, you move fast. When did you meet Saint again? You've never been the biggest believer of love at first sight."

"Well, you can't really believe in something you've never felt. My opinions changed after I bumped into Saint again." I started believing in hate at first sight... *fine, and a little bit of lust too.*

Another ping, and my leg started bouncing nervously under the table when they heard it too.

"Your fiancé is a little possessive," Irena said, no snark in her tone. Although she wanted to sound nonchalant, I could tell she was genuinely concerned about me. "That's like the third time he's texted you, in a five-minute interval."

Oh, how I wished it was my fiancé, but he didn't give a shit whether I lived or died. Saint spent crazy hours at Falco, certainly longer than he needed to, and I didn't know if it was because he wanted to avoid seeing me or ensuring a smooth merger took a lot out of him.

Dad was handling our side of things, though, and I didn't see him slaving away over a computer. But how would I know? I chose to stay out of it and work on my own thing. I didn't need anyone saying I got where I was because of my family or because I was fucking the boss.

Working as a lead designer for Falco and Fleur was a dream many creatives such as myself had, and I was sure the time would come eventually, but I wanted to prove myself first. I wouldn't take any hand-outs. My online store was launching in February, and I was dreading it as much as I was excited.

To commemorate Irena's words, my phone pinged yet again.

"He's catching up because I was supposed to take the dogs to the vet, but it's been a while since I left," I rushed to explain.

I should be concerned with how easily lies came to me. I was drowning in them as of late. Erebus helped me out with half a bark, resting his paw on my lap once he was done, and I smiled apologetically at Irena and Daphne, who eyed me with suspicion.

"Look, I really have to go, guys, but I'll see you next week for Thanksgiving," I said as I gathered my crossbody bag, buttoning up my faux fur coat. "Will you come, Daphne? *Giagia* is flying out early to be there for my wedding, December first."

"Family reunion? You know I wouldn't miss a Karaniko-laou versus Fleur showdown for the world," she said with a wicked smile.

Both Irena and I cringed. It was fun watching them bicker on the outside. Their insults were very creative, but after years of enduring them, the whole situation got stale quick.

With a hug and a kiss on Irena's cheek that she wiped off as soon as she got the chance, I left, heading to the beach close to my old apartment.

I didn't know what Harry wanted from me, nor did I want to find out, but he had been blowing up my phone with texts the past few days. At first, they were insulting, which proved how much a hurt ego could change men, and when that didn't work out, he laid it on thick, apologizing profoundly, and saying he was drunk when he sent those texts.

Not to mention he wouldn't stop calling me from unknown numbers when I blocked him.

So I caved and took him up on his offer to meet and hash things out. I chose a public location, shooting down his proposal for his apartment, and asked Saint if I could take the dogs out for a walk. I didn't think Harry would harm me, but I felt safer with Nyx and Erebus around.

I arrived at the beach twenty minutes late.

It was unusually sunny for a November day, rays kissing the shore as ocean waves slammed against the packed sand. Panting and sweating underneath my all-black outfit, I spotted Harry seated on a bench, wearing gray sweatpants, a North Face jacket, sunglasses, and a ball cap.

I had multiple reasons for not wanting to be spotted, but it didn't make sense as to why he had gone for an incognito look. My heart pumped in my chest as I got closer, and it often happened when he was around.

Something about Harry made me uncomfortable. He was prone to a quick temper and could be very pushy. I always made excuses for him, though. I also wasn't the easiest person to get along with, but that wasn't the case with my people. I would go to war for the people I loved, not at war *with* them whenever we disagreed.

Harry turned around when my footsteps drew nearer. The smile painted on his face faltered when he saw the huge Dobermans that were walking regally on either side.

"Ariadne," he shot up, ready to give me a hug, but Nyx and Erebus stopped him short with a few low growls. "When did you get dogs?" He removed his glasses, crouching to pat them first, and retreated when their tails swung up their bodies alert.

Okay... so maybe they didn't like male strangers.

I tugged on their leash, and they sat by my feet as I rounded the bench, a healthy distance away from Harry.

"Quite aggressive," Harry started, sinking down to the grain-filled bench again and eyeing the dogs wearily. "You should look into having them trained. I have a buddy that can help you ou—"

"They're already trained, and they're Saint's." I cut him off, scratching behind Nyx's ears.

My ring finger gleamed in the sunlight, and when I looked back at Harry, his lips were downturned looking at the ruby engagement ring. "Right... Saint's."

If he hadn't texted me all the nasty things he did, I would've felt bad. Some people took longer to move on than others, even if they were the ones that instigated a breakup.

"Are you going to tell me why you've been blowing up my phone for the past several days?" I cut straight to the chase.

"I lost my job." Harry's voice prickled with an edge when he completely bypassed my question.

"Well, if you expected a promotion, I don't think driving to your boss's house and screaming at him in the middle of the night was the right way to go about it."

"So you know."

He played with the zipper of his jacket, his head downcast. I expected sick satisfaction to hit me from seeing him at his lowest, but I couldn't rejoice in his ruin. Even though he called me every curse word in the book, there was a part of me that remembered my friend Harry.

The nice and kind one before he did a one-eighty.

Then again, people had multiple faces. One for their friends, family, love interests. You never knew who someone was when they were alone.

"Of course, I know. Ares and Saint are best friends. I would find out eventually."

"*Saint, Saint, Saint.*" He threw his hands in the air abruptly, and I stiffened, transmitting my energy through the leash and alerting the dogs. "Him again. First taking my girl, and then my job. I'm so fucking tired of people speaking about him like he's some sort of God."

"Harry..." My voice came out as a whisper, and I cleared my throat. "*You* broke up with *me*. No one took me away. *You* set me free."

"And it only took you about a week to spread your wings and fly." Spittle flew from his mouth, causing anger to brew inside me.

"Did you expect me to pine after you? Remain single for the rest of my life because some boy dumped me," I scoffed, my voice incredulous.

"I didn't dump you, Ariadne. I was simply giving you some space to think over things. Our relationship was progressing too slow to be considered normal. Is it because of him? Were you cheating on me with him?" Harry removed his sunglasses, poking the air with empty accusations.

A flicker of guilt simmered beneath my skin, even though I never did.

I wanted to. It was all I could think about at Siren's Grill. Saint's voice, rough hands, filthy mouth, they were all I could think about. Now I could add his kissing skills to the list of things my mind kept replaying.

"I never cheated on you!" My lips tingled as I replied, and not because of the North Atlantic ice-cold wind.

"Then what is it?" he asked, exasperated. "Why did you decide to get married? Can't you see that he proposed just so he can get between your legs sooner?"

If only you knew that Saint Astor has no intention of getting between my legs.

A bitter sentence filled my head, and it was true. That particular monster would never get inside my bed, but he loved filling up the empty space in my head like a parasite.

Remembering how Saint stood up for me, though, my sense of self-worth accentuated, and I realized I didn't owe Harry anything. Especially when his vocabulary was pulling short.

Lifting a cool brow up, I made a show of fixing my bag so I could get up. "I won't allow you to talk about my fiancé or me that way."

"Fine-fine..." Harry threw his hands up in surrender. "Just sit down. We can work something out. I didn't mean what I said, Ariadne. Sex is not a dealbreaker for me. I'm willing to wait some more time."

"Harry, this... you, me. It's over. I moved on, and so should you. I'm sorry things didn't work out, but it's for the best."

"Oh, yes, I'm sure you feel extremely sorry all cooped up in your mansion."

"I'm not the reason you lost your jo—" I cut my angry sentence off, not sure why I even bothered. Fixing myself up for real this time, I stood, and the dogs followed suit. "You know what? Have a good life, Harry. I wish you all the peace and love in the world."

His eyes flashed with panic, and before I could make it another step, he trapped my arm in his hand. "Where are you going?"

"Get your hands off me!" Nyx backed my order with a warning bark, and Harry pulled his lips back, his face almost resembling the dog's sneer as he let me go.

"I'm not done yet."

"Well, I am," I said, my heart beating out of my chest at all the commotion.

Harry laughed as if he'd lost his marbles, rocking back on the bench and shaking his head. "I tried. I really tried being nice about this, but you leave me with no choice."

"What are you talking about?" I snapped my fingers, so the Dobermans settled down again. They did, but their bodies stayed alert, pressed against either of my legs, eyeing Harry like he was their enemy.

"Do you remember all those times you did come to my

apartment, Ariadne? You're one selfish bitch, getting and giving little in return."

"You're still not getting much in return. I don't know why we're going around in circles here."

"I filmed you."

My reality collapsed, the world shifting beneath my feet when I digested his words. Everything hovered in the air when the first domino fell, motionless for a fraction of a second. I sucked in heavy breaths to make up for the lack of oxygen, but it only resulted in making me dizzier.

"What?"

My reaction got a smile out of him, straight white teeth gleaming in the light of someone else's misery. "That one time you sucked me off, with your tits on display for everyone to see, I filmed it. My face is not in the shot, but I made sure I got yours in 4K—"

There was no way. There was absolutely no way.

"Shut up," I forced out. "This is pathetic, even for you. You're lying. Stop lying."

This couldn't be happening to me. Things like this never happened in real life. They couldn't.

"Oh, you think I'm lying?"

I watched wordlessly as he pulled out his phone and pressed on it, turning the screen my way. All I saw was black before a fuzzy video started buffering, and I filled the screen, kneeling on Harry's marble floors, in a *very* compromising position.

Air fled from my lungs when I took in my naked chest, and my head bobbing back and forth on an intimate moment with my boyfriend, bile rushing up my throat at the ammunition that this unstable man had against me. I was a dead girl. My eyes were the size of the moon as I focused and refocused on the video, making sure I wasn't in a nightmare. I even pinched myself to see if this was real.

Unfortunately, it was.

People were mingling by the water, kids screaming at the pier farther south, and seagulls flying up ahead, reminding me of a world existing beyond my personal tragedy. I retracted my gaze when *video me* choked. My stomach lurched by the tape, and I stared at the sun, hoping the cruel rays would erase what my eyes had just watched.

But my mind couldn't forget. I was on my knees before Harry, my assets on full display, bringing shame to my family and myself with a single click of my disguised villain's sausage fingers.

My legs trembled, but I refused to sit down. *Back down.* I tried to see the light on the canvas that suddenly got ten shades darker.

"That's against the law," I parroted. "You can't release that, or you'll get in trouble."

Harry shrugged as he pocketed his phone again, satisfied with himself. "I'm already in trouble. I lost my job, and I'm behind on my mortgage payments. If I don't manage to find the money soon, I'll be kicked out."

There it was; the life jacket on my stormy sea. I grabbed it, my spirit fleeting, a cold robotic mentality kicking in to help me survive.

"So you want money? And then you'll delete whatever video you have?"

"I want my job back too."

"How am I supposed to do that? Ares is Saint's friend. I've only talked to him once."

Spreading his arms over the back of the bench, he

crossed his legs. "Figure out a way to make it happen, princess. Suck his dick too. That should do the trick."

For a second, I considered unleashing Nyx and Erebus on him. They hadn't stopped growling since I'd stood, feeling the shift in the air. I never in my life thought I'd ever consider murder. Find the sight of teeth tearing through skin almost orgasmic. A dark part of myself surfaced when pushed and blackmailed.

"Why don't you find another job?" I spoke through the scary thoughts in my head.

There were witnesses everywhere, and it was the twenty-first century. The law favored men way more than it ever had women. How many times had I watched as women were sent to prison for killing their abusers, sometimes even receiving maximum sentences for taking their life into their own hands when there was nowhere to turn to?

Countless.

"I've tried, but no one will hire me. I have a record, and not many employers are willing to overlook that."

"You have a record? I-I don't fucking know you at all." There was the second blow of the night, and I staggered back as Harry got to his feet, taking the dogs with me.

I wanted to light the smirk that spread over his face on fire.

"If you know what's good for you, Ariadne, you *won't* get to know me at all. Follow my instructions, wire me the money, and I'll make sure your tapes never see the light of day. Of course, go to the police, and the whole world gets a taste of Ariadne Fleur."

Tapes.

Plural.

Perhaps I was weak for the way I gave in so easily, for not

ripping the phone from his hands and clawing his face right then and there, but I had the disadvantage of being locked in the body of a midget, and I didn't want Nyx and Erebus to be put down for doing my bidding.

So I started with an offer, and then I'd plan.

"How much do you need?"

CHAPTER ELEVEN

ARIADNE

I rolled around in my bed for hours after I got home, hoping sleep would come and carry the panic and nausea away.

A difficult thing to do when you had an Albatross around your neck.

The sheets scratched against my skin, there was an annoying *tap, tap, tap,* against the window from a branch rhythmically slamming on it, and the wind howled across Saint's several acres of land.

The progression of the weather reminded me of how my life unraveled in under a month. A straight-laced girl, coming apart in a mess of loose threads. From sunshine and pink clouds to black ash raining over my heart.

In my quest to run from one monster, I'd willingly embraced another, let him in, only for him to slap me in the face when all was said and done.

I thought I knew.

I thought I could see the truth plain and simple.

Saint was bad. Saint wouldn't hesitate to crush my

heart into a thousand little pieces. So, I needed someone good to shield me. Someone safe and predictable. But desperation led to blindness, and blindness led to my demise.

Four million dollars.

He demanded four million dollars, and the thought of giving him my hard-earned money tore me apart inside.

Even though my stomach churned at the idea of food, I padded barefoot across the house to drown my thoughts with a tub of ice cream and rummage through Saint's alcohol stash.

I noticed a faint blue glow coming from the kitchen, but I figured it must've been from the outside. So, I flicked the lights on only to stumble on my steps when I saw a figure standing in front of the open fridge. A spooked scream bubbled out my throat, causing the man to bang his head against the plastic ceiling and curse as he turned around, cradling his scalp. I took a step back and stopped when I realized it was Saint scowling at me.

A shirtless Saint.

My heart raced as I stared at him. All hard muscle that looked like it could be made of steel, broad shoulders with pecs that beckoned you to take a bite, as the slopes of his abs led to a mouthwatering "V" that disappeared into his waistband. He also had a dusting of fair hair that made me bite my lip.

"Damn, Fleur, you move like a freaking ghost."

I schooled my expression, wiping my hand over my mouth to make sure no drool had escaped, and adjusted the height of my silk slip-on. "It's not my fault you're standing in the middle of the darkness at two a.m. What's wrong with you?"

Turning his back on me, he retrieved something from the freezer before slamming its door shut.

"Last time I checked, this was still my house, so I'll roam around whenever I want to," he grumbled, pressing an ice pack on the crown of his head.

Guilt fluttered in my belly, and I rushed forward to make sure he wasn't hurt. "Ugh, are you okay? Do you need me to look at that?"

Saint's eyes felt electrifying as they ran down the length of my body. The nightgown was no short of scandalous, seeing as I liked to sleep in as little as possible but not fully naked.

Fuck, maybe I should've slipped something extra on since I didn't live alone anymore.

Ya think?

A little voice in the back of my head chimed as Saint mapped the contours of my body, hanging over every curve— the embarrassing ones too. My pulse fluttered in my throat, and warmth rushed to my face. I sucked in my tummy when his gaze made its way up again from the tips of my toes to my cheeks, tinted pink.

"I'll be fine," he assured, scratching the no doubt bruised part of his scalp after removing the ice. "I came to get an ice pack for my knee. What are you doing up this late?"

Trying to run from my demons.

The sentence almost flew out of my mouth, but I held myself back as I crossed my arms over my chest, hoping my nipples weren't hard. "I had a sudden craving for Ben & Jerry's Cookie Dough ice cream."

He studied me before opening the freezer's door once more and pulling out a brown tub of creamy goodness. "Sorry, Spitfire. We only have Rocky Road."

"That'll do," I answered to his raised brow, and Saint set the tub on the aisle, gathering two large spoons from a drawer. I watched in fascination as he pulled out two seats and patted the one next to him. "Are you staying?"

He nodded as he settled down, inaugurating the open tub by taking the first spoonful, his biceps flexing as he brought it to his mouth. "I can't say no to chocolate."

I ignored the butterflies that took flight around my heart and sat down next to him before he left me with nothing to eat. His clean, citrusy smell tickled my senses, and I felt this sudden urge to lean forward until I ran my nose down the middle of his naked chest. *Like a proper weirdo.*

I grabbed my spoon before I did something I couldn't take back and shoved some ice cream in my mouth to cool down.

"So, what do you need the ice pack for?" I spoke with my mouth still full. I did put a hand on top, though.

See?

I wasn't completely classless.

"You mean other than that I banged my head because you scared me half to death?" he asked, and I rolled my eyes. "I jogged with Killian today, and my knee got a little sore."

"Because of your spinal cord injury?"

"Yeah, but I also hurt it in the gym the other day."

"Old age is catching up with you, huh?" I teased, knocking his spoon out of the way so I could get the little piece of marshmallow nestled in the ice cream.

He narrowed those feline eyes at me, leaning forward in a flash and wrapping his mouth around *my* spoon, an inch away from the carton.

I repeat.

He wrapped his mouth around my spoon, stealing my ice cream.

A shiver shot down my spine, and I was pretty sure it had everything to do with his full lips swathed where mine had been mere seconds ago. There was no inch of chocolate on the silverware when he popped it out of his mouth, grinning like a cocky bastard. The kind of smile that reeked of bad intentions and one you couldn't forget.

"You wouldn't be saying that if you'd sampled the goods, babe."

I was scared to know what would happen to me if I *did* sample the goods when the mere thought of an indirect kiss had wetness pooling between my legs. Safe to say, I didn't change my cutlery.

Because I could play too, I rested my elbows on the table as I licked the ice cream extra slow, giving him a show. I turned to smile at him when I heard him grunt, knowing the barely-there nightie was working in my favor this time.

"You got any alcohol too? I need to drink away the pain of not having sampled your goods."

"Ah, no," he responded, his tone grave. "You'll have to soldier through the pain, Spitfire."

A giggle escaped me at the whole situation. Saint perked up when he heard the sound, and a chuckle sounded from deep within his stomach (that was unfairly flat even though he was crouched). Never in my life did I think I would be eating ice cream with Saint Astor in the middle of the night while we exchanged jokes.

"For real, though, you have no liquor?"

"No. I emptied my cabinets a while ago. Sometimes I used to mistake the bottles of wine for juice." There was an unmistakable edge to his voice that had me shifting in my seat.

"Was that your way of numbing the pain of your injury? I mean, I've never suffered through anything like that, so I can't imagine what it feels like," I asked, eyeing the abandoned ice pack on the counter behind us.

"My impairment was incomplete. I was lucky because it could've been way more severe than just needing to attend rehab. I sometimes still feel an occasional stiffness on my legs and spine, but the fact that I wouldn't be able to play professionally again was more damaging than the injury could've ever been. Unless it killed me, that is. Can you imagine a world where you couldn't design ever again?"

No, no, I couldn't.

I couldn't imagine losing my one and only talent and passion in life. Sketching was when I could empty my mind of all worries and focus on creating. Sewing was magnificent because there was nothing more glorious than seeing your dreams come to life.

"I'm really sorry that happened to you, Saint." Genuinely sad for the agony he had to experience and probably kept feeling, I touched his arm, squeezing reassuringly.

His muscle flexed under my palm, and he faced forward, looking down at the now half-empty ice cream container. "You're not the one who should be sorry."

"What happened to the guy who hurt you?"

"His team won a couple of Super Bowls, but he died of an overdose last year," he said swiftly. Saint's eyes darkened and his white teeth peeked out, running over his bottom lip to contain a depraved smile. There was no love lost between them, and despite it being an accident, he enjoyed the outcome of his opponent's life. "But enough about me, Spitfire. What about you? How is this whole influencer thing going?"

I removed my hand from his arm, leaving my spoon inside the bowl when my stomach protested at the thought of another bite and fear at his bloodlust. "Well, my eyes are killing me from spending all that time on screen, but I'm getting things ready for the launch of my store."

"Is that why you look like you need a hug? Stress?" His thumb ran under his chin like he had a sixth sense or something.

Should I take offense to that? I touched my under-eyes, wondering if I had bags the size of those Paris Hilton used to haul around.

"I-I don't look like I need a hug."

I stopped breathing when he tugged my hands down, forcing the stool to spin and face him. Saint's face was a work of art. I often joked with my online reading buddies that we'd commit murder if it meant getting laid by our tall, dark, and handsome book boyfriends, but there was something so roguish and distinctive about this man's blond scruff and eyebrows framing his sultry eyes.

I was starting to understand why the media nicknamed him golden boy.

There was such a contrast between us. I had the whole Mediterranean, slightly uglier version of Cleopatra down to a T while he could pass for a posh English prince.

"It's almost three a.m., we're eating ice cream straight from the tub, and you asked for alcohol. Pretty sure that means you're going through a crisis, Spitfire."

Oh, you have no clue.

"Well, if I was, would you give me one?"

Obviously, I had no idea what the word platonic meant

when it came to Saint. I needed to feel an ounce of protection, though. Fighting all of this alone was wearing on me. My grandma was a wave I couldn't stop, but Harry turned out to be a tsunami ready to tear me apart with no remorse.

"I don't know," he mused over it, and something in my chest sank. It could've been my heart or my self-respect. "What do I get out of it?"

My throat closed, and I bit my lip to keep from cursing at him. We were having such a great time, there was no reason to ruin it now.

Hopping off my chair, I decided to leave. I didn't need to deal with this right now. I didn't make it far before he propelled me forward, his face troubled as I sunk into his chest. His warm, bare torso made my skin hum with excitement wherever we connected, which was pretty much everywhere given our state of undress.

"Come here, Ariadne." His big hand cupped the back of my head, and my full name on his lips unraveled me.

I allowed myself this rare moment of peace, my cheek pressed against his flesh, as I filled my lungs with his heady scent. Saint's palms were rough as they fisted the silk around my hips, pulling me impossibly tighter. His body temperature was comforting, like a lit furnace that burrowed warmth into my tissue and bone.

"That day after the engagement, where did you go?" I found the courage to ask while we were both relaxed.

For some reason, the answer was important to me when it shouldn't be. I was the one that proposed an open marriage, so I didn't have any room to complain, but it killed me that he never protested. That he could go to another so easily after stealing a piece of me on that dance floor. I was asking questions I had no right to, and I wished he didn't break the fragile cordialness that remained by answering.

"The boys had organized... let's say, a mini bachelor's party before the actual thing. They're extra like that."

"With strippers?" I stiffened.

"No, we drove down to Cape Cod and spent the weekend sailing and fishing since the weather forecast was good." My head shook with his dark laugh. "I'm pretty sure Eliana would castrate Leo if he ever got near a stripper."

"I don't think he ever would. He looks head over heels in love with her."

"He is. We all knew it since high school, but it took the bastard a while to figure it out."

"The best things in life take time to happen."

We stayed silent for a little while, our hug extending the length of time that was deemed normal for one, but I couldn't find it in me to pull away. Saint's palms had progressed to rubbing down my back, stopping when they reached the arch of my ass. His breaths got shallower every time he did so, and I was hit with this impending anticipation that maybe he would venture lower, blow all the invisible lines between us in the air like a house of cards.

I hated to ruin the moment, but even though Saint's arms were braced around me like a protective armor, he couldn't shield me from the impending cliff that was waiting to swallow me whole.

I had to be the one to pull myself from the edge.

"So I found out something today," I started as I pulled back, my fingers lingering on the wispy hairs of his chest.

"Are you going to say it, or do I have to guess?" He arched a brow down at me.

Here goes nothing.

"I found out that Ares fired Harry."

Saint's jaw popped as soon as he heard the second name, and his touch disappeared from my body so quickly I felt like I had imagined it in the first place. Even with nothing but empty air pressuring my body from every side, the imprint of his arms around me remained, gifting me a semblance of a repose as I leaned back to take his impressive statue in.

"Good." His tone was wooden.

"Don't you think it was a little harsh?" I whispered.

"What I think was harsh is the universe aligning so I wouldn't kick the cunt's ass." He barked a sharp laugh that made the hair on my arms stand up. "What's this about, Spitfire?"

"I guess I feel a bit bad for him. He was drunk, and we'd just broken up. It was a weak moment." I toyed with the edges of my hair.

Saint was an imposing presence even in just a pair of black basketball shorts. My thin nightie didn't stand a chance, making my stance vulnerable in this conversation. I moved a few steps back.

"You broke up?" He blinked as if in a trance.

"Yeah, I didn't think it was fair for him if we were still in a relationship."

"Why didn't you tell me?"

"It's none of your business."

That seemed to pop him right in the present.

"Right. Well, let me tell you what *is* my business, Aria." Saint edged forward. "When a loser screams in front of a whole neighborhood about how your fiancé is a stupid slut that only opens her legs for the rich. That is my business. When he goes on and on about how he would have at least liked to fuck the dumb bitch before *I* dipped my dick in.

That is my fucking business, and you best believe I'm going to do my best to bury that motherfucker a hundred feet in the fucking ground."

My soul teetered amidst the fine line of anger over Harry's statements and adoration over Saint's fierce protectiveness. He was a force to be reckoned with, his muscles bunching up with rage. It told me he cared, and I cherished that.

"How... how do you know what he said exactly?" My voice shook.

"Other than the little fact that Ares was there. We had to bribe the neighbors the next day for them to delete the videos they'd taken."

Fuck me.

There were more people who had witnessed him calling me names.

I must've seemed so stupid, sticking up for him, and I cared about Saint's opinion of me, but I would die if he ever saw the video. In all his years of debauchery, Saint didn't have one sex tape scandal, and then came me... the virgin with half a sex tape.

It was so ironic it made my eyes water.

"So you can't talk to Ares about getting him his job back?"

"Out of all of that, that's what you gathered? You're acting like a virgin infatuated with her first love even though he's the scum of the earth," Saint said, flabbergasted, and his eyes widened as realization dawned on him. "Wait... are you a virg—?"

"Of course I'm not." I didn't allow the idea to completely form in his head. "How many virgins my age have you met in this day and age? I simply feel bad for him. You don't have a shortage of scandals either, Saint. I mean, wouldn't you have liked it if someone stood for you back then?"

"Don't ever compare going off the rails because of a life-threatening injury to screaming and crying like a fucking freak because your girlfriend dumped you."

In all our back and forth, it took me a while to see that I was now backed into a corner, Saint's molten eyes pinning me in place and his tough body not allowing me to move.

I cringed because he was right. I was one insensitive bitch saying that after he somewhat opened up to me about it.

"You're right. I'm sorry. I just—"

"Keep your apologies to yourself. From the second I met you, you've done nothing but judge me and look down your nose at me. Do you think you're perfect, Ariadne? The prodigal daughter, the badass woman with a degree, a loved online presence, and a career that's catapulting to the stars at the mere age of twenty-one. You sound like every parents' wet dream on paper."

"What's your point?" I gritted my teeth.

"My point is to be proud of your character even when someone peers into your real life. From the outside, you might be all that, but from where I'm standing, you're nothing but a brat with a savior complex and a fetish for dicks that treat you like the dirt under their shoes." He dragged his tongue over his bottom lip in a lewd manner, fingering the strap of my nightie. "I mean, if that's what turns you on, I'd be more than happy to oblige."

Ouch.

My mouth went dry when his words touched base. They weren't true of course, I couldn't give a rat's ass about Harry, but I did paint a persona online that wasn't entirely mine. I photoshopped my pictures, smiled, straightened my hair, and sucked my stomach in to fit into the clothes designers sent me to be featured on my page. Sometimes I even altered them when they were too tight. Scared to ask for a different size, fucking terrified of allowing anyone to see my flaws in an industry that was so obsessed with perfection.

My mouth went dry, and his touch didn't carry that familiar welcome burn. This time it was scathing, wanting to hurt me.

"You could've just said no. That would've sufficed." I hated how weak I sounded, so I slapped his hand away for good measure.

"Fuck, no. I won't get him his job back," he snapped, looking me over as if I let him down. "Give it a rest, and grow some self-respect. Trust me, guys will walk all over you if you keep acting like this."

With that, he turned around and stalked out. I imagined if the kitchen had a door, he would've slammed it shut. I sucked my lower lip in my mouth, sliding down the cold wall until my ass hit the floor.

What the hell was I going to do?

CHAPTER TWELVE
SAINT

"And finally, the FTC ruled that our ads were misleading." Carson, our senior marketing advisor, a middle-aged man with a beer belly, stretching his suit, skimmed through the notes on his iPad.

"Which ads?" my father asked, on it like an angry Rottweiler.

Safe to say, he didn't have the best relationship with the Federal Trade Commission over the years. He was mystified as to why they wouldn't just bend over backward and showcase their assholes for a good fucking like his mistresses did.

I pulled my gaze from the purple and pink skyline beyond the skyscraper's glass windows and focused on the matter at hand. The sooner we were done with this meeting, the sooner I could get the hell out of here. It was nearing dinner time, and I'd skipped lunch.

Tapping my fingers on the clear conference table, I settled back on my spinning chair and stared at the image showcased on the TV across from me.

"The Renaissance painting inspired ones," Carson

explained, motioning to the text below the picture of a ginger model, featuring stitching the handle of a handbag. "A needle and infinite patience protect each stitch from the wear of time. With so much attention bestowed on every product, should we only call them details?"

My scoff cut off anything else he intended to say, and the room of about four men and two women turned to me when Noah addressed me with a question.

"Do you have something to say, Saint?"

"Only that you cannot get away with lying now as easily as you could twenty years ago. Advertising watchdogs have become more vicious than ever."

His lips cracked when he plastered a plastic smile on. "Where's the lie? We put an enormous amount of attention into every product we release."

I laced my fingers in front of me, glancing at him on my left side. If only I had a picture of his face when he entered the room and saw me sitting at the head of the table, I would stare at it daily.

"In the design aspect of it, sure. But people could not possibly believe that the highest-grossing luxury brand ever handmakes everything. We live in the age of mass production. If that was the case, we wouldn't have any products to sell."

"The consumer's reality is whatever we make it. To a certain extent, our products are made by hand." He dismissed my claims.

"Then why don't we divulge how much is made by hand? That should disprove their claims." I checkmated him, causing the purple veins in his hollow cheeks to deepen in color.

"You know we can't do that."

"He's right. We can't." Hunter Connolly, my father's favorite subject and biggest ass kisser, spoke up. "But we can argue that the use of hand sewing machines is part of what would be expected to amount to 'handmade' in the 21st century."

"That sounds like a good idea, Hunter." Father, of course, agreed.

"It sounds like a stupid idea." I countered, causing Hunter's pale face to twist in distaste. "The public will interpret the image of a woman using a needle and thread alongside the claim 'infinite patience protects each stitch' to mean that the bags are *hand-stitched.*"

"Well, what do you suggest?" Hunter knocked the ball on my counter, running his hand through the wispy brown hair on his mostly bald head, confident he had this argument in the bag.

"Pull the ads and make new ones. We can't release the evidence that demonstrates the extent to which Falco products are made by hand, and you know they're going to ask for them."

"We can't do that. That would mean admitting defeat." Dad sputtered like a headless chicken.

"You're going to lose the dispute anyway without sufficient proof and bring more attention to us that way." I could smell the headlines already. "Whereas if we roll with it and acknowledge the claims without projecting them to the public, this can go under the radar without being picked up by every major self-proclaimed fashion expert out there."

Hunter *tsked*, crossing his arms, his whole body turned in Dad's direction, even though he was addressing me. "Rule number one in marketing is that there is no such thing as bad publicity. Sure, it will get us some negative traction in the high fashion social circles, but all will be forgotten the next time *Vittoria Birmingham* starves her models for one of her runway shows. In the grand scheme of things, this is nothing. If anything, I guarantee you it will get us more sales because of the free publicity."

"It would also lose us loyal customers and credibility, which is what matters most for longevity. When someone is paying more than three thousand dollars for a handbag, they expect quality, even if that means the blood, sweat, and tears of some poor artisan in Mumbai."

My statement made everyone's eyes widen like they were hearing this for the first time. They weren't. They simply chose to ignore the facts so they could hold on to their designer bags.

"What do you pass us for *Zara?*" Hunter asked, affronted.

As if.

Fast fashion brands weren't the only ones quietly using employees from third world countries for their goods while offering little in the way of employment protection and compensation.

One of my first acts, when I started working at Falco, was to get us to sign a compliance project with other luxury brands to ensure factory safety for our workers, still unregulated facilities were not a thing of the past.

I had a reply on the tip of my tongue, and Dad rushed to speak over me just so I wouldn't make things worse. My differences with Hunter tended to stretch these already useless meetings longer than necessary.

"Anyway, I think Hunter's idea is the best, so we're going with that. That will be all for today, gentlemen—"

Slamming the case of my tablet shut, I sliced through my

father's words with a dismissing knife. "You can go now. This meeting is being postponed until tomorrow."

People's groans were inaudible. Problem-solving gatherings were no one's favorite, mostly because of the constant clashing of opinions. They all left, causing my father's face to sour at the easy abandonment.

"What did you say that for?" He snapped at me as soon as we were left alone.

"I think you're forgetting that you're not in charge anymore." I crossed my arms and legs, meeting his stare head-on. "And I really don't appreciate your patronizing tone."

"You don't possibly believe that you can work this all out by yourself, do you? You need someone to guide you through the process, and I have over forty years of experience on you, boy."

Except, I didn't want this to work.

Well, not the way my father originally intended to, anyway.

I put some thought into my original assessment and concluded that the complete dissolution of Falco was not the right way to hurt my father. It would devastate him, don't get me wrong, but I couldn't put everyone else's lives on the line just because *we* were in a dick measuring competition.

So, instead, I'd target his policies, completely overthrow his marketing techniques, basically shit all over his legacy until no one remembered who he was. Make Noah Astor blend into the background like he loathed.

"Haven't you gotten tired after all this time? I mean, forty years of acting like a tyrant and ruling with an iron fist must've taken its toll." I didn't feed into his hysterics, eager to leave, and shrugged my abandoned suit jacket on.

"If you want to be successful, you'll have to be willing to put in the work. Who cares what people label you as? They always have something to say for the ones at the top. That's why they're at the bottom." Father groused.

"Look at the bright side; you could become a motivational speaker,"—*since you're so good at spewing bullshit*—"but you'll need to research your quotes more. I imagine you'd be chased with tomatoes if you hit them with the 'It's lonely at the top, that's why a Lamborghini has two seats and a bus has fifty,' next."

His face twisted in a mean snare that reminded me of a constipated otter. "What do you want from me, Saint?"

"Absolutely nothing." I got on my feet. "I'm letting you stay until my wedding day to help smooth out things with the merger, but after that, you're done, old man."

"Done?" He narrowed his eyes. "You can't throw me out like that, I've worked my ass off for this company, and I deserve to leave with dignity."

"Then don't make this harder than it needs to be. December first, you're out." I gave him a final look. "Consider it forced retirement. Take Mom on a cruise, go visit Scotland like she always wanted to. She's your wife, in case you've forgotten, not this fucking company."

"And let Darian Fleur take over everything I've worked for all these years?" He hissed, crashing his fist on the table. "You know he's filling Ariadne's shoes, right?"

I knew. Ariadne was going to be a silent partner, and I was more than okay with that. I had to live with her at home. I didn't need her at my place of work too.

"You should've considered the risks before serving me with the merger papers and shoving her down my throat." I shrugged, turning to leave. "Oh, and by the way, I had

Yelena move your stuff to your temporary office on the second floor."

The conference room door slammed shut behind me as soon as the last word escaped my mouth, muffling a roar that brought a smile to my face.

"Saint!"

It didn't take him long to follow. I greeted some employees as he stewed behind me, and stopped short as I was nearing my office, a strained laugh catching my attention.

I didn't pay my father any mind when he crushed against my back, feasting my eyes on Ariadne, donned in a beige babydoll dress, and sexy as sin thigh-high leather heels that I found myself dreaming of unzipping with my teeth. My pulse raced faster when I saw that she was talking to Jane from HR—who I might've bumped uglies with once or twice in the past.

"Saint, our conversation—" My dad continued, oblivious to anything else but his wants.

"Is postponed indefinitely." I cut him off, rushing to the two women.

Jane was a deep-skinned woman with an afro that made her at least three heads taller than Ariadne alone. Even with the height difference, Spitfire held her own. Her chin was set at a sixty-degree angle, eyes emotionless as she listened to whatever Jane was saying.

"Sweetheart," the sound of my voice made them both jump. "What are you doing here?"

Jane spun my way, a dazed smile lighting up her face, but I was looking at Aria's, whose eyes clung to me like they were trying to peel away a layer of my skin.

"I was on the road and thought I'd stop by so we could

have dinner together." She held up a Panda Express bag in one hand, and I unloaded her. "You've been working so much. I felt bad."

"You should take breaks more often, Saint. It's not good to tire yourself out like this." Jane popped in, causing Aria's hands to morph into tiny fists.

"Yes, now he's going to take one with me. It was good meeting you, Jane." Spitfire showed her teeth, fisting the back of my suit, ready to usher *me* inside my office.

"Likewise, Ariadne."

I wondered if I had two cats instead of dogs if they would act the same way these two were doing right now. And then they said only men had pissing matches.

Loosening my tie, I acknowledged Jane with a simple nod and turned us both around before they resorted to hair pulling. Not that we'd have much privacy in the glass cubicle, but at least there'd be a barrier between them.

"What are you really doing outside of my office, Spitfire?" I asked, settling her chair sideways in front of my desk, and grabbed the one opposite hers.

"Technically, it's my office too. What's yours is mine, and what's mine is yours, right?" She crossed her legs and spared me the trouble of removing my gaze from them as she took out the takeout boxes.

Heels were sexy, but thigh-high ones?

They could lead you to an early grave *with* a hard-on.

"Annoying me is the answer you're looking for," I said under my breath, taking the food from her hands.

Aria's eyes narrowed, and she stabbed her noodles unnecessarily hard. "You're one ungrateful bastard, but I guess it's my mistake for trying to do something nice."

"Never asked you to," I shrugged, popping a piece of chicken in my mouth.

When she heaved a frustrated breath, my jaw tightened at the weird lump in my throat. Was I being a bigger dick than usual? Yes. Did she deserve it? Also, yes. So why the fuck did I find myself not wanting to disappoint her?

It was that nightie that she wore last night and her outfit today.

Ariadne wasn't model beautiful, certainly not swan-like and delicate like Eliana, or had an imposing presence like Jane. No, she sucker-punched you in the gut with her colorful palette, huge brown eyes with heavy lashes, and dark hair that would contrast perfectly against white silk pillows.

You couldn't ignore her presence or place her in a box because she didn't fit in any of them. Ariadne Fleur was in her own league, and I was fucking stupid for wanting to join. Maybe it was just an infatuation. I couldn't remember the last time I didn't get to have a girl I wanted.

Self-imposed sanctions were a thing of the present.

"Thank you." I managed to work around a bite. "Now, answer my question, *truthfully*."

"I want to get to know my *fiancé* better. This will never work if we keep fighting each other. People will see past our bullshit with little effort."

"And are we fooling anyone specific?"

"My grandparents from my mom's side, we're celebrating Thanksgiving together." Aria gave me a venomous smile. "My grandpa is a butcher, and he's not afraid to use his knives."

"I see where you get your fire from."

"I wouldn't use a butcher knife on you." She put a hand

to her chest. "I'd go for something more inconspicuous, like untraceable drugs."

"Good to know you've put some thought into this. I should probably inform my family that they should suspect you if I'm found dead in a ditch somewhere."

Rolling her eyes in good humor, she twisted the noodles around her fork and stuffed her mouth. My dick stirred in my pants, and I averted my eyes.

This was heading south quick—literally and figuratively. It was one thing masturbating after our fight last night but getting hard because of the way she ate was fucking unacceptable. I was acting like a teenager with no experience.

I needed to get laid ASAP. Who knew? This time could be different with all this pent-up sexual tension I was carrying.

"All right, I have some questions." Aria cut off the mental list of available girls I had on my phone who I trusted would sign an NDA if served with one.

"Shoot."

"Favorite color?"

I gave her a look that said she couldn't be serious. We weren't going to play twenty questions with her grandparents. She shot one back that had me swallowing my tongue.

"Blue."

"Mine's pink."

"Look at us. We're walking clichés," I deadpanned.

Her chatter grew comforting as we ate. I told her about my first job at MacDonald's (courtesy of my father, who wanted me to know how money was earned), and watched her eyes widen in horror when I rehashed the story about how the girl, who was in charge of the fries, got third-degree burns. Someone rushing down the aisle hit her in the back accidentally, causing her glasses to launch off her face and plop into the fry grease. Nonchalantly, she *thrust her hand into the boiling fry grease to retrieve her glasses.* A second later, she withdrew what looked and *smelled* like a cooked hand.

"Did she at least get her glasses?"

I shook my head. "No, they were made of plastic."

I reached the bottom of my Styrofoam container way faster than I thought, having to balance answering her questions and eating. When I did, my stomach was close to bursting. Not close enough, though, seeing as I all but scarfed down the Chinese sesame balls, Aria handed me over when I was done.

"What about pet peeves?" She continued.

"I hate loud chewing, breathing... anything loud in general."

Sudden smacking or popping sounds reminded me of the last time I was in the field.

"Do you have misophonia? My grandparents can get very loud."

"People should come with warning labels," I groaned. I already knew her whole family was loud and dramatic if Lydia Fleur was anything to go by.

"Well, what would your warning label say?" She dished back as if knowing where my thoughts had gone.

I didn't have to think too hard about it and replied with a smirk. "Caution: may cause pregnancy."

She choked on a ball. "You're so damn cocky."

"Hey, women have actually tried to steal my sperm before."

"Oh my God, how?" Second choke.

"You don't want to know." I handed her a water bottle.

"What would yours say?" I asked, even though I had a pretty good idea.

"Highly addictive."

She sure was to the point. I wished she was shoving different balls down her throat and licking white honey off her fingers.

"I think *flammable* would be more accurate." I stretched my legs to relieve the ache in my groin.

"No one asked for your opinion. Okay, last question for tonight; favorite childhood memory?"

Well, if that didn't clear the lust-filled smog around my brain, I didn't know what would. I had a cushy childhood, but I also wasn't farting rainbows. I had a ton of good moments—mostly with Killian, not nearly enough to over-shadow the bad. My father was neurotic as ever, ruining every achievement with his perfectionism, and Mom was the polar opposite. She didn't care what we did as long as we didn't bother her.

"You go first," I said as I dumped the now-empty boxes back in the brown paper bag.

"Hmm..." She pondered over it, her eyes lighting up with a newfound fondness. "When I was little, my mom was having an all grown-ups party, and all my cousins and I did was run around, hide under tables, play tag, etcetera." Aria made a dismissing motion. "Of course, she got mad that we wouldn't sit still for a single second, so they banished us outside, and we all sat down on top of a hill and talked. Then after a while, when she came out to check on us and saw us, she declared, *'that's not how you play!'*, and barrel-rolled down the hill, in front of half her guests."

"I know it might sound stupid, compared to all the Amalfi coast boat rides and Paris trips. Being carefree has always been my biggest weakness, though, and I'm sad I didn't take more from my mom on that aspect." Her slender throat bobbed with a swallow as she let out a nervous laugh, searching my face for any kind of reaction.

Whatever she found wasn't what she was looking for because her smile dropped.

I was jealous.

I was jealous she had something I didn't have, and never would.

A happy family.

"Are you sure you should be telling me your biggest weakness?" I leaned forward, probing her fragile trust.

"Would you use it against me?" Aria raised a disbelieving brow, crossing her arms. I was proud of myself for holding her gaze.

"It depends. Are you just trying to get on my good graces so I can talk to Ares about *Larson*? Because that's still not happening." I drawled, choosing ruin to avoid turning the evening even bleaker.

I couldn't think of a single happy memory that wasn't destroyed later on, one way or another. Be it catching my mother sneaking around with the gardener, or overhearing Dad on the phone with one of his mistresses, ordering her to get an abortion. The irony was that he claimed to be pro-life. To me, it seemed more like he was more pro-controlling women.

Heat rose up my spine when her eyes sparked immediately, and she pointed a manicured finger at me. "You're such a hypocrite."

"Excuse me?"

"Do you want to know what story your little friend Jane was rehashing before you walked in?" The question was rhetorical, and she paused for dramatic effect. "She was telling me all about your business trip in Milan and how the hotel had miraculously made the mistake of booking only one suite. I don't suppose you took the couch." Her voice held a nasal quality, imitating Jane's baby voice.

"That was years ago." I retorted, eerily calm.

"She's still hung up on you, and you're *working* with her, but you don't see me throwing fits because of it, even though she was undoubtedly rude."

No, she wasn't.

A cool settled over her like a protective layer as she dabbed her lips with a napkin before retrieving a red lipstick from her bag, painting her ample lips scarlet as if we were discussing the weather, and popping in a mint.

"Our situations are very different because *I* couldn't give a rat's ass about *her*."

Whereas you'd bleed on the side of the road for your loser ex.

To the employees outside that were surely trying to peak at their new bosses, it looked like we were having a normal conversation after finishing our food. They couldn't detect the silent anger and disappointment pouring out of us in waves.

I hadn't predicted such a tranquil reaction from *Spitfire*, but this time the burn was contained in her eyes when she also leaned forward, our faces inches apart.

"What are you doing?" I couldn't help the dive of my eyes to her perfect rosebud mouth, breathing fresh air to my face.

"Sending a message."

She elaborated further by breaching the gap between us and pressing her lips on mine in a sweet peck that had molten lava swirling in my gut and stirring the beast in my pants.

I hated the jealous kind. The clingy ones that went apeshit after no promises were made, but apparently, the same rules didn't apply to Ariadne. She was like an autonomous community, trying to break away from the norm and succeeding by finding the chips in my armor.

Good food, and a body made for sin.

I returned the kiss, splitting her legs so my thighs nestled between hers, and let her set the pace. It was slow and torturous. I was hyper-aware of all parts of her. Those taunting fingers, toying with my scruff, her nails biting slightly in my skin. Her mouth clung to mine like a sponge as she slipped her tongue inside leisurely like she wanted to enjoy the ride and not rush to the gold instantly.

She was decadent in her exploration. Licked, sucked, nipped, and soothed the sting of her teeth by lapping up my lips like I was a wounded animal in need of tending. And fuck if I wouldn't play dead for her open-mouthed kisses. There was an inherent innocence behind Ariadne's every move that craved to be corrupted.

With one last tug of my lower lip that had the back of my throat vibrating with unparalleled lust, she pulled back, resting her forehead to mine, both of us dry-heaving like we'd run a marathon.

If only a kiss from her had me—a thirty-year-old man— melting in a pile of hormones, then I couldn't fucking imagine what getting between her legs would be like. We humans surely loved the forbidden. Whatever you couldn't have tasted sweeter when you found a way to eat at the edges. But with Ariadne, I found myself wanting to taste more than just the surface level of what she had to offer.

And wasn't that a fucking swerve from my original plan?

"Jane can keep her job. I'm not feeling like ruining a *pick me girl's* life. She'll do that all by herself eventually, but do me a favor? Don't look into a mirror before you leave here."

"Two things; one, what's a *pick me, girl?* And two, why the fuck not?"

Done with the physical contact, she leaned back into her chair again, a drunk haze in her eyes. I didn't let go of her completely, trapping her legs with mine.

"Google it, golden boy," Aria said as she left my legs cold too, getting on her feet. I arched my neck back, catching a vixen smirk on her face. "Because I like my mark on you."

Her words fleeted through my ears as she winked and strutted out of the office in those fucking boots I'd most probably have dreams about. My chest squeezed with the effort it took not to follow, bend her over, and take her from behind while the whole floor watched open-mouthed.

Rules.

We needed ground rules.

CHAPTER THIRTEEN
ARIADNE

Grandma Chloe had always been huge on Thanksgiving. Besides having all the luxuries this world could offer, I was guessing she also needed to thank God for the number of times he spared her ass.

We celebrated the holiday at her manor, seeing as she employed an entire butler army to tend to our every need around the long table in the dining room, which was brimming with food. The centerpiece held a juicy roast turkey, and plates of mashed potatoes and green beans were being passed down. Candles and fairy lights strung on the wall assisted with the holiday spirit, and the scent of pumpkin and apple pie from the kitchen tickled my nose.

"Should we have asked your family to join too? I feel bad stealing you away for Thanksgiving," I asked Saint, who was sitting next to me. We were situated on the left edge of the table, our outfits matching—his an all-black suit, and I was wearing a dark Chanel dress with gold chains around my hips.

"Nah, it's fine. Killian is in Cali, and my parents are probably in the Philippines or Australia. Mom hates cold weather," he said as he dug into his food, barely looking at me.

Okay, so he didn't look like a stone-faced warrior because he couldn't celebrate with his family. I kept my wishful thinking up until the very last minute. The conclusion that he'd become colder than usual because of the kiss reared its ugly head in again.

I'd overstepped the boundaries. Both of us were so adamant on keeping planted between us. My cheeks flamed when I remembered I'd told him I liked seeing my mark on him. The faster the countdown ticked over my head, the more reckless I found myself becoming. Peppering Saint's face with red lipstick marks was just the icing on the cake.

Deteriorating was as liberating as it was nerve-wracking.

"So, Saint, are you planning on getting baptized?" Nico, my *pappou* asked in heavily accented English. He'd been scarfing down food since we got here and had a rule not to speak with his mouth full and his stomach empty.

He rubbed his round belly, ignoring *giagia,* who was glaring at him, and stared Saint down.

Saint took his time, cutting his stake in even pieces, cool as a mint before replying. "I already did when I was an infant, sir. I'm not planning on repeating it now that I have a say."

"The kids are getting married by a civil celebrant, Nico." Grandma Chloe cut my *pappou's* upcoming rant short.

"Can't say I've been called that in a while," Saint said dryly, a permanent frown etched on his face as he shoved a spoonful of mashed potatoes down his throat.

"I should've known you'd pull something like this," *Pappou* seethed, and the rest of the family gathered held back a collective sigh as they went at it for the thousandth time.

Irena had been glued to her phone, like a broody teenager the whole night, and even changed seats when I attempted to sit next to her. Mom and dad were cool toward each other, no doubt from the increasing pressure of picking sides. The only person who was enjoying themselves was Daphne, her eyes volleying between Nick and Chloe like she was watching her favorite movie.

"Like what? I don't understand what you're saying," Grandma asked, rolling her eyes.

"You're trying to turn my kids away from God's road." He waved his finger in the air.

"Should I tell him that it's a dead-end?" Saint scoffed, speaking to me directly for the first time since we got here.

"If you want him to bring out the butcher knives, go ahead," I whispered.

He shook his head. "Your grandparents are definitely something, Spitfire."

I studied him, my mind beginning to reel to keep up. He was the most frustrating, hot, and cold man I'd ever met. One day looking at me like he wanted to smoke me up, the next like I sickened him.

"Is that why you're moody? Are you having a bad time?"

"Moody?" Saint chuckled at my choice of words. "Yeah, I guess you could say I'm feeling *moody*."

"Why?"

"My mistress refused to sign an NDA."

Ever heard of curiosity killing the cat, Ariadne?

My mouth slammed shut as I stared at his cruel eyes, rejoicing in taking me off guard. Technically, he hadn't done anything wrong, just like I technically was supposed to stay away from him. It was within his right to fuck whoever he wanted. The knowledge still sat low in my stomach like a pile of rocks.

"So, Saint, Ariadne tells me you played Rugby, eh?" *Pappou* was back at it, moving on from Chloe.

"Football, sir," Saint replied as if he hadn't dropped a bomb on me.

"Really? Why have I never seen you in a championship before?"

"The only part of America that qualifies for the World Cup is South America." Mom put in her two cents.

"He plays American football, *pappou*. You're thinking about soccer." Clearing my throat, I wiped my mouth clean, not gracing Saint with any attention, and stood up. "If you'll excuse me, I need to go to the bathroom."

I got out of there like my ass was on fire, biting my lips savagely to contain the stinging in my eyes. I was halfway through the hallway when I felt him following me. His dark aura, a suffocating cloud.

I squeaked when a hand wrapped over my forearm, and I was dragged to a nearby supply closet smelling very intensely of fabric softener. *Laundry room.* I leaned against the thick wood, but Saint didn't give me any space, crowding me against the door and making my heart spin faster than the dryer.

"What's the matter, princess? What happened to '*I don't expect you to stay celibate, and you shouldn't expect that of me either?*'" he taunted, his hands bracketing me on either side.

My throat closed up, frustration leading me to latch my hands on his dress shirt dangerously close to tearing it apart in anger. "You're an asshole."

His eyes flared before they hooded as if enjoying the jealousy that ran through my veins. I couldn't even kid myself. Jealousy was an emotion I knew all too well, a green beast that pushed me to be the best.

In some cases, though, like this one, I despised it. I couldn't use it to my advantage this time. There was no denying it. I wanted Saint more than he wanted me. The scale between us wasn't even close to being equal, yet I couldn't escape the desperation inside me that begged to slam my mouth on his whenever he was in my vicinity.

I wanted him, dammit, when he'd done nothing to earn my fondness.

"Don't ask questions you don't want to know the answers to," he said, the low baritone of his tone playing up our proximity and giving me butterflies.

God, what was wrong with me? I shouldn't be attracted to him, but I was.

An infatuation, that was all it had to be.

Maybe I could work out the kink that twisted my soul to his by giving in once or twice, getting him out of my system. After all, there was so much hype around his unicorn dick that I couldn't help but succumb to it. Besides, might as well live up to the reputation that would soon follow if Harry's tape was released.

"What's bothering you, Spitfire? The fact that I wouldn't chase after you, begging you to split your legs like a rueful teenager after a few stolen kisses? I'm sorry to crush your dreams, sweetheart." He caressed the side of my head lovingly, a mocking quality to his movements. "But that mouth of yours is not that talented."

"Is it not?" I smiled, despite not feeling an ounce of humor. "Then why were you groaning like a mule, trying to get yourself closer?"

"Cause I'm a red-blooded male. Availability and desperation call to us like a siren." He stared at me expressionlessly.

That didn't explain why his body was flush against me, big and strong, his head slanted, our noses almost touching. I could feel his heartbeat under my palm, the erratic rhythm of it boosting my courage.

"You're lying," I breathed.

"How so?" He cocked his head, the side of his mouth curling.

"I would run out of fingers if I counted the number of times a woman made a pass at you at our own engagement party, then Jane yesterday. But I didn't see you show a scrap of interest." I looked on defiantly. "Why is that, Saint?"

"Believe it or not, Ariadne, I do have standards."

"Well, so do I. And I will not be with someone who belittles me so carelessly, parades his exes in front of my face, and tells me in front of my *family* that his mistress refused to sign an NDA. I am aware I'm not really your fiancé, your girlfriend, or even your friend, but I refuse to be your fool. You do whatever you want to do, as long as I am treated with respect," I seethed, annoyance spilling out of me in waves.

"This could be applied both ways, my judgmental, Spitfire."

Hysterical laughter bubbled up my throat, and my sanity held on by a thread. I felt so worked up all of a sudden like I always did when he was around and challenged me.

"Oh, please, I've only judged you unfairly twice, and

that was because I was..." I caught myself before I played into his hand.

Saint was fucking cunning, making your head loop in order to catch up with his mind games.

"Because you were what?" He snarled, his eyes thunderous and depraved. "Finish the sentence."

My mouth was wired shut, my hands tensing on his shirt until I heard a small rip, the fabric giving away under the pressure of my spiky nails that I'd painted black for the occasion. My lips wobbled like a pre-teen that couldn't handle a confrontation.

I didn't know what I was doing. Drowning in my thoughts, expectations, and reality. Saint the fucking almighty saw through me. One quality about him that unnerved me to the core was how easily he could decode me. Either he was that good at reading people, or I needed to get better at masking my emotions.

"Tell me what you were." He pressed, lacing his fingers through mine and pinning my hands to the door beside my waist.

My chest heaved with deep breaths, brushing against his taut muscles. I twisted my wrists in his grip, but they were like steel bands, shackling me in place and urging me to spill all my secrets.

"*Jealous.* Because I was fucking jealous." I turned my face away from him, squeezing my eyes shut as the words spilled out of me. "There. I said it. Are you satisfied?"

Saint's sigh feathered over my cheek. It didn't sound pleased. It sounded tortured. He released my hands, threading his fingers around my neck and straightening my head, so I was forced to look at him.

His ever-present potency shone through even in the

barely illuminated room. Those eyes that so often played a leading role in my dreams tore through whatever mental shields I still had present when he lowered his forehead on mine, our hearts beating in tandem in the dark.

"Not in the slightest. What am I going to do with you, Spitfire? You weren't supposed to turn out complicated."

"I'm sorry."

"No, you're not."

"No, I'm not," I parroted because, for the first time after a while, I felt at peace. Yes, asking for more out of this relationship was risky, but I couldn't contain the part of me that hungered for a deeper connection. It was human nature to want to make your dreams a reality, and he had been mine since I was thirteen.

"Would it be so bad to give this a try?" I whispered, my fleeting adrenaline exposing my raw emotions. "I like you, and you like me. There's no one holding us back but our damned selves."

I gulped when he shook his head, ice engulfing any sign of heat when he took a step back, disconnecting from me. I crossed my arms, kicking off the door. We'd definitely been gone longer than acceptable. Knowing my family, they would be too distracted by each other to notice.

"I don't do relationships, Ari—"

"Who's your role model? *Christian Grey*?" I cut him off with a scoff and a roll of my eyes. That was the lamest excuse ever, and if he didn't want to do *me,* he could say so.

"I really don't and despise everything that comes with them." Saint clipped. "I don't want kids, white picket fences make me retch, and I find dates an unnecessary prerequisite if we're just going to fuck anyway. Don't expect me to remember any anniversaries and the only romantic thing that'll ever come out of my mouth is when I tell you to lay on the table so I can have you for fucking lunch."

We were doomed. I knew we were doomed. The man had the emotional availability of fucking Bellatrix Lestrange, yet did that discourage me? No, it didn't. The thought of him having me for breakfast, lunch, and dinner reigned supreme.

"A true prince charming."

"This is who I am. Take it or leave it." He shrugged.

I pondered over it, wanting to knock that cocksure glint in his eyes.

"I want a trial period." I finally said with a nod. "The remainder of our year together, if either of us ever feels the need to be satisfied *sexually*... we go to each other. Exclusively, no mistresses and no more Harry. It's five years of our lives, Saint. No sane woman would ever be with a married man."

He looked at me like he couldn't quite believe I was negotiating with him about this—like he couldn't believe he was even considering it. Hope spread inside me like a balm. Saint eyed me up and down, and my chest puffed subconsciously.

"You're putting too much faith in your gender, Fleur." He reminded me in a withering tone that I chose to ignore.

"After the year is up." I continued as if I hadn't heard him. "If we still feel like it's not working, then we go our separate ways. No fuss, no scenes, an amicable split."

I walked over to the marble counter, sitting my ass down so I could give my feet a rest from standing up in heels. Saint latched on to the flutter of the slit on my left thigh as he spread his sinewy legs, his stance resembling that of a bodyguard.

"And you want this because? You'll still be young after

five years, twenty-six. Most people don't even start looking for committed relationships until well into their thirties."

"By most people, you mean yourself?" I questioned, adjusting the skirt of my dress over my lap.

"So what if I am? I enjoy sex, and I like to have plenty of it. Are you sure you can even keep up, Fleur? You said you weren't a virgin, but the way I cut it, you couldn't have been with more than one partner. You probably know the basics..."

I reared back when he rushed my way abruptly, and he caught my head with his hand before I slammed it against the cabinets behind me. I held my breath when he didn't let go, feeling something hard and long against the bare skin of my leg.

"My fist using your hair as reins while I ride your ass." Saint curled his fingers in my strands, tugging sharply until I was forced to look up at his eyes. The lust I found swimming behind the liquid gold shot a bullet of excitement down my spine. "My tongue shoved down your throat while your pussy milks my cock for all it's worth." He then grabbed my hips, dragging me, so I was perched right on the edge, cool air grazing my damp panties as he stepped between my legs. His nostrils flared, and I wondered if he could smell my arousal. "But what if I liked the darker side too? Edge play, voyeurism, masochism, *humiliation*? Would you be so quick to jump on my dick then, Spitfire?"

I didn't know how to explain it. It was like I was shoved underneath a stream of ice water and lava at the same time, dousing me with scorching heat and biting coldness. I turned solid as a rock, my body pounding with aftershocks of pleasure.

He was into all that? And I-I wasn't appalled—quite the opposite, I found myself intrigued.

"I'm open to trying new things." I found myself saying before I could filter my thoughts.

A part of me screamed that I was stupid and going straight off the deep end was not wise, but that part of me could shove it. I was tired of letting my fears rule me, of finding sexual satisfaction solely between the pages of my books, or by douchebags that took a mile when I gave them an inch and filmed me without my consent.

Saint's brows slammed together as if he wasn't expecting that answer like he was sure he'd scare me off. But I didn't give up that easily. This was a battle of wills I refused to lose.

"God, you're stubborn," he muttered, our faces angled so close I could feel his words on my mouth.

He had the smoothest lips I'd ever seen on a man, red and ripe like pomegranate. The urge to bite his bottom lip after he licked it teasingly washed over me like a small tsunami of horniness.

So I did.

I used the molten fire in his eyes as encouragement, his shoulders for support, and stood tall, taking his lip in my mouth and biting softly on the sensitive skin. Saint's grip turned bruising on my hips, a sweet pain that left me hungry for more.

More, more, more.

I wanted it all and then some. I wanted to be painted every shade of filthy under the sun because being a naive little girl with no experience had gotten me nowhere. And who better to show me the ropes than Saint Astor?

My future husband and irreformable sex fiend.

He didn't let me out without a fight, feeding me a guttural growl that hit the back of my throat and swallowing my mouth in a kiss that robbed me of my breath, and destroyed my already soaked panties. Sitting back at the dinner table with all my family would sure be fun.

"Your trial run starts after our wedding, Spitfire," he said once we came apart, our shoulders knocking as we sucked in air greedily. "I'm giving you time to reconsider your position until then. After that? You're all mine to do as I please."

CHAPTER FOURTEEN
ARIADNE

Between hiring a PA to take some of the load of remote marketing off my shoulders, fending of Harry's pushy texts, and sending him small sums of money to hold him off and buy myself time, December came in the blink of an eye.

Saint gave me the space I didn't ask for, and I was a rolling mess of nerves on my wedding day. The two bath with Epsom salts I'd already taken didn't help me out at all This would be the first time I'd see my groom after a week because *giagia* had deemed it inappropriate for us to be together before our wedding night. Little did she know that I could run around with my skirt up, begging to be fucked, and Saint's steely resolve wouldn't falter.

I was scared of staying at my old place alone, so I crashed at my parents' house. It wasn't all that bad, plus Irena and I needed some time together. I missed my sister or *skatouli* as I called her—little shit in Greek.

"Aria, stop sweating. You're going to ruin your makeup," Daphne ordered, fanning my face with her hands as Mom and *giagia* tried to squeeze me into the French Belle Époque inspired wedding gown. A strapless, lavish number with layered petals, decorated in silver threads, rhinestones, and pearls that increased in density toward the edges of each leaf-like surface.

I knew this dress was the one the second I saw it in the Falco archives. Designed by Marie Arsenault in the fifties, a legend with a penchant for innovation and leading the way with her pioneering ideas. We were taught about her in fashion history class, so I had a mini freak-out moment when Celia toured me about the place where they kept their crowd favorites.

"I can't control my bodily fluids." I groaned, holding on to the edges of the mirror with both hands as they buttoned the corset. You didn't alter a Falco wedding dress to fit you. You altered yourself to fit in it.

"Can someone turn up the AC here?" Daphne's request went ignored into the room of about twenty girls. All my female relatives had collectively decided to show up and watch me suffer as I was pinched and prodded the whole day, sprayed with enough hairspray to suffocate a small bear.

"Are you kidding me? It's freezing outside." Irena, clad in her blue bridesmaid dress, wrenched the curtains in my mom's closet open. "See? Snow!"

"Then someone get me some powder." Daphne snapped her fingers, and I sighed, sitting down after they were done with the dress and letting them pamper me while I drowned in champagne. I stopped when Mama gave me the side-eye, and I also didn't want to show up drunk at my own wedding.

Swallowing hard, I scribbled on the bottom of my white heels with a pen as the stylist weaved my hair into a romantic twist, with braids and wisps littering my temples.

"What are you writing there?" Irena hovered over me, peering down.

"Your name."

"Mine, why?"

"It's a tradition, Irena," Mom said, rummaging through her purse. "The day of the wedding, the bride writes the names of her unmarried friends on the soles of her wedding shoes, and the one that will fade out completely is the next to get married."

"Make sure you write mine in the middle." Daphne jumped in from her spot on the cream couch. "Phillip better propose soon, or I'm dumping his ass."

"Ah, you can't cheat fate. Your time will come eventually, but you can't rush the process." Ironically it was Mom that replied.

I shot a warning look at Grandma Chloe, who was standing on the far left of the room, away from my mom's family. I was already stressed enough as it was. I didn't need them fighting.

"It's funny. I've come to the conclusion that when it comes to relationships, it's always the ones who aren't looking for one that get hitched first," my cousin pointed out.

"Yes, funny how the world works." Grandma Chloe scooched off the windowsill and straightened up. "Shall we go now? Everyone is waiting. The pews are filled to the brim, and there's an army of paparazzi that's getting bigger by the minute outside right now."

"Just one moment..." Mom pulled out something shiny from her purse after rummaging through it for minutes.

"Another tradition?"

"Not that we need it, but you can never be too sure." She stole the heel from my fingers once I was done writing. "A gold coin goes inside the shoe. To symbolize financial fortune for the lucky couple."

Everyone in the stuffed room snickered as I slipped the heels on. I didn't. I had more than I'd ever need after the merger, but I wanted to hold on to it. Spend it and donate it however I liked. I wasn't willing to give anything to Harry, and he upped his price after I told him I couldn't help him get his job back.

Being blackmailed was like trying to breathe underwater. My lungs burned with the effort it took not to claw his eyes out when he had me in the palm of his hand. I needed a way out. I couldn't give him what he wanted. I refused to.

"Oh, and we made some adjustments to the wedding menu. Your *pappou* wasn't thrilled at the thought of eating escargots, so we shifted some things around to make him happy too. Not too much, though." Mom rushed to explain, and I swallowed a curse. "I hope you don't mind, my love. You're the first of your cousins to get married. Understandably this is huge."

Yeah, we'd already established this was everyone's wedding but mine. Saint got full control of Falco and Fleur. Grandma Chloe got her billions. And Mom fulfilled her dreams through me. And it wasn't like I was involved much with the planning either. Save for choosing a five-tier fruit cake and the venue, I left everything to the experts. I had enough on my plate already.

"That's fine." My smile was strained as I stood, gathering everyone's gaze. I resembled a sparkly puff-ball in this dress, but I loved the artistry of it too much to go for something else.

"You look like a fairy." Irena came next to me, and my smile turned genuine as I laced my arm with hers.

"Thank you, Ina."

"Now, let's go get you hitched." She patted my hand. "I hope you've prepared the groom for the madness that will ensue in the reception."

"I might've saved a few tricks up my sleeve to reveal later," I muttered conspiratorially.

"Oh boy, can't wait to see how the Astropolis's golden boy will react when *pappou* drags him to dance *Zeibekiko*."

"It will be a sight to behold, that's for sure."

And so, with my family ushering me forward, I started for the wolf's den, hoping the loyalty in his blood would encompass me as well.

SAINT

"Who would've thought?" Killian asked, standing two feet behind me.

"We'd be standing here." Leo continued, second in line.

"This snowy December day." Ares finished last, a stupid grin on his face as I glared at them.

It had started snowing this morning, and if that wasn't a bad omen, I didn't know what was. Flakes stuck on the glass roof of the conservatory. The outside, to inside contrast, stark. Our guests sat amidst lush tropical foliage. Green plants spilled from floating pots hanging on European trusses, koi ponds gurgled with artificial water streams, and toddlers tried to lick the rose gold marble archway when they entered because it reminded them of cotton candy.

Kids were dumber than rocks, but somehow people were mystified as to why I didn't want to have any.

"Thinking is not your strong suit, Killian," I said just to spite him, and he winked at me, unfazed.

"Overthinking makes you miserable, and I chose to be happy."

"He has a point, though." Leo picked some lint off his suit. "Out of all of us, Ares was the most likely to get married first, and look at him still single and ready to mingle."

"What happened to Sonia?" I raised a brow, continuing when Ares dropped his gaze. "Got the boot, eh?"

Killian turned toward him, the tattoos on his neck dancing with the movement. "Damn, man, you're like a closeted manwhore."

Ares's hazel eyes went hard, his lips tipping up in an arrogant smirk. "Someone has to take your brother's place now that he's getting married."

"Well, you just got a lot more interesting, Alsford." My brother mirrored Ares's expression.

"I'm glad I'm not getting married in a church. We would've probably been struck by lightning," I mumbled under my breath when a red-faced officiant glared at us from his place on the stand.

"Ah, I think God is way more lenient than you're giving him credit for." Leo's eyes glazed with a look I knew all too well as he stared at Eliana on the second row, rocking a squirming Bella on her lap.

"I'm not even going to ask." I shook my head, facing forward when a hush settled over the crowd. Scandalous displays of affection were Leo's thing. He stopped an entire graduation to profess his love for Eliana. Go big or go home was his motto.

Here Comes The Bride by Richard Wagner rolled through the speakers, and everyone scrambled to their feet, sending my pulse into overdrive. There wasn't much that could affect me. I'd lost my ability to care about bullshit at a young age, and rolling with the punches had become a personality trait at this point.

But getting married?

That shit had me sweating like a nun in a brothel every time I thought about it this past week. Not seeing Spitfire for seven days hadn't helped either, much to my dismay. I used my lust for her as a backdoor to escape the persistent thoughts of tying my life to another person for the immediate future. Taking a break from imagining her voluptuous body stretched out beneath me, twisting and turning to accommodate my thrusts had allowed for the harsh reality to creep in.

I was marrying for money, legally bound by a contract that didn't allow for any wiggle room unless I planned on losing everything I'd stolen from my father. And I couldn't let that happen. Not when I just got my opportunity to gloat.

My muscles bunched with the effort it took to stay rooted in place and not run for the hills. Ignoring the way the black tux constricted around my torso, I fixed my eyes on the patch of white peaking on the start of the aisle, working my way up the layers of tulle and silk, until the subject of my obsession filled my view, her hand clenched tightly around her father's arm.

My nails cut into my palms when a shot of warmth spread like slow poison from my chest up to the crown of my head.

So pure, so innocent, such a pretty liar.

She was hiding secrets behind the veil that acted as a protective film, disguising her reluctance from the world. I saw through it. Aria gnawed on her bottom lip, her steps down the walkway, scared and small. She had a white-knuckle grip around a cluster of pink peonies, keeping her posture straight, ready to take on the world, and perhaps that was what I admired most about this girl.

Ariadne annoyed me to no end, her reactions had me wanting to throw hurdles, but I also fucking loved how she didn't back down. She always had a response on the tip of her tongue, and if anything, I knew I was going to enjoy making her lose her words for however long this marriage lasted.

The bitterness on the back of my throat ebbed away when Darian kissed Aria's temple, glaring at me over her head, his gaze heavy with the promise of imminent death if I hurt his daughter before he handed her over.

"Take care of her." Darian's voice carried the tone of a concerned father.

"Yes, sir." I nodded half-heartedly. I wouldn't let anyone harm her, but I couldn't promise to be the white knight in shining armor.

I disregarded him pretty quick, finding my way back to Aria like a moth to a flame. She tilted her face up when I offered her my hand, staring at me through shadowed eyes, the brown swirling like malt in her irises. Placing her small hand on mine, Aria climbed the two short steps to the stand, her heels allowing her to reach my forearm in height.

"You look beautiful," I complimented her, and the guests aw'd as if on cue.

I made sure my voice was loud, partly for them, but I meant what I said. She was gorgeous. Her skin was smooth and tan, the wedding gown a mere accessory on her. Ariadne carried the show, and if this wasn't reality, I would have scooped her in my arms and had her down on all fours before she could blink, all that pretty tulle ripped to shreds.

But it was, and I'd made a verbal contract I was honoring.

She gave me a forced smile as Minister Parker started his speech, not fooled by my public camaraderie. I kept Ariadne's hand firmly in my grip, lacing my fingers with hers, and didn't let go even when our hold turned clammy.

We were navigating this side of hell on earth together. Intimate or not, she was mine for the next five years. I wanted to know her secrets before anyone else, and I wanted her complete submission—not an easy feat to tackle, but I vowed to make it work. If there was anything I wasn't going to allow ever again was making tabloids richer by profiting off our lives.

They'd done so for as long as I'd been alive, prompting spirals, capturing meltdowns, and making fun of tragedies.

"Please repeat after me," Minister Parker instructed, and Aria and I faced each other. She seemed oddly pale underneath her veil like she'd welcome the ground opening up and swallowing her whole over tying her life to mine.

A far cry from the woman who was begging for my dick while her whole family was having dinner a few rooms over.

"I Saint Astor, take you, Ariadne Fleur," I spoke over Parker's voice, my lines already memorized. "To have and to hold."

"For better or for worse." Aria's frail voice bled into mine, our vows intertwining as our lives linked with golden bands proclaiming ownership.

"For richer and for poorer." I held her shaking palm steady as I slid her tiny ring on.

"In sickness and in health," she echoed.

"To love and to cherish as long as we both shall live." I finished the lie.

Now's your chance to run, Spitfire.

Ariadne bit her lip, the guests blending into the background as she focused wholly on me for the first time. She matched the challenge in my eyes, her acrylics cutting into my skin as she arched her brow ever so slightly, making sure I was the only one that could see it.

I never bow first, Astor.

"I do." Her lips said one thing, but the words *I want this* floated in her eyes.

There was something very poetic about the connotation of desire versus compliance. Raw lust, the epitome of what led most couples to marriage.

It usually came before dinner with the parents or meeting the dogs, but Ariadne and I had a knack for doing things the unconventional way. And while she hated my guts, and I wanted to fill that mouth until the only sounds she was producing were gags, I wouldn't play dumb and deny my attraction toward her. The strain in my pants every time she entered a room wouldn't allow for a lie of that degree.

She wanted it; she'd get it.

But not in the way she dreamed. Reality had a terrible habit of not meeting expectations. I would protect Ariadne by becoming her lesson.

"I do." I mirrored her statement when the officiant asked if I consented to the marriage too.

His gaze bounced from me to Aria as he went through the *speak now or forever hold your peace* portion of the ceremony. When no one spoke or melted in a puddle of jealous tears, Minister Parker gave me the green light. "I pronounce you husband and wife. You may now kiss the bride."

I didn't understand the concoction of sensations that

swam in my chest right after the reverend finished his sentence. Dread, fascination, and worst of all, *excitement* took over as I removed Ariadne's veil, brushing my eyes over her fresh face with newfound urgency for my wife.

Wife.

She was the tiniest thing, so young it felt wrong to even touch her, but I'd never been one to stick to the rules. Cupping her cheeks, I lowered my lips to hers, going for a slow burn of a kiss that would linger until I knew the pads of my thumbs would heat by the intensity of her blush.

"Make no mistake, Spitfire. This isn't a vow of love." I whispered into her mouth, making her eat my words as our teeth clashed, prompting cheers and claps. "Keep that in mind, or it will turn into a vow of hell."

Ariadne grinned, fabricating a false narrative while providing me with the bite I'd found myself becoming attached to. "Are you sure you shouldn't be guarding your own heart, Lucifer? I'm small, and I can squeeze into places I don't belong in."

"And I'm big and could crush you just as easily." I made my point by digging my fingers into her skin. She retaliated by leaving crescents on my neck.

A display of affection among newlyweds, a dance of dominance amongst predators. There were two sides to every story, and manipulation came easy when you craved to fuck your burden as much as you wanted to get rid of her.

"Let the games begin, my dear husband." Ariadne got the last word, sealing her fate with brash boldness.

I looked forward to making her bend.

A party was thrown despite my initial denial of having one for our sham marriage. I'd suffered through enough family moments to last me a lifetime in our engagement. A man's opinion was trivial on matters such as this, I'd come to find out, though, and my wife's stubbornness, I was already aware of.

They should call me a seer because, in typical Astor and Fleur fashion, the reception had been a melting pot of under-cutting remarks, sprinkled with a healthy dose of sarcasm and tiered with a thick layer of resentment. One of the wedding planners had the bright idea of sitting our parents on opposite ends of the same table, and the only one who had a good time was my father, who thrived on chaos.

The commitment to which my new mother-in-law and mom were going at it, ping-ponging sentences with double meanings the entire night was slightly admirable since they didn't get tired for a fucking second. The plot twist came when Chloe Fleur sided with Mom on many occasions. At least for me, Aria, who was too busy playing a game of *critique the outfit* with her sister, didn't blink an eye.

Her grandpa, or *pappou* as I found out she liked to call him, was the true star of the whole ordeal, coordinating the dance floor better than a paid choreographer, dragging both of us with him like our asses were on fire, and we needed to dance in circles to traditional Greek songs to set them off. The budget of the wedding quadrupled when I factored in the cost of how many broken plates we had to pay for.

My feet thanked me for hiring a limo on the drive back home. In all my years of grueling football training, it was *pappou* Nico's insistence on not letting me rest for a single minute that killed me. Okay, I might've been avoiding rest a bit myself too, because Aria's *giagia* swooped in like a bloodthirsty mosquito whenever I sat down, eager to talk to me about all things that had to do with babies.

I'd rather go to rehab for a second time than have those kinds of conversations.

"Which word do you hate the most?" I asked Aria, who lounged next to me, mirroring me and removing her own shoes. I loosened my tie as the car skidded past busy streets, filled with fake Santa's spreading holiday cheer for a quick buck.

She gave me an inquisitorial look, rubbing her ankle to keep some of the swelling down. "I don't think I have one. Why?"

"Mine is fucking *opa*." Even saying it myself brought back nightmares.

Aria laughed as if I told the funniest joke in the world, but her grandfather only screamed the word in *my* ear while jumping up and down, confusing seventy-one, his actual age, for seventeen.

"That is not a word. It's an expression."

"Whatever the fuck it is, I don't want to hear it again."

"I quite like its versatility." She flung herself back on the seat with a heave, turning her body so she was staring at me. "Greek people use *opa* on a number of occasions, in marriages as you experienced. They say, *opa* in bad moments, where it's usually followed by *re malaka*, which roughly translates to *you asshole*. *Opa* is also used to warn someone to watch out, and—"

Maneuvering quickly, I drew her head under my arm, holding my hand over her protesting mouth. "Are you repeating it to get me even madder?"

I let go when she licked my palm. "Wow, you're so bright."

"Doesn't marriage usually make women more agreeable? How come I'm stuck on the other side of the aisle." I jutted my lip out, delivering a savage bite on it when I realized what I was doing—*pouting*.

"Mind-blowing sex might make women more agreeable. You've yet to deliver on that, *hubby*." Aria challenged me, and coincidentally, stumbled forward when the driver took a sharp turn.

Her curls spilled over my arm, and I steadied her with my hand on her back, not ready to let go yet. This walking, talking destruction was officially mine, and this was the first quiet moment I got with her since the altar.

"Are you holding your breath on breaking in your mattress tonight, Spitfire?" I skimmed my lips over her hairline, her shudder reverberating down my side.

"I'd much rather be at a hotel in the Bahamas, but since you're too busy for a honeymoon, my bed will do."

"So lenient of you."

"I'm giving you the benefit of the doubt. My expectations are high."

"Are they?" My brows rose. "Then I hope my wedding gift doesn't leave you as sordidly disappointed as I will."

"What are you talking about?" Her upper body detached from mine; her face was dumbfounded by my statement.

I found myself second-guessing my decision in the first place. I could follow her home, and sample everything my wife had to offer like a person in their right mind would, or take the scheduled flight to France, and bore myself to death, listening to shit I didn't give a rat's ass about, and that Darian could handle by himself.

Staying meant standing in the ashes of my previous conviction. At least by leaving, I'd exhausted all options of not giving in, which would definitely happen if I stayed. She had a body I wanted to enter and never leave; a trip wouldn't stop me. Maybe she'd be mad enough to tell me to fuck off when I returned like a smart girl should.

I had an inkling Aria was as dumb as me when it came to us, but I'd exhaust all my options, so at the end of the day, I could say I went down fighting.

"I'm afraid we're spending our wedding night separated, Spitfire. I have to attend a conference in Paris that was planned ahead of time, so you'll have to take care of your own needs."

No part of her connected to me now, her eyes rounding like they were ready to shoot laser beams at me. "You're leaving me alone? *On our wedding night?*"

"Well, look at who's not that bright now," I drawled, and I was sure she'd slap me.

Aria's nails dung into the seat, a silent current of anger spreading around the empty space and bouncing against the partition. "And oh, so disposable, I guess. You couldn't have postponed this conference? Or fucking canceled it." My silence was enough of an answer, and she snapped her head to look out the window when our driveway filled the view. "I see how it is."

She scrambled to get her hair tie and bag, and never had I felt like a bigger asshole than when I saw her eyes shining with unshed tears. I jerked forward, but she was out the door before the vehicle had fully even stopped yet.

"Have fucking fun then, and break a fucking leg." She slammed the door on my face, and something told me her wish was verbatim.

CHAPTER FIFTEEN
ARIADNE

I f Saint and I were competing in the Olympics, we would have certainly come last. Actually, who was I kidding? We wouldn't even qualify because that meant being in each other's presence in the first place in order to play.

That wasn't in the cards for us. Mister hotshot dropped me off home after the reception, and I didn't expect any clothes-ripping, hair-pulling type of sex before we even crossed the threshold or for him to even carry me inside. I was a hopeless romantic, not stupid, but him not to come in at all?

Now that put a dent the size of Pluto in my carefully curated plan of seducing him. And by seducing, I meant leather lingerie with scandalous cutouts beneath my flowy reception dress. I'd taken the plunge and got caught in branches when he abandoned me.

The idea of me not being enough, so he had to fly over-seas to get away, had my blood torching. My pride was more important than my libido, though, so I simply shut the car door to his face telling him to break a leg, hoping he broke both his legs for abandoning me the first night of our marriage like a common whore not even worth his time.

"Are you sure that's the picture you're going for? I happen to think the black, oversized blazer looked phenomenal on you." Hyram's eyes squinted as he looked at the monitor, a plastic smile painted on his face.

It looked phenomenal on me because it created the illusion of an hourglass figure due to its strategically placed cuts, and darker colors tended to slim you down as opposed to the silver mini dress picture I wanted to go with. My thighs did look like over-boiled sausages where the fabric ended, way too close to the arch of my ass, but I'd built this brand all on my own, and my values would be reflected in it.

Arachne was all-inclusive. I wanted every customer to look at my designs and not feel left out because of their weight. I had to start with tackling my own insecurities if it meant helping other people overcome theirs. No more internalizing humiliating comments flung my way years ago. High school was a vicious cycle I refused to let continue into my adult life.

"I'm not repeating myself again." My tone was stern as I pointed at the picture. "I don't pay you for fashion advice. Let me worry about the wardrobe. We're going with picture number four."

The finality in my voice made him grit his teeth. His brown eyes, hanging on my own a tad too long than I would've liked, but I didn't look away until he bopped his head in resignation. "All right."

Satisfied, I left it at that, cinching the robe I had on

tighter around my waist and turning to head to the changing room. Not even one step out, the continuation of his sentence had me stopping short.

"*So bossy,*" I heard Hyram murmur, probably to one of the staff members that were in charge of the lighting and maintenance of the set. A husky male chuckle followed his sentiment that had my hackles raising primed for battle.

I spun in place, my hands fisting at my sides with the effort it took to be professional even though he didn't deserve it. Hyram Black was a highly acclaimed photographer, and well... I certainly didn't expect this.

I should've. He was old and considered the cream of the crop. Different wasn't in his dictionary. He probably had a dusty one all the way from the early nineties when having Naomi Campbell in your fashion shows amongst an army of Dutch models was considered progressive.

"I'm not bossy. I am the boss." *And could quite frankly have you blacklisted for the rest of your life.* I watched the wrinkles on his forehead get deeper, and the employees around us snapped to action again, worried my reprieve would extend to them too. "I suggest you watch your tone, Mr. Black if you want us to have a healthy business relationship."

Translation: Keep your mouth shut and do as I say, or you're fired, even though it's too late for me to book someone else. Oh, and also, forget about taking part in any of my future campaigns.

Hyram pursed his mouth, primed to talk back, and I crossed my arms, making him think twice. Not only was I double the size of most women Mr. Black had the pleasure of working with but I was also half his age and his boss.

His eyes flicked behind me, and his frown got even deeper as he tried to swallow the bitter pill of being ordered around by someone he didn't consider his equal. I remained planted until he apologized, watching him wring his hands together in his lap and grapple to find the right words.

"Oh, I'm so sorry, Mrs. Astor." Hyram shook his head, his neck straining. "I think you misheard me. I said *you heard the boss*. I would never call you bossy."

The blatant disrespect made my palm itch. Violence wouldn't win me any brownie points, though, so I let him be. I wouldn't see him again after today, anyway.

"It's still Mrs. Fleur," I corrected as I walked out.

It was the twenty-first century. Women didn't have to take a man's last name anymore.

"Is that so?" That husky voice I could recognize even with my eyes closed made me stop short, my stomach bottoming out like I was on the peak of a roller coaster.

That was Saint Astor to me. My own personal roller coaster, with his highs and lows, and most importantly, one I was dying to ride. A towering presence, with tailor-made suits because he was that fucking big. He wasn't only sex personified. He had sass and wit too, making him annoying to deal with and hard to stay mad at.

Pretty privilege was definitely a thing, and the blond hunk with new highlights present in his hair was reeking of it.

"Saint." I edged forward, convinced I was seeing things. He'd left four days ago. I didn't expect him back until... Well, I simply didn't expect him to come back. "What are you doing here? I thought you were..."

Fucking everything that moved in Paris.

Saint kicked off the wall, his familiar cologne hitting my nostrils as he ushered me to my changing room by the small of my back. I held down the urge to kick him out, refusing to cause a scene in public.

In private, though?

You'll do what? You didn't say anything when he left. When it mattered. Who cares what you have to say now?

Tapping my foot on the parquet floor, I waited as his broad shoulders faced my way, taking up most of the space in the tiny dressing room.

"Came back late last night and was surprised when I didn't find you home. Where did you spend the night, Spitfire?"

I bit my lip to stop the incredulous laugh that bubbled up my throat. I couldn't believe his audacity, asking *me* where I'd been. Waiting until the next day to find me, like we didn't have phones. He didn't care, not really.

"I visited one of my side-dicks, invited some friends over, and had an orgy. Wild times," I mocked.

"Hilarious."

"That's my middle name." I threw my hair back, feeling hot as I disregarded his physical presence, and rummaged through the silver clothes rack, giving myself something to do. "What about you? Have a great time in Paris? I know Fiona Lee had a ton of nice things to say about you."

"Keeping tabs on me? How nauseatingly sweet."

"You wish. I was watching her interview, and she dropped your name. One conference *that* must've been, leaving your newlywed wife to hang out with models during fashion week."

There was a moment when I believed him. It was an

important event, usually, one where everyone who was anyone in the fashion industry attended, and if I wasn't busy, I would've been there too. A ton could go wrong. But my optimism went up in flames when the supermodel from Hong Kong gushed about *how nice he was, and how tall, and, and, and...* her list of compliments was never-ending.

Maybe it was me that inspired the asshole in him.

"I didn't leave you empty-handed." His voice was closer now, an edge present.

"Yes, thank you. I made sure Harry and I made good use of *Rabbid* 3000." I yanked a monogram jumpsuit out, throwing it on the tufted green couch. Holding the edges of my robe together, I locked eyes with Saint again, trying not to fall prey to the intensity in his gaze. "Do you mind? I need to change."

"I'm honored," he said, not making a move to leave.

"That I slept with someone else and used the sex toy you left on my fucking nightstand?" My brows bunched, all hope lost.

He cocked his head, a smirk perched on his lips like he had a built-in lie detector screwed in his mind. Saint struck before I could anticipate it. His big hand met my shoulder, and I was flailing back in no time, the hair on my face muffling my shocked gasp.

"That you'd lie to try to make me jealous, but let's make one thing abundantly clear, Spitfire. You let anyone touch you. I'll cut off their hands and shove them down their throats." *His* hand gripped around *my* throat once I managed to get my curls under control, and a fire cursed through my veins at the savage look on his face. "You asked for the full Astor experience. You're getting it."

Desire couldn't help but spark in my chest at the sexually charged atmosphere. If anyone could make me horny while promising to tear another man's hands off, that would certainly be Saint. His fury and ardor rubbed off on me as he watched me from above, his palm feeling the nervous bob of my throat. He seemed pleased with himself, having figured out all the words to a song that was just ours while I remained clueless.

I didn't like the powerlessness.

"And you agreed to celibacy but still broke that vow *on our wedding night*," I shot back.

"Kind of impossible to do that *on our wedding night*, seeing as I was on a plane with your father. Unless there's something else you'd like to accuse me of?" His dead eyes sparked with mirth, and I clawed at his hand.

Insistent knocks on the door lowered the temperature of the room, and we both froze as a thin female voice fleeted through the wood. "Mrs. Fleur? We're ready to wrap up the last shoot."

"She'll be there in ten," Saint barked.

"I'm ready now," I hissed back, mortified, but my P.A. was already walking away. I almost pleaded for her to come back when Saint settled his weight on top of me. Not to leave me alone in a room with a man who undid me with a few simple words and touches.

"The trust issues have got to stop, baby. You might be twenty-one, but I'm almost *thirty-one*. I didn't go through that shit in high school or college, and I'm not planning on starting now." His grip migrated to my hair, maneuvering my head until his full lips were almost touching mine.

"Because you've never been committed to just one person."

"Now I am. I might be fucked up, but I. Don't. Lie." He leaned to whisper in my ear. "I promised your daddy I'd take care of his little girl. And I'll use my tongue, teeth, and fingers to make sure I keep my word."

Saint's dirty mouth sent a shudder through me, making my body tingle in places I didn't know was possible without touch. My core clenched when he rolled his hips on mine out of the blue, and I felt him hard and pulsing close to my entrance, the only barrier being my panties and his slacks. My robe was almost undone at this point.

When the fuck did we get here?

"W-What are you doing?" I breathed.

Saint dropped his head and licked and nipped along my jaw, catching my jumping pulse between his teeth and digging in. The sharp pain made me cry out, my eyes closing and my hips lifting automatically as we dry-humped on the couch.

"You still have six minutes." His voice rolled over my skin like suede, business-like even though he was working his way down my neck, licking and sucking.

"I'm at work!" I protested, remembering the staff full of people outside, but my hands tangled in his hair. I loved it. It reminded me of sunshine on a rainy day. "Besides, six minutes is not nearly enough time for *that*, and I'm not done being mad at you."

"Good, use that anger." His answering smile was wicked as he peered up at me through hooded eyes. It was like I was merely a fly he could swat away because in the next second, he had my robe pooled under me with his expert fingers, and I was gloriously semi-naked. Only clad in some delicate lace underwear, beige-colored so they didn't peak through some sheer pieces.

A thrill went through me when he groaned at the sight. The bulge in his pants piqued with interest when he lowered himself down my body. I rested on my elbows as he bit each swell of my breasts, soothing the sting with lavish kisses and leaving wet trails with his tongue that glistened in the fluorescent lighting of the room.

The underwire felt constricting around my chest as my breathing picked up speed, and my heart pounded to the rhythm my clit had adopted. Saint made my whole being pulse with need as he put his mouth and hands to use.

"I'm a fast eater, especially when I'm famished," he reassured.

"Eater? Wha—" His teeth scraped a path down my belly button, hands fisting either side of my panties, and with a slight tug, the strings on either side gave away, melting off like scraps. "*Ohhh...*"

A small gasp escaped me, unsure if it was excitement or nervousness that gripped me. I'd asked for this, indeed, and Saint was keeping up his end of the deal. I didn't know whether it was out of pity or not, but I waited for him to pursue this further with bated breath.

I was truly pathetic, shouting his ear off one moment and shutting up when he dragged his calloused hands over my hips, disregarding the last of the material that covered me up.

Shame more intense than I'd ever experienced ran me over as Saint hovered above me, gazing at my bare pussy, stomach, and wide thighs. All my imperfections were on display for this seemingly perfect person, save for my neglected breasts, still confined in my bra. At least it was a push-up one.

"Fuck, I want your legs over my shoulders when you

cream over my face, Spitfire," Saint groaned as his breath cooled my heated core, and my eyes almost rolled back when he placed a kiss on my pelvis. "Your body is phenomenal, curves for days, enough to take the whole of me."

That's just him being polite.

A snide voice in my brain popped in again, but I didn't give her any attention, not when Saint used his fingers to spread my lips wide, diving headfirst like he was starving.

"Oh fuck, Saint." A moan slithered out at the first swipe of his tongue from front to back. My knees locked under the weight of euphoria, and he placed them over his broad back. They barely reached midway, curling up and squeezing his head in place as the feel of his mouth worked me up.

Saint teased me a while more, his whole mouth moving over my slit like he couldn't get enough, tasting and teasing as his tongue slipped inside me every time he swiped. He made me feel wanted, his rough palms under my ass, burying his face in me like he was addicted to my taste.

Stars bloomed behind my lids when he circled my clit, teasing me with his tongue before flattening it and dragging it over my nub repeatedly, making me wither by sucking it in his mouth and humming. I jerked in his grip, and he chuckled, sucking harder, then popping it free and blowing his breath across it.

"So responsive." His fingers probed my entrance as he looked up at me. Lips wet. Eyes wild. So fucking sexy. "Now tell me, Spitfire. Do I need to beat up that little shit out there?"

Fuck if that didn't make my hips dip when he slipped a finger inside, the thickness of it making me sting as I tried to adjust to the fullness. My God, if this hurt, I couldn't imagine what his dick would feel like. I was way out of my league. Even though I wasn't completely inexperienced, I knew it would still hurt, simply because he was football player big.

"No," I gasped when he continued to lap up my clit. "That would only say that I need a man to protect me, and I'm doing just fine on my own."

I wouldn't be doing oh so fine if he decided to stop. Nope, not at all.

A second finger had me squirming and panting, a thin sheen of cold sweat enveloping my limbs as I tried to relax. Saint didn't let up, unaware of the pain, fostering itself within the pleasure. "What did you disagree about?"

A crazed moan bounced off the walls of the room, and I prayed no one heard as I strained against him, wanting him deeper as much as I wanted to go slower. "We are not having a casual conversation while you're eating me out!"

"I'm not eating you out. I'm wolfing you down, sweetheart." He let a smile slowly curve over his lips as he *bit* down on my clit, making my ass scoot off the couch like I was burned.

"Holy fuck," I panted, completely breathless, clawing at his hair when he stretched the bundle of nerves in his mouth until my whole body was curved into an upside-down C. Any remnants of sanity fled my brain as uncontrollable whimpers of pleasure flooded every nook and cranny of the space around us.

"Use your voice *and* your words," Saint ordered, the tangible heat of his mouth never leaving my cunt even when he spoke, his fingers never ceasing their movement inside my wet folds. "What did you disagree about?"

"H-He preferred a different picture than I did for a banner, one where I was more covered up."

My admission made him pause, and I could've cried. My head popped up just in time to watch his gold eyes turn amber as he looked his fill, tracing my skin with his electrifying stare.

"Well, that's fucking stupid. Sex sells," Saint said, and with a slow blink of a lion on the brink of devouring his pray, he gave me one more lick from where his fingers slid in and out of me, to the hilt of my pussy. The visual of his tongue coated entirely in my wetness had my stomach quivering uncontrollably. I turned languid as I felt the threads of an intense wave building low in my womb, and if it wasn't for Saint's strong arms around me, I could've melted off the couch.

"Jesus Christ," I croaked, certainly getting sold on sex with Saint Astor.

He worked me up like no one ever had before. Building up a storm, letting it rest, and hitting me again with an onslaught of unbidden need, ravaging me until I was losing my sense of self. He gave my core the relief it needed by rubbing me faster and curling his fingers, the friction easing some of my discomfort, and lapping me up like I was his favorite flavor of ice cream.

Not even the knocking on the door for a second time could draw me out of the maelstrom he'd placed me in.

"She's coming," Saint barked against me, teasing me with his breath, and the filthy double meaning of his words was what sent me over the edge, catapulting me to my climax.

Wetness gushed between my legs as a vortex of fire and ice raged with a ferocity unlike I'd ever experienced. My core knotted tightly together, a lump of hormones, spasming and moving, following the weight of Saint's powerful physique between my legs, still taunting, still exploring. I held on to his hair for dear life as my climax pounded forth with the power of a thousand charging horses on an open field.

He was like a puppet master, knowing which strings to tweak, which places to press harder against, for my release to erupt like a suppressed volcano. The mastery of his craft, coupled with his beauty and confident movements, made me shake all over. I had no control over the sounds my mouth produced, singing as loud as the blood running through my veins.

My need for him was all around us, a mist of arousal that he worked down his thick throat with gusto. A blond devil, making a meal out of me, wanting me, needing me. For a second, I let myself believe that he did. That he was hooked to his wife like I was hooked to him, an opiate I couldn't kick.

That satisfying feeling of fullness dissipated when he withdrew his fingers from me, his digits thick enough to leave me sore. I hadn't been touched in a long time. I tried to regulate my breathing as he climbed up again, crushing me with his weight, my hands refusing to leave his hair alone.

"I guess I'll have to make you come more often if it turns you this speechless," he taunted with a cocky smile that I couldn't knock off because it was true. "Your six minutes are officially up, Spitfire." His hands firmly planted on my thighs, he flipped us right up, causing me to yelp and hold on to his shoulders as cool air rushed to my backside. "See? I told you I ate fast."

Rolling my eyes, I moved back, staring at his face and letting the nature of what transpired soak for a minute. I drew circles over his stubble, and he rubbed my thighs, a hum coming from his chest, the kind that signaled pure male satisfaction. He couldn't be—satisfied, that is, not when I felt his hard-on straining against my entrance over his lap. I couldn't do anything about it now, not with everyone waiting outside.

"They're all going to know what we did," I voiced my concerns. "You look like an army of monkeys was trying to pick lice off your hair, and I'm probably not faring any better."

Saint shrugged, fixing my robe over my shoulders again, and tying it. My heart warmed at his attentiveness. He was a lot of things, but you could never call him a selfish lover. Saint was always generous with his touch.

"Who cares? You just got an orgasm from your hot as sin husband, and they'll probably go home and jack off to porn."

Obviously, he wouldn't understand how hard it was to be taken seriously as a young woman by her colleagues, but I couldn't find it in me to lecture him.

"Hot as—" A laugh bubbled out my throat as I got off his lap, my body sated and boneless. "Modesty is not in your dictionary, huh?"

"Nope, but honesty is." He winked, sitting there a prominent bulge in his pants as he stared up at me. When I didn't make a move to change, he got the memo heaving a deep sigh and getting on his feet. "Looks like you have enough for the both of us. Take it from me, Ariadne, don't let others dictate the picture you have of yourself."

It didn't take a genius to realize he'd caught on to everything I wasn't saying. It wasn't a hard picture to paint. He had eyes and had witnessed the showdown outside. Come to think of it, Hyram only backed down when he saw Saint behind me.

"He has a point, you know." I hated admitting it, but it was plastered on every billboard out there. Hard to miss. "Sex sells, but not all body types do."

"Are you shitting me?" He blinked slowly.

"Let's not play dumb. You've been around plenty of models in your lifetime, and I certainly don't look anything like them."

"Why would you want to look like them? A model's job is to literally be a walking mannequin and show off clothes. As long as you're healthy and eat well, you're fine." Grasping my forearms, he twisted us around until we were facing the floor-to-ceiling mirror. "Show me. Tell me what you don't like about yourself."

"Saint, people are waiting for me." I squirmed under his touch.

"They'll still be there after I'm done with you. That's what you're paying them for."

Sighing, I forced myself to look in the mirror. At us. Saint's face was sharper, more symmetrical than mine, an edge of allure drawing attention to himself. He had that something extra, that star-power that washed me out.

"For one, I don't like my boobs. You'd think a plus to being on the heavier side of the scale would be having bigger boobs, but nope they're slightly larger than mosquito bites." My hand traveled to my collarbone as I shook my head. "I don't like this. I'm selling myself short."

"They're perky, and they remind me of two twin pears I'd really like to taste and eventually will. Keep going." He bent down, kissing my neck, and my mind turned to goo, mouth susceptible to spilling out all my secrets.

"My stomach isn't even close to being flat, and my hips are way too wide for my shoulders. My boobs aren't the only ones built like a pear. My whole body is. No matter how much I exercise, or even if I don't eat at all, it doesn't make that much of a difference. I'm built this way." Brick by brick, he saw through my fragile self-image. "Also, thank God for modern technology and leave-in conditioner, or my hair would be a frizzy mess all day, every fucking day."

"I'd never wanted to fuck someone's insecurities more than I do yours." He bit my earlobe softly, hands running up and down my arms. "Beauty is in the eye of the beholder, Ariadne. What to you seems fat, to me looks grabbable, kiss-able, and so utterly soft, I want to lose myself in your curves. The sweet arch of your ass has been calling my name since you first walked out on me, hips swinging like you knew where my eyes strayed."

His eyes never left mine in the mirror, and I was taken aback by his... *everything*. Never in my wildest dreams did I think Saint Astor would be the one to comfort me about the fragile image I had of my body, the man who had probably slept with so many models he couldn't count them on both hands.

He was damn swoony when he wanted to be, and I guess that was when he needed in my pants. At the fear of completely missing the last shoot and giving in when he deserved to suffer a little after abandoning me for Paris, I turned around and pushed him away.

Yeah, I was the one that begged for his dick, but I could wait a while longer until my pride had healed.

"You're absolutely filthy," I accused.

"And you were soaking wet, so I guess you like me filthy." We both glanced at his pants, stained with my arousal, and red splotches bloomed on both my cheeks. "For what it's worth, I'm sorry for leaving. I thought I could give you a chance to reconsider *this*, but I couldn't focus on shit while I was there if it makes you feel better." He sighed out his confession like it took a lot out of him, admitting it.

He was right. It did make me feel better, and I caved and kissed his lips one last time before throwing him out and resting against the door, trying to catch my breath.

Saint was lethal, and what was worse, he knew it.

CHAPTER SIXTEEN
SAINT

"Should you even be playing? What if you get injured again?" Aria grumbled as she followed me to the back of the Range.

I scoffed as I opened the tailgate, inhaling the fresh morning air, ripe by yesterday's shower. The field would not be in prime condition to play football, but I could use that to my advantage. It was easier to knock someone down when the ground was slick, less impact trauma too.

"By whom? Leo and Ares?" My voice was muffled as I removed my sweater and dropped it in the truck. The thermal long-sleeve I had on underneath let some of the cold seep in. I knew I'd be sweating my ass off once I got in my element.

"Why is that so unbelievable? They are as big as you." I noticed there was a hitch in her voice, and I turned just in time to catch her eyes roaming up my body, biting her lip like her mind was filled with some pretty NSFW thoughts.

I knew mine was.

After yesterday, nothing was stopping me from slipping

Ariadne into my daily menu. Seeing her completely lose her mind was like a drug, and watching her muscles flex with pleasure or her pretty pink slit engorged with arousal wouldn't be a bad reel to keep replaying for years to come.

I didn't perform oral sex often. It wasn't something I enjoyed doing with random people. Sure, penetration was personal, but having someone's genitals in your mouth was beyond intimate. I enjoyed the taste and smell of pussy, and Aria's was delectable. I didn't know if it was the pineapples she kept shoving down her throat at home, and I didn't care. All I cared about was for a repeat, and it was going to happen soon if she kept staring at me like she was wondering what *I* tasted like.

"No one is as big as me." I flexed my chest to drive my point forward, and she rolled her eyes at me. "Also, body size doesn't matter all that much when you don't know how to use all that muscle."

"So basically, I have no chance of survival whatsoever."

It was my turn to look her over, and I almost laughed. She reminded me of a Hobbit from *Lord of The Rings* in her compression tights, green Nike shirt, and hair hastily thrown in a ponytail. All she was missing was a pair of pointy ears, and the package would be complete.

I wisely decided not to tell her that mini people didn't have very high prospects when it came to this game, but I didn't give her false hope either. "If I pick you for my team, sure you do."

Her eyes rounded comically, and she caught the football I threw her way midair as I slammed the trunk shut, her hands shaped like a diamond, squeezing the oblong shape between her fingers. *Not bad.*

"What do you mean '*if I pick you*'?" Aria tried to mimic my voice.

"I play to win, Spitfire. I don't need any liabilities on my back, don't take it personally." I ushered her forward to join the others.

Their vehicles were already here. I recognized Bella's car seat in Leo's Mercedes and Ares's sleek Ducati parked right next to each other. Killian was also here. He decided to stay for Christmas break. Someone at the wedding might've caught his attention because he usually fled at the earliest opportunity. Our parents weren't the most fun to be around, so he always crashed at my place whenever he visited, but now that Aria was living with me, he was uncomfortable stepping on our toes.

"So not only did you cut me off in the middle of work and told me to get ready 'cause we're going out, but now you're also not choosing me for your team?" For all her talk, she melted by my side as we poured into the grass, borrowing some of my warmth.

"You have a flair for the dramatics." My friends came into view, exchanging thermos filled with hot chocolate, so I distracted her by biting the top of her ear, male pride uncurling inside me at the reaction I pulled out of her. "Besides, I did it for you. All that time hunched over a sewing machine is not going to do you any good. You'll be needing daily visits to the chiropractor before you even turn thirty."

Aria met my backhanded comment with her elbow on my stomach that tickled more than it did any harm. "I'm half Greek. Have you never watched *My Big Fat Greek Wedding*? It's not that far off from reality."

"You have a point. Your grandpa almost broke my legs dragging me on the dance floor every five seconds."

"Aww, I'm rubbing off on you," she said when I matched her energy.

"In more ways than one, Spitfire." I winked at her, and just because I could, I leaned down to kiss her parted mouth.

I wish I could've surprised myself and been stronger. No matter who chose who, who initiated the deal, and who wanted what, Ariadne was a *good* person. I wish I wasn't such a lousy piece of shit because this would end in eight months' time. I couldn't not take advantage of the situation, though.

She was the perfect medium to help me forget what I should be running from but was instead barreling toward with Leo's help.

"Ew, I did not need to hear that." A voice broke past our kiss, and we disconnected Aria's cheeks tinged in pink as she turned toward the source.

"Or see that," Killian added, never one to miss out.

"Ina," Aria met her sister halfway, greeting the teenager that was already taller than her with a hug. "What are you doing here?"

Irena resembled Eliana's sister more than she did Aria's. They had somewhat similar colorings and body types if you didn't take into consideration that Eliana was almost six months pregnant now and looking ready to pop as she sat on the back of the Chevy I'd instructed Killian to take.

"Saint sent Killian to drive me over. He said they needed some more members for the teams."

We were still eight players short on each team, but this wasn't a professional game by any means. Aria seemed quite estranged from her sister last time I saw them together, a cordialness between them I usually didn't see in siblings, so sue me, I took the initiative to invite her too.

"Uncle Saint!" A smile rippled over my face when I heard the excited squeal.

"Hey, beautiful girl." Dropping to my knees, I widened my arms, and Bella threw herself at me. I crushed her to my chest, basking in her warmth. Her sweet floral scent infiltrated my senses as the rest of the guys took their turn greeting us as well.

"You'll never believe what daddy said." Her green eyes crinkled up at me, little hands toying with the collar of my shirt.

"What did he say?" I glanced at Leo, tying his shoes a few feet away.

"He said I couldn't play with you because if I did, you'd squash me like a bug with your big as—"

"Bella, that's enough," Leo interrupted, looking at his daughter like she'd betrayed him. "When did you turn into such a snitch? You're supposed to be daddy's partner in crime."

Bella didn't pay him any mind. "Would you really squash me, Uncle Saint?"

"Of course not. I'll reserve all the squashing for your daddy, babe." I lifted her into my arms.

"So can I play?" Bella's legs swung back and forth over my forearm, and I threw a mean grin at Leo, whose face was etched with a frown.

"Isabella Bianchi, he's threatening your father with bodily harm," he said sternly, horrified by his spawn's lack of concern.

"But daddy, you're a liar. Uncle Saint would never hurt his favorite girl." The squirt talked back haughtily, her hair hitting me in the face as she turned to Spitfire. "Aria, you can be his second favorite. I don't mind sharing."

Now that pulled a laugh out of me. It felt good when you were a kid's favorite, even more so when she was Bianchi's. The two of us weren't the best of friends back in the day. Ares was the only one linking us together. I found him too rough around the edges and way too fucking serious, and Leo couldn't stand my brashness.

I've since calmed down, and he has pulled the stick off his ass.

"Thank you for being so gracious, Bella," Aria brushed up to me, a smile painted on her face. "Which days would work best for you?"

"I want him on the weekends." Bella patted my face with her sticky fingers, and my stomach hurt from holding back a roar. "Mommy won't let me have any fun during school days. Preschool is tough, man."

A collective wave of laughter rolled out of us, tumbling through the trees, and open space, and smoothing over the surface of the pond. Leo would have his hands full with her when she grew up. Not many kids her age were as bold or outspoken as she was.

"Pray you don't have a daughter this time, or else they'll both abandon you for a prettier guy. First crushes are hard to beat," Ares fluffed Eliana's hair, popping his gum.

"You're assuming the kid's going to be straight," Cole, Eli's half brother, argued, enjoying the sunny day with a Starbucks Frappuccino, as he looked Leo and me over, winking. "Don't get me wrong, Damon Salvatore is hot, but I would go for Klaus Mikelson any day."

"I guess everyone prefers my fat ass over yours," I bragged at Leo, hoisting Bella higher in my arms.

"What is this? National band against Leo day? First my daughter and now everyone else?" He complained, crossing his arms.

"Aw, don't worry, honey. I would still choose you." Eli blew him a kiss.

"You're saying that because he knocked you up," I said dryly, letting a writhing Bella go.

Her little feet blurred as she ate the distance to her father, changing sides like changing tides. She launched herself at him, and he caught her with ease as if they'd done the same routine a thousand times now, even though she hadn't been walking for all that long.

"I would choose you too, daddy," Bella squealed when Leo bit her nose playfully, and I heard strangled sounds coming from next to me.

"I think my ovaries just exploded." Ariadne was the first to say.

"I think I just fell pregnant." Irena followed up.

"Tell me about it," Killian completed the trilogy of sighs. I stared at him pointedly, and he shrugged. "What? That shit is cute."

Yeah, yeah... the bastard was living in domesticated bliss, disapproving my theory of relationships daily. I couldn't even be mad. They deserved the happy ending after the shit they went through. You either suffered in your younger years or later on in life. There was no escaping it. The world was purely made of fire, you just had to know how to navigate through it not to get burned, and my path had a single lane. So, I avoided the hope swimming in Ariadne's eyes like the plague.

I'd seen what a large age-gap and forced marriage had done to my parents, and I refused to let that be us.

"All right, enough with the chitchat," I instructed, my quarterback mode activated. My body straightened, muscles tightening, ready to let some aggression on the field. "Gather around, kids. You're in for the game of your lives."

We were losing.

How were we losing?

"Touchdown, baby!" Aria yelled as she threw the ball on the end zone doing a little victorious dance with her hips.

"Hell yeah." Killian high-fived her, and they bumped shoulders like old sporting buddies. "That's my sister-in-law!"

I ground my teeth, staring at my team that had the motivation of a fucking sloth. Irena and Ares chilled on the ground, dry-heaving as if they'd run a marathon when they could barely catch a pass and ran like they'd just learned to use their legs. I should've let Bella join. No one would tackle a kid.

"Man, are you sure you were in the NFL? We're wiping your ass," Ariadne taunted, hands on her knees as she looked up at me. Sweat dripped down the side of her face in distracting patterns. It would be deemed gross by most, but I didn't give a shit and leaned down, pressing my lips on her temple.

"Beginner's luck," I murmured, condensation staining my lips. And just like that, her smile disappeared, breaths getting shallower.

God, I needed inside this woman. If anything, to fuck the obsession off, see if the real thing held up to the hype in my mind. You didn't fight like we did without having mind-blowing chemistry in bed. I couldn't wait to uncover the ineffable mysteries of makeup sex.

"That's what you get for underestimating me. Keep your shitty players," her voice was hoarse when she replied.

"I'm offended," Ares complained, flopping back on the grass like a limp noodle.

"I'm not. We suck," Irena said, not faring any better. "Football was Dad and Aria's thing growing up. They've been playing together since she was a kid."

How little you know about your wife.

"Why didn't you tell me?" I asked, crossing my arms.

She met my stare head-on, biting her lip like she was demure, but I was starting to realize she was a lot more than met the eye.

Intelligent, savvy, a hard worker.

"You assumed that big is strong, and small is weak. People have been doing it my whole life. I didn't want to ruin your dreams." Aria shrugged, taking pleasure in proving me wrong.

Something very acute to respect warmed its way into my expression, and frissons zinged their way to my dick. Day by day, Aria was turning me into a fucking lotus-eater, leading the life of dreams because I fantasized about fucking her twenty-four-seven. I had to do something about it, and I hated how that trip to Europe right after our wedding set me on square one once again.

"Weaseling your way to the top, I see."

"One master at a time." She bopped her head like she had a whole mental list of names.

"How about one last game, Spitfire?" I tugged on her droopy ponytail, and she knocked my hand away. I bared my teeth. "Winner takes all."

"I'm sensing you mean more than bragging rights."

"You'd be right." We'd gathered the attention of the others as well. I didn't miss the way their eyes lingered on us, looking for tarnished spots on our shields. Our rush engagement and wedding were still at the forefront of every mind. I leaned close until she was the only one that would hear. "A date, that's what I want. Wherever I choose, and you have no right to ask me where we're going or storm out of the place when we get there."

I was taking quite the leap from eating her out to introducing her to all the things that would send her running. She was walking on a road paved with daisies. It would be quite the adjustment to find the beauty in thorny bushes.

"Well, that's not very comforting." Aria fidgeted with her sleeves.

"Knowing Saint, expect the worst, sweetheart," Leo warned, back from his water break.

Hell, if that didn't spark interest in her eyes. I felt myself tightening in my slacks in response.

Say yes, little fire.

Let me corrupt you beyond repair.

"And if I win, you do whatever *I* want?" She perked like I knew she would, and I nodded. "All right, let's do it."

"You can't be serious. He's a professional football player. You're going to lose." Her sister inserted herself from behind me, wiser than Ariadne despite her years, entirely too innocent as well.

Ariadne was tempted by the idea of losing, yearned to know what I was offering. I could read her like a goddamned billboard. She was both hellfire and holy water, too bold for her own good, and stupid enough to cave to her twisted fantasies.

Who was I to say no if she was offering me her heart on a silver platter?

"Team, on your feet," I ordered, giving Aria my back.

I wasn't losing even if I had to tackle both Leo and Kill at the same time, stacking them on top of each other. I gave Irena all my tough love and told her to cover Kill, who I knew would hesitate to tackle her if push came to shove, and Ares took the quarterback's role and a smack on the back of his head as a prerequisite of what was to come, in case he fucked up the throw.

"You're covering me? So predictable, Spitfire." I met her simmering gaze head-on, hyper-aware of my surroundings too. My blood buzzed, the hair on the back of my neck stood to full attention, and my feet took on a wide stance, ready to sprint when Ares sent the ball flying.

"Scared, Astor?" She squinted at me.

"I like my odds, baby."

"*Hut, hut, hike!*"

I kept my peripheral vision open when Ares yelled the words. Irena passed him the ball, and second nature took over as I rushed to the end zone, beating Aria, Irena, and Killian with my long, determined strides. Leo was well on his way to tackling Ares when I turned back, but he was a pinch too late.

Ares had already locked me as his target. His arm cocked back from the moment he caught the ball. When Leo was two short steps away from him, he propelled his hand forward, releasing the ball with the perfect amount of rotation.

Aria's tiny self was doing a bang-ass job, trying to intercept the pass from my much larger build. All I had to do was roll my back to her front, slightly push, and her legs twisted like a baby deer's, dropping back like a hot potato.

This was too easy.

"No." She gave a dramatic gasp when the ball fell to my hands perfectly, rushing to her feet. Smart man that I was, I let her jump me. Her chest crashed against mine, legs around my waist as she climbed me like a tree to get to the ball. Even then, she couldn't reach my outstretched hand, but I sure had a great time holding her up by her ass as I walked a few short steps and relinquished my hold on the ball.

"This doesn't count. You were holding yourself back before." Her breath tickled my neck, and I set her back on her feet, not wanting to scar little Bella, who was watching from the truck.

"Not my fault you got too arrogant, Spitfire." I shot her a dirty look. "This Friday, cancel all your plans."

There was more pink than blue in the sky when we decided to call it a day. It was a good one. Kill took a liking to Irena, and the two of them talked their ears off, fitting in better with each other than they did with the thirty-year-olds. Ariadne's interest in Eliana's pregnancy had my chest squeezing for some fucking reason. Maybe it was because she could get to have that in the next five years if she wanted, and I'd apparently turned unceremoniously emotional ever since she was thrust into my life.

"What did you need Ethan's number for?" Leo found an opportunity to corner me when we were walking back to the parking lot, jogging next to me and leaving the rest behind. I'd been avoiding any one on one time with him today because I didn't feel like answering any questions. As always, he was blunt as a razor's blade.

"To satisfy an itch." I rolled the football between my

hands, resisting the urge to sink my nails into the soft plastic. It'd been a week since I contacted the P.I. and was learning why people said patience was a virtue.

"The only ones that go to him are the ones that are in some deep shit, and as far as I know, your life is as rosy as a petal."

"And that's where your knowledge will remain."

"Hey." Leo gripped my shoulder, but I kept walking uninterrupted. This had to stay on the low-down for the time being. He was the only one that knew, and that was because I needed his help to get in contact with Astropolis's fixer. Ethan White went by many titles, and I would decide which mask he'd wear for me after he confirmed my inkling. "We care about you, man. If you need anything, you know our door is always open."

"I know, and you'll find out eventually." I nodded, but I didn't want to cry wolf without proof. "I'm just hoping to be proven wrong."

CHAPTER SEVENTEEN
ARIADNE

"Do I look fat in this?" The door to a changing room in the La Perla boutique flew open, and out came Eliana, only clad in some lace, black lingerie. Even pregnant, she definitely belonged in the upscale store, fully inspired by classic Italian architecture and the tulle associated with the brand's fine corsetry. Her blond hair was wavy and highlighted to perfection, lips pouty, and painted a sparkly nude color.

"You look perfect," I replied from the soft lilac couch, putting my phone down.

"I look like I'm about to explode." My words flew through her ears, and she pouted at the mirror screwed in at the end of the row.

"Well, in about three months or so, you officially will," Sonia announced as she flipped through some garter belts, her slanted eyes accentuated with a heavy dose of eyeliner.

The girls invited me out for shopping today, and I agreed, even though the last thing I needed was more clothes.

"Don't you usually find out the gender of the baby three months in? How come you don't know already?" Irena was here too, doing the lord's work and picking out something for me as I finished responding to an email.

"We decided to keep it a surprise."

"A surprise?" I butted in. "I could never. I'm way too impatient for that."

"That was me with Bella too." Eliana was checking out her ass in the mirror, and I promised myself to attend one of her dance classes, because holy hell, no pregnant lady had any business being that hot. "And if I could go back, I would still choose to find out early. I was hell-bent on having a daughter, and now that I do, I'm satisfied with whatever this little peanut is."

"Isn't it killing you? Not knowing?"

"A little bit, but mostly I'm looking forward to having it out of my body, so I can sit down without needing assistance and being able to reach my toes again."

"I bet Leo is going to appreciate you reaching your toes again as well." Sonia turned to me with a wicked grin. "Did you know they have a stripper pole installed in their bedroom?"

I choked on my next breath, more horrified by the interested glint in Irena's eyes than anything else. Eliana rolled her eyes like she'd been through this a thousand times already.

"There was no reason for her to know until you told her. We're having it removed, Bella is getting too old, and I don't want her—"

"Knowing that her parents are freaks?" Sonia cut her off, and Eli met her snark with a vixen smirk.

"If that's what you get labeled as for having a healthy sex

life and at least three orgasms a day, I'm more than happy to be called a freak."

"Ugh, I hate you," Sonia complained as we all gaped at the lucky blonde. "Whatever, I bought myself that toy everyone keeps raving about *Rabbid* 3000, and let me tell you... It's thigh-quivering good. Ares can go fuck himself."

Of course, Saint was up to date with the latest and greatest products from the adult community. I held back a wave of laughter, distracted by Sonia's last sentence and the fact that we'd missed her at the pick-up game.

"What happened between you two, anyway?"

"You'd have to ask him." She shrugged, flipping through the hangers faster. "I told him I loved him, which is a normal thing to say and feel after three months in a relationship, and it was like a switch flipped inside him. The sweet and loving guy I knew turned into a cold and brooding asshat."

"He's just going through a lot right now. He lost his parents in a car accident five months ago." Eliana was quick to jump to Ares's defense, and I could see that the subject caused a rift between the two friends when Sonia's shoulders stiffened.

Awkward energy stifled the air, and while I always was the first to preach about the wonders of how different the world would be if women supported women, I was aware that Eliana had known all of the guys since high school. That was a tough bond to break. Being friends for so many years wasn't easy. I would know. I only talked to a handful of friends from college, and that was when they needed a favor.

I stuck to family and look at where that got me.

Not partaking in the animosity taking place, I let them handle it and tuned in on my sister. "Why are you blushing and smiling at your phone like that?"

Her eyes snapped up, startled when I walked over, peaking at the screen. I only managed to see some green text boxes before she shoved the phone in her back pocket.

I raised a brow.

"Cause I have life, duh," Irena retorted, changing the subject by thrusting a royal blue set in my chest. "Here, try these on, and they might help you get one too."

I aimed for her head, but she side-stepped me, chuckling like she'd said the funniest joke ever. Sighing, because I couldn't pull an Eliana and claim I got three orgasms a day when I, in fact, got minus three, I went ahead and tried on the lingerie.

I was thumbing a silky strap, debating whether or not I should ambush Saint tonight, when the door's handle turned.

"What do you think?" I asked, thinking it was Irena coming to check, only the voice that answered made cold sweat formulate on the back of my neck.

"You could use a little trimming around your hips, but pretty good. You've lost some weight since the last time I saw you like this."

Fuck. Fuck. Fuck.

The F-bomb made its presence felt in my dictionary when I met my ex-boyfriends' eyes on the glass. My body startled by his sudden appearance, where everyone could find out at any given moment.

He looked appallingly put together for someone so vile and broke. It was my short payments that were keeping him tanned, muscled, and still in full possession of his teeth. One would believe that the rotten infestation in someone's soul would reflect on the outside, but that was very often not the case. Harry's brown curls were scattered about his head playfully, soulful eyes turning darker by the second, feeling comfortable enough to shed his snakeskin in my presence.

"*Harry?*" My mouth had a mind of its own, uttering his name to get verbal confirmation that it was really him. Hands around my midriff, I turned around. His eyes fell to my chest, and I despised having his slimy gaze on me. "My friends, they—"

"They are looking around the store. There's no one out of this changing room, Ariadne."

Harry's presence had fear cramming down my neck without Erebus and Nyx here to protect me. I wanted to reach for my clothes, but the bastard was in the way, and it meant I had to touch him to get to them.

"This is beyond creepy, but I guess violation of one's privacy is your thing, huh?" I faked it till I made it, acting as if I didn't have the bare minimum on it. "Does it turn you on, you sick bastard, perving on women when they aren't looking?"

It had to.

It took me a lot of self-reflection and time replaying that video back (he was kind enough to send me a copy of it) to figure out where the camera was placed. One of his countless TVs littering his apartment. Movie buff, my fucking stupid ass. Locking your doors didn't do anything when the bad guy had a key, but no one taught you to be wary of your closest people.

"You talk a big game, Ariadne, but let's not forget who's in control here." Harry invaded my space, fearless in the absence of a bigger predator in the cramped room. I refused to take a step back, tilting my chin up as his gaze rolled over my body again, violating my boundaries. "How come you never wore shit like this for me?"

"Because you are repulsive." I granted him the answer he wasn't looking for, and he matched it by striking out, hands around my throat. "Get your hands off me, or I'll fucking scream, and you'll be rushed behind bars before you could even protest," I seethed, clawing at his skin until I left it raw.

He held me in place with no emotion behind those beady eyes. "Don't even think about it, bitch. Anything happens to me, that video is scheduled to go live by the end of the month, and there's nothing you can do to stop it."

How did I miss this? My brain repeated the age-old question even though I already had the answer. *You were running from one monster, only to fall willingly at the hands of a beast.*

"I-It's scheduled?" I spoke around the tightness in my throat. A ball of puke blocked my windpipe, and I was blazing down the road of hyperventilation. A cold film of sweat covered every inch of my body.

"February first, the video goes live, and I'm the only one that knows the password to stop it. I'm done waiting, and I won't let you push your deadline anymore. All you have to do is give me the rest of the money in cash, and then I'll be gone."

"Why cash?" I challenged, wondering how many layers of skin my nails needed to sink through to touch his bone. The scent of iron invaded my nostrils, but he seemed unaffected, his hard-on pressing against my thigh.

"Do you think I'm stupid?"

"Well, I don't think you're particularly bright."

It was always my big mouth that got me in trouble. I saw it coming, really. His slap flying my way like a windmill slicing through the air. Warm metallic blood filled my mouth when my head snapped backward. Adrenaline ran rampant through my veins, and every cell in my body prickled with panic.

"You bast—" I didn't get to finish my sentence before another slap found me. My head slammed against the clear mirror, staining it red as my hairline took the brunt of the hit.

"Bastard!" I seethed, swiping my fingers inches from his face and aiming for his eye sockets. He dodged the attack by rearing back, not before I managed to fuck up his cheek with some scratches.

"Don't test me, Ariadne. There's plenty more where that came from." He shackled my wrists in his hands, and a whimper almost left me at the pressure. Weak, I was so fucking weak it made the food I'd consumed for breakfast churn in my stomach. "I've been kind to you, given you time, when you screwed me over and dragged my reputation through the mud. Don't make me get violent. You know you deserve it."

"I know you deserve jail, you fucking psycho," I provoked him again.

I didn't have much to lose, save for a trip to the ER. He'd be taken care of, and I'd be left alone, but Harry wasn't as impulsive as I hoped him to be. A stall door opened and slammed shut next to mine, and that sent him gearing to action, removing his hold from me. It was all I could do not to launch myself at his ugly face.

Harry's heavy boots clicked softly as he made his way to the door, glancing at my disheveled form with pride. "Clock's ticking, beautiful."

CHAPTER EIGHTEEN
SAINT

Awareness pulled my eyesight to the whirlpool tub when I entered the bathroom, like a line of static electricity. Water almost tipped at the sides, and Ariadne was at the middle of it, small enough she could lie her whole body down, like a freaking mummy straight out of a pyramid from Egypt.

Only her face showed out of the cloud-like foam, and her eyes popped open when the door slammed shut behind me, widening like she didn't expect me to burst into *my* bathroom, sweaty after my nightly workout.

"Saint! What are you doing here?" Water sloshed as she sat upright, acting modest and covering her tits with her arms, the only part of her I hadn't seen—*yet*.

"On my side of the house, you mean?" I countered, raising a brow, and because we'd established already that I was a pervert with serious needs for physical boundaries, I walked closer until I could make out droplets of water on the hollow of her collarbone. The need to lean down and lick a path up her neck flared inside me. "What are *you* doing here? The bathroom door was unlocked."

"That's still not an invitation for you to open it. Also, you have a bigger tub," she explained.

I couldn't focus on her words when I got a look at her forehead, tinged in pink and slightly swollen. Forgoing the fact that she was utterly bare underneath the steaming water, I sat down on the porcelain edge of the tub, my eyes surprisingly not veering off her face. Her gaze shuttered, lashes blinking rapidly, and my veins filled with boiling water because her wound didn't look like an accident.

"Tilt your head left for me," I ordered, wanting to get a better look.

She didn't do what I asked. Shocker.

"Do you mind? I'm all for having weird conversations while I'm naked, but I need to rinse off." Aria gathered some of the bubbles between her arms, relocating them closer to her chest.

"*Tilt your head left*," I commanded for a second time, and if she refused again, I had no qualms about jumping in the water with her and forcing her to do my bidding. The tone of my voice caused her to wince, and it was all I could do to keep my hands to myself.

"This alpha male attitude is not cute," she said but turned her head. Her forehead was pink and swollen, close to her hairline. A little dried-up blood sat around the edges as if it hurt her too much to wipe off. "Happy?"

Not in the slightest.

"What happened?" I reached forward, tracing the angry red bump. She watched me, fascinated that I even cared. The urge to punch a wall overwhelmed me. Was I really that much of an asshole that she thought I wouldn't care if she was hurt? Or that somebody hurt her?

Duh, Larry is still alive and thriving after running his mouth.

Was it him? My nostrils flared, and anger like a sleek blade sliced through my cervix. My personal vendetta against him ran darker. He didn't have her, but he was still in her heart. Only blind devotion could lead you to defend such absolute trash. I knew. I used to see it every day with my parents.

What did I see in this girl who had me twisted up in so many knots?

Aria bit her lower lip, cheeks filling with heat, her youth radiating from her in turbulent waves, making my brain play catch up. Her innocence, her goodness, her pure fucking soul, that was what I couldn't get enough of.

"It's embarrassing," she whispered.

"How come?"

"I was in a changing room when..." Aria squirmed under my stare, her shoulders prickling outside of the steaming bath. "I-I hit my head on the mirror while taking off a dress. The neck was too tight, and I couldn't get it out. I was sweating, I couldn't see anything, and next thing I know, my head is throbbing."

My chest squeezed one last time. Tension I didn't know I was holding in released as I breathed out a laugh, the visual of Ariadne running around like a headless chicken replacing the image of a discombobulated Harrold.

"It's not funny." Her eyes narrowed, and I let my hand drop on her temple, chasing away some water and bringing my thumb in my mouth, tasting the sweet orangey scent that was uniquely her.

Aria's shoulders rose with quicker breaths, and I felt every bit of tiredness after my workout ebb away and the need to experience lactic acid running through my veins again after strenuous exercise—the fun kind—rise.

"It's a little bit funny." I let my gaze wander to the swell of her chest, mad at myself for not tasting them when I had her spread eagle at her shoot. "Go on, rinse off, and I'll dress up the wound. You can't leave it like that. It'll get infected."

"You're staying?" She squeaked out when I headed to the sink, intending to brush my teeth. I had an early morning tomorrow, but either way, something was telling me I wouldn't be getting a lot of sleep tonight.

"Wouldn't want you to slip and bang your head on the tub this time." I winked at her reflection.

"Ugh, I'm never telling you anything again."

"Are you embarrassed by your own husband? I did see all of you almost a week ago," I pointed out the obvious, grabbing my toothbrush. The memory, coupled with the domestic nature of going through our nightly routines together, had me locking the muscles of my stomach to stop the nagging rush of tingles networking their way down my body.

Hesitantly, she tugged on the showerhead, letting the stream of water wash down her dark strands first before meeting my eyes again with fresh drops hanging from her lashes. I raised a brow, challenging her, and for the first time since I met her, she didn't fight me on it. We were on the same page, on the brink of control as our attraction thickened by the day.

Aria raised her body from the water without an ounce of shame. I stared abashedly, yet she didn't cower. She let the stream brush over her breasts, and the suds disappeared, giving the perfect view of the globes that would rain dominion over my dreams for the foreseeable future. They weren't huge. Not the kind you could thrust your dick into, and it would disappear under copious amounts of pressed velvet-like skin, but they were still grabbable, kissable, and fucking delicious, fully complete with fluffy dark pink nipples, beaconing me to clamp my teeth around them and get a taste.

"You like saying that, don't you? *Husband.*" Her fingers worked their way down her hair as she rinsed it out one last time, and

"I like seeing you flush when I say it." My voice was hardened with lust after I spit out the mouthwash. While dental hygiene was important, I found myself pulling out all the stops today just so I could see how the fresh mint in her pussy drove her wild.

I was more than ready for seconds when she pressed her dripping toes on the cold marble floor and walked my way, her skin peppered with goose bumps from the temperature change.

"Want me to let you in on a little secret, Saint?" She asked, wrapping herself with a towel and making my dick weep in the process.

I rummaged through the cabinet, pulling out some rubbing alcohol and bandages as she hopped on the counter, her feet swinging inches from my side. "How is that even a question, Spitfire? I want to know all your secrets."

She watched me warily as I dunked a cotton pad with antiseptic and pulled back hissing when it barely touched her skin.

"Stop being such a baby." I pulled her knees open, situating them on either side, so she had nowhere to go, leaning back as far as she could. She kept her eyes closed, nails digging into my arms as I meticulously cleaned her up. It was a nasty hit, and it would probably take a few weeks to go away completely. "My God, you're dramatic," I teased, blowing on her forehead, before sticking the skin-colored bandage on.

"I'm a girl. Calling me dramatic is not an insult."

"You'd be surprised by the number of dramatic guys. One of my teammates legit balled on the field one time because his name peeled off when he took a tumble."

"How is that being dramatic?" Her eyes widened in horror. "Do you have a heart of stone or something? That sounds painful as fuck."

"My heart melts only under the right circumstances." I skimmed my lips down the side of her face, pressing a peck below her ear and shuddering as I took in her scent. "Tell me your secret."

Her hands latched on my arms, holding me in place as I licked her skin before sucking it. My hands were on the curve of her ass, situating my hard-on between her open legs and grinding her on it. Aria's voice was weak when she replied, but her words still exploded like Fourth of July fireworks in my brain.

"I don't mind having you as my husband. My heart races when you simply look at me, and the reason I blush whenever you're around—which I hate—is not because I'm embarrassed or shy. It's because I want you so fucking much my blood heats up, my body flushes wherever your gaze is on me, and you're quiet thorough, Mr. Astor." Her nails came out to play, and I felt their teasing to the tip of my cock as she ran them down my arm. "So thorough, my blush extends to other parts of my body as well."

In a mad haze, my fingers worked the knot of her towel loose, my tongue having a mind of its own and wanting to map out where her blush began and where it ended. We both gasped when she stood gloriously naked against me, her nipples hard and pointing at my chest like rough diamonds in the wild.

"You don't mind, huh?" I taunted, my knuckles smoothing over her landing strip, finding what lay lower soaking wet and hot with need. "What if I make you do the splits on the counter, Spitfire? Open that pretty pink pussy up and let me see how raw it gets when I pound into it like there's no tomorrow? Will that elevate my status from 'I don't mind'?"

"You talk a big game, Astor, but so far, I haven't seen any action. Are you scared the hype won't live up to the expectations?"

"You should know by now I take insults quite personally." My teeth sank in her earlobe before releasing her and taking a step back to admire the confused look on her face as I cocked my head, watching her from head to toe. "On your knees, little girl. I'm all out of lube, and you're so tiny you're going to need a lot of it."

A white lie never hurt anybody. What did hurt was watching her lick her lips and staring at the imprint in my slacks like she couldn't wait to take me in her mouth? My heart slammed with anticipation against my cotton shirt, and I removed it when she hopped off the counter, giving her the perfect view to stare at from below.

If anything, I was considerate.

Her eyes left heat like an actual caress as they ran down my body, lighting my nerve endings on fire when she sunk to the ground in complete surrender, hanging her pride at the door.

"Do you know how to make it sloppy, or have you never sucked dick before?"

She huffed and dropped her hands to my waistband, tugging down until my hard length sprung free, bobbing against my stomach, engorged and eager to be licked, sucked, and stroked.

"I'll let you reach that conclusion yourself." She smiled, her full lips inches away from my dick, staring at it with hungry eyes.

Fuck me.

At the first teasing stroke of her tongue, her hand around my base, my hips drove forward before I could control them. Her wet heaven enveloped me with a gag that reverberated from my balls up my spine. A good man, *a gentleman*, would apologize for entering her so roughly, but I wasn't in a particularly kind mood, especially when she blinked back her tears like a pro and swallowed me down.

"You definitely have," I snarled when she didn't resist as I fisted her wet hair, guiding her to take more.

Aria's head bobbed every time I slammed back in, leaving behind pools of saliva that more than overcompensated for the lack of lube. Some of it dripped down her tits, and knowing someone else got to see her like this made murderous thoughts spring in my head. I had no right considering the number of holes I'd greeted with my cock, but I chalked it up to some stupid part of me that took the role of being her husband too seriously. At the end of the day, though, it was nothing more than a role with an expiration date, no matter how good she was at sucking me off.

"I don't know if I like that you're hoovering my soul out

of my body or if I want to cut off every cock that mouth has touched. I want a list of names." My mouth spewed out, insanely late to catching up with my brain.

"You're crazy." She popped me out of her mouth long enough to spew her retort and dove back in again, her left hand cupping my balls and kneading gently.

An overwhelming arc of pleasure slammed into the base of my spine, and I couldn't believe my luck as Ariadne Fleur, nine years my junior, fresh out of college, delivered one of the best blowjobs I'd ever had. She wanted to please me as much as she wanted to get herself off. This wasn't a chore for her, she was enjoying cleaning up my precum like it was her favorite vanilla milkshake.

"No, what I am is two seconds away from blowing my load down your throat," I argued, and she took it personally, relaxing her facial muscles until I was hitting the back of her throat, her retching sounding like filthy music my perverted ears wanted to hear on repeat. "You fucking tease."

With a hiss, I dragged her off, trying not to linger on how red and puffy her lips were, on how her neck and boobs glistened with our essences. She followed my instructions. Now it was time for me to keep my end of the deal.

"Wha-why did you stop?"

"Because the first time I come, it's going to be inside you, baby." We both sank on the heated floor, too delirious to make it into any kind of bedroom. "If your cunt is nearly as tight as your mouth, we've got a problem."

"What's that?" She purred coyly, sticking her chest on mine as I set her down, feeling up my abs with those talented hands.

"I'm going to come in two seconds flat like a fucking freshman touching boob for the first time," I admitted thickly, my pulse thudding in my ears. It had been a while—too damn long since someone evoked such a lack of control from me.

"I want us to go slow," she moaned when I captured a nipple in my mouth, squeezing the other between my fingers. Her hands laced in my hair, holding me in place until she was mewling when I clamped down on it, chasing the pain away with open-mouthed kisses on her tender flesh.

"I thought I made it abundantly clear that slow fucking, and missionary wasn't going to be in the terms and conditions of this relationship. You're going to take what I give you, and you're going to thank me for it," I switched tits and licked her other nipple, not wanting it to feel left out.

Aria's back arched as she threw her head back, and her inviting entrance was positioned directly in front of my straining dick. At that moment, I learned I possessed the patience of a nun for not plunging into the land of my dreams.

"Unless you want to rip me open my first time, you're going slow, or not at all," she threatened, making me pause abruptly, a cold rush boarding over the arc of my release.

"What did you say?"

"I-I might've lied about the status of my virginity." Her voice registered in my ears like a broken lullaby.

What the fuck?

I found that hard to believe, but at the same time, it made so much sense. How had no bastard gotten between the legs of sweet Ariadne, dripping honey on your tongue, and working wonders with those luscious lips? Ambitious, sarcastic, beautiful, and full of life, Ariadne.

If it was true, it must've been a personal choice, but I didn't cut her for the type to wait until marriage.

"God-fucking-dammit, Spitfire. There's no *might've* about it. Either you're a virgin or you're not. Which one is it?"

Her worried expression stared back at me, hanging on my features, pulled tight with surprise and something akin to pleasure. A bastard part of me, the one more in tune with my hair-pulling, cavemen ancestors, was fucking elated, ready to cream his cock all over Aria's pale stomach.

"I am," She croaked. "I'm not completely inexperienced. I've done other things, just never went full-out. I've hated my body for so long. I never truly felt wanted. I'm not saying that I haven't been pressured into it, but it was very off-putting when every guy I went out with would get extra touchy when I lost weight and would treat me as nothing but a hole with legs when I gained it back. I fluctuate a lot, Saint."

That list of names sounded more tempting by the minute.

"Look at me, Ariadne," I demanded, fisting my cock, and flushing that sad, faraway look from her eyes by sliding it up and down her folds. "Do you feel my dick against your clit?"

"Is that a rhetorical question?" She said in a half-moan when I drew lazy circles over her nub, willing my testosterone to take a dive.

"It's throbbing and hard to a point where I think I'll combust if I don't sink into you in the next five seconds. And it's all because of you, Spitfire. I'm going to let you in on a little secret too." I couldn't believe I was going to say it, but her transparency egged me on. "In the past six years since my accident on the field, coming inside a woman has been a rare occasion for me. It was a shock to the system because masturbating wasn't the way I rolled, but after going through something so life-changing, a part of me fucking broke. I was so over the fake moans, fake orgasms, and fake women who slept with me for two reasons alone. Number one; to see if my injury had also impacted my ability to fuck them until they saw stars, and number two; to brag to their friends that they'd bagged the ex-NFL player, Saint Astor."

The first time I didn't come, I chalked it up to whiskey dick. The second; weed. The third and fourth, I blamed it on the women I'd been with. By the sixth time, I was out of the denial phase and realized there was something seriously wrong with me.

Sometimes I got hard, was on the doorstep of release, yet whenever I attempted to cross the threshold, it dissipated into a thin cloud of smoke. My sanity was unraveling as much as my reputation, if not more, during that phase of my life. Only recently had I been able to get back into the gist of things, and it didn't happen often.

Being on the brink of control?

Now, that happened never.

The first time was with a hot little brunette that didn't know I'd pay gold to sink inside the cunt she was offering up so willingly.

"Saint, I'm so s—" She started, but I didn't let her finish.

"I'm not admitting this, so you feel bad for me. Fuck, I despise pity fucks. I'm saying it because you're the first woman to get me this worked up. While personality plays a big part, looks do too. And your body is fucking sexy. All woman, with silk-like skin that I keep fantasizing about decorating with ribbons of my cum, real, and so soft I want to scrape my teeth down the arch of your back while I take you from behind."

A shaky breath escaped her, but it came out like a needy

whimper at the angle of her head. "You're making it really hard to hold on to my virtue."

"Now we're talking. Open your legs wide for me, Spitfire."

Those thighs came apart in an instant, golden skin leading to a mouthwatering patch of pink and red engorged flesh, contracting as if needing something solid inside her. A lick of anticipation rushed over my skin, giddiness at the thought of taking Aria's first arose with a vengeance, and I let some spit dribble from my mouth directly onto her cunt, priming her for my dick.

"I'm assuming you're not on birth control." Somewhere around the haze in my mind, muscle memory kicked in, and I held back even though I was bulging and seeping precum.

"Can you pull out?" She shook as I probed her, getting her ready with my fingers, eyes on my cock like it was the winning prize. "I'll have my period in a few days. The chances of getting pregnant are pretty low."

"Tomorrow," I let out a rough breath, tempting myself by sliding the tip past her slick pussy lips. She was so wet she was dripping on the floor, so I knew she was ready to be filled. "Tomorrow, we're getting you on the pill."

"Fuck." She licked her lips as I crowned her entrance. I couldn't imagine what it felt like on her end, but to me, it was like my head was getting a very warm, very tight hug.

I edged her legs wider, digging my hands in her hips as I began the slow torture of thrusting inside her. One agonizing inch at the time that had both of us straining for oxygen.

"Ahh!" Ariadne cried out, her nails digging in my biceps and eyes shining with unshed tears when I finally pulled in all the way, breaking the invisible seal over her fragile innocence and letting blood rain all over my cock and her inner thighs.

My legs almost gave out. "How does it feel, baby?"

"Like I'm on fire." Her chest rose and fell with sharp exhales. "It burns, Saint. It burns so bad."

Bad. Bad. Bad.

No. I was determined to make this good, to make this last. The beautiful girl stretched out beneath me deserved a good experience after all the pussies she'd been with.

Wrapping her legs around my waist, I distracted her by leaning down and kissing that rosebud mouth until I felt her tightly coiled muscles melting inch by inch. "Listen to me, Aria," I murmured against her mouth, my lips ghosting over hers. "I want you to relax, and bite down on my shoulder, rake your nails over my back, do what you have to do."

"But I'll hurt you."

"Trust me, every minute I'm staying still inside your perfect cunt is hurting me more than you ever will."

Her breathing calmed as she nodded. Placing my head on the crook of her neck, I let her exert her stress on my body as I slid out, almost all the way, and then thrust, burying myself to the hilt again.

Aria arched her back, and I was glad I couldn't see her face, but I could feel her pain on my skin as she almost tore a good chunk off. I didn't care, lost by the hypnotic slide of my dick in the tightest hole I'd ever been in. I couldn't think of anything else as this girl gripped me so tightly the space between my muscles and bones charged with blue lightning, prompting me to drive my hips forward steadily again and again until Ariadne's painful moans turned into ones of pleasure.

"That's it, Spitfire," I soothed. "Slow and steady wins the

race. And you're doing so well, baby. I love taking my time, savoring every inch of you."

"God, Saint," her mouth unlatched from my skin, and I almost missed her bite when she replaced her teeth by scratching down my back, deep enough to draw blood as I thrust deep inside her. "Grip my hips harder," she requested, and I didn't have to be told twice.

Her pretty breasts rubbed against my pecs, and I blazed a path from her neck to her tits, nuzzling my nose over a hard nipple before I took it in my mouth, gazing up to see how her head bobbed on the floor by the force of my hips. Aria had clamped on her lip, holding her moans back as she watched me break her body down and loving all of it when little by little, she started meeting my thrusts, tilting her pelvis up, getting accustomed to our dirty dance.

"Don't hold back," I ordered, my hand wrapping around her throat as I pressed my lips gently on hers, a far cry from the brutal progression of my hips. I was being rough, but I only had so much control. "I want to hear what I'm doing to you; want to know how much you love unraveling on my cock."

It was as if my words broke a dam, and a mixture of soft pants, whimpers, breathy moans, and squeaky screams rushed out of her mouth like a waterfall she had no control over. I met her halfway with groans of my own when she got even tighter around me—if that was possible.

"My God, Saint, I've never felt this full before," she panted, holding on to me as she arched up to kiss my jaw, teasing my scruff with her tongue and a bite. "It hurts, but it's turning into an enjoyable pain, the masochistic kind. The one you can't stand but can't help but crave."

"My little fire is so filthy she loves getting fucked down

and dirty on the floor, doesn't she?" *Thrust. Thrust. Thrust.* "Tell me what you like, Aria. Do you like it when I go in deep, sweetheart, ruining your virgin cunt with my cock?"

"No," her muscles squeezed, and I narrowed my gaze at her, a thin layer of sweat lining up my entire body as I upped the speed, driving my groin into her relentlessly. "I fucking love it. I love how you stretch me out, how your cock feels like a velvet rod of sin, rubbing me down so good, inflicting the best kind of torture."

"You're so fucking greedy for it, aren't you, little girl?"

"If I knew it was this phenomenal, I would've had sex sooner."

I paused, ceasing all movement, causing her to cry out in frustration. "What the fuck did you just say?"

"I'm kidding," she backtracked quickly, thrusting her hips up and fucking *me*.

With a growl, I grabbed her hair, arching her chest into mine as my thrusts turned more vicious than before, rolling my pelvis every time I drove in and out in a way that I knew would drive her crazy.

"You better be. It's phenomenal because I'm the one giving it to you. No other bastards would know how to handle you like I do. You're covered in me. My DNA is all over you, and that's the way it'll be until I decide otherwise. Are we clear on that?" I barked over her mouth, riding her body like a wave, bouncing her on my dick like it was the last time I got to have her.

The air between us was drenched with the scent of sex and sweat, electrifying the hair on the nape of my neck as I frenched the side of her lips, occasionally stealing kisses from her mouth.

It took her a while to respond, but when she did, her response elated me. "Yes."

Small explosions of heat went off in the base of my spine, and Ari's cunt clenched painfully around me. I was ready to combust, and I would let go—we'd let go together once she surrendered one final thing I required from her.

Her complete fucking devotion.

I stretched her lower lip out with my teeth, prolonging her release with a sting of pain. "No one else gets your naked body but me. No one else sees your naked body but me. No one squeezes it, feels it, tastes it, touches it, or bites down on your supple flesh, but..." I growled over her tortured whimpers. "Finish the sentence."

"You," she cried out, her voice begging for relief. "No one else but Saint Astor."

Our orgasms detonated at the same time, going off like twin bombs in a minefield. A line of big eruptions followed by a cluster of more concentrated ones, going off with rapid succession, one after the other, evacuating all air and stealing every bit of sanity left in me. I was between worlds for a hot minute, jumping in fucking limbo as I spent every drop of cum in Ariadne's pussy. She milked me for all its worth, her velvet lips contracting around me as if she couldn't get enough of my essence.

"Holy shit," Aria's frail voice broke through the film in my ears as my lungs emptied, and I collapsed like a boneless pile of meat on the too hot floor, dragging her on top of me because I wasn't ready to let go yet.

"Holy fucking shit," I shared her sentiment, the only words I trusted myself to speak at that moment.

Hand wrapped around her waist, slowly softening inside

her. I held her pressed to my chest, scared she'd disappear if I let go. A virgin. I wouldn't believe it if I didn't see the wince on her face as she slid me out of her. We both felt the trickle of our mixed cum slip out of her abused pussy, and the sudden realization that I finished bare inside her gripped us both.

"Saint, oh my God." Aria's horrified gaze clashed with mine when I lifted my head, and I tried to calm her down by smoothing her wild curls back.

"It's okay, baby. We'll get a Plan B, okay?" I didn't stop petting her hair even when she nodded shakily. "I'll go get it, just give me a second to regain my strength."

"Is it always like this?"

I was torn between the truth and a lie. A part of me wanted to say *yes, it is*, so neither of us would get more attached than we already were, but I didn't know if I could pull a lie of that magnitude off.

"No, Spitfire. This was special." I cupped her head and slid her up my body, still finding the energy to kiss her somehow. "You are special."

So special I was losing track of the lesson I was embodying, the pages of my textbook approach flying off in the air.

CHAPTER NINETEEN
ARIADNE

"I had a dream last night." That was the first thing my sister said after I picked up and set her on speaker.

I lived out my dream last night.

I almost answered with that, and the unexpected turn of my brain had me pricking my finger while hand-pinning some flower motifs on the bodice of my launch dress. It was a month away, and I had to pull some all-nighters and drink copious amounts of Red Bull to make it on time.

I was a master procrastinator with a short attention span, and the nasty words Saint had whispered in my ear last night didn't help me out one bit today. He was so attentive and cradled me with gentleness and wanton desire I didn't expect from him. Although we didn't spend the night in the same bed, he drove to the pharmacy, got me my *no-babies before I'm thirty* pill, and kissed me good night, stretching out the connection long enough to make me want to pull him back down again. I would've if my body didn't need a break.

Having sex with Saint Astor was exhausting. I was sore all over, buzzing like a harp that had gotten all its strings tugged. Some parts hurt more than others, but the pain was as delicious as it was bothersome. Probably feeling bad for the workout he put me through yesterday, I'd found an Advil and a bottle of water on my nightstand when I woke up.

"Will you tell me what it was about, or are you going to leave me hanging?" I asked, licking the blood off my finger and continuing with the meticulous work that ensued. I didn't like this part of bringing something to life, worsening your eyesight just to make sure everything was evenly placed.

"You lost your V-card, didn't you?"

Another prick and I decided to stick my pins in the cushion for the remainder of this unpredictable phone call. Abandoning the mannequin, I settled against the window, staring at the sunlight weaving its way past the branches, and brought the speaker closer to my mouth.

"Wha—" I cut myself off. "Don't tell me that's what you dreamed of."

"Did you?" Ina pressed, and my silence spoke enough for me. "Oh my God, you totally did, you whore."

"Irena!"

"Oh, you know it's a term of endearment." She scoffed. "I want to know everything. Did it hurt? Was there blood? Did you come? How many times did you come if you came?" She spewed out a tongue twister that I could tell, confused even herself, seeing as she repeated the last sentence a few times over the static of the phone.

"Why should I tell you anything when you don't?"

"Ugh, don't make me drive there. I just got my license, and you know damn well I'm not afraid to use it."

"You're not, but the drivers on the road will be when you

start swerving in and out of traffic. I lost count. You got it on your sixth try, right?" I teased.

"Fourth. Okay? It was the fourth, and it's not my fault the world is not ready for my Vin Diesel level of awesomeness."

"Toretto would kick you off his team in zero point two seconds."

"Says you the miss with the dusty, crusty hundred-year-old Prius. You have billboards up on Sunset Strip and Piccadilly Circus. My ice-skating friends sent me real-life pictures of them standing under your half-naked picture. It's time for an upgrade, sissy." Irena had friends spread all over the world from the competitions she attended. I knew a few. I'd never heard of one in California, though.

"Which ice-skating friend lives in Cali?" My brows knotted. "And also my Prius does its job just fine, thank you very much. It drives me from point A to point B, safe and sound."

"A bus can do that too, yet I don't see you hopping in one."

"God, I've left you alone with Mom for far too long. You're starting to sound like her."

Meaning she had a response for everything. Irena had a razor-sharp mind and mouth. She could figure out what made someone tick in under five seconds.

"Are you accusing me of being unnecessarily sarcastic and remarkably witty? Because that sounds like a win to me." She snickered. "Do you know who you remind me of?"

"Who?" I bit the bullet.

"Grandma Chloe," she said, and any trace of humor wiped off my face. "Before you freak, you remind me of her in a way that both of you are super secretive and masters at changing the subject whenever you're pressed on a topic. Now spill, Ariadne. I need to know all the details."

Secretive.

Her voice was light and airy, with a hint of frustration eating at the edges. We were all hiding the truth from Irena, the baby of the family, even though she acted anything but. I knew she would blow up on my behalf if I told her the truth and invited her over and she saw that my *husband* and I lived in entirely different parts of the house.

"I thought you already saw them in your dream." I almost retched.

"I didn't see you actually doing it. That would be hella incestuous and creepy as fuck." She paused. "We gossiped about it. Dream Saint took you out on a picnic with chocolate-covered strawberries and all, made love to you while the sun was setting over the Atlantic."

Dream Saint didn't sound half bad, a true romantic through and through, whereas Real Saint would more likely pour chocolate on me than feed it to me and take his time licking me clean. I shivered at the idea, liking it more than I should, when an email notification spread over my screen, dousing any previous flowery thoughts away with a cold dose of reality.

"Tell you what, how about we go out for a walk at Bella's Pier and grab some popcorn like we used to after you're done with skating. I'll pick you up, and I promise I'll give you the PG-13 version of the story, not going full throttle with R, though."

The idea sounded appealing despite starting out as an excuse. My life was a revolving door consisting of Arachne, Saint, Harry, and keeping my family happy. I needed a break from getting hit on the face repeatedly.

"You've got yourself a deal," Irena agreed, and I wrapped up the conversation with her, heading to my inbox with bated breath.

The encrypted email stared back at me like the answer to all my questions after browsing through enough questionable websites to put me on the FBI's most-wanted list. When you primarily hung out with nerds throughout your life, it taught you a thing or two on how to browse the internet safely and where to look to find services that fell under the morally ambiguous category by the US government, particularly on the middle-end of the web iceberg.

I pressed on the attachment present and was delighted to see all the proof I needed. A picture of Harry, in his apartment, filmed by his own cameras. A poison that came back to bite him in the ass. He was lounging on his bed, a new girl by his side that had my heart squeezing with worry. She probably thought he was charming and sweet and all the bullshit he presented himself as when you first met him.

He was going to do it again. I didn't know in which other ways he was using this footage of girls he was collecting, but I was doubting it was only for money. He used it that way with me because he knew I had plenty. Not everyone was as blessed, though.

A current of determination ran through my veins. Harry wouldn't get anything more from me other than a wiped hard drive, and afterward, a trip to the local police department to rot inside a jail cell he was acquainted with already.

Pressing on my screen, I sent the deposit to the hacker I'd hired, who would take care of any leverage Harry had, which was required once I was convinced he was legit and prayed for the best.

SAINT

"You have to take him back."

My mother burst into my office without bothering to knock. Her hair was all over the place, as if she was so desperate she ran here. She was holding on to her white designer bag tight, like she was ready to throw it at me if I refused her.

I didn't have to ask who she was talking about.

Smoothing a hand over my tie, I settled back on my seat, abandoning the report I was looking over. "Why did you marry him if you can't stand him?"

Out of the two, Celia Astor was the better-looking one, the kinder one, and the one people actually gave a damn about. A beauty even in her late forties, with expressive blue eyes that reminded me of Killian.

"Because he was shoved down my throat by my parents like he did to you." Sighing, she fixed her skirt and took a seat on a leather armchair. *At least she was self-aware.* "Take my advice and divorce that girl once the contract permits you. It'll still be fairly easy to find another serious relationship at that age."

That was the plan.

Aria was nothing like Noah. Placing them in the same wavelength was alien to me, so I wasn't worried she'd end up like a watered-down version of a Disney villain.

It wasn't me I was worried about. Period.

If we decided to go two separate ways, and that was a very strong possibility, it would work more to Aria's advantage. She deserved a life of her own choosing.

So why did chugging a gallon of piss warm milk sound more appealing than not seeing my ring on Aria's finger?

"Thank you for your unsolicited relationship advice mother, I think I'll pass, seeing as you're not in a position to hand it out." Her eyes narrowed, but I kept going. "And to answer your request, *no*. It's been blissful around here without him, and this merger is stressing me enough as it is."

"He's going on and on about how Darian is stealing his son and company away from him." Mom's eyes flitted about the clinical space of my office and out the hallway, hoping to catch a peek of my father-in-law.

Unease churned in my stomach at her old infatuation. I was dicking down his daughter less than twenty-four hours ago and couldn't leave without dropping by her room today with the cheap excuse of getting her some painkillers.

She looked blissful in her sleep, lips slightly parted, producing soft exhales. I got the stupid urge to skip work while watching her, so I could wake her up with my head between her thighs. Edward Cullen would be proud.

"He's delusional," I said extra loud, snapping her attention back to me. "He handed everything over with his own two hands."

"I guess he assumed you'd take his side and fire Darian. He doesn't like him much, but he has always respected Chloe."

Knowing my father, that didn't sound too far-fetched. I had better things to do, though, than psychoanalyze his behavior. Flipping through the files on my desk, solely to look busy, I cut my gaze to hers.

"Is there anything else you'd like to tell me? I was in the middle of something."

"Why do you hate your father so much, Saint? Has he

done anything to you I don't know about?" Mom's eyes shone with crocodile tears. I'd seen her turn it on and off whenever she was desperate for something. "Have *we* done anything to both Killian and you to avoid us like the plague? He never stays at home when he visits."

Projected your dreams and insecurities on us? Is that a good enough reason?

"He's a teenager. Living with his parents is not his definition of cool," I excused my brother. "Especially when one of them doesn't even know what he's majoring in."

Being called out, put a pin to the waterworks, and she blinked at me as if she was seeing me for the first time.

I loved my mother and had a special place for her in my heart because I could see that she wasn't well after years of emotional turmoil. Her heart was fragile by nature, but she relied too much on letting Dad take care of her problems, including us. She wasn't a bad mother. She cared for us, remembered our birthdays, bought us gifts, and smacked me over the head the first day I got out of rehab and was found black-out drunk on my bathroom floor. Yet those moments of clarity were rare and far between.

"I-I..." She stuttered before giving a definitive nod. "Of course I know."

"Really? Refresh my memory then," I challenged, spinning a pen with my fingers.

"Graphic Design," she said after a few moments of stroking her chin in deliberation.

Not bad.

"Architecture," I corrected.

"But he... he used to talk about graphic design all the time. I *remember*," she remarked as if expecting a cookie for doing the bare minimum.

Stopping the pen mid-spin, I let the metal bite into my skin, calming down my inflamed thoughts. I was on a roll today, it seemed, and Mom was only throwing oil to the fire that already burned in the form of Ariadne's steady presence in my brain.

I was annoyed at myself for losing control like I did. I never came inside a woman without a condom before. And I knew those Plan B pills had some nasty side effects. I fucked up royally, and the worse thing was part of me loved having that deeper connection with her.

"Dad deemed architecture a more appropriate field for Kill to pursue. And what Noah Astor wants, Noah Astor gets. Hence why we cannot work together if he keeps challenging my place of authority."

She winced at my explanation, knowing full well that I was speaking the truth. Neither of us would back down —*correction*, I would rather shove a fork up my ass than make Noah happy. He deserved a dose of his own medicine, being controlled by someone else as opposed to having complete dominion. Watching your dreams wither away was a one-lane street to misery town.

A knock halted our conversation, and I waved my assistant in.

"Mr. Astor, this came in for you today." She strutted over to my desk, dropping off the manila folder I'd been dreading getting all week. I thanked her and rummaged through my drawers, shoving it deep into the last one, promising to look at it at the earliest convenience. Lying to yourself was inevitable when the probable outcome had your brain filling with all kinds of murderous scenarios.

Going to jail for patricide wasn't in my immediate plans.

"Look, Mom, if you're miserable, you could always move

out, go on a trip, hell even divorce him. Everyone can see that you two aren't working, but you're the only one who can do anything about it," I told her when Cynthia left, unsure as to why I was bothering.

I'd played Mom's psychologist one too many times in the past. Talked to her for hours, but my words went in one ear and out the other.

"It's not that easy. You wouldn't understand, Saint." She clutched her neck, blood-red nails popping against her ivory skin. "I'll be branded as damaged goods, and people will start thinking there must be something wrong with me after three highly publicized failed relationships."

Oh, I had an idea or two.

"They'll prey on your weaknesses, so you never show any sign of them, isn't that what you always taught us?"

"Precisely." She nodded, remembering her ingenious words.

"And then you spend your whole life living for someone else," I shot down her idea, but it was moot. The older we got, the chains around our souls became tighter, not allowing for us to see past the veil of our long list of experiences. "Anyway, this sounds like a problem you should discuss with your therapist. *I* need to finish up with this report. I have a date afterward."

"Oh, anyone I know?" She perked up.

"I assume you've met my wife," I said, my tone dry as a rice cake.

Our date wasn't until tomorrow, but she didn't need to know that.

She took me in with a flat expression. Her disapproval of Ariadne was obvious, even though Spitfire's only offense was being the byproduct of my mother's shattered juvenile crush.

Celia Astor took petty and dumped it in a bucket chock-full of bitter.

"Don't get too serious with her, Saint. The Fleurs are masters at manipulation."

I smiled.

She clearly didn't know her own son.

"I'll keep your words in mind, Mother."

CHAPTER TWENTY
ARIADNE

"**S**top staring at my boobs, or we're going to crash," I told Saint when he narrowly missed a Mini Cooper, my hand flying to the *oh-shit* bar.

He cursed under his breath, speeding up even more like he'd prevent any accidents by reaching his destination faster. To be fair, I'd have a hard time driving too if he was sitting next to me with his unbuttoned silk red shirt and striped, black pants, reminding me of a nineties male icon.

I may or may not have thumbed the wispy hair on his chest once or twice during our date tonight. Saint took me to a boat restaurant in Astropolis Harbor, fancy, but not so much so, I had to stifle my laughter or lower my voice while talking.

It was refreshing. The dynamic was different. For the first time, I felt like we were actually a couple and not stand-in actors for a real one. The conversation flowed with no insults, and I got to learn my husband better. Like his aversion to seafood, love of racehorses, and our eerily similar dream of leaving everything behind for a quieter life on the Mediterranean coastline.

"It's not my fault. That shirt—if you can even call it that —is distracting."

I knew what I was doing, going for some of the most daring pieces in my closet. A cropped white tube top that pushed my tits out, and a miniskirt that stopped at my upper thighs, half of my hair clipped back and falling in waves around my bare shoulders.

Saint's gaze on my body all evening made butterflies swarm my belly and me buzz with anticipation for what was yet to come. Our date would be split into two parts, according to Saint, and he was currently driving to our second destination.

"It's a crop top, Mr. Head of Falco and Fleur. You told me to dress casual."

"I'm not complaining, just admiring." His eyes cut to the top again as he took a right down a road with colorful lights and buzzing nightlife. "Aria, if you're not comfortable when we get there, tell me. I wasn't serious when I said you can't leave."

I watched his grip turn knuckle white on the wheel. "You're scaring me. Are we going to like a sex dungeon or something?"

"Yes, fully equipped with an underground crypt, where I'll chain you to the walls and have my way with you all night."

"Just one night?" I asked as he parked to an empty spot along the line of cars next to the pavement. "I see your stamina is weaning, golden boy."

"My stamina's fine, Spitfire," he chuckled roughly, his hand dropping to my exposed thigh, making me jump. "I wouldn't want your virgin pussy falling off due to rough handling."

"Did it ever feel like your dick was going to fall off due to rough handling?"

He grinned. "No."

I shrugged. "I believe that answers your stupid statement."

With an amused chuckle, he shut off the engine but didn't make a move to get out of the car. "I like your thought process."

I liked *him*. And it was getting to the point where I couldn't remember why I tried to convince myself to stay away in the first place. All the things I'd accused him of came back to bite me in the ass with Harry. Saint had a questionable past, but who didn't? Even Mother fucking Teresa, according to some sources.

"So are you going to let me know what I'm signing up for? The place looks like a sketchy club that allows underage customers in because they're short on cash."

I looked at the dark entrance of the club. It was the only place on the whole street that wasn't riddled with a line of people waiting to get inside, like a front used for money laundering.

I squirmed, sliding my ass back on the cream leather seat. Saint's fingers drew circles under my knee, lulling my brain out of its pre-freak-out stage.

"Don't judge a book by its cover."

I scoffed. "I can't *not* do that. I'm a bookworm. Explosions or swords on a cover mean sci-fi or fantasy, and half-naked men mean romance."

"Shirtless Fabios still sell?" He raised his brows, and my eyes dropped to *his* naked chest, illuminated red and blue by the artificial lighting outside our little bubble. I held back a frustrated sigh because he would so be a perfect cover model.

"No, we've moved on to Christian Hogue now."

An upgrade I wasn't mad about.

"Who's that?" His brows bunched, showing how out of touch he was with social media.

You, if you had blue eyes. My brain screamed, but I reined it in. Saint didn't need to be knocked up any more pegs.

Ignoring the question, I waved my hand to the entrance a couple had just gone through. "Spill, what's waiting for me behind those doors?"

Retracting his hand from my leg, he combed it through his blond waves, uttering the words like he had to physically force them out. "I used to come here quite often after I got out of rehab. When I was at my lowest, and in a way, it is kind of a sex club."

My eyes widened, and unease roiled in my stomach. I didn't even know what happened at sex clubs, like did everyone have sex with everyone? I explicitly stated I wasn't into sharing.

"Saint, what the f—" I started.

He cut me off with a rushed explanation. "I was looking for alternative ways to take care of my *problem*. And I knew that *Red Circle* hosted these voyeur slash exhibitionist nights where everyone interested in that lifestyle could attend. You have to pay a fee, of course, to enter and sign an NDA, protecting the identity of anyone you see inside."

My muscles loosened slightly when I understood his point of view. Albeit immoral, and what you usually did behind the comfort of your bedroom doors and a screen shoved to your face.

Of course, Saint took it to the next level.

"Holy shit, this is like rich people porn," I breathed, twisting my fingers in my lap.

"That's one way to put it. There's a slight difference, though." Saint met my stare. "The exhibitionists here are real couples in a real relationship and a shared interest in kinks which was what made it so good." I opened my mouth to protest, but he beat me to it. "Before you say it, no, there is no way in hell anyone is seeing you naked other than me unless they'd like to have a foot shoved up their ass. I thought we could go in and observe, widen your circle of experiences."

A part of me wanted to challenge him because Saint was anything but *saintly*, and I was sure he'd been both a voyeur and an exhibitionist at some point.

"But will they watch us, watching them? That sounds uncomfortable."

He shook his head. "There are public rooms and ones with two-way mirrors. We can see them. They can't see us."

"Like the ones they have in police interrogation rooms?"

"Exactly." His eyes sparkled at my cooperation. "Again, we don't have to go if you don't want to."

I wasn't going to lie. The idea was terrifying and tempting at the same time. This was way out of my comfort zone, yet I could see it as an opportunity to gain some more experience. I often heard guys say that virgins didn't do it for them because they would be a bore to fuck—*crude, I know*—and part of me took it personally.

I was willing to try it out.

"I mean, you *did* warn me about your tastes, and I'd prefer starting out with this rather than humiliation or masochism, which by the way, I highly doubt you're actually into." Voyeurism fit what I'd seen from him until now. Everything else he claimed to like? There was a missing link. "You have a terrible habit of saying the darndest things to push me away."

"You're like a dog with a bone, Fleur," he answered, making a dry, disbelieving tone on the back of his throat. It made sense; I'd chased him down when he wanted nothing to do with me.

"I bite too, especially if you call me that again." I snapped my teeth playfully, prompting him to dive forward and place a kiss on my lips that sent my heart into overdrive.

"I can't decide whether you're too smart or too stupid for your own good," Saint muttered roughly against my lips.

"I'm determined to get what I want, Astor."

"What if what you want isn't good for you?" His palms crushed my cheeks, and he squeezed another kiss out of me, stealing a moan too when he pulled back.

"I'll be the judge of that." I winked, knowing full well I was playing with fire and that there was a fun side to getting burned. "Let's go, shall we?"

Saint accompanied me through the thick curtain separating the reception from the main area, his arm steely braced around my shoulders. Dark floors spread beneath the soles of my Jimmy Choos, and velvet couches housed men and women, watching strippers swing from silver poles to the beat of a Cardi B song. It was like a full-fledged nightclub with pounding music and flashing neon lights.

One of the dancers did the splits on stage, garnering hoots of approval from the gathered crowd. My eyes bugged out of my sockets, and it wasn't because her asshole was out in her G-string. It was because my vagina hurt simply watching her do that.

I turned to see if Saint had seen it, but his gaze was focused down the hallway he was leading us to, doors zigzagging on each side. Just before the wall swallowed my view of the dance floor, I caught a familiar face in the crowd and stopped short, prompting Saint to bump into me.

"Oh my God, is that..." I didn't finish the sentence, cringing when our gray-haired senator tucked a hundred-dollar bill in a girl's thong.

"Sure is," Saint confirmed. "You'll probably see a ton of familiar faces here. Anonymity lures cheats."

"I'd rather drink bleach than watch our senator fuck his eighteen-year-old girlfriend. It's not them, right?"

"Patience is a virtue, Spitfire."

"You stole mine."

His chuckle echoed as he pulled me forward, opening a door on our left and shutting out the outside noise by isolating us. He flicked the light switch open, and I briefly took in the red walls and queen-sized bed shoved on one end. He had me braced against the double-sided glass in no time, his previously contained hunger on full display.

"The way I remember it, you gave it up quite willingly." He locked my wrists over my head, his lips trailing a tantalizing path down my cheek and to my mouth. "What was the first thing that crossed your mind when you found you were going to marry me, Ariadne?" He breathed the question over my lips, throwing me off with a dive to our turbulent past.

"Run as fast as my feet would allow me." I shuddered when his hand teased the top of my breasts, and then he fisted my top and pulled until my tits popped free, palming one roughly.

I didn't protest at how fast this was going. I'd been foaming at the mouth to have him again for the whole day.

"I appreciate your honesty." Saint nipped at my lips, sounding elated at inspiring fear in people. I was stupid for letting him know how much he impacted me. "Do you want to know mine?"

"No," I moaned out, scared of his answer. He ignored me.

"That your parents must hate you." The words crept beneath my skin and wrapped around my heart like barbed wire. I didn't have any time to dwell on them. He turned me around, and the view had a gasp spilling out of my mouth. I was so consumed by Saint that I didn't notice people in the other room. "Dropping their sweet, young daughter right at the wolf's feet, and baby, I certainly didn't hide in sheep's clothing. But the more I get to know you, the more I see you're not as straight-laced as I'd thought you to be in the first place, Spitfire."

The tips of my breasts touched the glass when he drove his hips forward, and I grew flustered by his words and the panic that the young couple on the other side could see me. Probably not. They were consumed in their own little bubble. The redhead palmed the muscled guy's dick, working her hand up and down his shaft as they kissed. They were already naked, and the girl was on top of him on the bed. Her ass was up in the air, so full, it put mine to shame.

My breathing grew shallow, and my thighs got slick. I'd forgone wearing underwear, shivering at the idea of Saint discovering that himself, and with the way he was working his hard dick between my ass cheeks, driving my skirt up an inch with each thrust, he was bound to find out soon.

I groaned loudly when he let go of my hands and fisted

my hair, straining my neck so he could lick his way up and bite my jugular. "No good girl would be dry-humping my cock like a night shift stripper short of cash."

"Angels are often devils in disguise. You should know," I mumbled, my voice thick. "Saint, if you keep teasing me like that, I think I'm gonna burst."

"Then tell me where you want me, baby. On my knees sucking the juices off your dripping cunt, on all fours pounding inside you until you can't stand straight, or in your mouth to see who'll come first." I saw his shadow nodding toward the couple. "Me or him."

The girl was working her way down the guy's body now, her red hair spilling over his abs as she sucked him in. I whimpered at the sight of his hips, bucking forward, and pushed my ass back, rubbing harder against Saint. He groaned in my ear, a rough sound that was pure male, his hand traveling to the front of my skirt.

"Goddamn, Ariadne," he growled when he found my flesh bare and moist from his taunting and wonderful idea of watching live porn while we fuck. The rough pads of his fingers swept over my pussy, making sure he wasn't imagining things. "This cunt has been bare the whole afternoon?" He slapped it lightly for good measure, and I all but screamed out my excitement.

Fucking hell, I was so worked up, I wanted to do everything at the same time, but that was humanly impossible. I was clenching around emptiness, and it physically hurt not feeling him rubbing against my inner walls.

"I want you inside me, but finish in my mouth. The pill takes a week to become effective, and I'm a sucker for some friendly competition."

"You'll have an unfair advantage," he teased my hole

with his fingers, and I almost begged him to stop. He was torturing me slowly, my body flushed, and my brain flooded with thoughts that would put Satan to shame.

"Where's the fun in playing if you can't cheat a little bit," I exhaled.

Saint huffed out a pained, "Fuck," as he took my instructions to heart and shrugged off his clothes. I didn't feel cold for a single minute. He was fast, and his hard... *everything* touched my back again in seconds.

"Throw your leg over my hand." He propped a hand on the viewing window, and I did as he asked, my flexibility coming in handy.

With both his hands positioning my body the way he needed, I helped out and wrapped my hand around his girth, lining him up on my entrance. He pulsed in my grip, and I pumped him twice, spreading his precum before letting him plunge inside.

Saint hissed, thumb caressing my underboob, and I sighed at the feel of him, so thick and hard, filling me up just the way I needed. A fire brewed inside me, prompting me to crane my neck so I could meet his lips, dying for everything he had to offer.

"Does it still hurt?" Saint asked, resting his cheek on mine, his surprisingly soft tone spreading fissures over the surface of my heart.

"When you don't move?" I mocked. "It sure hurts our chances of getting an orgasm."

"You know what sarcasm gets you? A red handprint on your perfect tits." He punctuated his statement with a slap on my left boob that stung in the most delicious way possible.

I groaned my approval, and he started fucking me with

deep strokes that hit *the* spot from this angle. "I should do it some more then."

"Please do. Nothing gets me harder than your smart mouth and pink flesh."

"And nothing gets me wetter than when you beg." I had no control over the volume of my voice and screamed out the sentence, stretching and impaling on his dick.

I predicted his second slap. I provoked him for it, and the generous bastard always gave me what I asked for. My breasts jiggled from him, bouncing me on his dick and his rough treatment.

"That hurt," I complained half-heartedly because my masochistic brain was begging for more pain.

"It was supposed to." Saint bit my lobe, and his eyes fell to the couple who were still going at it for the first time since we got here. I thought I'd be jealous, but he was hard because of me, and his thrusts were so fast and frequent it was like he couldn't get enough. "Tell me what you see, Aria. How does it make you feel?"

My leg over his arm trembled, and sweat ran rivulets down my back, causing my hair to stick between us. The guy was basically fucking the girl's face now, holding her hair and guiding her mouth to take all of him. I couldn't see their faces clearly, but I imagined she had tears running down her cheeks.

"I like it when he fists her hair, guiding her head. He's forceful, but not too much. He's showing her how much he likes what she's doing, and it's getting her excited."

My head lolled to Saint's shoulder when his left hand found my bundle of nerves and went to town by rolling his index finger over it. I was quivering all over from the intensity of fucking everything.

It was too much. The stimulation my body was getting was overwhelming. Saint's imaginative mouth acted as porn for my ears while he dicked me so good, I'd become a Slip n' Slide down there. The visual was just the icing on the cake that was going to be topped off with more any minute now.

My release built brick by brick, like a house that existed for the sole purpose of driving a wrecking ball through it.

"It's getting you excited too, huh, baby? My naughty wife, being turned on by the idea of a face fuck. You're contracting around me, tightening more with each thrust." Saint sucked on my neck, and at this point, I was convinced he was trying to build a collection of hickeys. "You know what I'm going to have you do, Aria?"

"What?" My back arched, tits smashing into the glass as Saint pressed harder against me, owning me completely at that moment, body and soul.

The couple on the other side paused for a moment, their gazes flying to the double-sided mirror, and I realized we were going at it so hard it was rattling under our combined weight. It didn't deter them, though. They returned to each other, more enthusiastic than before.

"Come on my dick, for one. Then force your head against the wall until your mascara stains your cheeks tar, and my cum tickles the back of your throat," he said, and uncontrollable moans fell from my parted lips. "Bet you'd love that enough to slip your fingers between your soaked folds and make yourself come a second time."

"Saint... oh God. *God. God. God.*" I chanted. "It seems blasphemous to even moan your name because you're so dirty."

"I didn't pick it, but I sure as hell love hearing you

scream it. Come on, belt it out for me. Let everyone hear how hard your husband makes you come."

I was embarrassed to admit it was the *H-word* that did it. I was only standing up because of Saint's support. My muscles embodied Jell-O as my body relaxed to the point where the only thing I felt was tingles on the tips of my toes, accommodating the rippling orgasm that came onto me and destroyed what was left of my innocence.

"*Saint. Saint. Saint.*" I did as he asked, chanting his name like a prayer.

My mind was a black canvas, and each electric shock that sent my womb quivering and my thighs shaking was like a violent stroke of paint running across it. Blue, yellow, pink, neon red, I was a mess. A byproduct of Saint's insatiable self tearing apart my insides and exploring every inch of me, hitting my G-spot with consistent strokes that had my throat sore from all my screaming.

"Fuck, Aria, your cunt is fucking addictive. It makes me want to die with you wrapped around me." He whispered his filth in my ear as he rode me through my crippling wave. "Death by cock asphyxiation. Doesn't seem like a bad way to go. Not at all."

I didn't expect to come off the high he put me in laughing, but that's exactly what happened. My giggles replaced my screams, and I felt his smile spreading over my skin.

"Jesus Christ, you're twisted. There's no such thing as death by cock asphyxiation."

"Sure there is. You're squeezing me so hard it's cutting the circulation off my dick."

His abs tensed against my ass, and he pulled out of me in a haste, letting my leg gently drop to the floor. I didn't waste any time getting on my knees, and my wobbly legs thanked me for it as I got to eye-level with his engorged shaft, keeping my end of the deal.

"I changed my mind." Saint's eyes burned golden, and his gaze touched me everywhere as he pulled my hair when I jerked him off with my hands, his length impressive enough to need both. "You can't touch yourself. I want to taste how ruined my dick made you, Spitfire. I want you to ride my face like you did your pillow when you had your first orgasm, drip cum down my chin."

That was it. Saint's words had me enveloping his throbbing member in my mouth without teasing him with licks. His head dropped back in ecstasy as I used both hands and mouth to get him off, humming whenever he hit the back of my throat.

"Shit," he cursed, driving into my mouth as brutally as he did my pussy. "Relax your throat, Aria. I don't have the patience to be gentle right now."

Pinpricks of pain along my scalp barely registered as I upped my suction, focusing on getting him off and letting him set the pace. It was fast and exhausting. I gave up on keeping up and let him take what he wanted, tasting a mixture of myself and him on his dick that had a newfound wave of hormones slam into me.

Our eyes connected when he held my nose to his base, his movements becoming jerky and shorter as he neared his release. I let my tongue roll over his balls, and that set off the loudest battle cry I'd ever heard in my life. Hot streams of cum flooded my throat, sliding down my esophagus, and I choked, raking my nails down his thighs, fueling his pleasure with a touch of pain.

"Holy mother of God," Saint exclaimed once sucked completely dry, withdrawing his cock, dropping to his knees next to me, and folding my body to his, like the first time.

I hadn't pegged him for the cuddling kind. Then again, I knew next to nothing about my husband at the beginning other than the narrative gossip columns led me to believe.

"I win," I said, borrowing closer to his chest, letting him shield me from the frigid tiles when another male cry followed one minute apart from the room over.

"No," he replied, and I snapped my gaze up, brows creasing. "*I* do. Now, legs on either side of my face, baby, let's see what that cunt is made of."

CHAPTER TWENTY-ONE
SAINT

"Where's the madam?" Ares played the first move, opening up the game with the queen's pawn.

I took a sip of whiskey, letting it warm my insides and numb the memory of Ariadne. Although, I'd found it was pretty fucking hard to stop thinking about her. My mind was stuck in fluffy Aria-induced clouds for the betterment of the past two weeks.

While I was at work, I couldn't stop texting her. It was little things, advice on things she was unsure about in her line of work, that progressed to asking her if she wanted me to bring something home for dinner. She sent me articles she found interesting and photos of a lingerie line she was designing, asking for my opinion. I told her I couldn't judge from pictures alone, so when I got to see her that evening she met me in the living room, clad in nothing but lacy scraps.

I took my time thumbing the material, getting a feel of its quality, leading up to the most important part of it all—how easy they were to rip off. I wasn't disappointed, and Aria was more than pleased when I chased the light of the fireplace shining down her back and over the arch of her ass with my lips.

"Missed her?" I placed my tumbler on the table, pushing my king's pawn to E5. The "Delicious" sounds coming from Leo's phone, lounging on the couch in my home office with Nyx at his feet, were starting to get on my nerves, prompting me to make my mental calculations between his Candy Crush wins. I'd be damned if I lost to Ares in chess. He was good with numbers, not with strategy.

"Just wondering why you said you needed our help and not hers."

The last thing I needed was to show Aria how low I thought of my family. When I agreed to give us a try, I didn't think we would last this long. She was too young, and we were in two different phases of our lives. And even though I'd been inside her enough times to memorize every inch of her body, it wasn't just sex. My curiosity usually weaned after I had my fill of a woman, with Ariadne though I found myself wanting to hear her moans on replay and talking shop daily because her enthusiasm got me hard.

A twenty-one-year-old with a mind for business—you didn't see that often. At her age, all I could think about was football and finding the best-looking hole to sink my dick into.

"I don't think Aria has the strength to stop me if I find what I think I will inside there." I cocked my head to the envelope that sat and collected dust until I pulled the stick out of my ass today and brought it home.

That got Leo's attention, and he dropped the phone in his lap—thank fuck, because if I heard the words *divine, sweet, and tasty* for a while longer, I would blow a fuse—scratching behind Nyx's ears when she dropped her head on his lap. "Is that the reason you contacted Ethan?"

I nodded, bringing my bishop out, and Ares countered my move by developing his knight. I moved my king's pawn, and he took, knocking mine out.

"So we have permission to tackle you? Man, I've been waiting to do that ever since you stole that house in Santa Monica from me," Ares complained.

"It's not my fault the owners liked me better." I kept my self-satisfied smile to myself.

"The granddaughter of the owners liked you better, and you paid her extra attention specifically for that fact."

"I never claimed to play fair." I almost groaned when I remembered the last time I'd heard those same words coming from the mouth of a destroyed Aria. Shifting in my seat, I resisted the urge to text her and find out when she'd get home.

I was not breaking societal norms by becoming the one that was stuck to her like glue. Aria split the stereotype of a virgin and didn't push for more. She simply took as much as I gave her.

"While I find this conversation completely riveting." Leo's voice dripped with sarcasm as he regarded me with as much interest as one had for a squashed roach. "Are you going to tell us what's up, or are you saving it for some big reveal?"

I already knew my next move, yet I stared blankly at the checkerboard, prolonging the inevitable. I'd never told anyone my suspicions. If I did, they'd think the inside my mind must be such a terrifying place. Cruel, blunt, always believing the worst, and never expecting anything less. They wouldn't be too far off. In the process of slaying your monsters, you often became them. Stare in the abyss, and the abyss will stare back and all that shit.

"I asked the P.I. to look into who caused the accident on the field," I admitted, sacrificing my knight to Ares's crutches. He fell into my trap as perfectly as I was hoping someone else would.

There was a pregnant pause in the room, the only sounds being the cracking wood in the fireplace. I was comfortable telling Leonardo and Ares my demons because I knew they weren't without their own.

"So you basically spent a shit ton of money—cause I know from personal experience that Ethan is not cheap—to get an answer to a question you and every football superfan already know?" Leo broke the silence, shaking his head. "Now that's some fucked up logic if I've ever seen one."

"Dude, you gotta stop living in the past." Ares mirrored his statement, mussing his hair. "Trust me, losing sleep over what could've been brings you nothing except for black fucking circles the size of Mars under your eyes."

"I'm not living in the past." I ground my molars, downing what was left in my glass to quench the sick feeling in my stomach, preparing to lead them down the well of my spotless intuition. "I was going through Falco's stocks a month ago and saw that there were some unauthorized investments made a year back in an up-and-coming restaurant chain in Dallas. And we all know, unless it's Mario Batali or Wolfgang Puck, that's one of the worst industries to invest in."

The air shifted, giving me the perception that I'd caught their attention. Bad business transactions were their kryptonite. Unlike me, Ares and Leo genuinely enjoyed navigating the cutthroat corporate world.

"I'm assuming it was neither of those," Leo said gravely, leaning forward, his hand on his knees. Nyx whined and rushed out of the room, bored of us. "So is someone stealing?"

"I don't suppose you could call it stealing when the head of the company is the one that chooses to spend the funds that way. But then, I looked into it and saw *who* owned the chain," I explained dryly, the back of my throat parched.

Sacrificing my bishop this time, I ate Ares's pawn and reached for the bottle of whiskey, topping off my glass one more time. Leo watched with wary eyes. I didn't drink much back in the day, only at parties I threw. Alcohol decreased aerobic performance. I'd come to appreciate the boost in serotonin levels more, though.

"I have a bad feeling about this," Ares spoke, his face set in a deep frown.

"So did I, and the feeling turned murderous when I found out my father was investing in Todd Brees's ventures."

Ice trickled through a thin line between us, sizzling under the twin melting stares on my face. My fingers tapped the oak surface of the table, letting them soak in the mind-fuckery of it all. My father, investing in the business of the man who sent me to rehab for six and a half months and left me with a limp to match.

"Holy shit, what are you saying?" Ares abandoned his focus on the game, keeping a white-knuckle grip around the armchair. "I understand not getting along with your father, but do you really think he would do something like this?"

"My mind can't comprehend it," Leo dropped his head between his hands.

I smiled with venom.

"Do you remember when you came to visit me at the

hospital the next day? Do you remember my father's smile stretching from ear to ear when the doctors confirmed that my chances of ever playing professionally again were slim to none?" My tone was grave, a part of my soul infusing with black ink when the suspicion turned to reality. "Because it's not something I can forget."

"So what are you saying?"

"That I wouldn't put it past him to go above and beyond to get what he wants. At the time, he was really pushing me to quit football so I'd take my position at Falco full time."

If it was true, I'd played into his hand. My career fizzled out, and I was burning to know if Noah Astor's wish was granted out of sheer luck or his pure immorality, craving to be matched. One thing was sure, if he took a piece of me, I'd take a fucking chunk out of him.

The father, son lines were blurred a long time ago.

"Yeah, I remember that time very well. You were a pain to be around," Leo sounded, breaking the tension like the ray of fucking sunshine he was.

"Thank you," I replied sarcastically, and Leo shrugged his shoulders as if to say *you're welcome*. "So, I hired Ethan to see if he could find any further evidence linking *Toad* Brees and my father together. I guess that's his report." I took the envelope in my hands, staining the paper with the moisture on my fingers.

"Well, what are we waiting for?"

They gathered behind me as I slashed the seal. It was like opening Pandora's box, and when we peeked at the contents, I knew the impending bloodstains on my knuckles were inevitable. According to a contract dated five years ago, Noah Astor promised Todd Brees financial support in his business and my position on the field in exchange for a non-fatal injury of Saint Astor.

Carbon dioxide left behind the scent of charred air as I exhaled through my nose, eating up the words on the paper faster than Leo and Ares. Noah Astor signed his death warrant the day he chose to hurt his own son for selfish gain.

ARIADNE

"Really? The dog again?"

My gaze drifted to Harry, sitting on the roof of his car, the only flashy one amongst a graveyard of them. The sun was getting dangerously low, and his eyes on my skin sprung shivers. My mind was in the, *keep the interaction brief, and get both Erebus and myself out unscathed* zone.

"Am I turning too predictable for you, Harry?"

"You're turning into a pain in my ass."

"Aw," I cooed. "How rude of me, not snapping my fingers and producing four million dollars out of thin air."

"I don't remember you being this much of a bitch when we were going out." He skittered to his feet like a bottom feeder, insulted by my language.

Erebus gave him a warning growl, and I saw Harry baring his teeth back in response like an idiot. The desperation called for my retaliation, and I decided not to hold back. The tables had turned even if he wasn't aware of it yet.

"I didn't know you were a delinquent loser either. Otherwise, I would've turned you in the first chance I got," I said with a sickly sweet smile. "How many other poor girls have you tricked this way?"

His eyes dropped to the hickeys on my neck, which I hadn't bothered covering up, and his nostrils flared. "If they're slutty enough to spread their legs, they should expect the repercussions that come with that. Nothing poor about bitches like you."

He must've been a high-functioning psychopath. There was no other explanation for the three-sixty degree his character turned. He used his fleeting charm to disguise the lack of empathy, impulsivity, and shallow emotions. When I thought back, I saw cracks in his facade, forceful touches, impatient tugs, and muttered curses. I never paid it much mind, too hung up on driving Saint away.

That restlessness inside me grew, even with Erebus by my side. Harry was as unpredictable as a toss-up. And I had no doubt he would come after me for freeing the bird he'd trapped in his rusted cage. I'd already wired him close to a quarter of a million. The last of which he was going to get.

Body tense and ready for action, I countered his insult. "Harry, I already know you have a small dick. You don't have to remind me with your energy too."

"I swear if you keep testing me..." He stepped forward, but this time I matched his gait, prompting him to stop short. One of the things I loved most in this world was watching toxic men lose their hold on power.

"You get within one inch of me, and you'll become the dog's personal chew toy. My wrist hurts from holding him back, don't make me release the leash."

Erebus barked at the right time for good measure, and Harry's shoulders bunched with repressed anger.

"Whatever, bitch. I don't have the time to deal with you. Give me the cash, and you won't have to see me again."

"You must certainly think I'm dumb." I cocked my hip.

"What guarantee do I have that you won't come back asking for more?"

"You have my word."

"Your word means shit to me." My responses were like rapid-fire, enjoying the agitation before lighting the fuse.

"Get on your knees, and maybe I'll sign a contract." Harry shrugged, carrying the audacity of a failed man.

"You'd jam your dick in peanut butter, so long it gets you some action. No wonder you call women whores. They must not give you the time of day."

He sniffed, proving my theory correct. "If you think you're going to annoy me, you're out of luck. I've had years of dealing with bitches that were less interesting than watching paint dry. Give me the money, or I'll carve you and your dog up like pumpkins."

"I don't think I will, Harry." I kept my voice loud and clear.

"The price goes up whenever you waste my time."

"I'm not giving you anything," I repeated, a strained smile on my face.

Harry glared, calling my bluff by crawling back to his blackmail. "I'm going to release the video."

The smile spread, and I shrugged, strength flowing through my veins. Who knew I'd feel my best in a pair of high-heeled booties and black tights? Every girl had an inner Black Widow, and I was embracing mine to the fullest.

"Go right ahead. See if you still have it."

His eyes turned into thin slits, and I waited as he checked his phone, my grip turning sweaty around my car keys. The deep web was the root of a lot of evils, but nothing was black and white, and not everything illegal was used for bad. If the hacker had done his job properly,

Harry should start spewing his venom in... *three... two... one...*

"You... you whore!" He shouted, his enraged voice echoing on the abandoned parking lot, and Erebus matched his vocals, spittle dripping down his chin as he dragged me slightly forward.

"Really? That word again? Your tiny brain is all out of clever insults, huh?" There was a mocking lilt on my lips, and I thought he was going to rush for me, uncaring for Erebus.

"I'm going to ruin you, Ariadne. I'm going to fucking destroy you." The veins along his neck bunched, and his eyes looked close to bugging out of his sockets. I didn't pay his fury any mind, lost in the highs of retribution.

"With what? Your word—" I stopped abruptly, baffled when Harry turned to his car, and my legs began a rapid run backward when I saw him reaching for something on his back seat.

"Oh fuck," My breath left my body in a whoosh, and I hauled Erebus behind me, practically dragging him by the collar to the Prius. "*Shit. Shit. Shit.*"

I'd shut the driver's door when the first shot rang, and I gunned it out of the parking lot at maximum speed. I must've had a saint looking over me for not running over anyone in my state of duress the entire drive home.

One thing was for sure, Harry might've lost his leverage, but this was far from over.

A sharp pain pierced my ribs, and I *oomphed* when someone stumbled over my body in the dark, causing me to roll on my belly as they got their bearings straight.

"Ariadne?" Saint's bewildered voice found me on the ground, spotting me from the faint light of the flickering stars beyond the sky bridge. *"What are you doing?"*

With a huff, I turned back around, holding on to my stomach, and glaring at his shadowed form standing over me. *Trying not to hyperventilate after almost dying today.*

"I'm stargazing." I settled for an answer that wouldn't have him throttling me after all the lies I'd spewed.

His throat produced a noise between a choke and a laugh, and he had the gall to probe me again with his foot to make sure I was there. I slapped his leg off, and his laugh developed to a full-blown chuckle that brushed against my skin like peach fuzz, soft and electric.

"No, you're freezing your little ass lying on the floor with no lights on."

I shrugged one shoulder. "You could always join me and warm me up. I know you like to cuddle."

There it was again, that little choking sound that had my hands sweating as he kneeled next to me and embraced my weirdness by flopping back on the floor. I attached myself to him like glue as soon as he was settled, throwing my leg over his waist as he fitted an arm under my shoulders.

"If you rat me out to anyone, I will deny it," he whispered over my forehead before dropping a peck on my brow.

"Your secret is safe with me, pretty boy." I nuzzled my head into his chest, my heart slowing down for the first time since I got home, and tried to wash the remnants of shock off me. It didn't work, my hands and legs still shook from the adrenaline boost, and paranoia lingered in my mind like an unwanted guest.

What if Harry showed up here?

He wasn't that stupid, right?

Like the moon gazing down on me, a war waged in my mind. One side burned with the need to say something, to seek protection. The one not illuminated by the sun ravaged me with fears of abandonment and shame if Saint found out all of what I'd kept sealed. We were on a trial period, and I didn't want to jeopardize this tentative ceasefire. Especially when I was discovering the big bad wolf was a puppy in disguise more and more every day.

Caring, funny, generous, and all alpha when need be. The perfect blend of *I'll bend you over the side of my desk* and *kiss you slowly under the stream of the shower.*

Thank God, dogs couldn't speak. I gave poor Erebus some extra treats today for putting him through what I did.

"What are you doing on this side of the house?" I asked Saint, basking in the slow rise and fall of his chest.

"I haven't seen you since this morning, Spitfire."

"Are you saying you missed me?"

He stiffened. "Came to see if you were still alive, that's all."

"You could've texted me if you just wanted to check on me."

"How would I know it was you that replied and someone hadn't stolen your phone?"

I laughed at his ridiculous excuse, and his eyes narrowed on the glass roof. Anything to not admit that he *did*, in fact, miss me. It was okay, I knew from the way his arm tightened around me, pressing every part of me against him like he found solace in my presence after a long day.

Settling back, I stared at the blinking night sky too. "Sometimes looking at the stars makes me feel safe. It reminds me of how small and insignificant I am compared to the entirety of the universe."

"We don't mean anything in the grand scheme of things, huh?" Saint agreed in a rare moment of clarity. "It's easy to forget that we're nothing but matter and bones. There is no grand purpose, no master plan, only to survive and make the best out of what we're given."

"What's one thing you want to do before you die?" I drew circles over his cotton T-shirt.

"You," he replied, making my stomach summersault, but I pressed for the real answer, and he gave it to me reluctantly. "Make sure my family is well taken care of. That Kill chooses to do whatever he wants no matter what is expected of him, and my mom finally outgrows her demons and insecurities."

Wasn't that sweet? And totally more heart-warming than my wish.

"Well, that just called me shallow in about three different languages."

Saint's stomach rumbled with laughter. "Why? What would you like to do?"

"See the southern lights."

"Are the northern lights too mainstream for you, Spitfire?"

"I like that not many people have seen them. There isn't land close enough to the southern pole, so the only time you can get a peek is under the right conditions, like a geomagnetic storm or if you park your ass in Antarctica somehow." An idea took shape in my mind, and I bit one of his abs through his shirt softly before staring up at him. "We could always travel to Australia, you know. You could get to meet your long-lost cousins, the Tasmanian devils too."

"Somehow, you always find new reasons for me to paint your ass red." I squealed when he reached down and spanked me, giggling when he kept his hand in place, rubbing some of the pain away.

Needing to forget about this shitty day, I pushed up and straddled him, finding confidence in the dark. I didn't know if Saint would give the time of day if he read my thoughts about him. They were obsessive, incessant, and full of maddening hunger, drowning me to the point of suffocation. It was scary when you were the first to catch feelings for a person who was an enigma.

"Why do you never talk about your dad?" I asked, wanting in, in that brain of his.

"That's a story for a different day, Spitfire." He shot me down, trailing his fingers on the back of my thighs.

I gulped, glad he couldn't see the vulnerability etched into my features, and leaned down, prolonging a breakdown by feeding off his strength. "Sleep with me tonight?"

"You don't have to ask for that, baby. Just take." He slowly hardened underneath me.

"No," I shifted my hands through his hair, and he raised a brow in question. "Sleep with me in my bed. Please?" I pressed a soft kiss to his Adam's apple, enjoying the way it bobbed under my lips.

A few seconds passed before he hauled us both up in that abrupt manner of his I'd found myself becoming familiar with because it kept me on the edge of my seat. Locking my ankles around his back, I let my husband carry me to an actual bed for the first time.

CHAPTER TWENTY-TWO
SAINT

The silver lining to falling asleep with Ariadne every night for the past month was waking up with her limbs tangled with mine—deliciously naked because clothes were forbidden as per the ground rules—sometimes her mouth wrapped around my cock, and other times me licking my way up her tits, and sinking into her warm cunt while she panted in my mouth.

Today I went for option number three, seeing as she'd been extra stressed, and I wanted to pay her extra attention. Ease the nerves that had her eyes wide as saucers until I got home from work so she could get some shut-eye.

Was I doing everything I vowed I never would with this woman? Yes, yes, I was.

Did I regret it? Hell to the fucking no.

The little virgin was milking daily orgasms from me, and I found myself growing attached to her orange scent and the random conversations she would strike at three am like whether men were truly necessary for the survival of the human species, now that scientists uncovered a new bone marrow procedure that allowed women to conceive without our help.

"Would you really be able to give this up?" I told her one of our nights together while she bounced up and down on me, under the stars on the sky bridge. It was her favorite place in the whole house.

Stargazing had become a tradition of sorts, and I bought us a fluffy white rug so her stubborn ass wouldn't catch pneumonia.

"I survived for twenty-one years without dick. Vibrators exist for a reason." Her boobs swayed tauntingly over my face, and I reached up, taking a nipple in my mouth. She shuddered, and I smiled around her hot flesh, her moans doing nothing to mask her lies.

"But you can't spell *coconut* with your hips while riding one, can you now?" I slapped her ass while she did the trick I taught her, and my eyes rolled to the back of my head, my lips parting with a hiss. "Don't lie to me. You've become more insatiable than I am."

"It's all your fault," she complained in my mouth while flooding my cock and balls with her release.

I never thought I would enjoy domestication. Throughout my life, I wasn't raised with the poster example of a happy family and parents devoted to each other—everyone cheated, it was a known fact, but I couldn't comprehend even touching someone else when I had a curvy brunette making me *Paximadi*, a hard heavily textured, traditional Greek bread for breakfast.

"Tell me again, why did we not sleep in the same bed before?" I half-moaned while taking a bite of the soaked bread, marinated with olive oil, and topped with chopped tomatoes and feta cheese.

Aria shrugged, and her robe fell slightly, exposing one of her shoulders, and I got the urge to get her filthy enough to need a second shower with me. "Because you were too busy fighting your blossoming emotions for me."

"If you use blossoming in a sentence like that again, those emotions will evaporate."

"Don't be so grumpy. It's okay to admit you fell for me, despite wanting to throw me off a cliff when I first got here," she pouted, and I wasn't surprised she thought that way.

I'd passed through douchebag academy with flying colors when I was younger, and some of the traits extended into adulthood. My stomach tightened at the words *fell for me*, and I took a sip of my Frappe—courtesy of Ariadne too—to avoid lashing out because of the murkiness that had overtaken my temporal lobe.

"Let's not run before we can walk." I settled for a neutral answer and proceeded to continue the joke. That's what she was also doing, *joking*. "And I never wanted to throw you off a cliff. Well, not without a parachute anyway. You were annoying, but not annoying enough to kill without remorse."

"Stop being so swoony. My heart can't handle it." She clutched her chest mockingly.

Checking the clock on the wall, I scarfed down the rest of the food, giving her some words of wisdom that she would heed if she was smart. "Better shield it, baby. You never know what might cause it to break."

"If I lived my life in fear, then I wouldn't be living at all." Aria gave me a haughty look that was all sass, and I had to remind myself that this was still a trial run and that I had to set her free once it was up.

"All this snow is making my hair frizzy. It's *March*. I long to see the sun again," Aria sighed dramatically, rearranging her scarf to cover her poofed-up hair as we made our way down a slick sidewalk.

"Want me to put a Shirley Temple song on when we ride back home?" I teased, drawing her close. She was so focused on maintaining the curls she defined before we left that she stepped straight onto a patch of ice. Rushing to the hospital because she broke her back was the last thing I needed.

She gave me the finger, and I laughed, blowing frigid air into the atmosphere.

"I want you to tell me why the hell you dragged me all the way to Boston on a Saturday." Her question was answered within seconds once we took a left and stopped in front of a Barnes and Noble. Aria's eyes squeezed in confusion, and she stared up at me, her windburned cheeks begging me to cup them. "A bookstore? Are you looking for something specific?"

I dropped my hand from her shoulders, squeezing my arms to my sides. It was cold, but I also avoided doing anything stupid. "I got a Facebook ad about an event related to one of the books you told me about. The one about the blue aliens with the ribbed dic—"

"Out of all the ones I told you about, that's the one you remember?" Her long lashes flicked to the sky in exasperation and humor.

"It was the most memorable." I shrugged, my lips twitching. "I was checking on a campaign with your dad, and you should've seen his face when I clicked the *Learn More* button."

"You did *not* tell him I like reading those types of books, right?" Aria clutched my forearm in desperation.

"No, I'm sure he thought I was booking tickets to the author's signing purely for my enjoyment," I mocked, shrugging some of the snowflakes that littered my coat.

"Okay, cool—" She sighed before doing a double take. "Wait, *what?*"

Lacing my fingers through hers, I ushered us past the double doors. "Come on, she's not going to wait forever."

Turned out, *we* had to wait forever.

The author was late due to the snowstorm, and even though I enjoyed the exciting kiss Aria planted on my lips when she saw Mariana Parker's banner—which was an iconic blue. However, I was not enjoying how she took advantage of the time we spent waiting by filling up my arms with special edition covers of Harry Potter because according to some online quiz, she was a Ravenclaw and had to have the blue box set.

At least her ass looked extra biteable in her white faux leather pants.

"Ohmigod, ohmigod, ohmigod." Her entire face lit up with one of the biggest smiles I'd ever seen when Mariana made her way to the desk that was set up for her, stacks of books on either side. "It's really her!"

I swallowed past the increasing lump in my throat and slammed the sudden urge to book tickets to Tasmania so she could see her fucking southern lights, and I could see an even bigger smile on her face illuminated by the green and blue sky, down. By the time it was winter in Australia, Aria and I would be on separate roads.

"I can't believe I married a dork," I complained but followed when she rushed forward.

Okay, blue aliens were more popular than I thought, and bookworms could remain silent as nuns. The line was fifty people long, and I was seriously concerned because one: I must've only caught like two customers lingering around the bookstore when we first came in. And two: The male species had some serious competition if so many women thought aliens were the next big thing.

I voiced my last concern to Aria and shut my mouth when she told me that it was because they were so tired of our bullshit. Even extraterrestrial love sounded better.

Couldn't argue with that logic.

After hearing girls squeal for about an hour, I was more than grateful to be out of that place. Ariadne's smile was still in place as we stared at the people skating about the ice rink in Boston Common, and I mirrored her, but mostly because I found watching people fall extremely entertaining.

"And here you said you there was no ounce of romance in you." Aria blinked innocently at me, taking a bite out of her cheesy pizza and chewing as fast as she could so she could shove her red fingers in her pockets again.

"Don't be fooled, Spitfire. I did this purely because it's not healthy living this dream world of yours. I hope meeting the author helped you realize that the characters are indeed fictional, and real life doesn't always have a happy ever after," I grumped, and the pit in my stomach grew when the next fall didn't do anything for me.

"Romantic *and* jealous of blue aliens. I like this two-for-one special." She grinned, reaching up to peck my cheek.

"Eat your pizza," I ordered, but as time went on, I was starting to forget why I was so averse to a lifetime with Aria.

I was happy—maybe too happy, and I hadn't felt like this in a while.

Sure, I had fun in my life, but fun was fleeting. Happiness was the extended version of it. And being with Ariadne

Fleur, my opposite in so many ways, surprisingly had me eating out of her hand to stretch the emotion.

My phone buzzed with a call once I'd gotten Ariadne settled on the passenger seat, and I checked the name as I strode to my side of the car, declining when I saw who it was.

The universe's way of showing me why we can't have nice things was cruel, but oh, so valid. Ariadne deserved someone better than a guy who was about to send his father to an early grave.

CHAPTER TWENTY-THREE

ARIADNE

I refreshed the local news channel website on my phone, checking for any updates like I'd done every day since Harry shot *at* me. The fact that the asshole was still roaming around free didn't sit well with me. He had a whole ass vendetta against me, and I had a family to protect. He was unpredictable, and I wouldn't put it past him to go after my loved ones.

Sighing, I grabbed the toy from Nyx's mouth, cocking my arm, and released, watching the black Doberman sprint toward the edge of Saint's property. I wished the cops were as fast when it came to making an arrest.

I did my research when it came to Harry's criminal record, and through an online database found out he was charged for drug possession and distribution. I wasn't all that surprised when the hacker informed me that he was selling again—online this time, on a marketplace called the silk road, an onion site on the Tor browser. I paid him extra to expose Harry's IP address, so the authorities caught up to his tracks.

Waiting was like sitting on burning coals.

I was fucking terrified of what he would do so long as he was free, but shame made my throat bunch up whenever I tried to talk to someone about what happened.

I was surrounding myself as much as I could with friends and family. I despised the tug of war my emotions played when I was alone. It led me down the road of mild panic attacks that kept getting progressively worse. I knew I had to speak to someone eventually, yet I kept prolonging it.

Things were going so well with Saint, and I didn't want to jeopardize that—*us*—with my questionable choices in past relationships.

"Holy shit, I don't think I've ever broken this much of a sweat before." Irena captured my attention, running back to me with Erebus zooming in front of her.

It was long overdue, bringing her here, and I honestly didn't know how she tolerated me sometimes. If there was a *rate your sister* scale, I'd be on the lower end of the spectrum. I was rectifying that, though, and had even started attending a few skating classes with her. My bum bore the brunt of that decision.

"Makes sense, the only type of exercise you get is on the ice." I threw another stick, diverting Erebus's playfulness to Nyx, and they ran around the open grass space together.

"Maybe I should get a dog too."

I scoffed, walking next to her as we made our way to an artificial pond in the garden. "Yeah, good luck convincing Mom to get you one. She's a germaphobe."

Irena flipped her auburn ponytail over her shoulder, the pout of her lips more pronounced. "No one ever understands the pain of kids that grow up without pets."

"Such a tragic way of living."

She ignored the sarcasm in my voice, kicking a stone into the water. "Where's your blond hunk?"

"He said he was stopping by his parents' place to say hi to Kill."

"Oh, Killian's in town again?" Irena chirped. "Wasn't he here like two months ago? Makes me wonder if he has any friends in California."

"From what I've seen online, he leads quite the busy life as every other college student." Parties, girls, random tattoos, ambiguous art. Killian was the dark and moody type. "Also, there's nothing wrong with him visiting often. I would certainly hope you'd come home just as much if you go to an out-of-state college."

"Yeah, *that's* not gonna happen. My skin can't handle all that traveling." She soothed her temples with her fingers. "So, how come you're not with him? Not mixing well with the in-laws?"

"They're nice. However, it's a little bit awkward. His mom doesn't like me much."

It was my turn to kick a stone, and we both watched it skip over the surface of the pond. I didn't blame her, and at least she tried to be nice when she was in my presence. I preferred it when people weren't rude to my face.

"Oh well, who needs them anyway?" Irena pushed me closer until she had my head on the crook of her neck, and I wrapped my arms around her. "If a woman can't move on after years have passed, then there's something wrong with her. You don't need that kind of negative energy in your life."

I nodded against her chest. If anyone saw us right now, they would never believe I was the older sister. "Although no one touches Mom and Dad's relationship, I do feel bad for Celia sometimes. It was a pretty brutal rejection."

She'd become a bit of a meme when a news article resurfaced recently, and the internet was a vicious place. I half-wished she didn't know how to operate social media.

"Yeah, Dad was a little bit of an asshole back then, huh?" Irena exhaled. "I don't get the obsession girls have with 'alpha males.' I'm gonna get me a cute beta that respects me."

"I think it's that adrenaline rush you get when—" I started explaining, but shut up. A cute beta was perfect for Irena. I wanted her to stay as far away from assholes who wouldn't hesitate to put your heart through a meat grinder as possible.

"Are you sure you don't want to come work for us? I mean, you also have a stake in the company. It's yours as much as it is mine." Saint dropped a kiss on the crown of my head, folding my body into his from behind.

The venue of my launch party was almost empty. The last of the people who remained, mingled with each other. Mostly my family and the employees that worked tirelessly to bring my vision to light. I made sure to give my PA, Alice a huge bonus because without her I would've probably drowned in a sea of responsibilities.

My first drop sold out in under a few minutes, and everything was going well. Too well. I was excited about all of it. Every day I checked off another steppingstone in my life, but there was this coiling anxiety that hung over my head like a grim reaper's scythe. I went ham on security, and you could see men with black suits scattered amidst the army of caterers and standing in front of light pink walls imprinted with my brand logo—peach spiders.

I twisted around, sounds of fluttering wings filling my ears and giddiness spreading like a balm, knowing that he followed me to the balcony. "Nah, have you heard what happens to couples that work at the same place?"

"Yeah, you're right. You'd be too much of a distraction." He dropped a kiss to my forehead, and I closed my eyes, holding on to the lapels of his suit.

Every day I sank more and more into Saint's ocean. He was the first person I saw every morning and the last every night. Married life suited us, despite our initial rebellion. Scrutiny was replaced with open fascination when we attended events together now. And even though offers from other women kept pouring in as if Saint was still single, he didn't show an ounce of interest, stealing thorough kisses in shadowed corners of public places because he couldn't wait until we got home.

My lungs filled with every drop of him. I just hoped that he wouldn't leave me to drown in two months' time. I wasn't ready to say goodbye. I didn't think I ever would be. Saint wasn't an addiction you could kick. He was turning out to be my whole world, the only one my heart swelled up for. My misunderstood man, hiding a heart of gold under all the articles that tried to bury him.

"That wasn't what I meant," I giggled when he kissed my neck.

"You realize I'm sleeping with the competition, right?" His bottom teeth scraped over my skin, and I pulled his head back, holding it hostage in my hands. My family could see us, and I could feel my mom's eyes rubbing over me, leaving an essence of an *I told you so* behind as they went.

"Oh, I'm no competition, just a tiny brand amidst a sea of thousands." I worried my lip, glancing down at his chest.

"About fifty percent of small businesses fail within the first five years, so who knows, maybe I'll take you up on your offer after all."

"No you won't," he said, his tone wooden. "I won't let you."

My stare turned into a glare. "All of a sudden, I like the idea of working at Falco and Fleur more and more."

His fingers squeezed my waist, and he fought against a laugh. "I won't let you because it would be sad to give all of this up, little fire. You have a genuine passion for design, sure, but you also built something from scratch, and not a lot of people in that room can say that, not even me. It takes a lot of drive and determination to open your own business, and when it's something you love, it would only fail if it lacked support. And no matter where we are in the future, one thing I can promise you, if you need me, I'll always be of help because you've earned my respect as an artist and as a fucking boss."

He cocked his head as if to say, *you got that?*

The thing was, I got more than that.

The cotton candy clouds that floated around my brain evaporated in a mist of painful truths. Saint Astor had managed to color himself outside the lines I'd drawn around him, dripping ink into my soul and hooking himself in deep until I couldn't think of anything else except how much I loved how he made me feel.

Powerful.

Beautiful.

Smart.

Worthy.

I loved him and everything that came with him. His rough edges sent my brain spiraling to understand him better. His dirty mouth had me melting in a puddle every time he uttered his filth when he was deep inside me. His sharp mind that he offered up willingly when I needed help.

Everything. Everything. Everything.

I fell hard and fast with no option of returning back to the land of dreams and thinking a year was enough to spend with a man like Saint. I wanted a lifetime, and I would do my damned best to get it because I knew he wanted me to, but something was holding him back. Something I would get him to open up about, eventually.

"God, I—" My mouth was miles ahead of my mind, but I caught my impulsivity and dragged her back by the hair. Saint wasn't ready for that yet. "I want to kiss you," I rectified, my chest heaving as if I'd run a marathon.

He gave me that cocky, self-assured smirk of his. "Yeah, I tend to inspire that need in women."

"If you kiss any other women, I'll cut off your balls while you're sleeping, *Sainty*." I tightened my hands on his jacket and brought myself to my tippy-toes, goose bumps spreading like fire on my skin when his minty breath fanned my face.

"Same goes to you, Spitfire with other men."

"I don't have balls."

"But you have boobs." He raised an eyebrow.

I cupped an arm protectively around my chest, an incredulous laugh escaping me. "My girls are hurt."

Saint leaned down and licked along the seam of my mouth, getting me to open up. "I'll kiss them better tonight," he growled against my lips, and family and guests be damned, I let him make out with me where everyone could see, realizing that, as always, a mother knows best.

Mama Lydia's intentions weren't pure. Nevertheless, if it wasn't for her, and surprisingly my rigid grandmother, I wouldn't be experiencing this whirlwind of love and high life so young—maybe never.

I hugged him close when we came out for air, both of us looking inside the double doors. Dad was twirling Mom on the dance floor, my creative team was showing off pictures of the designs pinned to the wall to the other guests, and Killian —the only member of Saint's family that bothered to show up—was talking with Irena, sparkly liquid on their hands that most likely contained alcohol and would have my dad up in arms if he saw.

She didn't make a move to drink it, simply talked animatedly to Killian, who had his full attention on her, and it made me wonder what the hell they were talking about that was so interesting.

"Your brother seems to be getting awfully close to my sister," I told Saint, letting the rise and fall of his chest lull some of the night's chaos off me.

"You should be glad they're getting along, unlike the rest of our families."

"Ugh, don't remind me." I rubbed my cheek further into his shirt. "It's ironic that they're the ones that pushed for this."

"Money brings people together, Spitfire. The synergy between Falco and Fleur was apparent even to casual observers. There is a very big buzz surrounding future collections. The spotlight will most definitely be on us for the next few seasons."

"Are you feeling the pressure?"

"Your dad has surprisingly been a huge help."

"My dad's super professional. I remember when I was interning at Fleur, he wouldn't let me call him *dad*."

His head bobbed over mine as if he was in complete

agreement with that attitude. "Trust me, that's better than dealing with temper tantrums."

Whatever it was he wasn't telling me, I knew it had to do with *his* dad. He never talked about Noah, and even when he did, Saint had this look of apathy on his face that broke my heart. But he would open up. I just needed to strike when his defenses were down.

CHAPTER TWENTY-FOUR

SAINT

"A little present for a successful launch by the three of us." Eliana held out a funky-looking gift bag, neatly tied with a red silk bow.

"Oh my gosh, you didn't have to get me anything." Ariadne's eyes lit up as we settled on a blue suede couch at Bella's, opposite Leo, Eli, and Ares. "But thank you so much." She gathered the bag in her hands, waiting until I sat next to her to open it.

I could've sworn the place looked different the last time I was here. Leo kept reinventing the decor every few years. With clubs and restaurants, you had to keep the customers on their toes, so they wouldn't get bored. He was adamant about not letting this place fail, and it was going well for years now. Not that he needed the money, he was a fucking oil tycoon and probably wiped his ass with cash when he ran out of toilet paper, but I knew there was sentimental value behind Bella's.

We used to hang out here at least once a month, and I showed up religiously for the dancing performances they did where the girls wore next to nothing. There was one going on right now, but the only one my dick got hard for these days was Ariadne. Even the voyeur club was moot. I might've glanced at the couple once, maybe twice. It should concern me, yet I couldn't find it in me to care.

"Are you kidding me? The site crashed, and you sold out in under ten minutes." Eliana pouted. "I didn't manage to grab anything for myself."

Leo grabbed a bottle of Armand de Brignac from an ice bucket, pouring some for us. "She's not lying. My finger almost fell off refreshing the page. It was a team failure."

"You should've just told me. I'll send you one of our leftover PR packages. We have plenty to go around," Ariadne offered, her tongue peeking out as she struggled to untie the present. "Ina snatched two already."

"How does it feel to fuck someone smarter than you?" Leo slid a glass of champagne my way, and Aria coughed out a laugh.

"I'm guessing the same way it feels to fuck someone prettier and more talented than you."

"Pretty fucking fantastic, huh?" His laugh turned into a cough when Eli side-eyed him.

She wasn't bothered by her husband's crude language but apologized to Aria, who wasn't used to his shit. "Please excuse him. He's a special needs type of guy. No matter how many times we go over his training, he still manages to say the wrong thing."

My girl took it in stride. "Don't worry about it. Saint's training just started, but he's proving to be just as challenging."

I opened my mouth to argue, but Ares beat me to it, shaking his head as he lounged back on the couch, his signature leather jacket on even inside the club. "I've never been more glad to be single than this very moment."

"Don't worry, honey," Eli cooed, patting his cheek. "Your time will surely come soon."

"Is this a... a..." I heard Aria stutter, and I turned to find her looking down at the bag with a frown on her face.

It took me a second to glance at the contents when staring over Aria's head gave me a great view of her rack in her cardigan-like top. It looked like some weird mini glass sculpture at first. I pieced all its compartments together pretty fast. The mouthpiece, followed by the smoke chamber that led to a wide base, didn't leave any room for doubt.

"A bong, really?" I deadpanned, eyeing the three of them.

"It was Eliana's idea." Ares ratted her out.

"Sure was." She gave a proud nod. "Just a little something to get you to relax. I remember how stressed I was before *and* after opening my dance studio."

"Epsom salts, a massage, a spa day." I checked off an imaginary list. "There were plenty of other alternatives."

"I love it!" Aria ignored me and subtly elbowed me when I chuckled. I bet she hadn't even seen one live until now. "Don't be mean. We're cracking into this thing together as soon as you gather the rest of the supplies."

"Are you asking me to break the law with you, Mrs. Fleur?" I crowded her, and her hand flew to my thigh under the table, a smile on her luscious lips.

"Seemed like she's asking you to break the law *for* her from where I'm standing. Smoking pot is not illegal. *Buying* is, in Astropolis," Ares ruined the moment.

Eliana clapped her hands, and it was almost inaudible over the Rihanna song pounding through the speakers.

"Okay, guys, you argue about that. I need to go to the bathroom. Aria, are you coming?"

Of course, she went. I didn't know what it was with girls and going to the bathroom in packs. The guys didn't wait long to bounce on my case when they left. "You seem pretty happy."

"Why wouldn't he be?" Leo asked rhetorically. "He finally got the girl, and his revenge plan is in motion as we speak."

"I didn't finally get the girl. The girl has been mine all along," I bypassed his last sentence, choosing not to tempt God by thinking about it. Everything was set up and ready to go. Now it was all on daddy dearest to take the bait.

"Right, and Ivana Trump really married for love," Leo countered.

"We know you, Saint. The last time you were in a serious relationship was in two-thousand and never. It didn't take much to figure out Ariadne wasn't really *your* choice." Ares emphasized Leo's assessment, and I knew there was no fooling them.

"She's my choice now, asshats." I gave in, knowing they wouldn't shut up about it, and I didn't want them mentioning it in front of Aria.

Spitfire walked into my life like she always belonged in it, broke down my walls, and made a competitive sport out of smoking out my demons. I was fooling myself by thinking I could stand watching her with someone else, letting some fucker touch all the parts of her that were uncharted territories before me, and not carve out his intestines like a sheep after slaughter. The mere thought sent my brain down a rage rampage.

I was throwing all of my worries out the window because

the feeling of being with Ariadne trumped all the reasons we shouldn't be together. Yes, I was way older than her, so fucking what? She acted nothing like a twenty-one-year-old. Sure, people cheated. I'd cut off the dick of any guy who came within a mile of her. And fuck, I wasn't her first choice, but I would make sure to be her last.

"We can see that otherwise, you wouldn't be sitting here while your daddy is about to get the shock of his life." Leo brought me back to the present.

I only hoped she wouldn't run screaming when I told her that my father was on his way to a hospital bed, and I was the reason.

I primed my mouth to respond when a loud pop had me swallowing my words. My body turned rigid as everyone froze at the reverberating sound that reminded me a whole fucking lot of a gunshot. I leaned forward, my head doing a three-sixty to see if anyone was down, bleeding, or if someone had a gun on their hands.

Aria. Aria. Aria.

I couldn't see her anywhere, and some of the tension between my shoulder blades ebbed away when I saw that she wasn't anywhere near the culprit. But then... we didn't fucking know where the culprit was. Fear mixed with adrenaline sparked in my veins, and the three of us stood at the same time.

"What was that?" Ares voiced his concern, looking toward where the girls had left.

"It came from the back." I realized, my brain working in slow motion.

"Eliana." Leo went pale, and the same panic that gripped his face I could feel, squeezing my heart.

There was a collective quiet, and we stared at each other

before scrambling to move. Everyone had the same idea, but where people were pushing for the exit, we were leading deeper, toward the bathrooms. My tall build allowed me to eat the distance faster, shoving people out of the way.

A sense of deja vu took over while walking to the place where Aria had seen me with another woman—I pressed it down, focusing on the matter at hand. Dread crept up on all four corners of the hallway when I latched onto the hole in the bathroom door. Rushing forward, I didn't give a shit about what might be waiting for me on the other side. I busted the door open.

Eliana was the first person I saw, trying to right herself on the floor. Leo was already storming in behind me, so I let my eyes search the room until I found Aria.

My blood ran cold when I saw her, a much larger body pressing hers to a stall, her feet swinging in the air and face red as she was held up by her neck. My brain short-circuited, and I flew toward the soon-to-be-dead man, hauling him off her by the shoulders. He tumbled to the ground, and Aria dropped to her feet, dry-heaving.

"Baby." I lowered myself next to her, and her eyes flashed with warning over my shoulder.

I spun around, dodging a fist to my face, my control snapping like a rubber band when I recognized her loser ex as I slammed him against the tiled floor for a second time.

My pulse raced.

My eyes burned.

He groaned, and I needed to hear more of his pain. The pent-up anger, worry, and fear uncurled with a swipe of my muscles, and I was on the asshole in seconds, fully intending to tenderize his meat until I could cut him up and use his skin as decoration.

"Stop. Sto—" he gurgled, his voice bottoming out when I delivered a blow to his lips, blood spraying across my knuckles.

I took it in stride, enjoying how the red glimmered under the fluorescent lights, allowing myself to lose my train of thought in slamming my fist on his face until he was as bruised as Aria's face had been when he was choking her. Welts on his skim bloomed purple like an opium poppy, and my ears rang, distorting all the noise around me.

All I could hear was the wet crunch of his skin and faded screams into the background that fueled my bloodthirst. I wanted to check on Aria but eliminating any threats against her got priority.

"The first time you went looking for her, there were no consequences for your actions." I fisted his shirt, watching as his head hung limply in the air before slamming his skull against the floor. "This time, I won't fucking stop until you're unable to think her name, let alone speak it."

"Virginal Ariadne isn't as good as you think." He still fought even though I was an inch away from cementing him to the floor.

"I'm going to rip your tongue off if you don't shut the fuck up." Saliva mixed with his life source at the edges of his mouth as he writhed beneath me. "Or you know what? Make it harder for yourself. Struggle."

He gave a few tired swings that were completely aimless; I doubted he could see much. His eyes were starting to swell. Something glimmered in my peripheral vision and I flicked my eyes there, seeing the weapon he intended to use on Aria. A black pistol sitting abandoned a few feet away.

He wasn't here to intimidate her.

He was here with the sole intention of killing her.

My wife, the woman who pierced through the fog of my inhibitions a little at a time until the warmth of her sunshine, had me shuddering at the thought of losing everything that came with her. And this motherfucker thought he could steal that away from me? Tough luck.

I reached for the firearm when he started speaking again.

"Did she tell you she has a tape where she does all sorts of interesting things? Like suck my dick like a whore—"

I brought the butt of the gun to his forehead, and the thump that echoed ricocheted through the room. Everything sat deathly still, and all the background noises ceased.

What the fuck did he say?

My muscles shook with barely controlled rage as someone tried to shake me off from behind. I felt hands on my shoulders for the past few minutes now, but only now did they register as they clawed underneath my arms, Aria's panicked voice breaking through the film in my ears.

"Saint, oh God, stop."

"We're in public," a harsher male voice whispered in my ear as he struggled to haul me off, dragging me to my feet. "You don't want to kill him while we're in public."

"The police are on their way." Someone else screamed in the background, but I wrote them all off, shaking the foreign grips off me and turning to Aria, my body sore from the excessive violence that coursed through my veins.

"Are you okay?" I asked her, my fingers slightly trembling to touch her. The purpling marks on her neck and the handprint on her face had me gearing to beat the shit out of the moaning son of a bitch on the floor all over again.

She leaned against a stall door, looking fucking exhausted, but I didn't get closer than need be. Her eyes were flighty, bouncing everywhere, forcing me to take in the room with her. The piece of shit was unconscious on the floor, bleeding underneath my designer loafers, Ares was talking to the security as they tried to evacuate the few brave customers that were trying to peek in, and Leo was holding a wide-eyed Eliana, who except for getting the shock of her life, appeared to be fine physically.

"I-I'm fine. He didn't manage to hit me, or Eliana," Aria said, hugging her stomach, and I stepped in front of the loser, so she wouldn't have to look at him.

"I think I've seen him before," Eliana piped in, her eyes wide. "That day at the La Perla boutique. He was there the same time we were."

The same day I popped her cherry and fucked her on the bathroom floor, with that damned bruise on her head. Things were unraveling, and I wasn't liking the conclusions my mind was reaching.

A tape.

Nostrils flaring, I turned back to Aria, whose fire had distinguished. "What was he talking about?"

Her throat bobbed, the forming bruises on her skin dancing with the movement. "I promise I'll explain everything."

You better, Ariadne, or I don't see this ending well for either of us. And most of all fucking Larry, because instead of unconscious, he's going to be dead if I find out you've been fooling around behind my back.

"Saint, I'm sorry about tonight—"

I let the door slam shut behind us, cutting off whatever she had to say. I'd heard enough and nothing at all tonight. I wanted to know more, but I didn't think I could escape the trip to jail. I hoped they locked me up with her loser ex, so I would finish the job I started.

The version she gave the police was that he was just a bitter ex that had trouble moving on, and while that was true, I knew it was only part of the equation after putting two and two together. I kept my mouth shut, playing the mummy when she talked with the officers. A storm was brewing inside me, the words *sex tape* being carried by the whistling wind of the unparalleled envy and mistrust blowing past every logic.

"Were you even a virgin?" I bit out as I blazed toward the kitchen because obviously, my priorities were set straight.

But why the fuck lie? About everything.

She followed in my tracks, desperation rolling off her in waves. "I was. You know I was. You saw the blood."

"Maybe you were on your period."

"You're reaching, and you know it." She raised her voice, and I searched the freezer for some frozen peas to avoid taking her over my knee to get her to understand what would happen when she lied to me.

I was teetering the edge between cracking my palm against her flesh for some behavioral lessons and licking her marred skin, so she felt better.

I was completely bipolar when it came to this girl.

"Fucking excuse me for reaching to conclusions when you tell me you're a virgin, but then turns out you have a sex tape." I dripped ice and menace when I turned around, shoving the bag to her chest.

Vulnerable eyes tracked my movements as I grabbed myself a whole bottle of whiskey, not bothering with glasses, downing a doppio when she sat on the counter, wincing as she pressed the bag to her neck.

"There was no penetration on the tape." She fumbled with her fingers, her eyes downcast. "I don't even know if you can call it a sex tape. He just had footage of me in a compromising position. I was, uh, giving him hea—"

Another wave of alcohol worked down my throat like medicine. "Spare me the details. When did this happen? Was it before you threw yourself all over me on Thanksgiving or while we were together? I might have to get tested for STDs."

My last comment was uncalled for, but my wings, as I knew them, were melting off. It turned out they were nothing but an illusion she'd fabricated. I had to hand it to Ariadne. She had me believing that this was real.

"The tape was filmed before we were together. Harry broke up with me the day we played pool because I wouldn't put out." She didn't retaliate verbally, and that annoyed me. "He started blackmailing me in exchange for cash and his job back soon after that, though."

"And you didn't tell me when it first happened because?"

"Shame? Fear? Take your pick. It's not the easiest thing in the world to admit, and I handled pretty okay myself—"

"You handled it okay?" I let out a bitter chuckle. "What if Eliana goes to early labor because of this? Will you still feel like you handled it *okay*?"

I didn't imagine getting shot at was healthy for the baby. She accepted Aria's apologies, but Leo was close to tearing a hole through every wall.

"I meant I got rid of the footage."

"How?"

"I hired a hacker from the dark web."

"You *what?*" That made me wanna hurl the bottle to the wall, a few inches away from her face.

"It worked out, he wiped his hard drive, and Harry was left with nothing. I paid him extra to tip off the police that he was dealing drugs online, and I guess when he realized it, he came after me."

"So let me get this straight." I paced the empty hall, ready to tear shit down for being so blind. "You went through all this trouble, spent your money, hired a hacker, lied to everyone about what was going on for months, and begged me to get him his job back with Ares, knowing full well what kind of a cunt he was?"

Aria squirmed when I turned to her. "It sounds bad when you put it like that."

My left eye twitched, and I couldn't hold back. "It's fucking horrible, juvenile, and stupid. You put all of us at risk today because you—"

"Because I what, Saint?" She hopped off the counter, squaring up to me. "Because I was blackmailed? Because I didn't want anyone to see Harry's revenge porn? I admit. I could've gone about it a different way. I could've talked to someone, but I am also a victim. There was no end to his daily threats, and I felt so fucking exposed, alone, and violated."

Her words inspired a cloud of violence, blurring my vision. Guilt, thick and palpable, turned my insides to slime until my breathing turned labored. "What else did he do? When you told me you hit your head while changing, was that true?"

She bit her lip. "Are you sure you want to know? You'll be sent to jail too if you go after him this time. The self-defense excuse won't hold." A growl from the back of my throat burst forth, and she shook her head, wiping her hands on jeans. They were ripped at the knee, and I didn't remember them being like that when we left the house this evening. "All right, all right, I'll tell you."

Maybe I should've heeded her warning because when she was done, I was clutching my hair in my hands, pulling so hard it hurt since the alternative was hurting someone else that was out of reach right now.

Car chases. Guns. I was looking at my wife through fresh eyes, not knowing her at all. At least she had the bare minimum of common sense and brought Nyx and Erebus along to most of her meetings, but the fact that he roughed her up *three* times, right under my fucking nose, would haunt me for the rest of my life.

"Fuck, Aria."

"What are you thinking?"

"Whether I want to throttle you, drive to the county jail and plummet the jackass's face, or fucking lock you in a room where no one will find you and hurt you again."

Her shock was audible at my last point, and I faced away when she neared, her hands going around my tense shoulders.

"You could just hold me." She sounded so fucking break-able, I almost fell on my knees to give her what she wanted. I was conflicted, fucking torn on how to deal with the blatant lies she had no qualms about telling me with a straight face.

Through the haze of lust, flesh hitting flesh, and droplets of water on bare, tantalizing skin, I remembered how easy it was for her to fabricate an entire story because she didn't trust me.

I shrugged her off, moving away from the aisle. "And I'd love it if my wife hadn't lied to me for months while sleeping under my roof and demanded a monogamous relationship where we genuinely gave this a shot. Well, news flash, Ariadne, it doesn't work if you don't trust me."

"The only reason I didn't tell you was because I was scared you'd leave me." She pushed past me, blocking my way, the pupils in her caramel eyes dilated. "I didn't want to lose you, Saint. I really like you. I-I lo—"

"Don't," I bit out harshly. "You don't think so lowly of someone you *love*. You don't think they're going to leave you because of something that happened before you even met. I'm fucking offended that's the kind of guy you think I am, Aria. No better than your ex if I was going to throw you out because a motherfucker was blackmailing you."

I could see the rise and fall of her chest getting faster now. She wrapped her hand around her neck, looking at me like she was scared I'd disappear.

And she was right.

Two parts of myself were battling for dominance. One wanted to chain her to the bed and lay with her until I was sure cunty Harry would rot in jail for years to come, and the other needed some space. Except for the fingerprints on her neck, Aria was fine. I made sure of that after I threatened the medics to make sure she had no holes in her body. Otherwise, I would put some in theirs.

"Saint, please, I would never put you in the same category as him. I love you. I do." Aria tried to hug me, but I held her back by her arms, ignoring the tears in her eyes at my rejection.

One thing I knew for sure; I was a goner for this girl. Even at her lowest, she looked so gorgeous my body was screaming to just give in, but I couldn't think straight right now. My phone was buzzing in my back pocket, reminding me that this night was far from over.

I had to deal with real-life karma.

"Ice your neck and face like the paramedics said, Ariadne. You have painkillers in the first drawer on the right." I moved her out of the way, her eyes sticking to my every move.

"You're leaving?" Aria's tear-thickened voice called me a bastard in all the languages of the world, including fucking Javascript, but I would deal with her later.

I didn't have the mental capacity to be extinguishing fires from every corner of my life right now.

CHAPTER TWENTY-FIVE
SAINT

"Where the hell have you been?" Killian badgered me as I passed by the beefy guards and walked straight into the hospital. A private clinic where Dad was most likely flown in.

Killian's face was pale and worn, clothes disheveled, and hair pointing in all directions. The gravity of the situation wasn't lost on me, but this turn of events was what I was waiting for, what I prepped for, what I *paid* for.

"Sorry, I was out and forgot my phone at home. I got here as soon as I saw your texts." I clapped him on the shoulder. A strong antiseptic scent assaulted my nose as we walked inside. "What happened?"

"A hit and run. He was on the road. We don't know where he was going to yet, but basically, someone crashed into him and left without notifying anyone. A passerby found his totaled car and called an ambulance and the police."

I knew I was sick when shivers of bliss made their way

down my body, my persistent limp gone for a few moments of elation. "Do we know who did it?"

"No, the police are looking into extracting footage from traffic cameras nearby, and we'll have an answer after that." His head drooped, and despite his strained relationship with Dad, he still cared for him. Good. If I could shield both him and Mom from the knowledge that Noah Astor was a massive sack of shit, I would. "They're saying it was most likely a drunk driver since nothing was stolen from the scene."

"And how is he?" I inserted some worry in my tone not to sound like a psychopath. Fabricated empathy would be the extent of my pity for my father.

"He was being transferred out of the operating room when you were parking. I told the doctor not to talk to Mom and wait until we got there. She's not in good condition right now."

Out so soon? The bastard must have had the devil looking over his shoulder. I didn't believe in the opposite saying. Good people went first. The bad stayed. Hence why in my mind, angels took lives they didn't give second chances.

"Is she worried?"

"Well, yeah." Killian gave me a, *why are you asking the obvious,* side-eye. "Her husband was in an accident. Aren't you worried?"

"Not particularly. Cockroaches never die," I drawled.

"That's fucking insensitive."

"Never claimed to be sensitive." In fact, I'd made it pretty clear my whole life that I refused to be fluent in bullshit.

"Don't say shit like that around Mom," Killian warned,

his fists tightening. Being the younger kid was nice. All the expectations were dropped, and the sense of responsibility was lifted off your shoulders. My brother was no brat, but he did get the longer end of the stick which allowed for more wiggle room.

Better than being a sociopath, so I bit my tongue, ruffling his hair with as much playfulness as I could muster. Spoiler alert, it wasn't much. "Come on, kid, I'm just playing with you. Let's go."

Mom was standing next to a doctor when she came into view, eyes bloodshot, talking a mile a minute. If there was one thing I was sorry about, it was the stress I was causing both of them with this recent development. I let her hug me longer than necessary when we reached her, supporting her weight.

"Oh, Saint. Thank God, you're here." She rose on her tiptoes and kissed my cheek, her lips trembling before she pulled away.

"I am also here." I heard Killian grumble. "Have been here for hours."

She ignored him, looking right at me, and tattled on the doctor. "They won't let me go in and see him."

"He probably just regained consciousness, Mom. Let us hear what the doctor has to say first." I patted her hair, and we faced the guy in the lab coat with no black circles under his eyes, despite it being almost three o'clock in the morning. "How is he?"

"We took some X-rays, ran a CAT scan, and everything seems normal. There is no internal bleeding. He has mild whiplash and will experience some pain and discomfort in his neck and back, but nothing that can't be fixed with some Tylenol and physical therapy if needed."

Perfect.

I thanked Satan while everyone else thanked the Lord for giving us free access to hitmen when we needed them. Since I was going to hell anyway might as well establish good relations when still situated on earth.

"Can we go in and see him?" Mom asked.

"The patient is resting. He still hasn't recovered from anesthesia, but once he's awake, one of the nurses will inform you." The doctor explained and nodded at us, rushing down the white hallway when his pager started beeping.

"Kill, can you go get Mom a bottle of cold water from the cafeteria?" I asked my brother as I sat Mom down on a silver bench, facing a row of rooms. "Grab me a coffee too, while you're at it." I needed one if I intended on staying awake.

"What's the magic word?" Kill asked, standing rigid.

"Now?" I raised a cool brow.

His expression soured as he turned. "I don't have the patience to deal with you today."

"You shouldn't talk to your brother like that." My mother was on my case when Killian disappeared down the corridor.

"I'm just bullying him a little bit, so he doesn't become a soy boy." I threw out an excuse I had on hand. Kill and I bullied each other all the time. It was our sibling love language. "Anyway, how are you feeling?"

"Like my whole world shifted." She exhaled. "I've never actually given your dad a proper chance before, Saint. I wrote him off from the start, my big *fuck you* to my parents and their need to control every aspect of my life, but today when I thought I'd lost him, I-I panicked. He's just always been there, taking care of everything, my crutch in life in a way."

I turned into a slab of stone. What a perfect time for her

to realize she was co-dependent. Celia Astor really couldn't do anything without her Noah, he was the one that sorted out all her shit, and she hadn't even realized until now. Exactly like she didn't care to know that he was sticking his grabby hands in too many jars, and the time had come when he'd gotten stuck.

"What are you talking about? A few months ago, you said—"

"I know what I said, and I'm not telling you I'm suddenly in love with Noah, but I respect him. I don't wish him anything bad."

I rested against the wall, hands hanging from my sides like limp noodles. There was a monster roaring in my mind, begging to be let out the more I locked it in. My respect for my father was lost somewhere near Atlantis, and the only thing keeping me from spewing facts that would ruin his picture-perfect image was Killian and Mom's fragile mental state.

Tragedies brought people together. I should've expected that.

It still stung like a bitch, though, knowing who stood behind your ruin and only repeating the sin, not repaying it ten times worse, like I carved to.

My phone danced in my slacks, and I pulled it out, checking my messages.

Spitfire: I just heard what happened.

Spitfire: God, Saint, I'm so sorry. Do you want me to come? Bring you anything to the hospital? You must be exhausted.

I bit my lip to clear some of the confusion clouding my brain where Aria was concerned. I wanted her here, it made watching your family worry for a man that didn't deserve it more bearable, yet I was the one that voluntarily left for this shit show. I didn't deserve her here, and she needed some rest.

Saint: No.

I typed out a blunt response, all I was capable of giving at the moment. The three dots didn't wait long to appear, but the message she sent for the amount of time she spent typing was ridiculously short.

Spitfire: Ok, I got you. I hope your dad gets well soon.

"Hey, Dad." I smiled, leaning a shoulder against his wall with my hands tucked inside my pockets. I rested my head beside an abstract painting and savored the view.

The man who'd ruined my life looked like a cheap carbon copy of the man he used to be in that hospital bed. Completely helpless, pale, his veins sticking out from his saggy, thin skin. Old age was catching up to him. That was why Mom came out with fresh concern on her face, recognizing it too. I'd cut off a few years from his median age.

He blinked, disbelief grazing his features that I was here. "Son, it's good to know you'll at least show up when I'm knocking on death's door."

"There's barely a scratch on you. Stop being so dramatic." I crossed my arms, walking closer.

"I'm in a neck brace." Spittle flew from his mouth as he glared at me. "A neck brace!" he repeated.

"You could've been in a coffin." My lips curved into a slight smirk. "Look at the bright side of things."

His face got so red I thought he'd have a heart attack. Maybe I didn't need to pay anyone to crash into him after all. "Would you have preferred that?"

"I wouldn't have been too broken up about it." I shrugged, getting comfortable in my position of power. "Tell me, Dad, where were you driving back from? The police are going to ask."

He found the asylum-like white walls more interesting than me as he answered. "A friend's place."

"And does this friend happen to have bleach-blond hair, silicone-infused double D's, and a BBL she flew to Miami to get with your money?"

His head snapped in my direction, momentarily forgetting his injuries, and hissed. "You went through my bank statements?"

I wondered if he'd drop dead when we got to the climax of this grade F comedy. I hoped so.

"Oh, I went through a lot more than that." I twisted the silver watch on my wrist. Seven a.m., I'd spent the whole night waiting for Cinderella to wake up from her deep sleep. "So you went to her house to... sample the product you'd purchased?"

My father's shoulders stiffened at the crude image I was painting. "Don't act like your mother doesn't cheat, Saint. She's as much at fault as I am. There is no singular bad guy here."

"No, you're right. You're not a bad guy." I moved closer to his bed, pressing some fancy buttons next to his resting hand until his upper half was sitting upright, eyes dancing with panic. "You're a moron that somehow managed to fly under the radar for so long."

His hand wrestled with mine for the controller, but I pushed him off. "You are out of your mind. How do you talk to your parent like that?"

"How does my parent pay someone to tackle their kid hard enough? I'll have a limp for the rest of my life?"

Dad's eyes grew big and perplexed, staring at my mouth like he couldn't believe the words that came out. When you were at the top of the food chain, you forgot where you started from. People at the bottom had sharper teeth to hold on to their victims as they climbed their way up, and I had Noah Astor in a fucking headlock, going straight for the jugular.

"Are you crazy? What are you accusing me of?" His gaze darted to the door helplessly, no doubt expecting the entire crew of Punk'd to pop in.

"You've been very generous the past few years, helping several start-ups."

"Is that what this is all about? You know we don't just leave money lying around in the market. If something looks promising, we'll invest in it."

"And a Hooters wannabe restaurant chain looked promising to you?" I sat sideways on his bed, making sure to crush his foot in the process. He glared at me, scooting his legs away. "Cut the lies for once in your life. You know very well what I'm talking about and what you've done. I saw the contract detailing how he'd be compensated handsomely so long as I was unable to play another game in my life."

Another glance, but it was futile. The old man was at my mercy and didn't want to accept it. "I did no such thing."

"Was it not you that had a grin the size of a Cheshire

cat's when I was in your very position? I think I was brought in at the same hospital. A poetic sense of justice, isn't it?" I tilted my head on the side, my lips tipping up when I saw the wheels on his head-turning.

"You... You..." he stuttered, growing panicked.

"Go on, use your words," I instructed.

"Did you do this to me?" Realization washed over his face, his knuckles turning white as he fisted the cotton sheets.

"Did you pay Todd Brees to tackle me because I refused to take over Falco?" I countered, my ears filling with white noise when the sound of his heartbeat grew static. It was the name that tipped him off, causing him to shed a bit of his composure as he banged his hands on the bed, hissing immediately at the abrupt movement.

"So you preferred me leaving you to become some brute? Chase after balls on a field and write off a billion-dollar company like it was no big deal?"

His argument was nothing original. I'd heard all his arguments before if only I'd connected the dots and realized he would have acted on his pent-up disappointment earlier. He wouldn't be moaning in pain for the next few months, and I wouldn't have met Aria.

I despised that I couldn't tell whether that made me happy or fucking depressed.

"I would've liked to have a choice." My voice raised.

"You don't get one when you choose *wrong*!" he yelled back.

His face grew impossibly strained, mouth foaming at the corners like he'd consumed venom. There was more that wanted to slip off his tongue, but he was physically restraining himself not to draw any attention. Knowing I got

under his skin and that he would remember me every time
he twisted and turned in pain, I straightened my back,
towering over his lying form.

"There is no changing you, Father." I *tsked*, buttoning up
my cuff links. "Consider this a warning. You mess up any
more shit, you play God again when no one asked you, and
you'll find yourself in a wheelchair permanently."

His gaze screamed horror as the trap I'd carefully placed
started rising around him, bars of steel materializing in the
shadows of his eyes. "You have no right to tell me what
to do."

"You should've thought about that before incriminating
yourself. That contract you kept locked up in your safe is
now in my possession. One wrong move, and the whole
world will know what a piece of shit you are. *Two* wrong
moves, and you'll be ten feet under with no one to mourn
you. Do I make myself clear?" I turned my back, not
waiting to hear more lies or an apology. I wasn't going to get
one, and frankly, it wasn't worth shit. "Oh, and the same
applies to if you ever open your mouth about this to
anyone."

"How—" The desperation in his voice made me halt.
"How did you—I never admitted what I did. Not even your
mother knows. Did someone from Todd Brees's life tell
you?"

Any sliver of guilt that managed to weasel its way into
my body was squeezed out when he gave me the confession I
thought he never would. Having it in writing was different
from hearing it out loud. One drew cold, calculating moves
on my part. The other had me wanting to punch a second
person in less than forty-eight hours.

I resisted the urge to knock him out cold because while

sharing a cell with Aria's ex sounded tempting, it meant not seeing her again, and I could not have that.

"That's for me to know and for you to try to fill in the blanks. Put that brilliant mind of yours to use." Swinging my head back, I feasted on his vulnerable side, his body writhing like he wanted to come at me. A slow smile spread over my face, and I winked at him. "What you're feeling right now? It's called helplessness. And the only reason I'm letting you get off with this much is because it would devastate Mom and Killian to know how twisted you really are, but I should warn you. I'm prone to changing my mind quite often."

CHAPTER TWENTY-SIX

ARIADNE

I knew when I wasn't welcome anymore. Every bone in my body protested as I wheeled a small suitcase with my essentials behind me, promising to have someone else pick up the rest of my stuff. I was cutting my stay at Saint's place short by a month. I didn't want to bother him with my presence when he had to deal with his injured father and judging by his curt texts, I wasn't his favorite person at the moment.

It stung like a bitch. Not to be needed, wanted, or loved back. To have a self-fulfilled prophecy hang over your head, laughing at you like you were the joke of the century while having a panic attack on your fake husband's kitchen floor, minutes after he turned his back on you.

My body still shook with the remnants of the day's lows on the drive back to my apartment, a conflict arising when-ever a part of me cussed him out for leaving me, for not loving me back. Saint didn't owe me anything, least of all his heart, considering all that I'd done.

My vision blurred behind tears and the glare of the sun

on the ocean as I let myself inside my waterfront apartment. There was an underlying musk in the air, carrying the knowledge of a space locked away for a long time. Desperation clung to my every step the day I moved out, but now that I was back, there was no serenity in my heart at being surrounded by my things again.

Where there were marble floors, I craved to replace them with wood. The elevated ceiling and open floor plan gave me anxiety, and the view of the beach had me missing the trees that so often lulled me to sleep in Saint's arms with the whispers of the wind shifting between their branches.

Once the first tears escaped, there were plenty more to follow, flowing down my cheeks like a broken dam looking for a way out. I let my knees crack on the ground, not even making it to a couch. I had no one to talk to, nowhere to turn, and the ball in my throat grew until I had to take heaving breaths to keep up with the despair that clawed at my chest.

Love was an addiction. All the signs pointed in that direction. Tremors ravaged my body as I curled up in a ball, depression waiting to snatch me in the dark when I closed my eyes, not even finding solace in letting my mind sleep. There was no rest for the wicked and heartbroken.

It wasn't anyone's fault but mine, though, for putting myself in this position. I lied, trusted the wrong people, and put others at risk because I was selfish. I wanted my cake, and I was stupid enough to take multiple bites too, not paying attention to the effects the overload of sweetness would have on my system later on.

Nothing good ever lasted. Every happy moment was brief to teach us to enjoy life but not take what we had for granted.

I crawled on my hands and knees to get to the bathroom,

not trusting myself to walk without splitting my head open in the process. The furniture was spinning because of the lack of oxygen in my lungs. The sobs that bubbled up my throat were too frequent, allowing for little air to travel past my windpipe, even with my mouth open.

Managing to climb in the shower, still fully clothed, I twisted the tap open, shivering when frigid water touched my heated skin like a cooling caress.

How did you salvage what was shattered?

How did you put a million tiny pieces back together?

You can't, not without getting your hands bloody and your knees red, agonizing over every little section. Rebuilding doesn't happen overnight. It's like a mosaic, requiring the utmost attention and meticulous work.

My skin turned feverish, the wet fabric suffocating me, and slowly I worked it off my body, letting it smack on the ground, outside the curtain with a plop. I went through the motions of a shower, wanting to get rid of Harry's ghost touch around my neck, the memory of his eyes glowering over me like he owned me because I made the terrible mistake of allowing him into my life. I scrubbed until I was red and raw, doing more harm for my injuries than good, but with each scrape of nails down my neck, chest, and arms, I regained a piece of my dignity, rubbing off the numbness that soaked my pores to protect me from the humiliation of the past catching up with the present.

My stomach growled for lunch when I slipped into my bed after being done. I had no power to dry my hair let alone cook, and I was all out of supplies. Grabbing my phone from the nightstand, I was glad Eliana's name was higher on the alphabetical list than Saint's.

I didn't trust myself with such easy access to his cell phone number.

Promising to mope some more later, I called Eliana, missing the opportunity to talk and apologize to her properly amidst all the chaos going down at Bella's. I had a lot to be sorry for, and one of the worst was putting her in danger. The thought of something bad happening to her baby because of me absolutely destroyed me with guilt.

"Hello?" She picked up on the second ring, and I flopped on my back, inspecting a black dot on the ceiling as I worked up the courage to speak.

"Eliana, hi," I breathed, expecting her to either shut the phone on my face or cuss me out and then shut the phone on my face.

"Aria." I heard a door opening and closing on her end and her sighing as if she sat down. "Are you okay?"

A hybrid mix of a sigh and a sob burst out of me. "You're asking me? God, girl, you're an angel."

She snickered. "I've been told I look like one once or twice."

She certainly did yesterday when she burst out of the stall some minutes after Harry appeared and started threatening me by pointing a gun at my head. If it wasn't for Eliana hitting him with the bathroom door, I could've been dead now. The safety was pulled, and when the pistol fell on the floor, it went off. Thank God it didn't hit anyone. Harry knocked Eliana down. However, he didn't get far before I jumped him, and his attention was back on me.

"Are *you* okay? I feel terrible after what you went through tonight. I really hope your pregnancy wasn't affected in any way."

"Oh, it was just a little shove. My ass is sore, and Leo is

being annoying, hovering over my head. Otherwise, I'm fine as can be."

My heart warmed despite shivering, wrapped in only a towel. I turned on my side, curling like a ball and urging some of that heat to travel to the rest of my limbs.

"You guys are adorable." My voice came out hoarse, emotion tightening around my throat like a noose.

"Aria, are you crying?"

"No," I said in half a sob, biting down on my lip to rein it in, but it was useless. I sounded like a whale separated by her calves, and the worst thing was, I couldn't stop.

"Honey, what happened?" Eliana asked, concerned.

Was it wise to burden a new friend with your problems? No.

Was I going to do it anyway? Yes.

I needed to talk, and since Irena was out of the question, Dad was... well, *Dad*, and Mom would take the opportunity to give me the lecture of my life if she found out what happened, Eliana would have to do.

"Let's just say, Saint didn't show half the interest in how I'm doing. And I guess I deserve it, I'm not blaming him for anything, but it still hurts knowing how insignificant I am in the grand scheme of things." Tears clung to my lower lashes, and my screen blurred.

"Insigni—what?" Eli released a sharp exhale. "Aria, I don't think I've ever seen Saint act the way he does around you with anyone else."

"How do you mean?"

"Like the world revolves around you, girl. I could probably count the number of times he looks *away* from you in one hand when you're in the same room, and he always has the biggest smile on his face when you're talking. This is the most realistic display of emotions I've ever seen from Saint. There is little that can affect that man, but whenever you're around, I swear everyone in the room can tell that he'll take them down in flames if they hurt you."

I knew what she meant. Saint was as aloof as they came. You probably had to do something extremely cruel to break down his defenses. Eliana was implying that I was his kryptonite, but I didn't see it, not when he ran away after I told him I loved him. He wouldn't even look me in the eye.

"I don't think that's the case—"

She spoke over me. "Of course, you don't. It's hard to believe we're worthy of affection, that another person can see past the flaws we magnify in our minds and love us regardless, but trust me, Aria, give him some time, and you'll see, you'll regret wishing for the same level of clinginess."

I munched on my lower lip, my head pounding after all the crying I'd done. A heavy weight pressed against my chest, and even though I knew it was moot, I hoped Eliana was correct in her assessment.

SAINT

Nyx and Erebus greeted me at the door when I came home. That should've been my first warning. They usually didn't stray far from Aria's side. She was more generous than I was with treats.

I didn't dare look toward her wing as I made my way to the bedroom, and despite the temptation lighting up my brain with thoughts of seeing her, I was out like a light when my head hit the pillow. The scent of her perfume clinging on my sheets made it easier for me to flush away the last twenty-four hours from my memory in order to sleep without nightmares.

After waking up with a death grip around the comforter, smothering my face on the cotton-like it was Aria's neck, I caught up on some work, seeing as I'd dropped off the face of the earth today, exercised, even finished reading a book I'd started a few weeks ago. All in my room.

As if I'd contract the plague by going outside.

I'd rather it be the fucking plague than what I had. A severe case of *Ariadnetitis*, similar to Huntington's Disease, in which it slowly deteriorated my physical and mental abilities until I rewired my life to be fine-tuned to Ariadne's. I made adjustments around her schedule, planned my days off from work to match her, and made plans according to what we would enjoy together.

My nerve cells were fried, and it took me staying away from her for a couple of hours to understand that I was living in marital bliss, and any change to my schedule threw me off the loop.

When the clock struck midnight, and I had enough of living off the packet of Haribos Aria had forgotten on my desk, I begrudgingly made my way to the living room, cursing my resolve for being so feeble.

She'd lied to me, but I hadn't been the most open husband either. There had been countless times where I wanted to open up about my father, my fucked up family life, and out of fear of judgment, I shut my mouth. Would she think I was a monster for what I did?

I didn't know.

Frankly, I didn't care if she did. She was stuck with me.

Every night we counted galaxies and forgot boundaries,

she chipped away at my soul with an ice pick, and I had a persistent Aria-sized hole I needed to fill. We were of the same breed, her and I. There was no point in fighting against my attraction. She'd consumed me completely.

I was fucking whipped, and blowing her off when she told me she loved me was one of the stupidest things I'd done in my life.

And I'd done a ton of shit I wasn't proud of.

The house was eerily quiet, and my parched throat watered as I patted barefoot across the sky bridge, but before I could reach her room, the doorbell rang. I considered ignoring it, but it did so again three more times.

Who the fuck was it so late at night anyway?

They kept going, and I pulled the door open with more force than necessary, a curse on the tip of my tongue that I audibly swallowed down when I saw who it was.

"Irena? Kill?" My brows pulled together as I stared at my sister-in-law and my brother.

"Finally!" Kill growled, blowing past me.

An equally annoyed Irena followed in his footsteps, and they left me standing in front of an empty doorway.

"*Make yourselves right at home, why don't you?*" I muttered, half tempted to kick them both out so I could continue with my original plan, which included kissing my way through every inch of my wife's body until the advantages of keeping my flawed ass outweighed the disadvantages.

"My God, your wife is infuriating. Why does she even have a phone if she never bothers to check it?" Irena whined, crossing arms when I turned to face them.

Her eyes dropped to my chest, cheeks pinkening, and I remembered I had no shirt on. Oh well, she'd have to deal.

"What are you guys doing here? Did you come together?"

"Dad was being prissier than usual, so I came to take advantage of your guest bedroom and the jacuzzi in your bathroom." Killian's gaze sliced to Irena, who gave an uppity huff when meeting his eyes. "Irena shared my idea apparently, and almost crashed my car on her drive here."

"Oh, come on, I barely nicked it." She slammed her foot on the ground, and it seemed like they'd had this conversation several times already. "And I was concerned for my sister, I've been calling her all day, and she hasn't answered once. Where is she?"

"Did it cross your mind that maybe they were busy?" My brother's face brightened with a smirk I'd taught him to use.

"The whole day? Doing what?" Ina bit the bullet.

"She's in her room probably. I was just heading there now." I cut in before Killian took it upon himself to educate my sister-in-law on fun activities that lasted all day long.

"*Her* room? You guys have separate rooms?"

"She uses it to sew and design and all that." Technically, I wasn't lying. We spent more time in *my* bedroom. Scratching my chest, I started up the stairs, trusting they'd come after me. "We had a fight, so she's most likely holed up in there."

"A fight? About what?" Irena echoed behind me.

My jaw locked, and my strides became longer. Why wouldn't she answer Irena? Shit, was she more seriously injured than I thought? The air shifted against my skin like sandpaper as I blew down the hall. Their voices became thinner and gait heavier to keep up with me.

"Calm down, Nancy Drew. Nosy much?" Killian snorted.

"I can be bitey too. Want to try me, Astor?"

"I might just take you up on it, Fleur." His voice held an edge I didn't like, and I gave him a warning look, stopping in front of Aria's room.

"He won't be taking you up on anything." A burn radiated through my chest when I knocked on Aria's door and didn't hear anything in response. "Aria?" I asked, but again nothing.

I took in a deep drag of oxygen, pushing the door open. That familiar throb right behind my breastbone missed me because her gaze wasn't there to bruise me with a mere look. The space was vacant, but you could still see her influence in the room. Her mannequin was wrapped with some sparkly fabric, scissors, and pins scattered all over her workspace. Still, there was only emptiness.

"Do you have any other rooms where she might be holed up after your fight?" Killian inserted himself when he saw that Aria wasn't there.

Frustration danced along with my nerves, and I focused on Irena. "Fuck, she hasn't answered you all day?"

Her hands fidgeted as she nodded, glancing inside. "Yeah. At first, it rang, but after a while, the line beeped as if her phone ran out of battery or was closed or something."

A bad inkling settled over my bones like a rush that ate me from the inside out. I didn't wait to hear anything more. I rushed forward, ready to tear my whole house apart, looking for her.

"We're splitting up," I commented. "Ina, you check upstairs, I'll take the main floor, and Kill, go look at the garage and see if her car is still there."

The next few moments were pure unadulterated torture as I tore down every door at my home, only to find empty space on the other side. No sweet laughter, no haughty retorts—nothing but vacancy.

As if someone had handcrafted my personal nightmare, we all wore similar expressions of dread when we met again. Nowhere. Ariadne was nowhere near me, and all this time, I hid in my room like a pussy, thinking she was here.

I let my wife slip through my fingers, but I'd spend this night—fuck, every goddamn night—awake as well so long as I found her.

CHAPTER TWENTY-SEVEN
ARIADNE

The mutters coming from the doorway woke me up. My emotions were muffled under a blanket that crushed my skull, a pain like someone was drilling my brain made my eyes heavy, and I couldn't open them to see who it was. The familiar tones spoke to me, and I relaxed on the mattress, rebuilding my strength little by little.

Irena raised her voice. "Why should we allow him to come? He's the one that drove her away."

"He's her husband. We can't keep him away," Mama reasoned.

"Yeah well, she can divorce him."

A dry cough came from who I instantly knew was Grandma Chloe. "You don't just divorce someone because of a small argument."

"Did she even want him in the first place?" Irena seethed. "I remember we were out riding, and she was telling me about how she'd broken up with Harry, then *you* came, and a few days later she's engaged to Astor, and the news of a merger is everywhere."

It wasn't rocket science to figure out. I shouldn't be surprised by Irena's knowing tone. She even knew I was a virgin, so the theory of me being pregnant out of wedlock didn't hold.

"Irena, you're too young—"

"I'm young, not stupid. I know, and the only reason I haven't pushed it is because I saw that he was treating her well." Guilt clogged her tone, and I opened my mouth to tell her not to worry, but nothing came out. "Now she's burning up, and there are *bruises* on her neck. I'm appalled you're not more concerned."

"She's right." The mattress dipped, and a cool cloth was spread over my forehead, providing some relief from the sweat that dripped down my temples. "How did I do this to my daughter? Darian is going to kill us both if he finds out."

"And then kill Saint too," Irena added, glee prominent in her tone.

Worry had me straining to speak again, and this time I managed to make some strangled sounds that had them all rushing to me. It was like someone was jamming a hammer on my forehead repeatedly, and even opening my eyes was a struggle. Three worried faces stared down at me. Mama, Irena, and Grandma Chloe. At least I wasn't as far lost as I thought and could still recognize their voices.

"No one is killing anyone," I croaked.

They all sighed, and Grandma moved to the foot of my bed as Irena settled on my other side, bringing her hand to hair, and patting the mess of curls back. I gave her a slow blink as a thank you, I hated when hair stuck on my temples.

"It's okay, Aria, you're okay. We'll gun him down if he touches you again," she whispered.

"You're a murderous little creature." A laugh burst out of

345

me, and I ended up wheezing, the upper half of my body straining against the blankets. I was tucked in so tight that I couldn't use my hands. "Why am I wrapped like a burrito? I can't move."

"You have a hundred and four fever, *agapi mou*. You have to sweat it out," Mom said, dunking the now lukewarm cloth that was on my head in chilled water. I let out a moan of relief when she put it back in place.

"I wonder who taught you to sleep with your hair wet, only wearing a towel while fresh out of the shower," Grandma interfered, making my hackles rise even though I felt like I was at the gates of hell.

"I am not divorcing, Saint, if that's what you're here for. Feel free to leave. Your company is safe."

That shut her up, the wrinkles around her mouth deepening. She was not fine with being told off, but I was all out of shits to give. Concerned family members I could deal with, ones that only sought me out because they needed favors, could fuck off. Mom didn't have the power to go against her the same way my dad and I did, so I'd be extra spiky around her. It didn't matter that she was old. She'd coasted through life unbothered plenty already. My sharp tongue wouldn't be the death of her.

Respecting your elders had a limit.

"Why the hell not? He hit you, Aria," Irena spoke up on my behalf.

I glanced down, thinking I had three-sixty vision and could somehow see how bad Harry's fingerprint marks looked around my neck. The movement made the room spin, and I could only manage an inch before my head hit the pillow again with a thump.

"It looks that way, but it's not Saint's fault. He's actually the one that protected me." I spoke up and didn't stop because outrage shone in Irena's blues. I didn't want her thinking this was a case of Stockholm syndrome.

"I will not scream at you now because you're sick. Some motherly advice, though? You better prepare yourself when this fever goes away," Mama muttered against my hair before dropping a kiss on my forehead after I came clean about what had gone down.

"I think she handled it as best as she could with the cards she was dealt." Grandma surprised me by taking my side, probably because if it wasn't for her all of this wouldn't have happened.

"Βέβαια, όταν η φωλιά σου είναι χεσμένη, δεν σε παίρνει να πεις τίποτα." Mama voiced out my thoughts in more colorful terms in Greek, well aware that it annoyed Chloe when she did that.

"Anyway, you should've told us earlier. We would've found a way to deal with him." Grandma acted like she hadn't heard her, and part of me feared this woman. She acted like she had ties to the mafia, and with all that she'd told me, I believed it.

"It's Aria we're talking about. She'd cut her left arm off before asking for help," Irena interjected, a frown etched on her face as she folded her legs underneath her. "So, Saint is the victim in all of this?"

Her guilt-ridden voice sounded suspicious, and I narrowed my eyes at her. "What did you do?"

She shrugged, looking sheepish. "I might've gone off on him and his brother when we found you."

I couldn't be mad. Not when she thought I was a victim of domestic violence. The word *we* struck out at me. The band around my heart let up a little, and my chest expanded with fresh air. *Pathetic is me* would be the most accurate way to describe how my chest expanded with hope.

"He looked for me?" My voice burned with yearning.

Irena nodded. "Was out of his mind until we found you. Searched up and down until he finally remembered to call his housekeeper. She was the one that told us you were here. I left them to get the spare keys from Mom. He didn't even know where your apartment was, by the way. Did the asshole even care to help you move?"

Mrs. Adkins only showed up for five hours a day but somehow always saved the day. Cooking, cleaning, and maintaining a house wasn't easy when you worked constantly. Saint and I were far from domestic, and we liked it that way. The few moments of peace we got together we cherished and spent them making memories.

A violent cough erupted from my mouth on my next breath as I readied to respond. I still did so, my voice a raspy mess. "I need to apologize."

Mama placed her hand on my shoulder when she saw that I was about to get up, and I didn't have any power to fight her. "I'll send him the address once you're a little bit better. Rest, for now, your immune system is weak."

"On that note, I will be leaving. It's good to know that this was all just a huge misunderstanding." Grandma clutched her designer bag to her side and patted my covered foot before she left. "Get better soon, Aria."

Sometimes I wondered if she only had a problem with us because I couldn't comprehend how my dad turned out so good with that kind of lacking maternal love.

"I'm surprised she lasted that long," Irena scoffed.

We shared a look before bursting out laughing. I cradled my forehead, moaning in pain simultaneously, but I didn't care. The isolation that sucked the life out of me was gone, and even though a piece of my heart was missing, I loved being surrounded by Mom and Irena, not having to hide anymore.

SAINT

The light in Ares's living room flickered, making my eye twitch. The tenor of the football commentator on the TV got louder, falling into a cadence, and my leg bounced violently with the effort it took not to haul the television against the James Turrell piece on the wall.

I enjoyed watching big beefy men get their asses tackled as much as the next guy, but I couldn't focus for shit. It didn't help that I knew they were throwing me a pity party because:

1.   Leo would rather eat bricks than leave pregnant Eli alone right now, which meant that she forced him to go out.

2.   Ares cared as much about the sport as I did about the Harley Davidson collection he wanted to build. Spoiler alert, I didn't. I was more of a Ferrari or—*anything that has a roof over your head because I live in a city that has been blessed by the rain gods*—guy. .

I powered my phone again, checking for a text from Irena, who was turning out to be my least favorite person in the world right now. I would've been more vivid in how deep my dislike ran, but she started sending me updates on how Aria was doing after I threatened to get her license suspended for backing up into my Aston Martin. Her driving points limit was pretty low since she was a first-year driver, so she didn't have much wiggle room.

I felt like a low-level crook, blackmailing a teenager, but I didn't regret it. Not when I knew Aria was sick and I wasn't fucking allowed to be near her. I'd never taken care of a sick person before, yet for her, I was all but ready to wear a pink apron and make her down so much soup she'd be peeing for days.

"How much longer am I supposed to wait?" I fumed.

My presence was like a dark cloud over the room, shrouding Leo and Ares's good intentions with ungratefulness. Ares's house, while big and modern, reminded me a little too much of my life pre-Aria. It lacked that feminine touch. There were no coffee mugs with lipstick imprints on his coffee table, no flowery perfume lingering in the air, and no thousand-dollar purses hanging from his coatrack.

The idea of going back to that fucked with my head. Made me want to destroy the furniture and inaugurate Eliana's bong all by myself.

"It's been like what? Two days?" Leo dropped his head back on the white sectional, and Ares sighed, lowering the TV's volume. "Fuck, you're whipped."

"Three," I deadpanned, not bothering to correct his assumption because he was right. I was whipped. It had been a gradual fall but no less painful. By the time I remembered I had to set her free, I'd locked myself into a cell with her and thrown away the key.

"What happened with your father?" Ares asked about the thing that would most definitely take my mind off Aria for a few seconds.

"He did not apologize if that's what you're asking for. As for the rest, you already know. He has to attend physical therapy for a while, but that's about it. He got out mostly unscathed."

"That's for the best. Better this annoy you for the rest of your life rather than the fact that you took his life," he remarked.

"I'm not so clear cut on that. The idea of shutting him up for good when he supported his decision certainly didn't sound all that annoying." I acknowledged the unsated blood-lust that simmered below the surface.

"He did?" Leo barked a laugh. "That man truly has a death wish."

Ares shrugged. "Hey, at least now you can embody your name for once. A true saint, gifting life left and right."

"Do you think your parents named you that, thinking it would be a good way to atone for the sins they'd commit-ted?" Leo's tone dripped with sarcasm, and I hated how his statement made sense in my mind.

"Normally, I would tell you to fuck off, but Killian's name means little church, so you probably aren't that far off."

"No way." Ares guffawed. "Has he ever even seen the inside of a church?"

"I wouldn't put it past him to be a regular at any Satanic Churches," I said, remembering that one time I'd seen him with cuts on his neck. I asked him what the fuck happened, the psychologist already on speed dial on my phone, and he took no shortage of joy in informing me about how he was into blood play.

I could've lived without being privy to that information.

My brother was a textbook freak. The only thing that kept him from being labeled as one was his genetics.

"You used to say that about me too," Ares complained.

"Because you dressed like an edgy teenager on the verge

351

of depression. You made it too easy to roast you," I said, and Leo choked on his next sip of beer.

My screen lit up with a text, and I missed Ares's reply as I dove for my phone like a man obsessed.

Killian: 310 Irving Rd.

Killian: That's Ariadne's address.

Leo and Ares's voices turned faint in the background, the sound of my heartbeat in my ears muffling every other distraction as my fingers flew over the keyboard.

Saint: How the hell did you find it?

Killian: I tailed her sister.

I shook my head. Of course, he did.

And why the fuck hadn't I thought of that?

Saint: Your delinquent ways came in handy for once.

Killian: You're welcome, and I'm inviting a few friends over tonight. I hope you don't mind.

Now it made sense as to why he went out of his way to help me out. Kill wasn't the type to offer his time willingly, but when he wanted something, he knew exactly how to get it. He figured I'd be too busy with Spitfire, and he was right because nothing was saving her ass from twenty lashes with my belt. Five for each day she stayed away.

Saint: Stay away from my bedroom.

Killian: Ok. No promises for your bathtub, though.

Saint: Your birthday gift will be a bucket of bleach.

Killian: I've never gotten high on bleach fumes before, but I'm sure it'll be something to tell the kids about.

I blew a frustrated breath at the ceiling, vowing to start looking for an apartment for Killian. With the way he was going, he wouldn't graduate anytime soon—or ever. I had to find him a place of his own to mess up.

But all that would wait until after I got rid of this hollowness in my chest.

I'd gotten a taste of how good life could get, and I'd take the whole damn cake too. So long as I regained Aria's trust. She fell, and I let her slip through my fingers like quicksilver. The shock had washed away, and this time when she crumbled, I'd be there to mold her back to her lively self.

"What's up, Lord McCuntson?" Ares asked over the rim of his beer bottle when I dug out of the body-shaped hole I'd left on his couch.

"Killian found Aria's address," I announced, watching their eyes round.

"I have a newfound respect for that kid," Leo expressed.

"Well, what are you waiting for, pretty boy?" Ares gave me a dry look, bending to retrieve some keys from his glass table, throwing them at my chest. "Take my Ducati. It'll help you cut traffic better."

CHAPTER TWENTY-EIGHT

ARIADNE

Luminescent blue lights blurred the surface of the water. A neon cast of brightness formed when the waves kissed the packed sand, breaking the monotony of the inky black night with their array of color.

The pains of an illness still loitered in the form of a dry cough and a dull ache beneath my eyebrows, but I'd finally gotten Mom and Irena to go home after babying me for three days. They didn't go without a fight, making me promise not to pick up my laptop and work while unwell.

Not all promises were made to be kept.

The house was empty, and my phone was too tantalizing, beckoning me to press the power button. So I caved and checked my emails on my computer to keep busy. Afterward, I got sucked in the hustle and tried to catch up with as much as I could while I was away.

When I had enough, I walked to the beach to enjoy the bioluminescent glow like I used to this time of year, when the water warmed and the algae bloomed. It was very therapeutic, considering the hell of a ride I'd endured since

September. Everything blew apart on my face in a steady stream of bad luck, adding new scars to my soul—ones that I was proud of. They made me who I was today, and despite all my shortcomings, I was alive and in *relatively* good health.

The reminder that something was missing didn't just disappear. You couldn't erase an organ integral on keeping you alive, but I was too scared to pick up the phone and text him.

What if he wanted nothing to do with me?

What if he told me to pack up my shit and go?

I needed to rebuild more than my immune system to face Saint Astor.

"You have a thing for sparkly shit, don't you?"

Of course, the universe took my words personally, chewed them out, and spat them on my face, giving me the exact opposite of what I wished for.

The salty breeze tickled my neck, my hair stood to full attention at the sultry, deep voice that played a pivotal role in all my waking and sleeping dreams. Fear and agony hit me in the chest as I twisted my body around, my breath escaping me in short puffs.

He stood a few feet behind me, his hands shoved in his pockets, feet buried in the sand. His gaze locked on mine, hanging on to the details of my features as if he was seeing me for the first time.

Or maybe trying to see you, since it's pitch fucking black, Ariadne, unless you're looking at the water.

An annoying voice of logic misinterpreted the look on his face, but it did nothing to stop the longing coloring my tone when I called out his name in a faint whisper that I was surprised he heard over the whistling of the wind. "Saint?"

"Spitfire," he rasped, the nickname so achingly familiar

and loved, it was all I could do not to launch myself at his arms like a loon in need of being reined back.

I didn't expect to see him here, and least of all for him to walk closer as if he didn't hate me anymore. My chest fluctuated, and there was a shaky quality to my voice when he sank down next to me, his jeans filling with grains of sand. "Doesn't everyone love what glows in the dark? A piece of safety amongst a sea of unknown."

I tried to be discreet as I took greedy sniffs of the air that held notes of his masculine perfume. It was crazy that even his scent made my pining rage harder, a clean woodsy aroma that touched me like I craved him to do so. Saint's illuminated face held signs of weariness, eyes a dark shade of whiskey instead of the golden fire I'd come to adore. He sat a foot away, and I had to restrain myself not to breach the gap and beg him to forgive me, *love me* like I did him.

Unspoken words stirred between us, shifting when his gaze danced over my body, clad in a sweater and tights, the most dressed down he'd ever seen me. I swallowed, knotting my hands around my legs and resting my cheek on my knees, readying for this lion of a man to tear me apart.

"Some of us are pure darkness. Light only disturbs that tranquility." His lips tipped up with a soft smirk, but there was no humor in it. He scrubbed a hand down the length of his face before breaking apart fractions of my sanity with his next admission. "When I was nine, my dad punched me in the face for the first time because I lost an heirloom watch. It fell while I was out playing with my friends."

I swore even the waves faltered upon hearing his words. The weight of his past hung heavy in my veins, filling them with tangible heat. The visual of a young Saint played like a movie in my mind, his blond hair twisting in angelic curls right below his ears, tear-stricken eyes punching a hole through my torso.

"Is he crazy?" I sputtered. "You were just a kid."

Saint shrugged as if it was no big deal. "Which was perfect because I couldn't retaliate," he said, seemingly at peace with what had happened. "Noah did a lot of fucked up shit whenever I *displeased* him. Until one day, when I was fifteen. He shoved me because I'd failed a math test, but by that age, I was fully capable of defending myself."

I dug my nails into the material of my pants in an attempt to keep my hands to myself. Something told me he didn't want to be touched while relieving that part of his past.

"I hope you broke the hand he used to hit you with," I spat, not looking forward to seeing my father-in-law again. I didn't know whether I could hold myself back from clawing his eyes out.

Parents hit their kids, it wasn't anything new, and I myself was spanked a couple of times when I misbehaved. But punching a child? Shoving them? That went beyond discipline and blew straight into the territory of abuse.

Saint chuckled, and the sound made my lips tip up ever so slightly. "Unfortunately, I didn't." He sighed, reaching down to take a handful of sand in his hand. We both watched it trickle back down again as he hit me with news that made my stomach erupt with horror. "But I was the reason he was sent to the hospital this time."

"What?" I quaked, turning alert. My first instinct was wondering what this meant for Saint and not giving a shit about his father's health. He could've been dead, and the only reason I'd care would be because I didn't want Saint to get in trouble.

Inhaling a deep breath, he began to tell me about what he did and how he did it. Everything from the money missing from Falco's funds to the contract between his father and Todd Brees, him telling Leo and Ares, and how they helped him hire a hitman to hurt his father like he hurt him.

Nausea churned inside me the more I listened to him relay the story, and by the time he was done, my palm was pressed against my stomach in an attempt to keep down the chicken soup leftovers I had for lunch. His eyes chased after every expression, the vulnerability I found lying beyond, stunning me in a state of carefulness. I kept my features smooth, scared he'd stop talking if he saw the depth of my pity for what was done to him.

"I didn't want to tell you earlier because I didn't want you to know that I was capable of such revenge. I didn't want you to be scared of me."

My heart sputtered in my chest like a fish out of water. Oh, I was scared of Saint, all right, but not for the reasons he thought. It terrified me how I could love someone so much. How unconditional that love was, reckless and blind. He had done something completely illegal, and I found myself wanting to join in on the action. He was unaware of the power he had over me. At this point, I probably would've followed him off a cliff.

"He deserved it, Saint. He stole the one thing you loved doing away from you." I couldn't hold back anymore and caved, caressing his forearm. I'd really done my damage when we first met, constantly throwing my vitriol around because the only way I knew to defend myself was by bringing him down. Of course, he didn't trust me enough to share this part of his life with me. "God, I'm fucking furious *for* you."

The disbelief in Saint's eyes when I aligned with him broke me. I didn't even know what to feel anymore as I shifted closer, brushing up my shoulder with his. My soul churned like a vicious sandstorm, and for a second, I hated that he took the option away from me to enjoy the view of a banged-up Noah at the hospital. He hurt *my* person, and I wanted him to hurt twice as much.

A stillness settled over Saint's body when I got closer, watching me through narrowed eyes, his hands twitchy on his lap. I pretended I was using him as a shield against the wind that had my hair waving like a flag behind me, even though there was nothing I wanted more than for him to hug me.

He didn't, and my shirt was itchy over my skin without the added weight of his protective arm. Saint marveled at the shore, and I followed his gaze, ignoring the warmth running a languid path between my legs.

"You see, you weren't the only one to lie about aspects of your life, Ariadne. To smile when all you wanted to do was raze everything to the ground. We both didn't trust each other enough to open up." His gravelly tone made the hair on the nape of my neck stand up, and I didn't like where this was going.

He was right, and I hated that I couldn't dispute his logic. It made us sound dysfunctional when the only thing that kept my head above water all this time was him.

"You're right, but you also made me feel safe, Saint. Whenever something bad happened with Harry, I knew I could count on falling asleep with your arms around me and waking up to a much better day than the one I had before." I voiced my truth, watching the way it made his jaw clench.

"I can't believe I didn't kill him when I had the chance."

Saint's hand tightened around the sand, and I imagined if the grains had souls, they'd be dead by now by the brute force of his white-knuckled hold.

Breaking the partition between us one touch at a time, I slid my pinkie alongside his. Saint heaved a breath, and next thing I knew, my entire hand was enveloped by his much bigger one, sand and all. I didn't complain. With the way I was missing his touch on me, I would've let him lie on top of me even after a stroll through the sewers.

"I would've never forgiven myself if you went to jail because of me." My lips pursed when a smile that said he wouldn't mind at all spread over his face. Straight white teeth glimmered in the velvety night, and his muscles rippled with movement that reminded me he could probably kill a person just by wrapping himself around them and squeezing.

And here I was. Finding comfort in the arms of one of the biggest brutes to grace the face of the earth, nine years older than me and enough inches taller to pass as my big brother.

Saint's head snapped to me when I smoothed my finger over his wrist, willing some of the tension to ebb away from his hold.

"We aren't the first or the last couple to suffer from miscommunication, Spitfire, and wanting to hide our darkest parts from our people is second nature because we would hate to see them leave."

Was it bad that all I got from that was him referring to me as his person and hating seeing me leave? *Probably.*

Did my soaring heart care? *Not one bit.*

My mouth opened, trying to combine words with

fighting the breathlessness that took hold as a result of my need for forgiveness.

"While revenge doesn't fix anything, I'd never judge you for what you did. I don't think I'll ever be able to stomach being in the same room as your father now that I know, and the fact that he's still breathing annoys me immensely. He deserves to suffer through more than just a few bruises for hurting you." I said in all seriousness, and his answering surprised laugh at my bloodthirst did strange things to my nervous system.

"He will. His bruised ego will hurt him plenty for years to come. He lost everything, and the only person capable of loving him is the one that stares back at him in the mirror whenever he wakes up in the morning. Letting him live is worse than taking his life," he supplied, cold and calculating before his stare melted into something hotter, digging a hole through my cheek like a laser. "So as much as I hate that you hid a huge part of your life from me, I can't say anything without looking at how much I kept to myself too."

We were truly a match made in heaven.

So similar, we were dysfunctional.

I kept my excitement to a minimum, even though I knew he could feel my accelerated pulse with his fingers around my inner wrist.

I needed him to give me verbal confirmation before I let myself dream again.

"Is this your way of saying you forgive me? For lying?" My voice was barely audible, but the wind carried the whisper in his ears, extracting a dry amused sound from the back of his throat.

As if in tune with my hopeful heartbeat, his hand abandoned mine to slide around my waist and tug me impossibly closer. My whole side tingled as I let out a sigh of relief, and uncaring crept over his lap, refusing not to feel his body on mine for a single second more.

Hard muscle bunched beneath my fingers as our foreheads met, and my legs settled on either side of him.

"So long as you promise me not to freak out if Larry ends up passing away by a mysterious stab wound in prison." His sentence brought an alarming smile to my face.

"Your mind speaks to my mind, Sainty." I nudged his nose with mine, and his chest vibrated with a growl as his fingers sifted through my curls, holding my head hostage and lining up our mouths, so I felt his next words on my lips.

"Your soul speaks to my heart, Spitfire."

He peppered his revelation with a toe-curling peck, not quite the makeup kiss I was expecting, but phenomenal nonetheless as it started a slow simmer underneath the surface of our reconciliation.

"I missed you so much." I breathed, spreading more small kisses over his face. On the corner of his mouth, his jaw, his scratchy chin with all that delicious blond scruff that was often the cause of the burns on the inside of my thighs. "How pathetic does that make me? We were barely separated for a week."

He made a quiet noise of satisfaction, his hand tightening in my strands. I welcomed the bite of pain on my scalp, all too familiar with his rough touches as he tilted my head up, his hardened gaze contrasting his sweet answer.

"Certainly not as pathetic as it makes me. I'm a simp for you, baby. I apologize for turning my back on you. I regretted it the second I stepped foot out of the house."

It was like fire ants spread over every part of me, lighting up paths of the sweetest kind of pain as they marched over my heart that pumped blood a little bit harder as the seconds trickled by.

"Don't ever do it again," I said on a broken whimper, breathing in his scent with a shudder.

Home.

The sense of home predominated my mind, saffron, vanilla, and pine mixing in my nostrils until all our memories flashed behind my blink. When I opened my eyes again, I knew that there could never be anyone like Saint. The way he cherished me, my body, and my mind was uniquely his.

"I'd rather cut my legs off," he said, and I gulped when I didn't hear a mocking undertone.

"That's not very healthy," I murmured, caught up in the intensity of his amber gaze.

"Who cares?" he growled. "You tempt me, you consume me, and you fucking ruin me, sweetheart. You could be radioactive for all I care, and I still wouldn't let you go."

My breath hitched, but I still found it in me to joke. "What if I had extra limbs?"

Saint shrugged as if it would be the most normal thing in the world. "That just means more skin for me to kiss and explore."

I choked on my saliva. "You're ridiculous."

"But you love me anyway." His deep voice chased away the last of our secrets, drowning them under the tide.

The ocean air mixed with our heaving breaths, and my legs shuddered around his waist as he smoothed his palms down my back. I couldn't deny it, not when the stars overhead lined our heartbeats, and I fell a little bit harder as I ran my fingertips over his high cheekbones.

"I do. I love you." I breathed hard, enduring his eyes that

burned dark and hot over my face. "You're supportive, smart, savvy, funny, and the sexiest man alive, golden boy."

A harsh curse fell from his potty mouth, and I clamped my legs around his waist, needing to be even closer if possible.

"Don't be shy. I'm sure you can find more adjectives to describe me with." The bastard teased, and I flashed my teeth at him for stalling. He appeased me with another peck the last step before the ground gave out. "I love you too, Ariadne, so much it's like a constant flow spilling into my soul. You taught me how to live again, and in a world without you, I would merely be surviving."

We couldn't wait anymore, diving for each other at the same time.

His lips clashed with mine fiercely. Our volatile moods mixing, embers aligning with the bioluminescence in the water until blazing blue was the only thing that remained behind my shut lids. The vivid color pulsed as my heart mended and pieced itself back together in the arms of my husband, so savage and loving that dying in his embrace seemed like a good time.

A greedy sort of madness filled us as our teeth met, tongues dancing sloppily with each other as if we were too far gone for any sort of tact. I didn't care. Sparks burst into flames, eliciting the wildest kind of urgency inside me that only the devil hiding beneath my Saint could sate.

Reality faded. The fact that we were on a public beach and that anyone could stumble across our jumbled forms missed me as I tightened around him, loving the way his hold spread the best kind of ache over my bones. Our kiss was laced with longing, anger, and best of all, pure want and love.

I didn't want to stop, but we both recognized that in

order for this to trickle into something more, we had to get inside where it wasn't freezing. Saint dragged the kiss out, holding my face hostage in his big palms, and our giddiness combined as our breaths mixed.

Then I did one of the most embarrassing things one could do after professing my love to my significant other and being kissed senseless... I sneezed.

Right. On. His. Face.

"Oh my God," I gasped, and Saint's scrunched-up expression didn't take long to dissolve as he burst out laughing, his neck straining with humor as he stood, his protective embrace never leaving my body.

"Let's get you to bed, Spitfire. I would like to have a few more years on earth with you before we retire together in hell."

EPILOGUE
SAINT

One Year Later

"Aria," I held the gurgling baby a safe distance away, his stench reaching my nostrils and making my eyes water. "I think it pooped again."

The one-year-old blinked his emerald greens at me, drool pooling at the corner of his lips, feet swinging like the air had wronged him. He was a menace that never stopped crying, farting, eating, and sleeping. I didn't understand how Eliana and Leo dealt with him daily. We had to babysit him for a week because Bella had chickenpox, and they didn't want her near Matteo, and I was ready to throw in the towel from the second day in.

"Stop calling him *it*," Ariadne sing-songed as she bounded into our bedroom, her bright and airy mood lighting up when she saw the little squirt. Her body was spilled into a romantic fuzzy pink dress that had *me* drooling now and forgetting I was holding a baby like it was an atomic bomb in my hands.

I traced her every move with my eyes, unable to shake her off when we were in a room together. Her presence was magnetizing, and I hung over her soft features, willing my thoughts back to PG territory.

"He doesn't even understand what I'm saying," I said dryly, and Matteo confirmed my words by smiling brightly and clapping his hands in front of him as if I was the funniest person in the world.

She rolled her eyes, picking up the grabby kid away from me. He giggled as she cooed at him. "Who's a good boy?" Aria's nasally voice bounced off the walls, and Matteo's eyes got moon big as he looked at her and smiled like a loon. I wondered if we had matching mesmerized expressions on our faces. "You are! Yes, you are."

"He pooped himself. That's not good." I ruined the moment, spreading a towel on our bed which had become a temporary changing station.

"He's a baby, Saint. He doesn't have control of his bowel movements. You pooped yourself too when you were his age," she said as she lied him down.

"Whatever." I watched as she expertly cleaned him up with the wipes, even though he didn't stop kicking his legs for a second and dropped a puff of powder on his squirming ass.

"How are you so good at this?" I walked to the side of the bed, resting my weight on a pole.

She shrugged. "I used to love watching Irena when I was younger. Would fight with my cousins for how long they got to hold her too."

"My, my, quite the dictator, Mrs. Astor." The smile on my face spread automatically as I crossed my arms.

"*Fleur-Astor*," she corrected haughtily.

"My mistake, I always seem to forget the first hyphen," I said, not sorry at all. It was a miracle I'd gotten her to agree to add my last name to hers anyway, so I planned on taking full advantage of it.

"It's okay. I'll keep reminding you for the rest of our lives." Aria mirrored my smile, and I almost caved and told her that was exactly what I wanted. Her fire. Some things in a marriage should remain a secret, though. "And how are you *not* good at this? You're eleven years older than Killian."

It was my turn to shrug as I handed her a Pampers. "We had an army of nannies that allowed me to stay away as much as possible."

She got the stretchy material over Matteo's squirming hips, dropping a kiss to his forehead before holding him up again. "You really hate kids, huh?"

Not when they're around you.

"I don't hate them. I just don't particularly enjoy being around them unless they're past the phase where they'll spit pudding all over my face when I'm trying to feed them." I directed the sentence at Matteo in Ariadne's embrace, hand smashed against her tits, and for a second felt immensely jealous of a toddler until I remembered I got to sleep with her every night.

"Can you really stay mad at a face like this?" Aria rubbed her cheek on Leo's clone, letting her nose graze the wispy brown tuft on the top of his head. "Or that baby scent that fills your lungs with joy?"

They both stared at me, doe-eyed and hopeful, and because I wasn't heartless, some of the frost around my chest melted when Matteo clapped his little hands.

"Da-da!" he squealed, bouncing up and down in her grip.

"Look, he called you *Da-da!*" Her eyes sparkled, and she didn't even complain when he clutched one of her locks in his unyielding grip.

I kicked off the bed, one arm curling around Ariadne's hips, the other taking hold of the little guy's fist. "He calls everyone that because it's the only word he knows, much to Eliana's dislike."

"So, kids are out of the question for us?" she whispered, glancing up at me.

A tiny fist wrapped around my index finger, and I knew instantly I eventually wanted a little piece of Aria and me. The therapist I started seeing after my father's accident and his continuous calls that led me to block his number had helped in explaining that parents, in general, had no clue what they were doing, but at the end of the day, love and understanding was all you needed to raise a healthy, happy child.

Corny—I know. But with Aria by my side, I knew we would make for some kick-ass parents.

Plus, our genes were too good *not* to pass down to future generations.

"I may not like them, but I love you, Spitfire, and will love anything that is a part of you just as much." Her breath hitched, and I swooped down to brush my lips over hers, grinning wolfishly. "Besides, our kids are going to be smarter and cuter."

Her head snapped back, and she held back a smile as she pressed Matteo's head to her chest so he wouldn't listen to my boasting. "That is so bad."

"I choose to live life on the edge like that."

"Really?" Her brow raised. "If I told you I wanted to get pregnant by the end of the year, what would you say?"

"That we can certainly have fun trying, challenge fate too by leaving your IUD in and see if you're the exception to the ninety-nine percent effectiveness rate," I drawled, and she rolled her eyes, slapping my chest. Matteo followed suit, and I leaned back laughing.

I wanted a daughter because boys were always closer to their moms.

"You make my blood boil," she complained half-heartedly.

"You make mine rush south." Matteo set my finger free, and I took the opportunity to attach both hands on Aria's hips, leaning her weight on me. We stood in the middle of our room together, staring at the giggling little guy as an April shower started descending outside, the shifting winds setting the tone of my words. "I'm just kidding, baby. I would like us to have a few more years to ourselves, but we could start trying as soon as tonight if that is truly what you want."

Aria let go completely, melting her back to my front, and I held both of them, their matching expressions shining with happiness from below.

"I'm just gauging your reaction. I'm not ready for a baby, don't think I will be for at least five more years. You're all I need for me to be happy," she breathed, and my heart beat a little faster.

"You were always what I needed," I confessed back, one of the most genuine things I'd ever said, pressing my lips on the crown of her head and tightening my arms, her small build sparking a blazing protectiveness inside me.

She was my light, my wife, my life, and I wouldn't give her up for anything in the world.

THANKS FOR READING!

If you enjoyed Vow of Hell, please consider leaving a review! Your support means the world and helps other readers find books.

Join Clara's Firehearts Facebook group for exclusive excerpts, giveaways, funny memes, book talk, and more.

Scan the code to join the group:

Excerpt from *Kiss of War*, the first standalone book in the *City of Stars* series.

PROLOGUE
LEONARDO

A FIELD OF DEATH surrounded me as I kneeled next to the marble crypt. The color was stark, a beacon among the tilted and moldy gravestones planted in the cemetery for much longer.

Young blood had been spilled, fresh soil had been dug.

Pebbles poked my knees, the steps leading to the entrance were littered with them. I could feel the pieces of gravel through the thick material of my jeans, a reminder that this was indeed real.

The Massachusetts summer heat was no match for the war brewing inside me as I traced the letters on the plaque. I worked my way up the epitaph—*Beloved Daughter, Sister, Granddaughter & Friend. You are always in the hearts of those you touched. For nothing loved is ever lost, and you loved so much*—to the dips and the curves of the year of her death—*2017*—to her name. My sister's name.

Isabella Bianchi.

Blood roared in my ears, and an outburst of warmth burned a path from my heart down to my veins and onto my hand as it curled over the engraved *I*, my nails digging into my palms.

The end.

This was the end for my twin.

We all died eventually, be it humans, plants, or animals. Death was inevitable and a stepping-stone to utter oblivion. It surrounded us every day—sick patients in hospitals, old people in walkers, and junkies in alleyways. We lived it, and we breathed it, but we never grasped the full cataclysmic impact it had until we experienced it.

I had a habit of being the most confident person in a room. The one people always tried to please, the one whose smile they tried the hardest to earn. It was a mindset, one my family held close to our heart. Lead and others will follow.

Nothing touched us.

Nothing harmed the third richest family in the United States of America, sixth in the world.

Yet... my sister was dead.

The dirt on her grave still hadn't settled. We buried her a mere five hours ago, and I stayed planted in the same spot I'd been in since the start of the funeral. I watched as the lot emptied and relatives and friends returned back to their glitzy cars, some of them chatting lively as if this was a social gathering, a chance to catch up, and my twin wasn't lying dead, six feet underground.

No one cared. No one ever truly cared.

The apathy was a real eye-opener. It forced me to harden my shell, locking in my anger and grief until they overflowed. I felt them everywhere. They drowned my senses, muting my touch with reality. My ears rang, and my eyes stung. I lived in the City of Stars, yet a vortex of darkness hung heavy over my shoulders.

This was Isabella's end, but it felt like my beginning.

One born out of shadows and blood.

I didn't realize Francis Roux traded in his paintbrushes for swords and spears until it was too late. I didn't know he'd developed an interest in the art of war too, until my sister's violated body washed up ashore on Long Beach.

The back of my neck was burned to a crisp, and I tilted my head up, facing the cloudless sky and letting the cruel rays of the overbearing sun ravage my green eyes.

Every breath I took dragged with unearned privilege. Guilt that I hadn't protected Isabella stirred the blood in my veins, and my need for revenge made it race faster. I was blind to my enemies before, but I wouldn't forget their names anytime soon.

So, with wrath as my witness, I took an oath not to fucking rest until the entire Roux clan faced a worse end than Isabella. The countdown started the moment the thought filled my head, and each sharp inhale coating my lungs counted as a day lost for them.

CHAPTER ONE
ELIANA

Four Years Ago
Eliana 16; Leonardo 17

THE WHISPERS.

That was what I hated the most.

Not that my father was being charged for murder. Not that life as I knew it was coming apart one brick at a time. It was the whispers I cared about.

It started with one person, then spread like wildfire. The whole pier circled around me, sneaking not so inconspicuous glances at the bench where I sat.

I glared at a woman with a stroller, and she wheeled off faster, scared the cornered animal would attack. Scoffed at and looked down upon, that was what I was reduced to.

My skin crawled. I questioned my decision to come out in the first place. Staying home seemed like the wiser decision when my family name was plastered on every social media news outlet out there, but I couldn't. I'd rather suffocate in judgment than the lies the Roux Manor fostered.

Another lady with a stroller wheeled by incredibly slow, and I sighed. What was it with these baby mamas?

Abandoning the bench because I knew they wouldn't stop looking, I reached for the rusted green railing, giving them my back to disguise the fractures on my surface.

And it was a good thing I did. I cringed when I caught my reflection on the waves, aided by the lampposts hanging over my head.

My face looked borderline unhealthy. Deep black grooves decorated the surface under my bloodshot eyes, making the clear blue color of my irises stand out like a blot on the landscape. Hollowed-out cheeks followed before the bloodless form of my lips tied the knot on the badly wrapped present. I resembled a zombie in its prior to devouring brains form.

Pale.

Alone.

Miserable.

"Are you expecting flowers to spring up in your stead, little vain monster?" a voice spoke behind me. That familiar low timbre sprung me back to the present, my body locking at the sound. Warning signs flashed behind my closed eyelids as I blinked slow.

Leonardo Bianchi.

He had a special aura about him, one that sucked up all the oxygen from a room, replacing it with danger. Breathing became harder as fear coated the walls of my throat. A prickle of awareness ran down my spine even before seeing him sometimes, and this time was no different.

My body protested as I turned around, but I had to before he sank his claws in my back when I wasn't looking. Brown hair, the color of chocolate dreams, decorated the top of his head in unruly curls. Eyes like two uncut emerald shards pulled me in, and the slope of his aristocratic nose threatened to slice me if I made a wrong move, right along with the sharp line of his jaw.

In the span of a week, he'd turned a one-eighty. I couldn't blame him, but I also couldn't help mourning what I'd lost. I used to love basking under the light of the candle Leo always kept burning for me. But the boy with a crush had developed into a man looking for someone to ruin.

Me.

His black shirt was open at the collar, framing his lean, muscular body well. Grass stains decorated his knees as if he'd taken one too many tumbles on a soccer field, but I knew it wasn't that. His all-black outfit told me all I needed to know.

He'd visited Isabella.

"What are you doing here?"

"Enjoying my front-row seat to a drama called *Roux Family: A Shit Show of Epic Proportions*," Leo taunted. "Gotta say, Narcissus, you make it extremely easy for me to do so."

I smiled, not buckling under the weight of his swift judgments. Keeping up with the charade of the put-together girl was turning painful, though. My mask struggled to stay in place.

"You must be proud. Displaying your obsessions with such arrogance takes a special kind of stupid to pull off. Should I get a restraining order to get you to keep your distance?"

I never wanted him close.

Not when we were ten, and he managed to steal my first kiss, even though I wasn't past the age of believing boys were riddled with cooties. And certainly not at sixteen, when the only way he'd attach his lips on mine would be if he gained the ability to provide me with death's kiss.

"Go ahead and give it a try, sweetheart. Seeing your family swimming in further shit will only make my day brighter." My mock smile shattered, and my heart pounded so hard it hurt. He leaned forward, his six feet, three inches making me crane my neck. "My word is law around here, Narcissus. I own the fucking world you live in, including the authorities. There is no version of this story where you come out on top."

"And somehow, that still wasn't enough to find your sister. I think running the town with an iron fist is doing you worse than it is good. You're unearthing enemies every-where, Bianchi." I regretted my words as soon as they left my mouth.

He had every reason to be mad. To hate me. What my father did I—I didn't even want to think about. I avoided it at all costs, but that didn't stop people on social media from tweeting, sharing, and posting about it. It was flaunted in front of me during every waking moment, and that took a toll when there weren't many sleeping ones.

My father killed a girl. He raped her, killed her, and then left her for dead. I couldn't sleep. I couldn't eat without bile assaulting my throat. Isabella was just one year older than me. I hadn't the slightest idea what Francis was capable of. My dad wasn't *my* dad anymore.

Leo's eyes lit up, and the blood vessels on my cheeks expanded, painting my face scarlet. I wasn't a cruel person, I'd just been poked restlessly for the past week, and Leo brought out the bitch in me.

He lowered his face to mine, obliterating my personal

space. The world around us paused. A mesmerized public prepared to witness the lion tearing into his lamb. A hand curled around my blond hair, and I froze under his touch, my heartbeat erratic, fear mixing with exhilaration.

"It might not have been enough then, but you'll come to find I'm very insistent on getting the things I want. And what I want, my little vain monster, is your father's head on a pike if proven guilty." He tilted his head, eyes focused on mine. "I wouldn't mind seeing yours standing next to his either."

That hand tugged on my strands. His face was so close, his intoxicated breath fanned on my cheek. I didn't doubt he could do it. I pulled, but when it came to pushing, no one stood a chance against his barreling form.

"An eye for an eye, Roux."

"Makes the whole world blind?" I spoke past the lump in my throat, quoting Gandhi. "I am not my father, Leo. Don't box me in with his sins."

"The apple doesn't fall far from the tree, and you, Eliana Roux, *you* are the whole damn harvest. I'm past sparing people when the same compassion wasn't shown to my sister."

Leo's green-eyed twin haunted my dreams enough as it was. I didn't need him piling on more guilt. I moved, aiming to detach my body from his, but like a python, he wrapped me tighter in his asphyxiating grip. I sucked in a breath, fisting his shirt.

"Don't you have a better way to spend your time, Bianchi?" *Asshole.* "Or do you enjoy being a bastard far too much?"

"Hm... being a bastard to you *is* starting to become my favorite pastime. What can I say? Your daddy's cruelty lit a spark in me."

A spark? Yeah, no. The blazing heat his body emitted hinted at a ten-foot-tall fire, waiting to consume me whole.

"So what? Are you gonna start stalking me now? Did you follow me here?"

"Stalk you?" A condescending smirk bloomed on his lips. "Nah, sweetheart. I'll save you the Ted Bundy experience until after the trial." He twirled a strand of gold hair between his fingers. The jut of his jaw was so close to my lips, his stubble left a trail of electricity and what-ifs dancing on my skin. "But if you must know, I'm meeting Serena. You know? The pretty to your ugly?"

I flinched. The angry little green monster inside me that lived and breathed for moments like these rose kicking and screaming like a drunk, awakened sailor.

Serena had been my best friend ever since we used to wear diapers to make fashion statements. And Leo was right. She *was* indeed the pretty to my ugly. She had everything. Her mother was there for her while I only saw mine once in a blue moon. And her dad was a respectable lawyer while mine was the one needing his services.

Serena was the perfect to my flawed.

"Green looks rather ghastly on you, Narcissus."

I flinched again and pushed at his chest until he finally released me. I gulped in the fresh air that traveled to my lungs, now that his overbearing presence wasn't stifling it.

"You know, with such high self-esteem you possess, Bianchi, I wonder if that Narcissus nickname should be reversed."

The mop of curls bounced as he shook his head. "The pet name is here to stay, Roux. It suits you perfectly."

I strived to argue, but the butt of the cigarette (I hadn't even noticed he had), came dangerously close to my pinky.

He rolled it closed, a few inches away from my hand on the railing, and I tugged my arm back, shocked.

"Some advice for old time's sake, Narcissus. Be a good little girl tonight. Get on your knees for me—" A wicked smile illuminated the contours of his face. "And *pray*. Pray for your father's pardon because if he had a hand in my sister's death, you won't like the outcome."

A pang made a mess out of my insides. They were all over the place, twisting and churning with anxiety.

Much to Leo's disbelief, I did pray. Every day, I prayed that this wasn't real. That the next day I'd wake up, and this nightmare would be all but a memory. I didn't want Isabella dead, and I didn't want my father to be a murderer. Why couldn't he understand that?

"Leo!" a high-pitched voice called from behind us. Our gazes both snapped to the source.

My stomach got hollower when a genuine smile pulled on Leo's lips when he caught sight of Serena. She looked like a fairy—a brown bob framed her heart-shaped face, and the knee-high blush dress she wore flowed with the wind as she waved to Leo like a maniac.

I bit my bottom lip, a stinging sensation overtaking my eyes. Serena was supposed to be my best friend, but it seemed like she was settling in on the opposite side of the camp. Her excitement stagnated when she saw me. Suddenly, her wave felt more like a goodbye rather than a lackluster hello.

I didn't bother returning the sentiment.

"See you tomorrow, Narcissus." Leo clucked his tongue on the roof of his mouth as he retreated backward. "Can't wait to see how busted those knees look."

"You're late," I spoke as my mom breezed inside the courtroom. She garnered double glances from everyone, reminding me again why she reigned supreme in the trophy wife department. Her chestnut brown hair was highlighted and styled to perfection, eyeliner sharp enough to gouge someone's eyes out, and lips painted blood red.

"What are you talking about? The trial hasn't started." She took a seat on the wooden bench next to me, her Chanel N°5 perfume wafting to my nose. I resisted the urge to retch .

Yes, because showing up a few minutes early would be such a bad thing. Riding with me to court, sparing any of your words for me like a fucking mother is supposed to do, would be the end of the world.

I bit back my words like always. Mother and I didn't have a conventional relationship. Her signature frozen glare had shut me out a long time ago. I no longer asked for questions when I knew I wouldn't find any answers. Trying to reach out to her was like drawing water from an empty well.

"All rise. This court is now in session," the bailiff said.

A blanket of dread fell over my shoulders when the judge entered. I was hyperaware of Leonardo's presence on the opposite side of the court. It forced my muscles to tense into immobility.

Opening statements began, and my father's resigned stance had my heart pounding. Why would someone who was innocent look so ashen? Fear and uncertainty were palpable around him, dripping onto the tawny floors of the courthouse. He glanced back at me—his crystal blues were glass-like, and his blond hair askew as he rubbed it to oblivion.

Anxiety twisted my stomach in knots, but the lawyer—Carter Laurent, Serena's father—cherry-picked for us was impeccable. He held his ground with compound sentences that left even me feeling confused by the end of the questioning.

"Your Honor," the opposing attorney motioned to a flat-screen TV. "According to the witness's statements, Isabella Bianchi was last seen alive walking out of a restaurant on Elm Street with her friends. She got in her car and simply vanished until she was discovered three days later on Long Beach, a mere ten-minute drive from the place she was last seen. Now, I think I speak for everyone when I say that alien abductions are not recurring anomalies."

The ice of the murder trial melted slightly as the lawyer garnered a few chuckles from the jury. I coiled further, drawing invisible tic-tac-toes on the skirt of my gray dress, waiting for the other shoe to drop.

"Let's all witness as Mr. Roux is spotted near the location, Isabella Bianchi, but also three more girls, Zena Steele, Kira Vang, and Emily Haviliard, were reported missing the very same day and still haven't been found."

"Objection! Assumes facts not in evidence." Mr. Gideon popped out of his seat.

"Sustained," the judge ruled. "Mr. Hunt, please stick to the information in the record."

XXX, *cross.*

OOO, *cross.*

I doodled harder on my thigh when my father's silver Mercedes flashed on the screen like a beacon of guilt. Security footage from a store nearby caught his license plate and profile as he drove. There was no mistaking the aquiline shape of his nose. At the bottom of the screen, a white time-stamp linked him to the wrong place at the wrong time. He wasn't seen doing anything incriminating, but the coincidences were too many to sweep under the rug.

My ass was numb by the time Dad was called to the stand, and Mom kept throwing me *"behave"* glares because I couldn't seem to keep still anymore. My feet bounced, fingers twisting and overlapping.

"Mr. Roux, would you agree that you looked up to Lorcan Callahan? You found inspiration from him, isn't that correct?"

I swallowed hard, knowing where the prosecution was heading with this. They wanted to take a hit at Dad's character, and this was the perfect place to strike. Dad knew it too. Shadows gathered in his eyes, but there was no point in denying it. He'd only dropped Callahan's name about a thousand times during interviews.

Keep your head up.

Don't let me down.

I can't lose you too.

I traced the words on the roof of my mouth. I was Daddy's girl, always had been, and it was hard being anything else when Mom was never there.

"That's correct. I think he was brilliant."

Indeed he did. Art should always be telling a story. It wasn't about how beautiful a painting was; it was about the message behind it. My dad lived by that mantra. His art centered around depicting the most immoral parts of our society, psychotic, just like Callahan's.

"Lorcan Callahan passed away in the early twenties, out of self-mutilation, right? His cause of death was widely reported. It's not every day someone drinks paint or tries to carve his body to become 'one with his art.' So how brilliant can a man be when he harms himself as part of his creative process?"

"Art isn't sane or logical, Mr. Hunt. It takes you where it wants to take you. Sometimes you just have to hold on and hope the ship doesn't capsize."

I squeezed my eyes shut, recognizing my father's colossal mistake. Our lawyer tried to object again, but the judge shut him down.

"And where did your art take you, Mr. Roux? Your paintings feature mostly human subjects in various stages of duress, particularly females. How do we know you didn't try to become one with your art as well?"

"I didn't!" Dad raised his voice. "Art is subjectiv—" he started, but the prosecutor cut him off.

"Thank you, your honor. I have no further questions."

Irritation dilated my father's gaze. He sat back in his seat, muttering words I couldn't make out.

I risked a glance at Leo when the prime piece of evidence was brought forth. My stomach churned as Ms. Bianchi broke down crying in his arms when the lawyer uncovered that pieces of Francis's hair were found on Isabella's clothes the day she disappeared.

"Don't look at them," Mother snapped, her cold marble gaze fixing me in place. "You're only giving them more power that way."

"They lost their daughter," I croaked out. "Because of Dad."

"We don't know that yet," she hissed. "Now keep still and stay quiet. Don't attract any unnecessary attention."

I couldn't.

I couldn't keep doing the same thing I'd been doing for the past two weeks. Ignoring the evidence that kept piling on. Supporting Dad when he was the villain in this story.

A growl of irritation rumbled from Mom's throat, but I didn't care. I had to get out of that courtroom. Keeping my head down, I exited the trial, my black pumps clicking on the laminated floor. Bile rushed up my throat, and I managed to reach the bathroom in time, spilling my guts all over a porcelain sink.

I gagged. My tears burned as they slid down my face, leaving a charred trail forged by Leo's loathing. There was no turning back after this. He'd ruin me, for that I was sure. Heaven had no rage like love to hatred turned. Nor hell hath no fury like a Bianchi scorned.

ALSO BY CLARA ELROY

City of Stars Series

Kiss of War #1

Vow of Hell #2

Lick of Fire #3

Sting of Ice (TBA)

Scan the code to read the books:

ACKNOWLEDGMENTS

This book was challenging to write. It took a lot out of me mentally and physically, and I wouldn't have made it if it wasn't for:

My family—I took a lot of inspiration from their craziness when creating Aria's family dynamics. Things are a bit exaggerated in fiction as always, though. I promise we're not that wild, just a bit... eccentric.

The readers—I can't put into words how much you guys have changed my life and how much brighter you make my days when you contact me. I love getting in touch with you and reading all your heartfelt messages (even though, it might take me days to respond sometimes cause I'm notoriously bad at checking my inbox. Thank you for not hating me.)

My incredible beta readers—Ariel, Brianna, and Mia. Thank you so much for your valuable input and enthusiasm when it came to this story. I'm so grateful for every minute you spent helping me out.

All the amazing bloggers and bookstagrammers—thank you, thank you, thank you! I feel so blessed to have you in my life, and I appreciate everything you create and share simply because of your love for books.

The kickass authors that offer up their advice so willingly and support each other's success. Ladies, you know who you are, and if it wasn't for you, I would've sunk under a long time ago.

Books and Moods—this cover is incredible, and you always manage to bring my vision to life. Thank you SO much.

Ketlli and Jessy—the two most special girls in my life. I don't think I could function without you, so thank you for being always there whenever I need your support.

And finally, myself, and all the empty coffee cups and RedBull cans that helped me stay awake so I could finish this book. It's not my intention to sound vain, but I pushed myself to new limits while writing Vow of Hell, and I deserve a place in my own acknowledgments lol.

Always grateful,
Clara Elroy

ABOUT THE AUTHOR

Clara Elroy is an Amazon Top 100 best selling author of romance novels that make your heart clench. Her love for reading began when she was a young girl, and would lose sleep because she wanted to read "just one more page." Clara lives for reading and writing about flawed and relatable characters. She loves making sparks fly between stubborn men and the badass women that make them kneel. When Clara's not typing away at her computer, you can find her with her nose buried in a book or writing biographies in the third person.
Yeah, she's cool like that.

You can find Clara at these places:

Website:
www.claraelroy.com

Newsletter:
https://bit.ly/3voOhiz

Follow on Amazon to be alerted of her next release:
http://author.to/claraelroy

instagram.com/claraelroyauthor

facebook.com/claraelroyauthor

goodreads.com/claraelroy

bookbub.com/authors/clara-elroy

Made in the USA
Las Vegas, NV
17 September 2022

55485993R00225